THE COLLEGE OF SORCERERS TRILOGY

THADDEUS AND THE DAEMON

BOOK THREE

LOUIS SAUVAIN

Book Three: Thaddeus and the Daemon
The College of Sorcerers Trilogy
© 2023 Louis Sauvain.

All rights reserved.

P R O T I N U S
Published by Protinus Press

Development Editor: Judith Briles, TheBookShepherd.com
Editor/Proofreader: Barb Wilson, EditPartner.com; Peggie Ireland
Original Cover Concept: Michael Yuen-Killick, Rainy Dog Studio
Cover and Interior Design: Rebecca Finkel, F + P Graphic Design, FPGD.com
Maps and Illustrations: Sean Bodley, Mount Nittany Studio
Lingua Imperatoria translations: Laura Barnard, PhD

Books may be purchased in quantity by contacting the publisher through the author's website: AuthorLouisSauvain@gmail.com

Library of Congress Control Number: 2023902757
ISBN trade paper KDP: 979-8-9859482-9-5
ISBN trade paper Ingram Spark: 979-8-9877650-0-5
ISBN eBook: 979-8-9859482-8-8
ISBN audiobook: 979-8-9877650-1-2

Fiction | Epic Fantasy | Teen & Young Adult | Sorcerers | Magic

First Edition
Printed in the USA

To the Flower,

the Butterfly,

the Dragon and the Wolf –

Four who would make

any the proudest of parents,

especially this one.

Contents

Prologue 1

CHAPTER 1: Letters I: *Litterae I* 5

CHAPTER 2: Letters II: *Litterae II* 15

CHAPTER 3: Headlong Flight: *Praecipiti Fuga* 27

CHAPTER 4: Tombstone: *Monumentum Sepulcri* 35

CHAPTER 5: Care from a Goblin and a Centaur:
Curare a Cobolorum et Centaurus 43

CHAPTER 6: Children and the Hall of the Seniors:
Liberi et Atrium Supremorum 55

CHAPTER 7: The Young Horse-Master:
Magistrum Equitum Iuvenem 65

CHAPTER 8: The Offer of a Quest and the Speech of a Daemon:
Inquisitio Prolatus Et Daemonis Oratio 75

CHAPTER 9: The Mad Hermit: *Solitarius Insanus* 85

CHAPTER 10: The Blinded Eagle: *Aquila Caeca* 95

CHAPTER 11: The Curse of the Red Dragon:
Maledictio Autem Rufus Draco 105

CHAPTER 12: The Old Woman of the Sea I: *Anicula Maritima I* . . . 115

CHAPTER 13: The Old Woman of the Sea II: *Anicula Maritima II* . . 125

CHAPTER 14: The Queen of Sea Dragons I:
Regina Draconum Marinarum I . . . 135

CHAPTER 15: The Queen of Sea Dragons II:
Regina Draconum Marinarum II . . . 145

CHAPTER 16: Loving I: *Amo, Amas, Amat* 155

CHAPTER 17: Loving II: *Amamus, Amatis, Amant* 165

CHAPTER 18: Goblins I: *Coboli I* 175

CHAPTER 19: Goblins II: *Coboli II* 187

CHAPTER 20: Goblins III: *Coboli III* 197

CHAPTER 21: A Daemon Speaks: *Daemon Dicit* 205

CHAPTER 22: A Traitor Is Uncovered:
    Reus Laesae Majestatis Reveletur 215

CHAPTER 23: The Loss of Three: *Tres Pueri Perditi* 223

CHAPTER 24: Into the Mirror I: *Per Speculum I* 233

CHAPTER 25: Into the Mirror II: *Per Speculum II* 241

CHAPTER 26: Choices: *Electiones* 253

CHAPTER 27: The Loss of Belief: *Fides Concidit* 263

CHAPTER 28: Death of a Daemon: *Mors Daemonis* 273

CHAPTER 29: Cleansing the Land: *Terra Purgata* 283

CHAPTER 30: The Secret of the Mirror: *Speculum Arcanum* 293

CHAPTER 31: Reunion and Explanations:
    Reunion et Explicationes 303

CHAPTER 32: A Judgment Rendered: *Iudicum Factum* 313

CHAPTER 33: Women Warriors: *Amazones* 325

CHAPTER 34: Thaddeus Decides: *Thaddeus Iudicat* 335

CHAPTER 35: The Pain of Farewell I: *Abitus Dolorosus I* 345

CHAPTER 36: The Pain of Farewell II: *Abitus Dolorosus II* 355

CHAPTER 37: A Purchase: *Mercatura* 363

CHAPTER 38: Dragon Legacy I: *Draconis Legatum I* 375

CHAPTER 39: Dragon Legacy II: *Draconis Legatum II* 383

CHAPTER 40: Leaving the Westlands: *Praeterirns Occidentem* . . . 393

Epilogue 405

Appendices 419

Imperial Cinnian Family Tree 420

Molly-o'-the-Willows Family Tree 421

The Lay of Man 422

Character Log 426

Glossary: *Lingua Imperatoria* 446

Discussion Questions 454

Excerpt from Book Four: *Thaddeus and the Ancient One* 457

Meet Louis Sauvain 461

How to Work with Louis Sauvain 462

Book One: *Thaddeus of Beewicke* 463

Book Two: *Thaddeus and the Master* 464

Next from Louis Sauvain 465

x

List of Illustrations

Frontispiece the Westlands xii

Specus in Study 17

The Hall of the Supremi 59

Osiric, Lord of Eagles 97

Mari, Regina Draconum Marinarum 138

The Vengeance of Sonnia 199

Brother Longbone's Tale 238

The Agony 272

The Iron Company Stands 288

The Intelligentiae 342

Scralia Pass 401

THE GREAT GLACIER
THE FROZEN SHALLOWS
THE WEST
ICE PORTS
THE ICE
LAKE ILG
INFORN FOREST
IGANZ
GAGDELLE RIVER
ICCEN RIVER
Somerset
NORDEN ROAD
N
NEEDERN
Tarandon
NORDENNE ROAD
THE NORZIL PLAINS
LAKE NILIN
NORTE RIVER
NORDENGELL
LUDIA
NORTHFAST
MIDINA ROAD
PONTES PORT
LAKE NOREN
BEAST WOOD
TRAILIC ROAD
THE SEASIDE FOREST
TETHYS SEA
TOPE WOOD
THE HORN COAST
THE INNE SEA
TAPILL FOREST
MERNEN RIVER
TECEN MOUNTAINS
TOPIAN
Dorset Downs
PATI ROAD
TRESHWINN
PARI ROAD
SUT ROAD
COBBLY E KNOB
THE RED FORE
BELI RIVER
LEGEND
WESTWALLIA
RIVER
ROAD
CITY/ TOWN
MOUNTAINS
TUR
TURIAN RIVER
HILLS
Glascoton
FOREST
THE WALLIAN MARSHES
WETLANDS
ADALANTINE OCEAN

LANDS
THE GREAT ICE WALL
IREZ
COLLEGIUM SORCERORUM
NORTHIRST PEAKS
THE NORTHERN ROAD
Walworth County
LANDS
ARX MONTIUM (MOUNTAINGAARD)
THE GREAT FLATSTONE RIVER
THE BARREN FLATS
BULCORAN FOREST
THE SOUTHERN CAVES
GAGDEN RIVER
BANNOCK
THE GREAT STRIUNN FOREST
MEF WOOD
LAKE CIRUM
THE GOLDEN RANGE
LAKE MARN
MERCEA
Copperville
LAKE GERNEM
THE
BAKEM ROAD
MEKERN
GREAT
MERNECA
NORTH
RURGEV FOREST
ROAD
FREMOR ROAD
THE GREAT BRAMILL FOREST
ARDENNIA PASS
RIVER'S WOOD
MOORSTOWN
BRAMILLEAN WETLANDS
CITY ON THE PLAIN
BEEWICKE
MOORSLAND
LAKE THEAN
FOUNTAINDALE
FRANTILLIA
IP WOOD
RICKLEWOOD
SCRALIA PASS
FRANTILLE ROAD
FRANTIL ROAD
THE GREAT FRANTILLEAN GRASS LANDS
THE GREAT FLATSTONE RIVER
BONEDELLUM SWAMPS
FROCEAN WOODS
FRANTILLA
Maritanius
VEXARE
BLACKCOVE
PORT STELLATUS
PORT OSTIA
FRANTILLAN SEA

Prologue

The tall, fiery-haired figure regarded her silvery companion.

"And wilt thou, fair Equus, now deign to bear me to that place of which we have spoken in time past?"

"Aye, my Lady. I stand ready to ferry thee, as always, even unto the heart of yonder star, should thou wish it. You have only to bid me."

"Ah, sweet steed, I did well with thee and thou provest it at every turn."

"Thank ye, my Lady, but there is a thing I wonder concerning which I would raise it as a question to ye if ye would consider to reply."

"Ask, brave Equus, and I will respond."

The glimmering quadruped looked away, then back again.

"Ye have told me the place I am to bear ye, but not the purpose of the journey thereto. Now that, I know, is none of my affair, yet ye did breed into me a certain curiosity. It is my impression that you have not left this same plane in millennia that I can reckon. Yet you now pick such a time. I would know that which you can relate to me."

"Fair enough, silver fellow. I shall reward your impertinence this one time. I go to meet a man. By him shall I deliver twins, each with a certain destiny."

"Hmm. My Lady, your daughters—the Four. Know they of these additions to the family tree?"

"Just how would that be important, Equus?"

"Well, it is not my place to say, but siblings are siblings. Sometimes they rejoice in the advent of rivals, sometimes not."

"Whether they do or not is not the concern presently. They are good girls and they shall continue to play their part and do their duty however it may come to pass. In the meantime, if your nose has now grown any shorter, let us away."

"Aye, my Lady. As you say."

The taller figure approached her mount and sat astride him. "Go," she commanded.

All around them melted away in an instant, and clouds and stars flew together and rushed by and were gone. The lady noted their entry into a long twisting tunnel, pursing a pinpoint of white light at its end; so small, yet so blindingly bright as to be almost unbearable.

Shortly, the other-worldly woman stood on a lush, grassy knoll overlooking a sparkling river. Her unbound red hair reached her ankles and trailed into the tall grasses.

"I will be here in this place for a few years only. Come to me when I call."

"So I will, my Lady."

With that, the silvery beast faded off into the forest, leaving no hint of his passage.

The tall lady smiled to herself and, with a passing glance of concentration, made her way to a modest, dilapidated cottage that stood near at hand. As she walked toward it, the glow that had surrounded her began to fade and was gone by the time her hand touched the structure's door latch.

She entered the musty dwelling and paused to look around critically. This was going to require some work, but no matter.

The drizzle that had been annoying all day now turned into a serious downpour. The man cursed as he made his way through the forest following the faint deer path. Darkness was coming on, and he was getting soaked. He hated this yet tried to appear in control as if it was all no bother—not, of course, that anyone was watching.

Abruptly he stopped short. A faint yellow light beckoned. In the middle of the forest? Yet, there it was. He advanced cautiously. The *Fey* were commonly seen in the forests at night, and they did so enjoy their little diversions.

Closer, he could make out what appeared to be a small and tidy cottage with warm light streaming from the windows and the aroma of woodsmoke escaping from the tall chimney.

Observing from the trees, he took pains to be sure of his safety. All he saw was one cabin with one occupant, a redheaded woman. The smell of warm stew latched onto his nostrils and would not let go. Finally, he approached the door and knocked softly.

The door opened, and there she stood. The home, when he could take his eyes off the woman, was spotless, cheerful, and seemed comfortable. The lady moved toward him, smiling.

"You," he said.

The Lady sat squatting in a field rich with flowers, their delicate scents mixing deliciously. She grunted. The birth was imminent.

Obviously, she did not have to endure any discomfort whatsoever, but it was her way. Another spasm came, and another grunt escaped her lips. She judged it was time to begin to push.

Once born, the two babies suckled effortlessly, and why should they not—their world flowed with milk and warmth; as much as they could wish of both.

The woman tenderly brushed a bit of leaf from the girl's brow and shifted slightly, so the boy had greater comfort. They were both comely but not breathtaking. Better not to draw too much attention right away. She could have looked to see what lay ahead for them but chose not to at this time.

Noting the tiny, fiery curls on their heads, she saw that both her daughter and son would take after their mother.

Naturally.

She had arranged for the twins' care. For what would be demanded of them, it would be better for them to rely on others. Perhaps she would look in on them from time to time, however. Why not—it was her right as their mother.

Soon it was time to call her mount. He appeared in no time at all and bore her back to that other world that was both between and among other worlds.

"Fare-thee-well, my little ones. Fare thee very well," she called out.

It had been a pleasant and welcome interlude. It was not exactly an adventure; adventures implied things that could occur beyond one's control. In her world that, of course, was not possible.

Now back to work. There was so much to do. Always.

Letters I
Litterae I

Dear Father,

I am writing to let you know I had a wonderful Holiday. My three good friends and I spent it together and shared many instructive entertainments. Our hosts were gracious and saw to our every need; we wanted for nothing. I received many fine gifts and presents, including a pair of homespun woolen stockings. It is the custom here to wear these during the winter, as they are quite effective in keeping one's feet warm. I will bring a pair home to show you when next I visit. As these people were ever kind to me, I feel they have earned our special thanks and consideration.

My schoolmates and I are getting on very well now, and I believe we are all heading in the right direction. Our instructor has been impatient for this to be the case, and it appears his efforts are bearing fruit. But as to what specifically lies ahead … who can say?

We have had many new adventures and learned much in our studies since

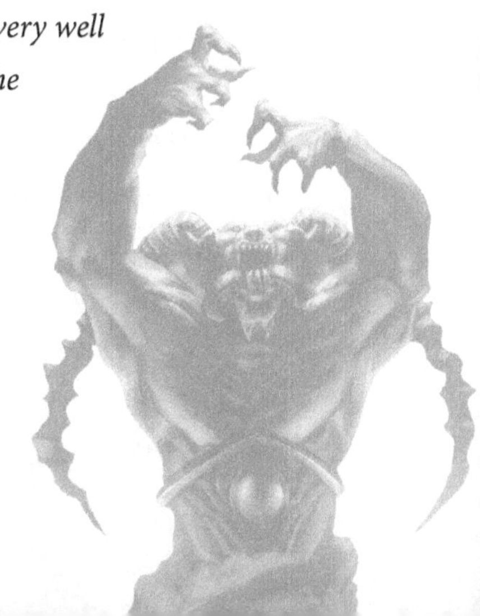

the start of the new school year. You will recall I had written to you concerning our music. I'm glad to say it is progressing well. I hope you will be able to hear us perform one day.

We had an interesting trip back to the Collegium from our Holiday. We stopped in a small town for refreshment and were greeted by members of the Borrower Family. You recall them, I'm sure. Unfortunately, a disagreement arose between them and one of my friends, but I was able to hold a number of discussions with them—thirteen, as it turned out—and they were satisfied to go on, and all was resolved.

Later, I met with their new Father—you will, perhaps, be saddened to learn that their old Father had cause to join his ancestors rather recently—and he was quick to apologize and did his best to make amends. He was hopeful that our Family would not hold the actions of one rogue against his Family. It is my opinion that he did well in this arbitration, and I think we should bear him no ill will because of it.

But this is, of course, your decision.

In addition to the Borrower Family, several members of the Merchant Family were present as well, which I also found interesting. The Father of the Borrowers was at a loss to explain why they were there, and I believed him. We held some further discussions with the Merchants as well, with a similar resolution.

Sadly, I learned that they had wanted me to accompany them. They thought to sell me some of their trinkets—a necklace, bracelets, and anklets, mainly—but I declined. I was surprised, though, as they had come such a long way to distribute their goods at such an inclement time of the year.

As I considered the situation, it occurred to me that some of our friends at court—especially those who have always been so supportive of you—may have considered to establish relations with the Merchants so as to bring this about. I wondered if you might wish to investigate their need for further instruction in the timing and purpose of their sales and merchandise management.

Otherwise, my own studies are going very well. I am learning much that is both interesting and certainly useful— both for now and in the future.

I miss you and Mother very much. My embraces to you both. And tell little Jadell she is ever in my thoughts. I have acquired some special items for her and cannot wait to see her expression when she sees them. Assure her, however, that they are inanimate.

My love to you all. I will write again as soon as I may. Psittaca sends her affections as well.

Your son,

Zoarr, Prince, House of Abdomoolano, Mauretesia.

Post-Scriptus: I have met a wonderful girl, and I have asked her to marry me. I believe, in time, she will accept. I will tell you all about her in another writing.

Post-Post-Scriptus: If you happen to think of it, please tell Pertangus he was right.

—Z.

The Old Man sat at his desk, guttering candles giving off a flickering light. A breeze blew into the room through the Sorcerous window from time to time, causing the candle flames to dance a jig. Although the window showed a scene of snowdrifts and ice-frosted trees, the wind gusts were temperate and refreshing.

Silvestrus touched quill to tongue, dipped ink, and applied feather to parchment.

My Dearest Geanninia,

I hope this letter finds you in the best of health and spirits. Events are afoot here. My thoughts increasingly turn these seasons to my young charges—during those few moments I am not thinking of you and your charms. However, these days have been long in coming, and events are unfolding apace.

The Prince has at last found his heart—your Molly o', as I understand it. Though I have not met her, I have heard enough concerning her to believe she is the one, just as you have said. So now each of them has his partner, though I believe the last two do not yet realize it.

I continue to keep an eye on Perditus. I also continue to believe he does not knowingly understand what lies at the end of the path he is choosing. I think, at the climax, it will cost him the greatest of sacrifices—along with any number of others along the way. How foolish and for what? Just to right an old wrong? Just to suckle at the largest teat? Ah, what futility.

Our House-Mistress demonstrates an increasing affection for our boys. She continues to try putting the puzzle pieces together. And then there is Brother Longbone. I hope someday their long ordeal can come to an end.

What a turmoil those lads cause! Over the Holidays, some rogue member of the Thieves' Guild attempted to lay hold of Rolland to collect the bounty that stood on his head. I was furious and ready to crisp the lot of them. And had it not been for Specus' petition, I would have done so.

It is strange....

When first I brought the Master Cook that snot-nosed red-headed street-thief he was to adopt, I had thought how clever it would be to have access to the inner workings of the Guild— forgetting, of course, that every byway runs both ways.

Specus pleaded Faran's case rather well. Apparently, Rolland's torture had not only not been condoned by Faran; it had been strictly prohibited. But Faran had not counted on a rogue agent.

The Cook showed me the fellow's tongue and finger with signet ring—at least what he claimed to be the tongue and finger. I gave them to Antigonis as a treat. He did not seem to object to them being a bit ripe.

Specus told me Faran had requested the four boys accompany us to the "parley," as he called it. I refused his initial request, as I was not about to put these Keys to the Future in any further peril. But the Cook bent my will again. He is quite good at that. I think he senses I have always felt sorry for him and his people … being the last living representative and all that … well, you know.

Besides, I thought, with the Cook, me, and the four boys, there would be enough Vires to blunt all but the most pointed, determined, and desperate attacks. As it turned out, my concerns were unfounded. I wished that I had known that in advance.

In any event, I demanded we meet at the foot of Mountaingaard. Only a fool would try mischief in my presence and under the eyes of Captain Geoffrey's Iron Company. And as we all know, Faran is no fool; it seems Nytus at long last discovered that to his dismay. So, Faran agreed to the site immediately, and I began to feel, perhaps, the Guild might be spared.

Specus drove us down to the rendezvous in the cart with Asullus, who complained all the way. A convocation tent had been erected, containing all manner of luxury. Then I entered, only to find Iacus—that black heart —passing his ease. I demanded to know why he was there, and Faran mumbled something about "balance." I considered removing Iacus' liver on the spot.

I have still not forgotten how he tried to take liberties with you. He is lucky he yet lives. If not for your intercession….

However, my biggest surprise was yet to come. I had planned to issue a number of impossible demands, then ruin him utterly when he could not agree. But my thunder was stolen by those boys. Almost before you could detect it, they were doing the bargaining themselves. I have to credit them, though; they did very well. Who could have thought they would have the audacity to make the bargain for the College with the new Grand Master of the Thieves' Guild?

I have given the matter much thought since, but I am still undetermined as to whether Faran intended this from the beginning or not. I think not, but I am unsure. Perhaps, we were both bearing further witness to the power of the Prophecy. Or perhaps it was all coincidence—random chance. But you know what I think of coincidence….

In any event, the lads weaseled the Thieves' Guild Master out of a thousand gold Imperials. "Rolland's tuition," Zoarr called it. Ha! Faran looked as if he had swallowed his spleen. But, again, it could all have been an act. He must have felt considerable pressure to make the settlement go well, considering the potential ruinous consequences—both for his Guild and himself personally—if it did not. He may have thought it better to act the wounded dove and draw the serpents off, thinking themselves satisfied.

I will likely never know for certain.

So, this adventure came to an end. When first they matriculated at the College, I thought it wisest to remove myself from the boys' instruction directly. I truly felt it would be better for them to obtain their training from others. Besides, who knows what jealousy such attention would have stirred in the hearts of their peers?

But now I am considering I may have played my hand too subtly. I think it would be better were I to be more direct. It may be that the time has come to take the boys firmly in tow. Yet, something inside me resists that pose. I do not know what.

Mayhap you can tell me, my love.

So many threads these four lads weave together. Then there is our old enemy, and beyond them, our Oldest Enemy. I do not know if we will survive this, dearest one, but I will pledge that if we go out, we will go out in blazes of glory with lightnings and thunders abounding. Who could ask for more?

Well, the hour is late, and your lover, old. I will write to you again in near time.

All of my love,
Silvestrus

The dark-haired young maiden pressed several coins into the porter's hand.

"Now, as we discussed," the girl said, her tone businesslike, "you will see this missive to the village depot and arrange for its posting."

The silver-haired man knuckled his forehead. "Yes, Mistress. Straight to the depot as you have said."

Dismissed, he turned and mounted his old mare. He smiled to himself. If he'd had an Imperial for every time over the years, one or another of these girls had sent off a heart-scroll....

Worse, though, were the times he'd handed some young lass a scroll sent from another, declaring an end to all between them. Those were definitely worse, especially with those ladies who were older and could use the Art.

It was worth a man's hide to be heading for the gate at a good clip after handing off bad news such as that. Yes, those were worse.

Within a month, Anders rushed up to his room, clutching the precious letter. He sealed his door and carefully opened the scroll, hands trembling.

"*My Precious Bubo,*" it began, while Anders reflected he would be forced to open his veins with a knife should Rolland ever learn of Nannsi's predilection for tender, yet odd, salutations. He read on.

> *All is well here. I am writing to bring you up to date on our adventures.*
>
> *As you no doubt know by now, the crèche girl, Molly o' the Willows, has joined us. She seems nice enough and is very good about doing her part of the chores and keeping up with everything.*
>
> *Marsia, as usual, has taken this bird under her wing and is assisting her in getting used to our lady's life. You are most perceptive in observing her great affection for your Prince. She never speaks of him—not ever—but you can see affection in her eyes whenever he is mentioned. She seems to be deciding something about him, so her feelings must run deep.*
>
> *Sonnia could be kinder to the girl, I believe. But you know Sonnia. She is ever conscious of where everyone comes from. I think she should consider more about where everyone is going to. But she is my Sister, and that is that.*
>
> *I wouldn't mind at all, however, if our Molly and the Prince ended up together just to see the sour plum Sonnia would be called upon to swallow at the news.*

As things turn about, I have a deep suspicion concerning Sonnia, which I will share with you, my beautiful one.

Here Anders had to pause to catch his breath and reread the passage more than a dozen times before going on.

I believe there is something about your rude Rolland that has caught in her teeth, as it were. She rarely speaks of him, but when she does, it is always disparaging. Now, people may often criticize others they do not care for, but not with every mention! That takes effort, and effort is spent only where it's willingly invested.

But we shall see.…

We are learning much and, hopefully, will begin practicing at some time in the near future. Mistress Geanninia looks after all of her children here. Belief, indeed, appears to be the key. I have carefully considered your ideas on this and find your reasoning flawless—as I expected.

I have been thinking it would be good for us to enjoy a holiday together, perhaps sometime this spring or summer. It would be interesting to share our thoughts on our teachings and compare notes and such. Mayhap something could be arranged with your classmates and my Sisters as well.

I am sorry to make this letter so brief, but the porter is leaving soon, and I want to get this scroll to you.

Be sure to take care of yourself and remember to dress warmly and eat well. Please know I think of you fondly always, my gentle Anders.

Daring to end with my heart,
Your Nannsi, forever

2

Letters II
Litterae II

The giant figure sat hunched over a small desk in a corner of the kitchen, its surface lit by a solitary candle. His heavy hands forced the splintered quill to the parchment, only to tear it anew at regular intervals. His features were contorted with concentration and effort, and his wrists cramped with the unaccustomed movements. Sweat beaded on his brow. His task was exceedingly difficult and required hours. However, he begrudged not a single one.

In the study at his headquarters in Fountaindale, the robed man quickly dismissed his Accounts Factor and the two feather girls once Macro had placed the newly arrived scroll in his hands. Alone, he broke the seal—red, which meant no bad news—and settled back in his pillowed chair with a glass of the old vintage.

My son Faran,
I write to say good to view of you this past
time. I am well and you I hope. I feel bad
to not to writing more to you but you

think back to how this is hard for me your Pa-ap. You and I say always your peoples and my peoples are always the same kinds in many things. But it cannot be just every thing and this is difference. My peoples had not writing from that time. You know the songs for us are singing but no writing. Of those times I think I am only one people of my peoples who does do it. I can not know all about this with my peoples gone now so long time.

These days I was scared for you safely. Master Silvestrus was angering toward you for Apprentice Rolland hurt beating. Your man mistaking order you had give to him about that. I am glad he is now all dead by you.

My fear you for living made me remember your Ma-am Coqua and me having you at the first time. So writing I am so you having this story for your tikis of you some day they coming. It is best of my stories about son I am loving.

Your Ma-am Coqua was being my wife since our beginning loving. She had so small and tiny a looking by a flower in our meadow so was not so big ugly as your Pa-ap.

Can not know when telling you back before days. All my peoples your peoples killing over years and years and so your Ma-am Coqua and your Pa-ap me had no others ever. Once Great Pa-ap Threkor is killed by Others spear so just now she and me is us two living only. Only thing thinking about she living and me living by living together. So thinking and thinking and running toward Great Stone Ring. A boy I was when seeing it first when hunting and spying Others and remembering the Stones. Big two or three peoples on top each other as big for the Stones. My peoples knowing the Stones but no building Stones that were so big.

SPECUS IN STUDY

First peoples of you building them all. Tiny, tiny First peoples and smarter. My peoples not knowing smarter and hiding good not so much. Your Ma-am Coqua and your Pa-ap are running to the Stones. And all new peoples chasing and yelling. But we see these two Stones of all the Stones standing so they are very tall. They call me and your Ma-am and we run so we are going. Your Pa-ap's legs longer so carry your Ma-am while I running.

Standing by Stones, one of Firsts looking surprised to see your Ma-am and Pa-ap running by so fast. So I run through the Stones arching over all our heads. Next knowing thing is us by all Stones now crumpled up with growing vines and looking old to we. Not hearing others. They just gone a sudden. Walk and walking and talk and talking to your peoples. Some give money to work us in fields with cropping. Learn cooking kitchens not such bad a thing. People like fooding of Pa-ap even Others so some even word telling Pa-ap cooking good.

So many changes. Others in huts when I tiny but through Stones go and now towns and clothes and farms not before seeing ever. Think I too have changes going through Stones. Try always am I to learning new things. Always learning speaking but writing stay bad. Our peoples can not do it good.

Hard being quiet with your peoples pointing us often. No one understanding with us looking big ugly. Some pointing Others throw rocks and bad name calling. Not all your peoples but some. Keep Coqua safe sometime breaking necks and having to moving on and on.

Then come to big city water fountain. Then one night you come to we at home with door knocking. Old man peddler standing hooding head with dirty boy of eight years you. Saying you in troubles and troubling others. Old man say no one wanting dirty redhead boy young thief. Says gaol or worse if not taking in boy of Others not our own. Old man saying we no tikis of our own so we take dirty redhead boy. Questing always about him knowing us never with children but always wanting. Never we telling him that.

By our luck we got home toward forest with not so many Others there and not troubling happy home by brook your Ma-am and Pa-ap and you son. Those happy days brook living but think you not happy with new Ma-am and big ugly Pa-ap. Think maybe missing you own Ma-am and Pa-ap. Old peddler say they gone long time leaving you. Wonder always how old man knowing these things? Who tells him things from past?

Slow, slow you come love your new Ma-am and maybe Pa-ap hoping I? We loving you always from first with dirty face and red hair only we ever see. Love you our Others boy even though not Fathers of Man. To your Ma-am and Pa-ap it make no difference our son in small house by brook.

One times seven years we by brook living. Sometime you missing biggest towns and I think wilder life stealing exciting for you. But by brook you always good to us by that time of years.

Then come the Bad Night. Others come having torches looking for us last of Fathers of Man for killing. Over past years I thinking sometimes someone has told them about us by brook. Others come in night middle us sleeping they all awake yelling cursing. So coming in house jumping on us many and many.

Your Pa-ap stronger in those days than now and crush little Others every one he catches. Soon blood coming to feelings roaring our Peoples battling cry loud out and killing puny Others.

Finally all a ways go and no Others behind and quiet now. But worst now is my Coqua your Ma-am with Others colding steel in pretty flower tummy used to always kissing and patting in your Pa-ap loving his Coqua.

Call I her name over and over but she is gone beyond holding her for time but moving not again. Then looking for son mine and looking and looking but is gone too know where not. Your Pa-ap crying and calling Fathers of Man Gods but not one coming though waiting by house by brook for hours days weeks.

Your Pa-ap heart broken into pieces. Finally doing Rites taught Elders to me time after time and when rites done with hole buried Coqua and stones mound. Put your Ma-am things with her those she cared for. Your forest lion tooth that time you and Pa-ap fought it and took it and that jay feather I found her in woods those colors she liked. And her necklace her Ma-am had from her Ma-am and backward some.

So at last ready your Pa-ap with Great club skull crushing on way to village to find Others. But then come old peddler from before. How know he and find me by brook? No one ever telling Pa-ap.

He sat down and to me talk and talk. Said sorry and sorry for the Others and do I know not all like those ones. I think I knowing that but too angry to be caring how Others feeling when my Loves all being gone.

So he saying a place he knows for me. A choice for me he saying to make. But I wanted you my son loving. So old peddler said wait and he going among Others and looking for you he said. I knowing not if he being true but talking and talking finally said I yes and put Great club down.

Old peddler said wait in house by brook for new man of Others to come by and by. He was saying this new man knowing way to new starting over place. Then peddler going off looking to town for my loving son redhead.

And finally few days after that new man he promised coming. And know you who? Was Master Silvestrus! Not knowing him so close back then. We talking and he saying about Sorcery and Collegium and my good cooking and so coming I to here.

Strange things see at first but after time not being so bad and all the Apprentices doing good things there.

But best thing after two of the years past was Silvestrus telling he heard from old man peddler having found loving son at a long last. He telling me of loving son and growing up. Sad hearing of son stealing things but every man is making own choosings and to have to live with them.

More importance loving son is alive and not harmful to self. And so my loving son making living taking from Others gold for what precious they taking from him his Ma-am. Hear word Justice. Maybe this is but not your Philosopher is your Pa-ap so not knowing for certain.

Then better of all nights getting first of scrolls writing to your Pa-ap of yourself and things you knew and saw and were doing. Taking hours it to read though caring not at all.

Then best of all nights was finally time of seeing you loving son at the last long. Pa-ap was hoping to be remembered by his loving son but years had been long time and scared things and feelings maybe changing but then you coming and you did gave Pa-ap your hug and kissing like in those long times ago by house by brook. And your Pa-ap day was full and his heart singing was in heavens all above.

And so now telling you old story one more time hoping no tired of it you hear. But in telling your Pa-ap lives over old time with his Coqua and you little dirty redhair by brook so is pleasure but hurting too so is life full.

Of course Pa-ap must be adding how old Father of Man feel life completing his loving son nice girl meeting mating and having own loving tikis so Pa-ap becoming Great Pa-ap some one day. That happening your Pa-ap ready to for going Far Land and seeing his Coqua at last. Then all complete being for ending peace.

I must now going on with next meals for fixing Apprentices. Am putting bit of each these fixing meals out each night every for your red sister-cousin as have I over every years since you asking me to do for her memory since her killing that time. Hoping you of her thinking all those years ago. Am keeping word though so young redhead Apprentice knowing not relations as was I told. Someday maybe he knowing be all right and telling.

Just glad being son alive as Others saying close of call since Bannock night. Taking care greatly for yourself my loving son.

Your Pa-ap loving much to you,

Specus, Pa-ap

"Aye, Thaddeus," Rolland called out, holding up a scroll case. "This came for you. I was on my way back from Master Beatus and Porter Modus spied me. It must have come with the evening route. He said I should pass it on, so receive." The redhead tossed the battered leather cylinder to his back-country Brother. "Who sent it?"

Thaddeus was surprised. Who would be writing to him? Certainly not his parents; they were illiterate. He could think of no one else until he saw the seal on the scroll case—a rose in white wax next to a deep red wax seal imprinted with a bunch of grapes. He knew the sigil immediately.

The tall Apprentice mumbled an excuse and, half-running, made his way out of the quadrangle and across the snow to the stables. He took a lantern from a peg and set it alight, being careful to guard the flame.

The old mule looked up when Thaddeus entered, but as the boy did not approach or address him, Asullus remained silent.

Thaddeus placed the lantern on a low stool and put his back against the wall, sliding down the boards until he was sitting. Carefully, he examined the scroll case, studying the leather and the seals.

He took out his knife, opened the catch on the lantern and placed the cutting edge over the flame for a brief moment, then applied the blade gently under the wax seals, loosening one and then the other.

Closing the lantern and sliding his knife back into its sheath, he opened the leather case and cautiously withdrew the beribboned scroll. The young Apprentice gently turned the rolled parchment over and over in his hands as if holding a most precious possession—which he was.

Glancing quickly around the stable, he pressed the missive to his nose and inhaled. *Ahh, yes, her fragrance.*

With trembling hands, he pried loose the white rose seal on the scroll. He slowly removed the ribbon and stared at the parchment, not wanting to miss any detail. Then he carefully unrolled the parchment. He gazed at the writer's hand, recognizing it immediately as well.

Ethne's.

> *My Sweet Thaddeus,*
> *I am writing to break the silence I have so harshly and purpose-*
> *fully—but not thoughtlessly, I hope—imposed between us.*
> *Perchance you will want to discard this letter. Perhaps you*
> *have already. Yet I beseech you—please read on. Fates greater*
> *than our own depend on it.*

I realize this is a very peculiar beginning for a love letter, but you will see.

First, let me tell you that I love you. I have loved you since I first saw you and even—if you can believe it—before that. This secret is a part of what I have to tell you.

You see, I knew we would meet long before you came to Figberry.

How is this, you will ask? Well, it is from a Prophecy. My mother was once visited by four old women. Women of Power, she called them. They told her that her daughter—me—would one day, if she so chose, have a child. That child, they prophesied, would grow to become a great ruler and the savior of the Westlands.

Were I you, I would think this was all nonsense, but hearken to me, my love, and know it is true. I know this down to my bones. And this wonderful child is the product of our Love.

There is another part of what I have to tell you. You see, I am having your child. It happened during that precious time we spent together when you gave your gift to me. He—I already know it is a boy—is coming any time. I think, perhaps, tomorrow. I even know his name, my love, yet I am not permitted—by Forces greater than I—to tell it to you. I do not know why.

There is nothing you need do. Our son will be raised well. When you are both ready, it is said you will meet. If the Prophecy holds true, you will grow to love one another as you should. So it has been foretold.

My love—and this is the hardest thing I must tell you— this wonderful miracle we bring to the world has, like all precious things, a cost. A price. It is a price I pay willingly, my Thaddeus. I wish you to know this. I would not undo one moment of any of it. And I pray you will come to feel the same over time.

The price, my love, is my life. I was told that after I have our baby, I will die. It was hard, at first, to accept this. But please know I have now come to embrace what must be. If truth be told, I think we both knew this was bound to happen, in any case, from the consuming illness that has plagued me so.

Dearest Thaddeus, please do not grieve for me. Let us both always remember our love as a wonderful fulfillment of our brief time together and think on it with kindness—a true blessing.

Do not think to come to me, for by the time you read this, I will be no more. By then, there will be nothing to see, dearest Thaddeus, only wonderful moments to remember.

I am sad to leave this world, but I know your future stretches out before you, and I know you will go on to become a most potent and powerful Sorcerer.

You may remember I predicted this; so long ago, it all seems. You will do well, more than well. You will love, marry, have children. This is not part of any Prophecy. It is just what my eyes have always told me. What worthy maiden of any station and substance would allow you to go on alone in this world? Ha! I know the answer to that question. I admit I am a bit jealous of whoever it is that comes to share your life with you, but I hold in my heart the knowledge that I was your first love, and from that love, a salvation.

Well, my love, I will end this now and gather my strength for what must come. Be well, my Thaddeus. You are the most handsome, the sweetest, the most gentle and caring, the best and finest man I ever truly loved. That is also easy to say, as you are the only man I ever truly loved.

Perhaps a part of you will find this an amusing declaration coming from a common courtesan of the House of Lilies in the city of Fountaindale, but it is true, nevertheless.

Farewell, my dearest, dearest Thaddeus.

Ethne of Tarandon

3

Headlong Flight
Praecipiti Fuga

Thaddeus sat stunned, the scroll in his lap as if he'd been hit in the stomach by a *Pugil*. A tear trickled from his eye, then another, then a stream, a river, a torrent. Howling and sobbing, the Apprentice shook with unending waves of shock, sorrow, and loss.

Of a sudden, Asullus was there, nuzzling Thaddeus' cheek.

"Now, now, laddie. 'Tis all right. Yer old mule is here, an' together we'll make it whole again, whate'er it may be. No one there is'll be givin' ye a hurt while I'm here wi' ye an' breathin' still. Now, now…."

The boy threw his arms around the neck of his trusted friend and cried until he could cry no more. Slowly, the storm spent itself.

"I canno' read it upside down, laddie, but I'd bet me portion o' oats this month yer grief is tied up to what ye've been readin' in that there parchment. Ha' I the trow o' it?"

Thaddeus' tear-stained face shone wetly as he nodded. "Y-yes. It-it's from Ethne. Oh, Asullus, she's dead!" Another storm of tears unleashed a new flood of pain. Eventually, it spent itself as well.

"Aye, laddie, I know it," the mule answered softly.

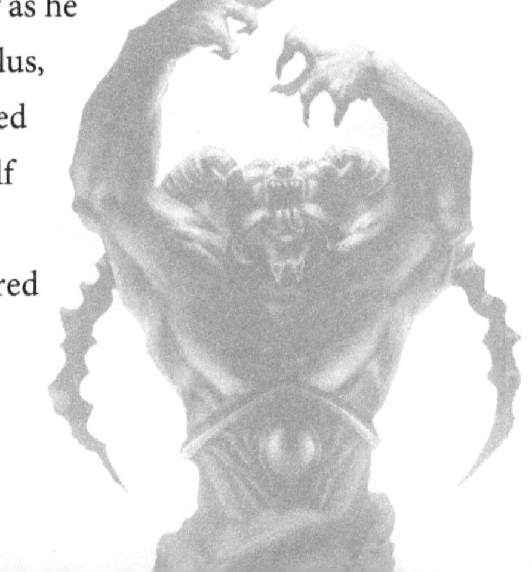

"W-what?" Thaddeus started. "How is it you know that?"

"I knew a bit ago, laddie. Ye see, 'tis connected wi' the lass herself, I am, on account o' this garland I ha' been wearin' all these months. The lass gave it to me wi' her own hands that time we passed through Figberry an' stayed wi' the vintner there, Ormerod.

"She came to me in the stable that evening an' took o'er me groomin', sendin' the stable boy away. She said she ha' a way wi' plants an' such an' ha' wove that garland a-purpose to gi' to me so I could keep a better eye on a certain one. She told me then, o' a foretellin' she'd had as a slip o' a girl concernin' a young lad an' a child o' some import they were to be havin' together." Asullus looked directly into Thaddeus' eyes. "I ha' the impression all this might be tied together, an' that she might ha' been talkin' aboot a laddie I might know. What think ye now?"

Thaddeus lowered his head, his face reddening. Then he swallowed and returned his friend's gaze. He swiped his eyes, sniffed, and cleared his throat. "It's true. Ethne and I … we were together at Figberry. Her letter says there was a child from our love … a boy. She says I have a son. She says he's to save the Westlands. But she said she has to die for it! That can't be, Asullus! That must not happen!"

"Aye, laddie, I know yer feelin' but 'tis done already. Ye'll be remember-in' that time no' so long ago in Bannock, and I ha' me spell? Well, the sickness was brought on by the lassie breathin' her last. As I was wearin' her garland at the time, the force o' her dyin' came to me directly hard, bein' connected as we were through the flowers."

The mule looked away for a moment. Thaddeus saw pain writ large upon his shaggy features.

"An' then I saw the sun, blazin' entire, fillin' up me vision from one side to the other. Thought to meself, me eyes'll be boilin' in me sockets soon enou', I did. But I knew I ha' ne'er seen a sight so grand in all me livin' days. Was like the glories o' all the heavens above, an' I knew somethin' o great import ha' occurred. I didno' know then what it might be, so I held back from tellin' ye the scraps I had. Who's to know? I could ha' it all wrong, an' sent ye into the pit fer no reason. So, now I thinks I knows. 'Twas the birth o' yer son, come to save the Westlands, entire. A mighty one among all the mighty ones there e'er was. He's yer son. Once ye can put yer grief aside, laddie, 'tis rightfully proud ye should be."

"But, Asullus, even if that's all true, Ethne says I'll not be able to see him or even meet him until years and years have passed. I won't have the raising of him. She wrote I couldn't even know his name!"

"Ah, laddie, take ye an e'en strain. There must be a reason fer this all to fall out the way it has. Think, how is it ye could his parent be? Ye've just started yer schoolin'. Ye know the Master ha' said ye're the main point o' the Great Compass. Ye ha' much to learn, much growin' t' do an' many deeds to accomplish. Think ye, ye could do all o' that an' be a proper parent at the same time? A fifteen-year-old lad?"

Thaddeus shook his head but looked defiant.

"Nay, o' course no'. Now, yer own letter's yer own letter, an' I do no' need to be knowin' the details, mind ye. But did the lass mention to ye any provisions fer yer son's raisin' an' such as ha' been made?"

Thaddeus nodded slowly. "Yes, she did, but she did not tell me that, either."

"Thaddeus, me lad, ye must know yer lady. Ye must know her heart was the grandest thing aboot her. Goin' bravely on to meet her doom all these years an' ne'er complainin' if I ha' me guess correct. An' a doom it was—endin' all an' ev'rything. An' we both know she loved ye fierce if only fer a splinter o' time. Ye no' think she'd keep from tellin' ye all that she could now, do ye?"

"No. No, she wouldn't."

"Well, there ye are, then. She's told ye' what ye need to know fer now. Otherwise, perhaps ye'd be steppin' in when ye shouldn't, an' a fine mess ye'd be creatin'. Or, mayhap, knowin' somethin' as ye shouldn't at this time would only lead to danger comin' to the wee one or yerself, don' ye know. Take me word, laddie. 'Tis fer the best."

Thaddeus was silent for a long moment before answering. "No, Asullus. Nothing that you said or she's written proves she's really dead. No one can predict when a baby is to be born. Most ladies in Beewicke had their babies and they lived, not died. Nothing is certain. She could be living but be in terrible distress." Lines of decision formed on his face. "I must go to her."

"Thaddeus! Are ye daft, lad? Ye canno' jus' march off in the middle o' winter like ye ha' no other plans fer the rest o' yer life! The lass is gone, I tell ye. An' all yer wishin' an' denyin' willna' make any o' it be different."

"Tell the others I'll be back as I may."

So saying, the tall Apprentice began rummaging around the stable for gear and supplies. Soon enough, he had snowshoes, a backpack, bow and arrows, and a mix of other provisions and tools for his journey. Throughout his preparations, Asullus alternately pleaded and scolded the youth for the risk and his stubborn foolishness. But Thaddeus' mind was set, and he was determined.

"Goodbye, Asullus. Tell the others." With that, he went out of the shed into the early wintry night. He didn't bother to hitch up the cart, feeling it would only slow him down. Also, Asullus' increasingly frantic pleas and diatribes made it unlikely the beast would willingly assist in his journey.

He crossed the meadow to the forest, selected a path at random, and took it. He was the best tracker in the College, and he knew it. He just hoped there'd be no pursuit.

Asullus paced back and forth in the stable. "Aye, here's a fine kettle o' mule stew, ain't it now? The lad's run off wi' ne'er a thought fer tomorrow—runnin' away from his trainin', his school, his Master. And fer what? Ye must face the fact, laddie. She's gone from ye. What good is it ye think ye'll be doin'? She canno' help ye, nor ye she. Aye, 'tis a son ye ha', but as I ha' told ye, ye canno' be a father to the lad just now. There'll be another in any case to take care o' yer bonnie boy. Trainin' him up to accept the heavy load the Fates ha' spun out fer him."

The mule snorted and resumed his pacing.

"Yet, here I be. An' what was it the lass ha' said t' me, gazin' at this ol' mule wi' those huge eyes o' hers? 'Take care o' him, Asullus,' she says. Aye, an' what was it I ha' said in reply? 'Aye, lassie, that I will.' An' yet, here I be, on account o' the most stubborn o' all the creatures o' the Gods—a lad o' fifteen years entire."

Asullus shook his head, the slobber of disgust flying everywhere.

"So, what is it I'm to do, then? Stay me ground? Inform the Master an' let 'em as run things sort it out while warm an' well-fed I be here in me stable-home? Aye, an' while all that would be goin' on, the poor lad is out in the wind an' cold, ne'er thinkin' aboot how to make his journey. Freezin' an' starvin', ne'er knowin' how best to fend fer himself. Canno' count on his Sorcerous craft to help him none outside the school. Wolves an' bears an' worse, just waitin' to make a mid-winter snack o' him. Or, them as is brigands wantin' ta finish the job their friends started back when first we set out."

Asullus stopped abruptly.

"Nay, I'll no' be left behind. I promised the lass, an' I do care fer the boy in any case, even though he be more stubborn than any twelve o' what I'm accused o'. So, laddie, ye'll no' think ye kin get away from me so easily, havin' all yer adventures to yerself, claimin' the glory at the end just so ye can come back an' rub me tail in it. No, me Bucko. No' this time. No' this day."

So saying, Asullus trotted back to his stall, nudged the garland from its hook, positioned it around his neck, turned, and cantered out the stable door. He had no difficulty following the tall Apprentice. Snowshoes in freshly fallen snow presented no great tracking challenge.

Thaddeus marched steadily over the frozen whiteness, arms swinging rhythmically. He was confident he could reach the vintner's estate. He had a bow and arrows as well as a small trap for rabbits, all borrowed from the shed and stable yards. A rolled-up blanket sat atop his backpack, cushioning his neck as he walked. Stockings and gloves he had as well.

Unfortunately, he had no ambrosia that would really have been welcome. What he did have in greatest commodity, however, was determination. Nothing would keep him from Ethne. If he hurried, he might even be in time to save her—somehow—though the portion of his mind that usually questioned such peculiar non-reasoning was currently being ignored.

As time passed, he began to think of other things he should have taken time to gather before he left. He also began to wish for his three friends. Their companionship always shortened any journey and blunted any anxieties.

Well, there was nothing for it but to hurry. Soon it would be totally dark, and the temperature would plummet. He knew what to do and how to do it. He only wished he needn't be alone when it was time to act. He didn't even have his faithful old mule with him. Perhaps he should have asked Asullus to accompany him. With a little persuasion, the old one might have agreed. Even his crooked grin, outrageous stories, and bad accent would be welcome.

Several hours passed. The moon rose, its beams dancing' off Thaddeus' steaming breath. Finally, cold and weariness were sufficiently daunting, and he stopped to make a forest camp. He started a small fire and melted snow to drink. It was then he began thinking about his meal back at the *Collegium* compared to his dinner this night—that is, nothing.

Perhaps he should have given this journey more thought. Perhaps....

His head whipped around, his senses alert. Something was approaching from the southwest and was now very close. His knife was out in a blink, and he assumed the crouching position favored by Master Luctarus. The sounds of approach increased.

There … a dark shape taking form. It was….

"Aye, so I've traveled all this way, leavin' me warm stable an' its comforts fer no good reason I ken, so I can be greeted by someone anxious to open me innards? Humans!"

"Asullus!" Thaddeus' heart leaped with joy.

"Aye. I know o' no one else who'd be trekkin' after the most stubborn —in the middle of winter—seeking a no-sense … ah, *pfah!* I'll no' be goin' to be wi' ye at the beginnin' when all is easy, then stay to home when it gets a mite sticky. An' in addition … ah, *pfah* again … makes no difference. Are ye well, lad? Ha' ye at least brought yer warm stockings?"

"Oh, Asullus. It's … it's good to see you. I … um, you don't have anything to eat, by chance, do you?"

Anders questioned Rolland closely. "And you just let him run off to who knows where after you saw how agitated he was by that scroll you'd given him?"

Zoarr's eyebrows rose. "Ah, Anders, let's be fair. Rolland couldn't divine the import of the message. And, I believe … ahem … he may not be the only one to run off from time to time and wish to be undisturbed after receiving special mail. Yes?"

Anders' face suffused with a rapidly spreading crimson glow. "Perhaps, but he's been gone all evening. And we're sitting here playing our instruments, waiting and waiting. He's never missed a session, you know. Besides, since when did you start defending Rolland, anyway? I think we should check his room again. Come on."

Three boys stood in front of Thaddeus' room, alternately pounding on the door and shouting his name. One by one, the other hall doors opened with either curious or irritated faces peering out.

"Aye, we're studying here, you know," one said.

"Everyone should experience new things at least once," Rolland gibed. "By the way, *Anima Inflationis,* have you seen Thaddeus this eve?"

"No, I have not seen him."

"Nor I."

"Nor I," chimed in the other half-*Aelvae.*

"We had best go out and search the grounds. I think we should try the stable and shed first," Anders directed.

The three boys had just reached the landing to their stairs when Lilyput appeared—per usual—as if out of thin air.

"Ah-heee! And where do you three see yourselves heading this evening, hmm?"

"House-Mistress, we go to find Thaddeus. He's been missing all evening. He ran off after receiving a scroll, and no one has seen him since."

The ancient Goblin turned to gaze down the hall and was silent for a long moment. "You three must return to your rooms. Some need journey while others need wait. It is the way of things. I know you miss your fellow but become used to this. This is but the first. He will be one of many journeys, I think."

Lilyput stared at the floor for another long moment, then raised her head. "Do not be concerned for him. There is one who accompanies him. He will be safe. Now, to your beds, all of you, or shall I speak the words for Brother Longbone, eh? Be off!"

Tombstone
Monumentum Sepulcri

ord Geoffrey looked after the tall boy leading Asullus out the gate toward the wide world outside Mountaingaard. The lad's story had the same feeling as those Geoffrey's men told of why they were late while smelling of ale and cheap perfume on Moon Day's morning muster after a weekend off duty—just barely plausible and lacking the ring of truth, yet not worth the effort to fully challenge. And as he'd heard nothing to the contrary, and with that old mule vouchsafing the tale, he'd let both of them through. But he'd had a word with Asullus before they left.

"Hark ye, old hayburner. I don't know what game is afoot here, but you've not been contradicted, so I'm obliged to let you pass. But this is a highly irregular sortie. If you allow the Old Man's prize Apprentice to come to harm, it's both our heads."

"Now, laddie, what sort o' tone is it ye take wi' yer friendly ol' mule, then? Why I but remember the time when…."

"I said I was letting you through, but I have my duties as well this day, and waiting for you to finish with one of your stories will not allow enough hours to accomplish all I must do."

"*Harrumph.* Well, ye no' ha' to be so bold now, me Lord. Ne'er it was did I do ye a hurt. Intentionally."

"True enough. And this is no time to start. Well, you've enough provisions to last the week you've asked for. So, on your way then. Take your best care of him, Asullus, and yourself as well."

"Aye, laddie, that I will."

As they traveled, Thaddeus paid particular attention to Asullus, frequently stopping for rest, watering, and feeding. The last was accomplished by the old mule pawing at some spot in the ground, after which Thaddeus took his hand shovel and turned the frozen earth over to disclose a tuber or parted a bush to expose a swatch of coarse grass. Boiled versions of these same served as the main course for his own meals.

Thaddeus imagined Anders' amusement at telling his Nannsi, should he ever learn of it, how the Beewickean had used the girls' vegetable lore from their experience together over Mid-Summer past to identify and forage for edible plants.

Fortunately, unwary rabbits and similar small creatures, including the infrequent squirrel, provided a welcome, albeit periodic, addition of meat to his diet. And on one occasion, his bow and arrow brought down a giant red-beaked strutting grouse unwise enough to take a turn around his realm that day.

Once Thaddeus sighted along his shaft toward a tawny hind innocently feeding on tree bark. But just before release, he dropped his arm. He could not take the creature's life.

The animal regarded the Apprentice a moment before bounding away into the forest. Thaddeus followed the hind's tracks until he lost sight of it. The spore vanished abruptly as if into thin air. He stood for a moment regarding the scene, then shrugged and returned to Asullus.

Toward evening, the boy led the mule up the long curve north of Figberry, past fields of fired vineyards now partly covered in snow.

At the top of the slight rise stood the burned and crumbling remains of the vintner's manor. The smell of char still hung in the air, a faint but pungent presence.

Thaddeus' mouth dropped open in shock. He stood stock-still, staring, unable to move as his eyes drank in the desolation.

"Laddie, this place ha' the smell o' death. There be nothin' here for ye. Whatever there once was ha' passed."

Thaddeus shook his head in denial. "No, Asullus. We have only just arrived. I must know what happened here. I must find her."

It was now growing dark. Thaddeus fashioned a pair of torches, lit them, and set forth to explore the grounds while Asullus foraged for a meal. A tickle of something brushed Thaddeus' cheek. Holding up his torches, he found it was snowing again. After further investigation, he rejoined the mule.

"See the ground? Two groups of men came from two different directions. It happened at night—torch markings all over the ground. Hmm. Some conflict … it looks as if the groups fought, so they had to have been here at the same time. There are no bodies in what's left of the big house."

"Aye, then the lot servin' the master ha' all left. 'Tis no' likely two opposin' groups would ha' carried them away out o' respect. So, the manor was deserted. The word ha' gotten around, an' the scavengers came to claim what they could then fell to wi' the competition. Aye, 'tis a common enou' occurrence. But the question is, how did the manor come to be deserted?"

Thaddeus searched behind the ruined manor, coming to a halt facing the southern exposure, overlooking what remained of the vine-yards. "Asullus, to me a moment. The answer may fall here. What do you make of this?"

As the mule drew near, the tall boy gestured widely with an arm sweep that included several paces in either direction. "Look you. It's bones. Human. See there, a skull. It was a person. But the bones are all scattered. Why … oh, I see. Someone died here, and then the wild dogs came."

"Ye Gods! That'd no' be—"

"No, Asullus. It was a woman, though. See the tattered remains of her shift and shawl? Yes, it was an old woman. Look there; the skull. Toothless."

Thaddeus' eyes marched up the incline and paused. He rose and walked a few paces further away from the house. "Asullus, there are two headstones here." Thaddeus crouched again in front of the markers. He brushed debris off the larger, more ornate of the pair.

"Oh, Asullus. It's Ormerod. That's why the manor was empty, with no bodies or vases, bowls, or jewelry in the ashes. The Master had died, and with no one to carry on, he was buried, deserted, and then after, the manor was looted by the servants. But, then, whatever happened to Eth—"

Thaddeus halted in mid-speech. Crouched down on one knee and holding the two torches aloft in one hand, he swept more debris from the second headstone.

"Oh, Ethne!" Thaddeus stared at the grave marker, then dropped both torches, hands springing to his eyes. "Oh, Ethne!" Collapsing in a heap, he wept.

"Aye, laddie, ye've found yer lass, ye ha. 'Tis all right, me boy, her sufferin's o'er an' she's gone on to a better place. Ye weep now. Yer journey's been hard an' yer loss is great. Ye weep. I'll be just o'er here a ways."

Asullus left the sobbing boy alone with his sorrow and walked slowly over to a shallow rise that presented yet another panorama of the abandoned and desolate vineyards, though the pale moonlight made all appear ghostly. The mule sighed deeply.

"Ah, lassie, I hope 'tis all true. If there e'er was one as deserved a better place, surely no one save yerself. I hope 'tis all true."

Thaddeus' torches, cast away and ignored on the ground, sputtered and went out. A chill breeze sprang up but died quickly as a pale glow illuminated the ground.

"Why do you weep, boy?" a faraway, hollow voice said.

Startled, Thaddeus jerked up his head, his tears interrupted. Sitting there on the gravestone was Ethne, his love, except she was the palest of pale and of no substance. Translucent. He noted with a start that he could see through her. She was as beautiful as always, but her eyes were hollow pools … otherworldly.

Thaddeus jumped to embrace her, but his hands passed through the figure as through empty air. He recoiled with the effort.

"Ethne? Are you … Is that…."

"Thaddeus, I am she, the spirit of she who was." The figure reached out to touch the boy, but her hand passed through him as well, and she sighed.

Thaddeus was not frightened. How could he be frightened of one who had loved him and whom he had loved? But his tongue clove to the roof of his mouth. What could he say? She was beautiful, but she was—

"Thaddeus, you must needs listen to me, my love. You have received my letter? Ah, yes. I see it. That is why you have come, though, dear Thaddeus, I forbade it." The figure smiled wanly. *"I have moments only, my love. I have been waiting here for you. Our son … Aki— Ah, I cannot say it, even now. No matter, the servants have him and will tend him well until … the other comes. Oh, Thaddeus, if the Ladies told us true, our son will be a great leader of men and will save his people. And … oh, my time is past, my love. We will see each other again, at the end of things. Remain steadfast. Farewell, my love."*

The figure faded into mist and was gone.

Mute, Thaddeus sat staring at the gravestone. The snow spiraled down ever thicker as the silent storm increased in intensity.

Asullus made his way over to the boy kneeling in front of the smaller headstone. He bowed his head in respect and waited a goodly while as the snow flurries flew ever faster before he spoke.

"Aye, laddie, she's gone. A beautiful, wonderful girl she was, full o' life an' joy. She shared her love wi' ye an' ye an' she ha' gi'en to the world its salvation if I ha' the right o' it. But, laddie, she's gone on as she ha' told ye herself. Ye know her chief concern is fer yer welfare. She'd want ye to live an' go on to develop yer powers an' see to yer boy later on. So, there's nothin' fer us here, my lad. I say, let's be aboot findin' our way back to the College. A fer piece it is, e'en if we cut a corner or two. So best we get started, aye? What say ye, lad?"

Thaddeus did not answer the old mule, then or later. Every few minutes, Asullus would try again, reasoning, pleading, arguing—but to no avail. The snow was flying blindingly by now and had begun to accumulate, thickening at an alarming rate.

Finally, Thaddeus spoke. "You. Go on." He then lay down on the gravestone, pulling his snow-covered cloak over his head.

"Thaddeus! Oh, me boy! 'Tis no' the time to be givin' up, lad. The world's at risk, an' all's a gamble. Oh, teeth an' tails! What to do, what to do? Here I be, leagues an' leagues from home, an' I canno' go an' I canno' stay! *Equus!* God o' those as has four hooves, I call on ye to save us here. Come ye now!"

The blizzard continued and nothing happened. Moments stretched out before the old mule's words were whisked away by the storm.

"*Pfah!* Never were ye worth a turd in me or anyone else's memory, in any case, truth be told. What can I do now? Well, there is that, but the Lady ha' said I should use it only sparingly an' only in the most dire o' circumstances. Well, now, if this do no' qualify, then I ha' no idea o' what might. All right then, we'll have a go at it. Hope this tree'll bear the right-most fruit. *Commuta!*"

Asullus' garland began to glow, whiter and whiter, till it hurt the eyes to look on it. A pulse of blazing light shot from it in an expanding sphere brighter than a thousand torches.

In the part of his mind still attached to this world, Thaddeus was aware of the painfully bright light. Then two sharp bands gripped him around his middle as if he'd been grasped by two great scythes. Suddenly, he was lifted up and away and, at the fringe of his consciousness, became aware of the cold.

The sound of howling wind filled his ears and something else in the background, some sort of rhythmic *schiss*ing noise, rising and falling. And a distant part of him realized he himself was rising and falling in time with the pulsing sound. He had only enough strength to open his eyes but closed them quickly, rejecting the improbable sight.

Stretched beyond endurance, he gave himself up to oblivion.

5

Care from a Goblin and a Centaur
Curare a Cobolorum et Centaurus

Ever so slowly wakening, wakening, Thaddeus was vaguely aware of being warmer than he had at any time in the past two weeks. He sensed the weight of covers — toasty, pleasant. His forehead was being patted with—yes, with a damp cloth of some kind, and then his cheeks as well. Soon enough, he had the strength to open his eyes a slit.

He was in his own room, in his own bed. The House-Mistress stood over him with a look of concern on her countenance. She had a folded linen and was carefully and gently applying it to his face. When he opened his eyes fully, she drew back and regarded him levelly.

"Ah-heee, young Thaddeus. Back from yet another adventure, eh? What a trouble you are! All the College in an uproar these three weeks past, and you at the center of it while not even here. You and that old mule, eh? But found you out some things, I imagine, yes? Yes, I see it." Her gaze softened. "Ah, poor boy, you've had a loss, you have. But then you've gained something as well, have you not? But you don't even know what it is, nor can you come to know, perhaps not for years. That is a hard one for a boy so young."

On impulse, Thaddeus reached out and grasped the green Goblin's wrinkled hand in his, giving it a gentle squeeze.

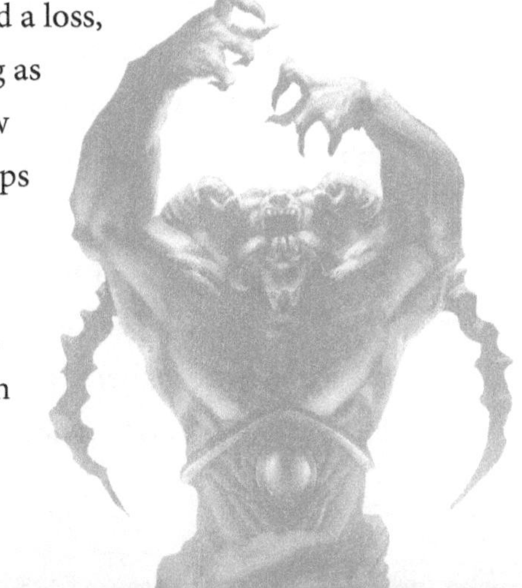

"Thank you, Lilyput. You always take such good care of us. I don't know if anyone ever says so, but thank you."

The House-Mistress inhaled sharply but did not take her hand away immediately. A trace of moisture rimmed those ancient eyes.

"Ah, it's true, the One you are." She withdrew her hand and returned to her ministrations. "Not so glad was I at the first, compelled to care for young boys and all. But over centuries, a person will get used to anything, I suppose. Now you come, and the others, and maybe things will change, eh? Well, we shall see. In the meantime, take you better care of yourself, young Apprentice. Eat your fill…." Lilyput nodded in the direction of a covered tray sitting on a low stool. "And then rest or Lilyput shall have to summon Brother Longbone, eh? Ah-heee!"

But the Goblin was smiling a sharp-pointed, yellow-toothed smile, and Thaddeus knew he had nothing to fear. He smiled back in acknowledgment.

"By the by, old Asullus is fine but concerned about you. Your fellow Apprentices are jumping up and down to see you—equal parts relief and curiosity, I trow. And Master Silvestrus has been keeping an eye on you for certain. It is my feeling, boy, that none of them, however, has any idea what it is you've been about, eh? Except, perhaps the Master— a bit."

"And also except, perhaps, the House-Mistress—a bit, eh?" Thaddeus said in a moment of insight.

"Ah-heee! More trouble from a troublesome boy. Always the same. Not sure why Lilyput even puts up with it anymore. Next time, Lilyput will stay in bed all day, snoring like lazy Apprentice here. Then would we see how well things run, so? Ah-heee! More than enough time is wasting on this overgrown one, useful only for taking up space."

Dabbing Thaddeus' face a final time, the Goblin carefully straightened his covers, then gathered her washbowl and cloths and, with a nod, made her way out the door, quietly closing the portal behind her.

Aromas Thaddeus had only been peripherally aware of now registered on his senses. Slowly, he raised himself on one elbow and drew the stool and its anticipated contents closer to the bedside. After removing the cloth, he fell to eating immediately.

Sometime later, replete, he lay on his back and turned his head to gaze out the window.

His thoughts ranged wide as he reviewed his experiences of the past year. So much had changed, as had he. Some changes would probably have come his way in any case. He was taller, stronger, and hopefully wiser. He now knew more about himself than he ever had.

He could defend himself in an organized and effective way and mete out significant punishment to any serious opponent. Reading and writing were familiar tasks to him, as were the classics: *Mathematica, Scientia,* and the rest were all less mysterious than before. He could now converse in the Speech of Learning. He had acquired manners, always expected in public. In short, a bit of polish had been put on the apple, though his father would have said a sheen on the honeycomb.

Thaddeus knew his mind was expanding; he could reason more rationally. Master Logus had striven mightily to pound logic, rhetoric, and analysis into his thick-skulled charges. Though with a wry smile, he had declaimed, "It may not all sink in, lads, right this term. But fear not, I'll have you for the next three years. You'll absorb it all, believe me—one way or another." The Master's smile had broadened ominously at that point.

The greatest change of all was his own growing ability to perform Sorcery, to create something out of nothing.

Thaddeus smiled.

Anders and Master Beatus had spent hours debating that particular point. Anders held the view that, by *Leges Naturae,* nothing could be created out of nothing. He used the argument of predecession and a line of reasoning involving how the substance of something was always 'conserved,' as he called it. All serving to prove how it was not possible for him to be doing what he was doing.

Professor Beatus tolerantly wondered aloud what it was concerning the particular prospect of wondrous and unknowable creativity that appeared to disturb the young scholar to the point he'd felt forced to invent all manner of rationalizations. So, it had gone on, week after week.

Thaddeus did not find abstract arguments involving such things as causality, free will versus determinism', the nature of structure, or the origin of the soul particularly edifying, but he did find the practice of Sorcery especially satisfying. He still considered each act he accomplished under the watchful eyes of his Masters a work of awe and wonder. It gave him special pleasure to perform the Art, a feeling that was at once indescribable and humbling.

He marveled yet at the concept of Belief. If it was Believed with sufficient strength, then it was possible.

Master Beatus seemed to feel Thaddeus had a knack for the Art, along with his three Brothers, though it was harder to include Zoarr in this group since he'd already had a year's practical experience. This accounted, perhaps, for his Royal Brother's flair and seeming ease of execution, not to mention his wider range of skills.

Surprisingly, Rolland tended to use Sorcery only sparingly. He had apparently taken to heart the admonition concerning diminution of the life span as the penalty for each Sorcerous application. However, when the thief did use the Art, he invested it with a mix of dash and verve, perhaps a manifestation of his more recent good-natured rivalry with the Prince.

Anders was also frugal with the use of Sorcery, though in his case, it was probably an extension of a parsimonious trait already present in his character rather than any motivated by anxiety.

Thaddeus reflected that he'd already had a life full of experiences, and all in less than a year. He had killed people, saved people, gained

Brothers, loved, then lost others, and begun to open his mind. But overriding all was his burgeoning sense of purpose. If he was, as others claimed, someone special, then he must have a special responsibility for which he'd been given these special abilities.

On the one hand, it seemed very grand, particularly at the beginning. Now, however, doubts were beginning to creep into his sense of accomplishment. Just what was it he'd be called on to do? When? And by what means? He didn't know and might never know until too late. Perhaps that was the point, in part, of all this preparation. And underlying it all was Belief, the means to the end.

But did this end justify these means? He did not know that, either.

One thing he did know was that the feelings inside him were churning as they had back in Beewicke when someone married, and the village men tossed the lucky groom on a blanket, usually until he threw up. He hadn't had a chance yet to absorb all that had happened to him, let alone process it.

Some of those very feelings he'd successfully kept submerged now began to intrude on his consciousness. Feelings concerning his first love, her loss, and the fact he was now a father. A father! It made his head spin. And he didn't even know his son's name.

He had no idea how he should feel about it, but he did know it would remain a secret he'd not divulge to anyone. Then, as soon as he could travel again, assuming he wasn't going to be confined to the College for this last unauthorized venture, he'd begin a journey to search for the boy. He wasn't quite sure where to start looking, but he reasoned something would occur to him—an inspiration, perhaps. He seemed to have a certain facility with inspiration. In the meantime, he'd share with his friends everything—everything except that.

A muffled *thump, thump, thump* coming down the hallway interrupted his train of thought. It stopped at his door. A loud knocking came next, followed by a pause.

"Come in," Thaddeus bade.

The door opened to reveal the massive form of Chiron the Centaur, Horse-Master, filling the doorframe. "Have I leave to enter your room, Apprentice?" the tall figure asked formally.

"Master Chiron! Yes, of course. How is it I may serve you, Master?" Thaddeus asked, starting to rise to make the Greeting of Respect required for all Masters.

The Man-Horse held up a restraining hand. "Do not leave your pallet, Apprentice. I know you are just come back and may yet have the effect of fatigue. I understand you have been traveling. It is, perhaps, a hard thing to reveal now, but I must ask: do you have a son?" The question hung in the air.

"Master, I have just been told this, but I do not know whether or not it is tr—"

The Horse-Master shook suddenly, as if struck, closed his eyes, and tilted his head back as far as it would go. After a moment, he seemed to regain his composure, opened his eyes, and spoke.

"I see. Ah, well, I knew it must come some day, as was foretold. The *Sidera* do not lie. Very well, so be it. Apprentice! Tell your Master Silvestrus that Chiron, the Horse-Master, has left the College. I do not believe I will be returning. If you wish, you may add that I consider myself blessed among all those who possess a mind and walk the Earth. Come I to think on it, you should feel that same way. *Ave!*"

As abruptly as he came, the Centaur backed out of the room, the door slamming shut behind him, though Thaddeus had not bid it so.

Only a moment and a half passed before more knocking—this less measured than frantic—assailed his door.

"Come in," Thaddeus called again.

His door sprang open. Three familiar forms stood there for a second before rushing into his room and immediately closing the door behind them.

"Aye, Thaddeus! Are you well?"

"Aye, Thaddeus! Where the Hells have you been?"

"Aye, Thaddeus! What was the Horse-Master doing in your room?"

Some resolve lasts less long than others, Thaddeus considered, and some lasts hardly any time at all.

Chiron assembled his field pack with practiced care, selecting only those things he would truly need. He believed he would never return, so he had no need to weigh himself down unnecessarily.

Yes, the Sidera do not lie….

Now he would make his way to the town of the birth. That would be Figberry. Once there, he needed to trace where the babe had been taken and by whom. Next, he would track the party to its destination. He knew it not for certain. It could be any place in the world. But he had a guess from a sign seen in the Constellation of the Fountains this past spring.

Following that he would obtain the boy. For years, he'd been saving the greater portion of his Master's pay for this occasion. He would do whatever was necessary to save the child.

Once all that had been achieved, he would take the boy to Fornia, or rather to some hill caves he knew of in the area of Fornia. And there they would live, and he would teach the lad; teach him everything he knew. The boy must learn these things until they became second nature to him. It would take time. But then, time was what the Horse-Master had in greatest quantity.

Afterward … well, what would be, would be.

He had no control over that. He had read little in the Heavens concerning his own fate beyond completing the boy's instruction. It was as if all would come to an end after his task was done. But who knew for certain concerning the Future? He did not, and that he *did* know for certain.

Now to his uncle's to obtain the mare and her foal they had discussed. The babe would be in need of sustenance—and what better? But first....

The Horse-Master, his long cloak trailing down his back and his head hooded against the cold, quietly opened the armory door and entered. Locating what he sought did not take long: a heavy long sword with an engraving of a lion near the hilt, facing right rampant, and a shield, a long oval affair with a faded white rose on its face.

Yes, these would do. In fact, they were necessary for the father, so for the son.

The Centaur carefully closed sand locked the armory door and locked it in place, leaving the keys in their accustomed place on the frame's hook. *Now to the journey....*

He believed in his soul in what he was doing, but he was not entirely certain as to how he was going to accomplish it. And the cost, personally, the cost would be … high.

But the reward: salvation! Well worth that and any other cost he could imagine.

As he placed his hands on the sword and shield, a name came to him. It blazoned forth, a searing white light in his brain: *Akireu!*

Startled, the Centaur staggered sideways a pace. Yes, now he had it. The boy's name—a warrior's name—an Emperor's name!

Gathering himself, the Centaur surged forward at a canter, down the hill toward the forest and away from the College.

He never looked back.

The talking had gone on for hours. As a measure of their excitement, the boys had not even stopped for Even-tide.

"And you remember nothing about how you came home? Thaddeus, 'tis a week or two's journey at the most serene of times. How did you make it in just hours?"

"He flew. Just like he said, Stumpy. Weren't you listening?"

"He didn't say he flew. And don't call me that. He just said he felt like he was up in the air. Besides, he can't fly. And neither can Asullus, come to think."

"Yet, they both made it back as described in no time at all. How do you explain that?"

"I can't. It's a mystery. But a mystery for another day. Of more import, I think, is his son."

"A son! *Iovis!* Thaddeus, what does it mean?" Rolland asked.

"I don't know," the tall Apprentice replied. "Perhaps it has no meaning at all. Nellia, a girl in our village, got pregnant once. I never knew who the father was, but there must have been some difficulty. Because one night she was there, and the next day she was gone. No one ever heard from her again. Maybe it's just something that happens. Only this time, it happened to me." Thaddeus turned his head to the wall for a moment, then turned back.

"I don't think so, Thaddeus," Anders said. "I think it was meant to happen."

"Meant to happen? Bughouse, Anders! How do you...." Rolland sputtered.

"Peace, brother mine," Zoarr interrupted. "Let us hear from our Resident Scholar. You say you think it was meant to happen, Anders? How do you mean?"

"Realize I am putting this together as we go. Ah, all right. Zoarr, you weren't with us then, but you, Rolland, and you, Thaddeus, remember that night with Merriwhiddle?"

"Hard to forget that night. Kill every bug or fly I've seen since, whenever I can," Rolland replied.

"Yes, well, I was in a bit of a fog myself but I remember. I remember Master Silvestrus speaking with Merriwhiddle before, well, before that. They were talking about the Great Compass. Don't you remember, Thaddeus? Merriwhiddle had hoped to interrupt the Prophecy by killing her own children, fathered by Silvestrus.

"But then Master Silvestrus said something about how there was more than one way for the Compass to work. He said one of the *Cardines*—the four of us—could give rise to the *Ordines*. There were to be four of the *Ordines*, the complementary points of the Compass. And they had to be there as well. And then, do you not remember what he said? Something about an old rhyme…."

"The Flower, the Insect, the Serpent, the Beast," Thaddeus said, a faraway look in his eyes.

Anders nodded. "As you say."

"Well," Rolland interjected, "what's all that gibberish got to do with anything?"

"Just this, my fiery-headed pickpocket. We all know Thaddeus here, for some reason, is the chief point of the *Circuitus Octipes Magnus*—the North, or *Septentrio*. This has some meaning beyond what Master Silvestrus has said. Look at the actions of Charles that time just before you were about to become hash—"

Rolland shivered.

"—and then how Perditus reacted, Thaddeus, you remember?"

"Yes."

"So, it all must have meaning. Well, if Thaddeus is the chief point on the Great Compass, and the secondary points—the *Ordines*—are to come from one of the main Compass points, then it stands to reason that they would come from the leading point. Yes?"

"What 'secondary points' are you describing here? I'm not following," Rolland said, plainly exasperated.

"The 'secondary points,' or *Ordines*, Rolland, are children—specifically, four children—that I think our Thaddeus, here, is supposed to sire. Children who will then grow up to help us in our Great Compass task."

"You know, this doesn't make a lick of sense, Anders," Rolland said. "What children? And what task?"

"I don't know the task yet, though I have an idea or two in my mind. But I think I know who the children are."

6

Children and the
Hall of the Seniors
Liberi et Atrium Supremorum

The moment stretched out.

Rolland sighed. "All right, learned scholar, who are the children?"

"Well, apparently, Thaddeus has already had the first."

"How do you mean, Anders?" the tall Apprentice asked, his attention riveted to his friend.

"Your first child, Thaddeus. Your child by—Ethne, is it? Yes, Ethne. The girl from Figberry. Weren't you always saying she had a certain gift with flowers?"

"But what of the others?" Zoarr asked.

"Well, what was it Master Silvestrus said … the second child was listed as 'the insect'? And a butterfly is an insect, according to my tutor, Primus. And Thaddeus, I know you dislike talking about it, but were you not, um … with the blue butterfly lady—what was her name?"

"Caerulea," Thaddeus replied. "Yes, Anders, but she and I do not have a child … I mean…."

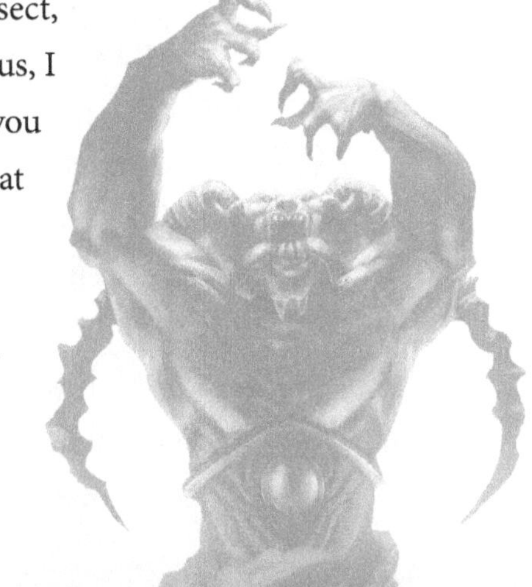

"Ah, not one that you know of. But think back, Thaddeus. Don't you remember telling us about your Mid-Summer's Night's Eve—that's really hard to say, you know—when you saw the Butterfly Queen, and you said her abdomen was all swollen but that she did not appear sick. Well, mayhap she was carrying your child."

Thaddeus blushed but carefully considered his friend's words. It might be true … possibly.

"Anders! That is the most ridiculous—" Rolland began.

"Peace, Brother," Zoarr said, holding up a restraining hand. "All right, Anders. Your thesis is plausible, though barely so. For the sake of argument, let us assume for the moment you are correct. Then what of the serpent and the beast?"

"Well, yes. I have not worked everything out yet, but Thaddeus … I recall you saying something about dragons and wolves in your dreams that time."

"Yes, but those were just dreams, brought about by Rolland's having put the Master's special pipe-weed into the fire that night. I haven't had relations with any snakes or whatever and certainly not with wolves—nor would I wish to, in any case," the boy insisted with some heat.

Anders shrugged. "Um, yes. Well, it was just a thought, as I said."

"Horse dung! My Brother does not couple with animals!" Rolland returned.

"Not to contradict you, Brother, but that is a rather interesting idea," Zoarr said. "And, it has the advantage of being provable by that old element, Time."

"Well, yes. Time, I suppose," Thaddeus said, bringing that part of the discussion to a close. "Anything else of interest while I was away?"

"Well, we have been keeping an eye on Master Perditus," Anders said.

"Oh? Why so?"

"I never liked him anyway," Rolland responded. "Truly a strange one, he is. Always skulking around that damn Tower at all hours. One of the nights we sneaked out looking for you, and he was up there again. And we heard some more of that garbled conversation coming from the top floor. I swear there was more than one person up in the Tower, but when he finally came down, he was alone. There is something not right about it all."

"Perhaps we should be more organized about this. We could seek out Master Silvestrus and Asullus, maybe even Master Cook and Lilyput. We could ask them about him," Anders said.

"Hmm. Not a wise path for us," Zoarr said, stroking his chin. "I think that would only serve to alert everyone, which might then get back to our quarry. Also, I believe they would just forbid us, and it would only lead to increased observation of ourselves. We have been let a fairly loose hand so far, and we should be careful not to place that advantage in jeopardy."

"One small point, fellow Apprentices," Rolland intervened. "Lest we not forget, we are—at least three of us are—*Tirones* in our first year of study, and that year not even completed. How is it we think we have the *adrogantia* to harbor suspicions concerning a Master of the College while, apparently, the entire Faculty fully trained and so far above our own level does not?"

"Excuse me, Rolland," Anders said, "but don't you find Master Perditus' activities suspect?"

"Of course I do. To me, he seems a sneaky little *stercus*, but for the sake of fairness, I just thought I would mention the other."

"There is one thing further," Zoarr said.

"Aye?" Thaddeus said.

"Well, you should know, as long as we're seeking information, um, informally, Wil Rathboneson was once a pupil of Master Perditus but left him for some reason. I heard about that last year. He might possess a reservoir of information concerning the Master and be willing to share it without our other Masters being made aware. However, I do not believe he would do it for myself or Anders here or Rolland, but he might—"

"For myself." Thaddeus nodded. "It's a sound idea and a good place to begin. Getting in to see him might be a little stiff, though. I have heard the *Supremi* do not welcome the Underclass on their wing."

"Doubtful you will have any trouble getting in, Thaddeus," Rolland said, grinning. "If anyone wants to prohibit you, just rattle off a long sentence of explanation, including the two words *Daemon* and *Charles*. I will wager those three gold pieces of yours that you will have no trouble." The thief laughed at his own joke, leaned over, and clapped his friend on the shoulder.

Thaddeus grinned, too. "All right, that will be our plan. I will try tonight. But Rolland, out of curiosity, how can you bet something you do not have? Is that some sort of thieves' logic?"

"Not at all," Rolland said, fanning the fingers of one hand wide to display the Beewickean's trio of worn yellow coins. "Logic has nothing to do with it, actually … except, perhaps, to deduce that a recently-till-now unconscious person may not be at his most alert."

Laughing again, Rolland flipped the gold coins back to his Brother, who caught them left-handed, also with a laugh.

Thaddeus topped the last landing of the stairs leading to the *Supremi's* wing and faced a pair of heavy oaken doors set with massive brass rings and what appeared to be a Cyclops' severed head nailed to the center of the door on Thaddeus' left. A dense fog seeped out from under the lintel, evaporating a short distance from the portal. Sounds—muffled and vaguely threatening animalistic howls—came from behind.

Of a sudden, the single eye flew open. In the left-hand corner of the landing, what had appeared to be a quarterstaff rack transformed into a tree with malevolent features and long-limbed, branch-like hands

THE HALL OF THE SUPREMI

that reached out for Thaddeus. In the other corner, a waist-high black dragon—not there a moment before—bristled its claws, reared back, and shot out flames a pace in length.

The head's single eye regarded him hostilely. "What in the Hells do you want?"

"I have come to see Wil Rathboneson," Thaddeus replied steadily.

"Well, he don't want to see you. If you value your skin, *Tironis*, turn around and march your ass right back down the stairs. Otherwise, there may be … trouble."

At this, a chorus of raucous laughter arose from everywhere at once. The tree became more menacing, and the dragon reared up on its hind feet and fanned its wings, snarling in threat.

"Nevertheless, I have come to see Wil Rathboneson, and I will see him. I have no time to argue with you, but if you wish it, my servant, Charles, *Daemon Minor,* will be glad to address any concerns you may have. Shall I summon him now?"

"Uh … a moment," the head replied, then the eye closed, assuming a posture of repose. The tree and the dragon backed off a step, waiting.

The eye opened again.

"No need to be so surly, young Master. Just doing me job. Aye, *Supremus* Rathboneson's in and will see ye presently."

The head cleared its throat and intoned, "Know all that now you enter the Hall of the *Supremi*. Bring respect and forbearance to those Great you encounter here." The head paused. "Yes, I think that's it." Once again, the voice declaimed, "Enter now the Hall of the *Supremi*."

The thick doors swung open. The tree resumed its quarterstaff form, and the small dragon disappeared.

"Thank you," Thaddeus said as he passed through the now-open portals.

"No trouble, young Master," said the head, which then closed its eye and resumed a slack-mouthed posture.

Thaddeus looked down the hall. A fog did indeed roll a pace above the floor, and the random wild calls were clearer now. Ivory torches sporting variously colored flames were set in copper sconces along both walls. It may have been a trick of the eye, but the corridor appeared to go on without end. Further away and to his right, a pair of small fauns tussled on the floor.

The doors to the *Supremi* rooms were set at intervals similar to those on the *Tirones'* floor, but there the similarity ended. Each door here was different. Some were ornate, made of gold, and bejeweled; others were sturdy with forbidding iron gates. Some were tree-like or covered in vines. One appeared to be a giant, hairy, clenched fist with pointed claws.

Of a sudden, it opened its fingers, and a thin, dark-haired boy walked out holding a scroll, yawning and scratching absently. He crossed the hall and knocked on a door covered with writhing serpents, which parted and let him pass unscathed, then resumed its previous configuration.

Two green-tinged, black-haired Sirens lounged in front of one of the few plain oaken doors. They were beautiful, and as he passed, they beckoned to him suggestively, revealing much about themselves.

A tall, blond boy Thaddeus recognized from the *Supremi Pila Ludere* team walked down the hall toward him, giving a number of instructions over his shoulder to a winged orange sprite who carefully transcribed them onto a small scroll and flew off when the youth had finished.

Thaddeus caught his eye. "Your pardon, *Supremus,* and all Honor to you." He waited.

"Ah, yes, the *Tironis Pila Ludere* captain. What seek you here?"

"I'm looking for Wil Rathboneson's room, *Supremus.* I must speak with him."

"Oh, you'll be wanting the last room but one on the left. Just knock, but then I would step back a bit, if I were you, till it opens."

"Thank you, *Supremus,* all Honor to you."

The fellow acknowledged the salutation with a wave and continued on his way.

The next door appeared to be bricked up with only a small, barred opening showing. A pale, almost skeletal hand stuck through the grated hole. As Thaddeus passed, a voice assailed him.

"Someone, help, please! For the grace of the Gods, someone help me!"

Thaddeus stopped, half-turning toward the door when another voice spoke from over his shoulder. "Aye, lad, keep on marching. He's only a perception."

Thaddeus turned to behold the door across the hall. The door had a face and arms which were folded in front of it.

"He thinks it's amusing, but after the five-thousandth time, it gets a bit wearing."

Thaddeus nodded to the door. "Thank you."

"Don't mention it." The door reached into itself, withdrew a lit pipe and started puffing it into activity, then waved the *Tironis* off.

Thaddeus ducked as some sort of flying creature flew by his ear and sailed down the hall. It had an elongated crest and beak, but a small body in proportion. Its front arms formed the wings with claws while its feet and a stubby tail trailed out behind. It had a respectable wing span and gave a shrill cry as it passed.

Thaddeus finally reached the end of the corridor. He knew it was the end because it looked out onto empty space. The hallway simply stopped at the edge of open air, three stories off the ground. The meadow, the forest in the distance, and the star-dazzled sky harboring a quarter moon were all clearly visible.

Thaddeus approached the edge cautiously and put out his hand, touching stone. Closing his eyes, he felt a solid wall, just as in his own hall. He opened his eyes again and beheld empty air. Shrugging, he turned back, passed one door, which appeared to be in flames, and stopped in front of the next.

Curled up in front of this door was what Thaddeus recognized as a griffin. This one was pure white and seemed to be sleeping.

He stood forward, knocked, and stepped back quickly.

The griffin opened its eyes and jumped up, claws springing from its paws. "You have good reason to disturb the Captain, yes?" the beast asked.

"Yes," the boy replied carefully. "Please tell your—Captain—Thaddeus of Beewicke has come to see him."

"Oh, Beewicke. Hmm, isn't that the place where the honey comes from? I once—"

A muffled voice came from within. "Who is it, Atreus?"

"That *Tironis Pila Ludere* fellow, Thaddeus of Beewicke. Says he wants speech with you," the griffin replied.

"Oh, right. Let him by."

"Aye, Captain, my Captain. By the way, when are we going rabbit hunting again? You promised, remember?"

"Soon, Atreus, soon. Now allow the *Tironis* in."

The griffin moved to one side. "You may go in."

"Thank you," Thaddeus said as he moved forward.

"Do you like to hunt rabbits, Apprentice Thaddeus?" the creature asked.

Hand on the brass doorknob, Thaddeus answered, "Yes. I used to do that back home."

"Ah, excellent," the griffin replied. "You know, the Captain will be moving on fairly soon, and I will require a new employer. Perhaps you could keep me in mind?"

"That I will." Thaddeus nodded to the griffin, turned the knob, and entered.

7

The Young Horse-Master
Magistrum Equitum Iuvenem

The room of the *Supremi* was spacious and well-appointed. A number of carved statues of horses in various poses and different groupings were placed throughout his quarters. Though thick, textured rugs covered the tile floor, they were plain rather than decorated with the intricate designs of Faran's rugs. Multiple brass stands held candles that provided brightness to the room. Two large tapestries, also depicting horses, hung on opposing walls. Sturdy oak furniture included chairs, a wardrobe, a desk, and two chests of drawers, all matching. A large fireplace blazed in one corner. While it gave off heat and light, Thaddeus detected no ash or smoke from the blaze. His eyes turned to the young man approaching him.

"*Ave,* Thaddeus of Beewicke," the black-haired fellow said. He wore a green leather jerkin and pants. His tunic was emblazoned with a horse's head, obviously some sort of sigil.

"*Ave,* Wil Rathboneson—all Honor to the *Supremi,*" Thaddeus completed the formal greeting.

"All right, that's out of the way. Please be seated." Here the Captain indicated one of the chairs. "Care you for some refreshment?" At the shake of the Beewickean's head, he seated himself across from his guest. "Now, how may I help you?"

"I am sorry to interrupt your evening, *Supremus*," Thaddeus began.

"Please, call me Wil."

"All right, Wil. I have come looking for some information concerning one of the Masters."

"Oh, someone you will be taking studies with next year, and you wish to know something of him?"

"Um, not exactly. You see, Zoarr, the Prince … you know him?"

"Yes, the Prince. I know him. Not well, but I know him."

Thaddeus continued, "He told me that, in the past, you had worked with Master Perditus. Well, I am wondering what you can tell me of him."

"Hmm. Perditus, eh? Are you certain you wish to take studies with him?" the dark-haired lad asked carefully.

"I have no plans to study with him. Rather, my friends and I have found his behavior to be … well, a bit strange … and we wondered if that was, um, always the way it was with him?" Thaddeus let the question hang.

"I see. Is this something that might warrant approaching the other Masters about?"

"No, *Supremus*—uh, Wil. Not yet at this time, I think."

"Perhaps you should tell me of your concerns."

Thaddeus was unsure how much he should say. What if this youth still had ties to his former Master? Then he and his three Brothers would be in the toast for sure. But something told him that was not the case. He took a deep breath and forged ahead.

"It's the Tower of the East and his connection with it. He seems often to be there. And lately, well, on several occasions when he's in the structure, we have heard voices coming from the windows, mainly from the top floor.

"Voices? Plural?"

"Yes. Loud, harsh voices sometimes laughing coarsely."

"That's … very interesting. Hmm. All right, I will tell you what I know, and you can make of it what you will." The youth leaned back in his chair, tenting his fingers.

"It's true. I was approached by Master Perditus in my second year. He told me he thought I was showing a great deal of promise, and he asked if I'd favor coming to work with him. It was all a bit flattering, you know—a Master seeking out a boy only in the second year. So, I said yes. Initially, I met with him in his laboratory, a cold and unwelcome place that was, I will tell you. Then, after a bit, he began to take me into the Tower. I never felt very comfortable up there, either. It was … unsettling … and sometimes made me feel a little wild, almost as if it were a place where one could lose oneself. Then at the end of the year's study, I left and went home. When I returned last year, I approached Master Logus about working with him, and that was that."

"Did Master Perditus object to your leaving him?"

"No, strangely enough, he did not, especially after all his courting at the beginning. At first, he asked me what I knew of Compasses and about the Power of the Heavens, as he called it. I remember he used to mention something concerning the 'Cauldron of Creation.' But I had no idea about any of that. After a time, he stopped speaking of such things. Instead, he began talking about sources of power and how an individual might have advantages in harnessing such power, whereas a group might not. It made little sense to me. After several more months of the same, I think he got bored with me, and the remainder of my year was spent in simple fetch and carry. It was almost as if he'd thought at first I was someone else, had later come to realize his mistake, and was glad when I left him."

"What was he like? What sort of person was he?"

"Well, he has a brilliant mind; there's no denying that. But he seemed a bit erratic to me. Or, perhaps he was just preoccupied. He was always alone, too. No one ever came to see him. I think, except for my time with him, he had few, if any, other contacts with the Faculty or Students here, excepting, of course, during his attendance at Council Meetings." The *Supremus* paused and barked a short laugh.

"He always used to rant on and on about how the *Collegium* spent its funds unwisely. He seemed to feel too many resources were being diverted toward Sport, as he termed it. By this, he meant the Arts of the Arms Masters. I gather he and Master-Knight Eques had many contentious arguments in the Council room. He thought very little of the intellectual integrity of those gentlemen. His position was that all funding should be directed toward Research. Very one-sided he was about that. I think part of the reason he used to go on so about it was that he knew of my own interest in *Pila Ludere* and the modest success I'd had in my own Arms training."

"Did he say much when you were in the Tower? Did you see anything of interest?"

"Very little, actually. He used to require I write while he spoke. It seemed to me more his random thoughts, and some of it made no sense whatsoever. Once, he had me transcribe two complete scrolls regarding the topic of portals."

"You mean doors?"

"No, it seemed he meant portals as in going from one place to another. Are you familiar with the *Orbis Magnus,* the Great Ring?"

"Um, yes, a bit."

"Well, then, you may know that it is said the Stones there can, on occasion, and under the right circumstances, transport a person from one place to a completely different place, perhaps, even a completely different time."

"Yes, I have heard that."

"Well, his talk was much of that kind. Though it seemed to me that he did not mean for someone here to go elsewhere but more for someone elsewhere to come here—someone or something."

"Something—how is it you mean?"

"Well, it was just the way he said it. Very odd. As for the place itself, it was just a Tower with winding stairs and a lot of empty rooms. I spent as little time there as I could. As I said, it made me uncomfortable. There was no furniture on any of the other floors, save the top round, and there just an old broken table, and some chairs. Also up there were a number of large lenses and mirrors. He never spoke of their purpose, however."

The *Supremus* shifted in his chair and continued.

"Sometimes, especially toward the end of my time with him, he would have me carry scrolls filled with arcane symbols and numbers up there. Some even had drawings of strange shapes and beings."

"Beings? What sort of beings?"

"I could never tell for certain. An artist, the man was not. They were more like crude sketches. Onc scroll had several figures that looked a bit like *Spritae,* only with tails and bat-like wings—some with horns and long teeth. It was all very peculiar."

"Did you ask him the meaning of those symbols and figures?"

"Oh, yes. Many times, in fact. But he was always evasive in his answers and being a *Secundus* only, I was too timid to press a Master. Then, toward the end, when it became obvious we were not going to fit well together, he would not answer any of my questions. He would just change the subject. These days, if we meet, he ignores me, which is fine with me. The man has terrible bad breath, in any case." The *Supremus* grinned.

Thaddeus grinned back. "Yes, I know."

The Apprentice fell silent for a time and looked around the room again. "You favor horses?"

"Oh, yes. I'm from Westwallia, and our family has a large stock of the beasts for our breeding stables. We are well-known in the area for it. I believe I was riding before I was walking. In fact, we will soon be working together on this," the *Supremus* said.

"Oh? In what way is that, Wil?"

"Sir Eques came to my room earlier this evening. He said that Master Chiron, the Horse-Master, had left the school. Some pressing family matter, I believe. In any case, I think your class has begun their first horsemanship courses this term. Am I correct?"

Thaddeus nodded. His Brothers had mentioned this up in his room.

"Well, he knew of my experience—limited though it might be—and asked if I would take over the instruction of your class in the Equestrian. I agreed. So we will be seeing more of each other." The *Supremus* smiled.

Thaddeus nodded. "I'd like that. But I must say, I have never ridden a horse before."

"That's all right," the older youth said lightly, "I have a horse for you that's never really been ridden before." Both boys burst out laughing.

The lads fell silent for a time, then Wil Rathboneson rose and poked at his fire before he spoke again.

"I will tell you, Thaddeus, Master Perditus is an odd fellow, even for a place such as this. He follows naught but his own precepts and cares for none other save himself. But I believe he is working toward something, however, that totally occupies his attention and commands all his energies. I have no sense that it is Evil, shall we say, or even criminal. But whatever he's working on, it has absolute control of his entire awareness, and he will see it through to its conclusion—whatever the cost—allowing none to stand in his way with impunity. So, knowing that, I advise caution in any dealings you may have with him."

The *Supremus* glanced to his right and left, then lowered his voice. "I am serious when I say to you, Thaddeus, use extreme caution. I have heard soft talk lately that Master Perditus has been making small inquiries concerning you, just as you are now doing of him. This Master does nothing without a reason, my young friend—*nothing*."

The upperclassman rose, signaling the interview was at an end. Smiling, Wil said, "Besides, it would be a pity for the Sorcerous community to lose such an upcoming and talented *Pila Ludere* player, eh?" The older youth proffered his hand, which Thaddeus took.

"Thank you, Wil. This is all very helpful."

"It was my pleasure, Thaddeus. Do be cautious, though, right?"

"Right."

The *Supremus* saw the younger boy to the door. The griffin started up.

"It's all right, Atreus. Our guest is just leaving. Why don't you go on along with him to the hallway door? See that he's not bothered by the others, eh? Good night, *Tironis*."

"Good night, *Supremus*. All Honor to the *Supremi*."

Nodding, the older youth closed the door, and Thaddeus followed the griffin back down the hallway. Little had changed in the corridor except that halfway down the hall, a table and chairs floated two paces above the floor. Two *Supremi* faced each other across the table, their attention focused on several small items resting on a patterned board. They appeared to be playing Stone Throws.

Zoarr had recently interested the Brothers in the game. Anders was already practiced at it, having had previous instruction from his tutors. He seemed taken with the use of strategy and logic the game required, and his contests with Zoarr were all-out campaigns. Rolland's progress was somewhat slower, but he was the more highly motivated. He hated to come out second-best in any activity that included his newfound Brother, though he was loath to admit it. Thaddeus was a plodding learner, but whatever he did learn, he seemed to retain, as Zoarr often told him.

At the door, Thaddeus bade the griffin farewell and, again, promised to keep him in mind for possible future employment. After he passed through the portal, it closed behind him.

The Cyclops' eye popped open again. "Aye, Thaddeus of Beewicke. Had your nice chat with your better, did you?"

"Yes, I did. And I am sorry, but I do not have your name."

"It's Polyphemus."

"All right. Well met then, Polyphemus. Not to pry, but I was wondering how it was you came to be, um, attached to the door here?"

"NoMan did this to me," replied the Cyclops as a large tear trickled from his eye.

"Ah, some other agency, perhaps. So, Good Repose, Polyphemus."

"And you, *Tironis*."

Once Thaddeus had vanished down the stairwell, the severed head sighed. "They never understand. Not once. I don't know why I try."

Thaddeus' Brothers were anxiously awaiting his return. It took another hour for him to explain his experience and answer their questions.

"Aye, Thaddeus, it sounds more and more like Master Perditus has a sinister agenda that is currently unknown. The question is, what should we do about it if anything?"

"We do what we have been doing. Observe what we can. If we discover anything of import, we take it to Master Silvestrus, but we must be absolutely sure. Perditus is, after all, a Master at the College. We cannot charge such a one lightly. Not to mention the fact that if we are wrong, we will have made a powerful and potent enemy who, over time, will likely become less and less concerned with our welfare."

"What about his asking after you, Thaddeus?"

"Well, as Rathboneson warned me, I will be cautious. By the way, how far along are you two in the Equestrian studies?"

"Some lectures on anatomy, some laboratory work, an introduction to grooming, and a fair amount of horse turd shoveling. Asullus has been out in the stable yard about the same time each day for our lessons, and I'm certain 'tis not by accident. He says very little, just snorts and makes faces. Master Chiron had to go talk with him at one point. But now, with Chiron gone…."

"Have either of you actually been on a horse?" Thaddeus asked.

"Um, Mater always said they were unpredictable," Anders replied.

"How can you really trust something that much bigger than you are?" Rolland queried.

"I see," Thaddeus said. "Well, I am not so far behind as I thought. Rathboneson said now that Chiron has left, he would be teaching the Equestrian classes."

Rolland grimaced. "That stuffed *Supremus* tunic?"

"Rolland, I think you may have the wrong impression of him. He was very forthcoming when discussing Master Perditus with me and he shared his experiences freely. He treated me with respect. More than I expected, all things considered."

Zoarr smiled. "If you remain hesitant regarding your horsemanship, Brothers, I will gladly offer whatever help I may on my Diator. We have always kept horses, and I raised him from a colt. My father says he is the best piece of horse flesh in our entire kingdom."

"Yes. Yes, I would like that, Brother," Rolland said gratefully.

"I would as well … I think," Anders offered.

"I think we need to talk more about this, but I am near to falling over. Actually, I am surprised Master Silvestrus has not put in an appearance, asking for details of my trip. I would have thought—"

A series of knocks at the door halted the tall youth's reflection in mid-sentence. "Come in," Thaddeus called.

The door opened to reveal Master Silvestrus. The boys looked at each other.

"Ah, excellent. Thaddeus is up and about. We can talk here, then. Good Repose, other Apprentices."

No one had any difficulty understanding the old man's intent.

As Silvestrus inquired only about Thaddeus' adventure at Figberry and nothing concerning Master Perditis, that was what he heard about.

Finally, the Apprentice was released and ultimately, he slept.

8

The Offer of a Quest
and the Speech of a Daemon
Inquisitio Prolatus et Daemonis Oratio

eginning abruptly and for no discernible reason, Master Silvestrus started leading the Tironis class in a series of discussions supplementing Master Beatus' own seminars on Belief.

These seminars took the form of demonstrations and tutorials of practical Sorcerous applications. They were primarily concerned with formulating attacks and defending against attacks of all kinds, ranging from the mundane to the arcane. The sessions were informative, and the boys' skills grew apace.

For the three Brothers, it seemed like old times, just as when they were riding the barge upriver.

Winter gave more and more ground until it was banished entirely. Snows melted, flowers bloomed, insects buzzed, birds sang. Spring was in the air with all its trappings. Soon the Spring Equinox would occur, followed by Thaddeus' birthday.

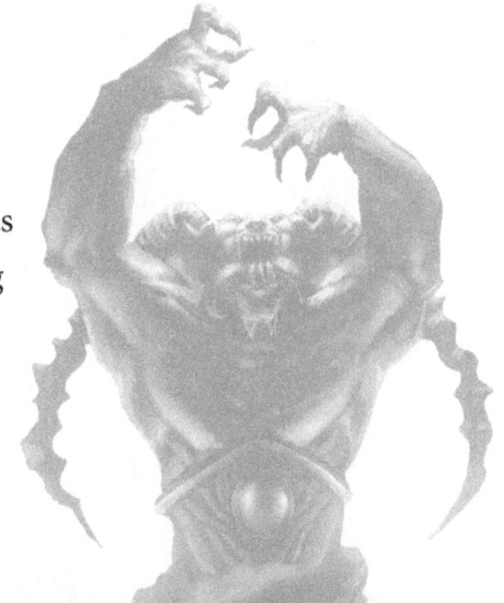

Anders never celebrated his own birthday as it fell on Year's Day, and the honoring of it was subsumed in the events and present-giving of the Saturnalia.

Rolland did not know when his birthday was—or at least he said he had never been told—so he was happy to celebrate it with his Brother, Zoarr, whose own birth occurred on Mid-Summer's Day.

Thaddeus' spirits were high. He was quickly becoming, for his age and experience, an accomplished rider as well as an accomplished Sorcerer. He was occasionally lonely for his parents, but the wonders he saw and practiced daily were potent distractions.

Master-Knight Eques seemed pleased with Thaddeus' progress in Combat Arts training, though some difficulty arose when his sword and shield went missing. The substitutes he'd had to choose did not seem to fit quite right, but he was making do.

Thaddeus felt guilty, thinking of Ethne more frequently than his parents—and thinking of Marsia more frequently than Ethne. He wondered about his son: Who was caring for him, where was he, and what, if anything, would he know of his father? And most importantly, what would he be like, and when would he be able to see him?

He had recently received a scroll from Marsia. She spoke of her activities and reminisced about their time together over the summer. She mentioned that Nannsi and Anders had apparently been in communication regarding a possible meeting at some convenient midpoint between the two schools during the Spring Equinox.

The girls had decided to bring Molly o' the Willows with them since they had become close. She wondered if Thaddeus might wish to join Anders, providing he had no other commitments. She added that the three girls were seeking to convince Sonnia to accompany them as well, though they were meeting resistance. Of Rolland and Zoarr, she made no mention. In closing, Marsia signed her missive but had not included a written signature. Instead, she had drawn a heart onto which a scent had been marked.

Thaddeus' head swam each time he read it and smelled it, which
was often, very often.

And that was where things stood when Lilyput appeared to the boys
in Zoarr's room one evening as their group was practicing their music.
The Goblin allowed as how they were making progress. She even
demonstrated what she called a *jig* to accompany one of the livelier
tunes. She had learned the dance, she said, a long, long time ago.

For the other tunes, she clapped her taloned hands together in time.
Although she attempted to hide it, she clearly seemed to enjoy the
music. After listening to several songs at the boys' request, she drew
Thaddeus aside during a rest.

"Ah-heee, Apprentice, I have been distracted from my original
purpose, which was to tell you that you're wanted in Master Silvestrus'
study. Tell him it was my negligence in making you late, eh?"

Thaddeus thanked the House-Mistress, left the grumbling group,
and made his way to his Master's laboratory.

At his knock, the door opened. He entered but found only the lizard
in residence.

"Hail, Antigonis, how fare you?"

"Have you seen the *Supremus,* Wil Rathboneson?"

Startled at the unexpected query, Thaddeus responded quickly. "No.
Not lately, I have not. Why do you ask? Is he missing?"

"The Master's been asking after him all afternoon. Seems he's been
unaccounted for several days now. It is upsetting the Master, and it is
not good when the Master is upset."

"Why is that, Antigonis?"

"Because when he is upset, he forgets to feed me," the lizard replied.

At that moment, Silvestrus strode in, appearing preoccupied, and
took a seat at his table. The sorcerous-suspended window opened, and a

pleasant, early evening breeze wafted the smell of a spring meadow into the room.

"Thaddeus. How are you, my boy? How do your studies go?"

"Well, Master, and well," the tall youth replied, himself preoccupied with the news regarding the *Supremus*.

"Good. I have been reviewing reports from the other Masters who instruct you. They are uniform in their praise and in their expectations of your developing prowess and competence. Actually, rather unheard of in one so young, though not entirely unexpected. Leastways not by me."

The old man smiled and stared absently out the window at an early-rising moon. Presently, he came to himself and began shuffling through the stack of parchments sitting at his elbow. After a moment of rummaging, he withdrew one missive and began reading it silently, lips moving.

"In fact, so highly do your Masters sing your praises, my young Apprentice, that they have put forth the exceptionally irregular recommendation that you be given a Quest."

It took a moment for this pronouncement to penetrate the boy's consciousness.

"A Quest, Master? Me, Master? I do not understand. I thought Quests were given only to the Upperclass: the *Supremae*."

"Quite so, my lad, quite so. However, I did say it was irregular. And you may be further interested to know that I myself have endorsed this venture. So, Thaddeus, what say you?"

"I-I am taken aback, Master. 'Tis all—unexpected. I would consider it a great honor, but, um … what would the Quest concern, Master, if I may ask?"

"Best to ask, Thaddeus. Only a fool says yes without asking questions. All right, lad, here is the task." The old sorcerer glanced again at the parchment and cleared his throat.

"I have here a letter from the Chief Magistrate, one Pontius, of a small fishing village on the southern coast of Frantillia. He writes of a calamity his community suffers due to the curse of a Red Dragon. He says that all sea life is dying—fish, crabs, porpoises, dead and dying—washing up daily on the beach to rot. He believes the Red Dragon has poisoned them because of a dispute between that creature and a Green Dragon, said to have its den in the locale. It is a beast, however, that neither he nor any villager has ever seen, though the serpent is central to a legend of the town and said to be centuries old."

Silvestrus paused in his tale to pull a candle closer to the parchment. At that moment, Thaddeus glanced at the suspended window to find the moon had come from behind a cloud to cast even more light on the petition.

"He goes on to say all concur the Red Dragon is responsible for this disaster, as it has turned the sea red as far as the eye can see. He requests, therefore, that a Sorcerer be sent to deal with the Red Dragon's scourge, while at the same time taking care to avoid annoying the Green Dragon, and thus freeing the town from its terrible curse. Doing so would unleash a torrent of affection from said villagers, resulting, for example, in the payment of two thousand gold Imperials for our time and trouble, the lasting friendship of the village and the undying..."

The old man looked up expectantly, then squinted his eyes and frowned. "Thaddeus? Thaddeus!"

The boy jumped.

"Thaddeus, what ails you? You sit there with a frozen expression of consternation upon your countenance."

"Excuse me, Master, but did you say Dragons?"

"Oh, that. Yes. Yes, I did. Why?"

"Well, it's just that they're said to be formidable opponents, and there has seldom been found a way to vanquish them."

"True enough, lad, true enough. And so...."

"Well, Master, I am not sure how I'm to go about accomplishing this task, given the low chance of…."

"Ah, well, I see. All right, hear my proposal. If you accept this Quest, I will share with you several strategies you may employ, with a good likelihood of success. What say you?"

"Very well, Master. Please know I understand that you and the Faculty honor me by assigning a *Tironis* a Quest, especially one of this import. I hope I will not betray this trust you place in me, and I hope I can find a way to relieve the suffering of the village people."

"Well spoken, lad. You put your words together usefully."

"Master, when am I to take my leave of the College to set out upon this Quest? I think I should want to prepare, and—"

"I advise you to set out this very week's end. The village you seek to save is a fishing village, and if the men there cannot fish, the village and its people cannot survive."

"This week's end? Oh."

"What trouble do you have, Thaddeus?"

"Well, Master, it's only that several of us sought to spend the weeks of the Spring Equinox celebration with some of our friends from the *Ludia,* whom we had met this summer past with Mistress Geanninia. You recall—"

"Ah, yes. Most certainly, I recall. I recall most especially one honey-locked tall lass named Marsia, I believe. Might she, perhaps, be counted among those 'friends' you hoped to meet?"

"Yes, Master," Thaddeus said, his ears turning red.

"I understand, Thaddeus. However, I consider this Quest most important, particularly important, in fact. But you must decide. I will not compel you to accept this honor. The choice is yours."

Thaddeus was silent for a moment. "Yes, Master, I will accept the Quest and hope to comport myself so as to be a credit to the College." But the taste in the Apprentice's mouth was of ashes. He could not decide at first which was worse: having to face a Red Dragon or missing the chance to spend several days with Marsia. As he thought it over, he knew the answer to that question with certainty.

"Excellent. Good choice, Thaddeus. And be aware that I appreciate your sacrifice. Though, you never know how things will work out. We are all surprised from time to time. Now, let us see to those strategies I spoke of. Then I will prepare some documents and a Letter of Credit for your use. Oh, and you will need a map of the region. See Brother Cartographus in the Library. He can help you with your route. Have you any questions at this point, my boy?"

"None at this time, Master," Thaddeus replied, his resignation accompanied by a sinking feeling.

The old man turned, pulled a rucksack from a shelf and placed it on the corner of his desk. "Very well then. I am also sending with you several scrolls of advanced studies. Read these carefully during the course of your journey, and we shall discuss them on your return. Consider them your work from home, if you will. So … now to strategies. Are you familiar with the concept of *Scientia*?"

In his room, Thaddeus composed a painful reply, telling Marsia that he would not be able to see her and why. Afterward, he sought out his three Brothers to advise them on how things stood with him.

"You cannot go alone, Thaddeus. We will abandon our plans immediately and accompany you as you challenge this peril. Brothers face adversity united!"

"Thank you, Zoarr, but Master Silvestrus specifically said I was to go alone. Perhaps he wishes only to risk one Apprentice rather than four at once," the tall boy said ruefully. "But 'tis hard not to go with you."

"Aye, Thaddeus, that's a stone to your knee sure," Rolland said. "I know you have been wanting to see your Marsia. But a Quest—*Iovis!*—for a *Tironis,* that is quite an honor. We will surely miss you though, Brother."

"You will miss me? Are you going as well, then?" Thaddeus asked, surprised. "I thought you had no use for Sonnia?"

"Uh, this has nothing to do with Sonnia. It's just a chance to get away from this place—get a little fresh air, as it were. Spend some time of quality with my Brothers here."

"Of course. But, wait … Brothers? Are you going along, too, Zoarr?"

"Of course. I will see my fiancée," he added, his tone matter-of-fact.

"Zoarr, are you sure about that? That is, I know you proposed—after your fashion—but I do not remember Molly o' the Willows agreeing to your proposal."

"It is only a matter of time and details, Thaddeus," the Mauretesian replied with equanimity.

"Those can be fairly big details, oh, Prince. Well, you know your situation best."

"Thaddeus, when were you planning on leaving on your Quest?" Anders asked.

"Venus' Day, following afternoon classes."

"That's when we plan to leave as well," Anders explained. "Master Silvestrus has allowed us the use of Asullus and the cart. Rather, Asullus said he was 'no' goin' to be left behind,' and Master Silvestrus gave his consent after the fact, as it were. The decision to take the cart, once we replace the wheels, was made by us informally. In any case, I propose that we head out together. We can always divide up later on."

"Yes, that's a good idea. Done!"

"Done! Now, out of curiosity, how is it, exactly, you plan to defeat a Red Dragon?"

"… and so there was sufficient supply of the blood, then? You do appear more substantial," said the one.

"Yes," said the other, licking his muzzle. "More than sufficient and of exquisite taste. You know, you ought to try it sometime. You might be surprised."

"No. Thank you all the same. You are now, therefore, stronger in your presence here?"

"Yes. I think only two more should complete the phase-in. Do you have any prospects?"

"Yes, the same prospects, as it turns out. But they are now fled to the West. A Holiday, I believe. I think Silvestrus' plan to send them away, however, is his method of trying to keep them safe from us. Additionally, I have learned they will be meeting up with those same girls from the summer—and the slave girl."

"Perhaps then, something can be made of this that would work to my—that is, *our*—benefit."

"Yes, that was my thought as well. But an intercession surer than those Graecolian fools and their puerile attempts at capture. They could not even hold onto a seventeen-year-old girl or obtain the *Solaris*, despite their vaunted reputation. Well, they have received their reward."

"Then what is your plan?"

"I have made arrangements for a troop of warriors to pursue and capture the lot of them. They will then be brought to us to use as our needs direct."

"And how do you propose to bring a group, especially *this* group, past Mountaingaard, through the surrounding forest onto this campus, and into this Tower?"

"Leave that to me. It will not be so difficult with only one old man to thwart. It will be done."

"Then I will return to complete my repast. There are few things so satisfying as the company of a Sorcerer, especially a young Sorcerer."

9

The Mad Hermit
Solitarius Insanus

"Aye, an' ha' ye somethin' now personal against our sweet *Naturae Materna,* that ye wishes to end her eternal life, premature-like, wi' all yer caterwaulin' and carryin' on? Mind ye, I do no' claim to be the fairest voice in all the land, but this—singin'—as ye calls it … well, ye must know ye be drivin' away the game in three shires already an' probably causin' a stampede an' many unnecessary deaths an' such down the line."

"Oh, Asullus, we are practicing one of our songs. It does sound better with our instruments accompanying it, though," Anders offered from the driver's seat of the swaying cart, continuing to snap the reins in time to the music.

"I ha' no trouble in imaginin' that, laddie, an' that's fer certain," the mule shot back. "Any change could only work to the good, don' ye know."

"Aye, Asullus, the bookworm is right. With our instruments, it sounds different," Rolland said, jumping in to defend his Brother.

"Grant ye, seven is different from six—but on yer scale to a hundred, 'tis a wee difference, would ye no' agree?"

This observation caused the boys to give the mule and the surrounding countryside another rollicking chorus of "Bill, What Do Ye with the Sheep, Lad?" as the cart rocked back and forth in the sodden, rain-rutted trails that dominated that particular stretch of their overland route.

From the beginning, the boys had felt the now-familiar excitement that always accompanied the initial phase of their journeys together. Their spirits were high, and the thought of the upcoming sundering— albeit temporary—of their fellowship was far from their minds.

Many jibes were traded among the four of them, but it was Rolland who seemed to suffer most of the outrageous barbs. These, it turned out, tended to center around the general disbelief accorded his declared disinterest in Sonnia. And the more he denied it, the stronger became the chorus of naysaying, goads, and taunts.

The principal subject of conversation, however, was the Release from Constraint the Apprentices had been given by Master Silvestrus prior to their departure.

"Given your recent history, the Council and I have decided that during this particular time, and for this occasion only, you are to be given permission to practice Sorcery beyond the borders of the *Collegium*. This release is unique in the annals of the school, so appreciate this act in the fullest sense of the word. You are, thereby, given significant responsibility —use it well, and further benefits may follow. Use it poorly, and the opposite may be your fate. I am sure you take my meaning."

The second subject of conversation was the upcoming Holiday with the girls. Anders suspected he was the only one of the group who understood—he believed—the real purpose of this Holiday the girls had proposed. But he kept his speculation to himself. It would clearly not affect Zoarr or Molly o' the Willows. He was somewhat undecided regarding Rolland and Sonnia, though he favored a pairing there; and he felt badly for Marsia. Still, he understood what he thought must be the basis of Thaddeus' choice: duty.

Any melancholy generated by his Brother's absence, however, was blotted out by the anticipation of his meeting with Nannsi. With such thoughts in his head, he blushed, and his mouth went dry at the same time. His main concern, though, would be in not making any mistakes. The Scourge of Shame was the ascendent Deity in his Pantheon of Suffering, a fact always in his awareness.

The boys were first to reach their past Mid-Summer's Eve encampment and scurried about setting it aright. Thaddeus laughed to himself. Their frenzied activity reminded him of how, in springtime back home, the brown male snippet frantically clears a nesting space, arranging it in a manner hopefully pleasing to the female to ensure she will favor him over his fellows.

The thought, however, resurrected the ache, knowing he would not see Marsia and would consequently lose an opportunity that might only come once. In Nature, he believed the female was often mysterious, and one little frustration might cause her to fly off, never to be seen again. The same possibility played on his mind for Marsia's visit.

The following day, he bade farewell to his friends, who shared their sympathy for him. Clearly, however, they were distracted by their own anticipation, and there was only so much empathy to spare.

Thaddeus took his time to say goodbye to Asullus, who he bade stay with the group, as its need for the beast's services was the greater. The grizzled gray one didn't like being left behind very much and fussed and fretted about the boy's decision. The mule went on to offer much good, albeit unsolicited, advice concerning his route and mode of travel and how to keep safe with Dragons about.

With a heartfelt farewell, Thaddeus shouldered his pack and struck out cross-country to the Southwest, where he hoped to pick up a barge heading downstream on the Greater Flatstone River. He could have, of course, headed due West to River's Town, but he might run into the girls coming East, and that would make everything ten times harder. Also, the town itself held little interest for him, and, therefore he felt it best to avoid it altogether.

Near evening, he was looking for a campsite when he espied several cave entrances by a creek bed, probably limestone, as he recalled from his field classwork earlier that year. A cave would offer good protection from the spring chill, though sometimes such protections were occupied by animals frequently unwilling to share their homes. The cave he settled on, however, was different from the others in that it already had a fire glowing in its mouth.

Approaching the cave, Thaddeus was unafraid but cautious. He stopped a hundred paces from the entrance and hailed the cave's tenant.

The response was immediate. "*Ave* yourself. I've been watching you for some time. Lost, are you then?"

"Nay, sir. I travel southwest to the Greater Flatstone River and thought to overnight in this area. Can you recommend one of the caves hereabout for a campsite, so not to intrude on any belonging to you, of course?"

"Ha! No cave in Nature belongs to me or any Man, young one. We are all but guests here, and that only briefly. But come up half the distance, so I may see you better. And do not think to try to take advantage. I am a Mad Hermit, you see, and have many wondrous and terrible devices at my disposal."

Thaddeus found himself drawn to this fellow. His declaration, at least, was intriguing, if not downright amusing. Thaddeus felt it might be best to present himself seriously to the man, an old man, if his eyes spoke truly from this distance, allowing for the small cook-fire's roiling smoke.

"As you wish," the Apprentice replied and walked forward slowly.

"That is far enough, boy. Now tell me your name and wherefrom you hail."

"I am known as Thaddeus, sir, and I am an Apprentice from the *Collegium Sorcerorum.*"

The youth heard a sharp intake of breath. "None of your tricks now, young Sorcerer. Harm my flesh, and you will have to deal with the Devils!"

"Peace, sir. I only seek to pass through this place on my way to the River."

"So you say. Well, it is darkening and getting cold. Perhaps, you should come on up. I have some extra beans and lentils cooking here if you wish to partake."

"Thank you, sir. 'Tis true; soup would fill a void." Thaddeus approached the cave entrance warily. There he beheld a thin, wiry man with feverish eyes. But the old man's most striking features were his two hands supporting but one finger between them.

The old recluse followed the boy's gaze and held his hands and remaining digit up for closer inspection. It was an odd sight. All the fingers were missing on his left hand, and only his index finger remained on the right.

"Yes, what you see is no illusion. There is, of course, a story as comes with it. So, I will make you a proposition. You eat my soup, then you listen to my tale."

"Yes, sir. That is more than fair."

The little man stood aside, and Thaddeus entered the cave. The Hermit indicated a worn and somewhat soiled grass mat, and Thaddeus seated himself.

With little difficulty, the man untied a dirty, thong-knotted canvas sack and withdrew two bowls from it. "Robbers everywhere, you know," he said, scanning the forest. He filled them with soup from a ladle, passing one to his young guest.

Thaddeus was amazed at the Hermit's dexterity, given his lack of fingers. Within moments, he and his host were busily eating the hot soup. After they finished and following a few pleasantries, the old man put his bowl down. "Now, I will tell you my tale."

"My name is Digitus. Not so long in the past, I was Master of Philosophy and *Rerum Mathematicarum* at the Court of the Consul of Frantillia. All there looked to me for the understanding of the Universe, and my studies, over time, led me to the greatest discovery of the Age. Now I realize this is a great boast, but it is, nevertheless, the truth. And, not to continue you in endless suspense, what I discovered was *Lex Numeri Decem*—the Law of Tens." The man smiled and waited expectantly, then frowned at the silence.

"Well, perhaps I should expound. Look at your hands, boy—see, ten fingers. Now, make two fists—there, you see it? No fingers. So, no fingers —none—then all fingers—ten of them. Now, imagine a group of ten people standing here, all showing their fingers. You see—ten of ten— one hundred fingers. Next, imagine ten groups of ten persons each, and what do you have? Ten of ten of ten … so, that is one thousand fingers. And it goes on forever; row after row, column after column, and so on. That is my discovery: the Law of Tens!"

Thaddeus considered what he had been shown and wished mightily for Anders. "Ah, Master Digitus, I see. That is an amazing discovery."

"Ah, yes, of course. I'm glad you understand it. Many do not, especially at first."

"But how does that lead to your hands as they are now, sir?"

"Ah, well. You see, there was a time when I was not so shy as I am now. I, ahem, rather sung my own praises regarding my discovery. And why not? Who could sing them better? But it fell ill with others at the Consul's court. Some took it as boasting and began to murmur amongst themselves. Jealous, they began to poison the Consul's ear, saying that either the wondrous discovery was nothing of the sort, or else I had borrowed it from others."

The old man spat in disgust at the outrage and paused to drink from an old wineskin.

Thaddeus declined the Hermit's offer to share the wine, as it smelled sour.

"They kept up their complaining. Finally, one night I was taken before the Court of the Ecclesiastes. There I was charged with corrupting the youth. Several suggested I take a bowl of hemlock."

The old man held up his hands. "But this was my punishment. All my fingers were taken from me, save this one. After, I was banished to this wild wood, and here I remain. All my work burned, all my possessions cast away. 'Go, teach your Ten Digits now,' they mocked me. It was all very disheartening. Since that dark day, this cave has been my home, with madness, my companion."

The Hermit sat lost in thought while the fire burned lower.

"Well, enough of this maundering. Let us to sleep. A new day can sometimes bring new insights."

Thaddeus gave his condolences and his thanks. Sleep came late as he ruminated over the old man's plight.

Morning dawned cold and crisp, and Thaddeus awoke to the smell of gruel boiling in the pot used the night before for beans and lentils.

"Ah, lad, good morrow. The gruel is just finishing. Normally, I would have added blackberries, but it's a little early in the season. Come, help yourself."

Thaddeus reviewed his thoughts from the previous night, then looked again at the old man's hands. *Wait…. What if….? Yes!*

"Master Digitus, I have been thinking about your problem, and I believe I may have a solution."

"Do you now, boy? Well, that would be wondrous indeed, considering some of the best minds in the land—principally mine—have been at this for a time. Pray tell me your postulate, then."

"Well, Master, you used to have ten fingers, five on each hand, and all of them had meaning, taken together. But now, see … you have no fingers on one hand, and but one finger on the other hand. You could think of it as a different way of describing things—or ciphering. None and one. Nothing and something. You accomplish all that you do here in this cave, the many and myriad tasks—with none and one—and thus, perhaps you could do the same with your *Mathematica* as well."

The old man stared at the boy as if thunderstruck, then jumped up and cried aloud, "Aiyee! None and one! Yes! I see it! Of course! Why did I not think of this before? I can do all this, explain everything with none and one." The old man began laughing hysterically as his face turned purple. After the paroxysm passed, his breathing returned, and he addressed his guest.

"Thaddeus of the *Collegium,* you have done me this day a great service! Now I can return to Court with this new discovery—a discovery, perhaps, even greater than its predecessor. I will have all restored to me. My life is saved."

The man paused, wiping tears of joy from his eyes. "I shall have to change my name now, however. Digitus certainly no longer applies. Let me see now … hmm. Ah-ha! I have it! My new name will be … Binarius!"

The old Hermit rushed to Thaddeus and shook his hands as best he could.

"You have saved a life this day, lad, and a reputation—not to mention, made a discovery of some import. For this boon, I shall impart to you a vision I had concerning you this night past. You see, since I have lived alone in this place over the years, I have come to experience visions in my sleep, all of which invariably come true. I have seen that on your travels this day, you shall meet a presence that shall be a companion and aide to you until your last breath. Small payment for a great gift and again, my thanks!"

The Hermit laughed, shaking so that his grimy hide almost fell off. Coming to himself, he turned to the boy. "Oh, and Thaddeus, keep the cave! Keep the contents! I am off to spread word of my new discovery! None and one! Oh, joyous day!"

With that, the old man began to dance a jig, twirling his way out of the cave, across the stream, into the woods on the other side, and finally out of sight.

"*Your* discovery?" Thaddeus laughed to himself. "Well, Master Binarius, I hope you have learned how better to comport yourself, or you may risk losing your remaining finger. Then you will be truly out of luck, for I have no more theories to lend you. Nothing from nothing leaves nothing, after all."

Thaddeus made good use of Rolland's ferreting skills in looting the old Hermit's cave and thus was rewarded with several useful items. Some of the things he discovered, however, he did not think it would be a good idea to take or even touch. And several others he could not even identify.

Thaddeus strode overland, continuing southwest until he stopped for Mid-day. After finishing his meal and repacking, he resumed his trek. He'd gone, perhaps, three hours with the Sun halfway down the Westering sky when his Tracking Eye, as Anders called it, detected a series of signs in the brush and on one patch of soft earth: a paw print.

He slipped off his pack and bent down to examine the trace. Yes, indeed, a paw print. It was a hunter—a wolf! But it was a young wolf, an adolescent, that had only recently passed by. Interesting. A wolf alone— assuming he was separated from his group.

Thaddeus traced back and forth across the trail but detected none other than the solitary wolf.

Curious, he reshouldered his pack. Carefully and quietly, he followed the signs of the animal's passage. He was downwind, which would work to his advantage. Advancing cautiously to the edge of a small clearing, he gingerly parted a stand of tall grass.

There before him was a sight he'd never witnessed before.

The Blinded Eagle
Aquila Caeca

A quarter of the way around the edge of the clearing, a young wolf crouched, half-hidden in the bush. The fact that Thaddeus could see the creature at all was undoubtedly due to the latter's youthful inexperience.

The wolf was not looking at him. Instead, his attention was entirely focused on a bird, one of the largest birds Thaddeus had ever seen, standing on a fallen tree trunk in the middle of the clearing. The feathered creature stared straight ahead, only ten paces from where the wolf hid. Given its legendary sight, it must have seen the hunter, yet the bird made no attempt at flight nor gave any sign of recognition. The feathered one simply stood with its talons clutching the rotting log.

The only sign of life it displayed was the occasional blink of its eyes, which appeared pale rather than the typical dark color. *Curious….*

The wolf seemed puzzled by the bird's unusual behavior and appeared undecided about what to do next.

Thaddeus was puzzled as well, and his curiosity was roused. Why would the King of Birds stand there, such a tempting target for an ancient ground-based enemy? It was almost as if….

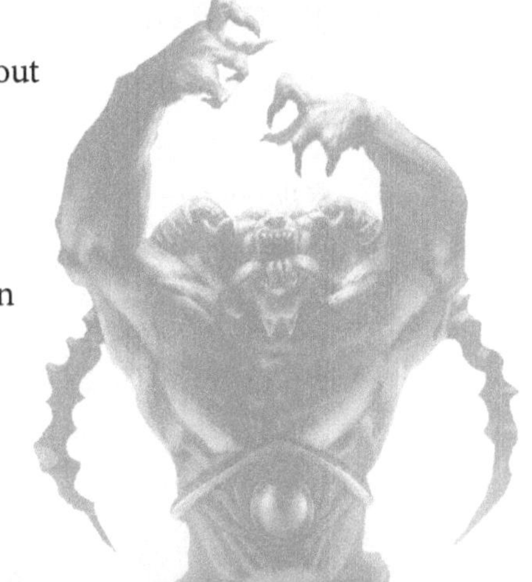

He concentrated, as he had on other occasions, reaching out, reaching out....

"Lupus, what do you here?"

Startled, the young wolf looked around quickly, locating where Thaddeus knelt.

"Ah, a Speaker. I have not met your kind before. Great-Father has always told stories, but you know the elderly—"

"Aye," Thaddeus responded, *"and they are often worth listening to."*

"Well, yes. Perhaps the first several times. But to answer your question. I was only passing through this wood seeking to rejoin my pack when I detected the scent of this eagle. Interestingly, the smell lingered, ground-bound. I thought to investigate and have found him, as you see. I had never seen this before nor heard Great-Father speak of it. As I have been traveling in search of my pack, I have become hungry and am now considering making him my meal. But his odd way has put me off a bit, though I think I could pounce him at this short distance. Perhaps he has fallen from the sky and is injured, or perhaps he has a sickness."

"If you will but forbear your assault for a moment, I shall try to speak with this one and see how it stands with him."

"Very well," the young wolf said. *"But please proceed quickly. It is getting late, and my hunger grows."*

"As you say."

Thaddeus slowly stood, making no attempt to be quiet. He was directly across from the bird. It showed no sign of acknowledgment.

How odd....

"Oh, mighty Eagle," Thaddeus began in the Language of Those Who Soar. *"Chiefest of all those who rule the Great Sky above, what do you here?"*

The great bird of prey shifted its head slightly in Thaddeus' direction but was silent for some time before answering. *"I wait."*

Osiric, Lord of Eagles

"What is it, Lord of Wings, that you wait for?"

"The end of things. Or, at least, my part in it."

"I have never before heard of one of the Great Ones acting thus. Have you some deep purpose in so doing that I and this young wolf cannot detect?" Thaddeus thought it would be polite to mention the wolf's presence in the extremely unusual case the Eagle had not detected it.

"Yes, I know of the wolf. I smell him and you also. As to my purpose … it is a long tale, and I am too weak and too uncaring to relate it. I wait only for my fate."

"Hmm. Great Eagle, under all other circumstances, I would respect and honor your desire in such things. Yet, I must tell you, I have become quite curious regarding this situation. Is there any inducement I may offer to persuade you to share this tale, though I realize it is in no way my business to intrude in this rude fashion?"

"Yes, rude. You have said it. Well, perhaps I might have earlier, but time has run its course, and I have no strength remaining. I am standing now by will alone. I have not eaten since … well, not in some time. I am content to let the wolf do as he will. In fact, I welcome it."

"Not to thwart you, Great One, but I have here in my pack—this bulge I carry on my back—some dried fish. It is not as fresh as what you are used to, but it mayhap suffice until such time as a fresher repast can be made available to you."

"Now, it is my curiosity that is roused. What is your concern in this?"

"I am unsure, Wind Lord, yet it is there, and I cannot deny it. Well, what say you? Will you have my meal?"

"You tempt me, Primate, yet I do not believe the wolf will allow me the leisure. I sense his time has run its course and mine has now as well."

"Abide, yet, Lord. I may be able to influence the outcome of this tableau."

Thaddeus turned to address the wolf, which had tensed, preparing to attack.

"Hold, Lupus. I am near to solving this puzzle. I petition you to withhold your death lunge."

"I cannot, Speaker. I must eat, and my prey is here. This you must understand."

"I understand. Perhaps, more than you think. Nevertheless, I say, forestall."

"Nay, I will not," the wolf snarled and started to leap.

Thaddeus thought furiously. *"Halt, I say, in the name of the Great Golden Pack Leader!"*

The young wolf spun around in mid-lunge, nearly breaking its back. It rolled over, jumped up, and faced the Apprentice.

"You! I should have known it! Great-Father has said it of Luperca. I meant no offense, Lord Consort. I will submit and do as you wish."

Thaddeus was amazed at the designation and unsure of its meaning. Yet he was not above taking advantage of a situation handed him this readily by fate.

"Yes. Know I will not let you go a-hungered. If you will abide yet a moment more, I will share with you some provision, then you may go on your way to rejoin your pack."

"Yes, Lord Consort. It shall be as you say."

Lord Consort? Well, that was a question for another day.

Thaddeus slid his pack from his shoulder and dug around until he found what he thought might be sufficient. He placed the meat halfway to the adolescent lupine and backed away. The young wolf cautiously approached the collect, sniffed it, then picked it up in his jaws. With a quick nod to his benefactor, he loped off into the forest.

Thaddeus dug again in his pack, found the dried fish from Binarius' cave, and came as close to the Eagle as he thought advisable. There, he laid down the food and backed away again.

"Lord, the wolf has gone. I have placed food in front of you from which I hope you will draw strength. After, perhaps, I may hear your tale."

The Eagle did not reply, nor did he look at the food, but instead seemed to be smelling for it. With obvious effort, he unsteadily jumped down from the log and slowly hopped nearer the fish. He leaned forward and beaked the earth several times until he hit upon it. Once located, he gulped it down greedily. As close as he was now, Thaddeus could see that the Eagle's eyes were covered with a milky white film as if scarred.

After the Great Bird finished, he was silent for several moments before speaking. *"You will have observed by now that I am blind,"* the bird began.

"Aye, Lord. I had guessed it."

"Yes, well, that, then, is the tale. An Eagle with no eyes is no Eagle. I have no tongue for such a story, and to tell it is to relive its pain. Yet you have been patient, and I gave my word. So, it is as follows.

"My name is Osiric. In times past, I was King of my peoples. I had my mate, Qinda, and we bred our young, year after year. They prospered, were fine, strong, and soared as they should. Many lead the tribes and sub-tribes of the land even to this day. We were content.

"Then, season last, a great storm came, as storms do, and lines of blue fire traced the night sky. One must have struck a stand of pine near our nest, for a blaze started, and soon the great trees surrendered to the flames, one after the other. Closer to our home came the danger-death. I flew to fight it. I skreed my call and flashed it with my wings, but to no avail. The fire was mightier than I and came steadily on.

"Suddenly, I heard the call of my mate. I wheeled back swiftly, but not swiftly enough. Our own tree-home was overcome by the flames. I flew into them to save my Qinda, who had stayed with the two we had that year. I … I tried to save them, but the heat was too bright. My body failed. My feathers were aflame. And my eyes burned. Suddenly, I could see no more. I fell."

The Eagle paused before continuing. *"When I awoke, I was on a rock in the middle of the stream that flowed beneath our great tree. My Eagle's eyes were no more. I did not know where I was at first. I called and called and gave my great cry. Soon my children began to come to me; those as could hear it. They told me our tree was no more. They said they could find no trace of Qinda or the fledglings. They did not say she had died, but they did not have to.*

"Then they bade me farewell. You see, with our peoples, if you are blind, having lost your Eagle's eyes, you are no more. I became as a cast-out, and they left me. I did not blame them. For us, it is the law, and I would, in their place, have done the same. Sennead, my eldest, became the new King in my place.

"I understood my plight and determined to face it with dignity, but for some reason, two of my daughters came to me and lifted me up to be safe at night and brought me fish while I healed as best I could. They should not have done this, and they risked much, but I was grateful.

"In time, my wounds, grievous though they were, healed, and my feathers grew anew. I could again fly, though I made many missteps. With the loss of my vision, however, came new awareness. I found I could smell more keenly than ever before. And I could hear! These advantages often saved me from flying head-on into a tree, although not always, especially at first.

"So passed the fall and the winter. And now I judge it a year since the fire. One day this past cycle, my daughters stopped coming and have come no more. I imagine they were finally found out and chastened, or, perhaps, at last they grew weary. I felt the loss of dignity keenly and knew I was a burden only. I took wing to I knew not where and flew until I could fly no further. Then I landed here. Not with grace, I am afraid and so I found this log. I felt it was time to stop being a weight on life, so I decided to wait. And so I did."

The Eagle again fell silent. *"Thus, stranger, have I spoken. Now it is to you. You have reawakened me, so now you have a responsibility. What is your tale?"*

Well, fair was fair. Thaddeus introduced himself and gave the Eagle a brief version of his personal history. He ended with his Quest.

"So, you are a Sorcerer-to-be—one of the Mighty, then. And you now embark upon your Great Peregrination: to find and challenge a Red Dragon. Interesting. I wish you well, Thaddeus, Sorcerer. I hope the outcome will fall your way. Thank you for your earlier kindness. Farewell." The Eagle finished speaking and put his head under his wing, making no effort to flee or even save himself.

A plan had formed in Thaddeus' mind as the Eagle told his tale. "Osiric?"

The Eagle cocked his head. "Yes?"

"Excuse me for intruding further, but know you anything of Dragons?"

"Dragons? I have heard from our legends that in the first days, our Great-Fathers and their Great-Fathers were in contention. In those times, our Great-Fathers were of a size with Dragons and their battles titanic. The Serpents, however, had fire—always our weakness—and they had the advantage. Our size dwindled, and our range diminished. But they had not taken into account Man. As Man prospered, he came and smote the Dragons, hip, thigh, wing, and scale, and their numbers grew less. Now, we see one another only rarely. I, myself, have never chanced to meet one. Otherwise, I can tell you naught of them."

After a moment, Thaddeus spoke.

"Still, your wisdom outweighs mine in this and, I am sure, in other matters as well. Would you consider accompanying me on my Quest for the Dragon? I must tell you frankly, however, standing by me against the Great Serpent must surely mark you for death."

The Eagle was silent for a time before replying. "A Sorcerer you are for certain, casting a spell with your words. So obvious your intention, and yet … yet am I constrained. To move me would require a sign from the Heavens, I believe. Having none, I bid you pass on and relinquish me."

Inspiration flashed in Thaddeus' mind, and he reached into his pack. It took but a moment to locate what he sought and another moment to extract it carefully.

"Very well, Osiric. Behold, with the senses that remain to you, the sign you demand of the Heavens."

With an unnecessary flourish, he held up the Great Crested Golden Eagle feather he had received from Iam at the *Orbis Magnus* and laid it on the ground across from the Eagle.

"The sign you seek lies directly in front of you." Thaddeus stepped back and waited.

The Eagle, appearing intrigued, hopped forward somewhat awkwardly until it stood directly over the feather. It sniffed and nudged it with its beak, then stopped suddenly with a sharp intake of breath.

"Aquilla's crop! By what miracle have you come by this feather? It speaks of lines of generations, stretching back to time beyond time. I have no words for it. Pray, tell me of it!"

"Of course, Mighty Osiric. Some short time past, I chanced in my travels to visit the Great Ring. Perhaps you know of it? In any case, through a wondrous circumstance, I was, I believe, able to look back to a time past. And there I met a man—Iam, of the First. He it was who gave me that feather and told me to save it. Later, as I came to myself, many of my memories of that time were gone, but the feather remained."

"Very well, Thaddeus, Sorcerer. You have rescued me, succored me, and shown me a Great Sign. I can argue no longer and must relent. If my purpose is to die, then let me die not in surrender but in combat. I will accompany you."

"Excellent! I am honored and heartened."

As Thaddeus looked more closely at the majestic Eagle, proud, even to the sightless ruin of his eyes, inspiration visited him again. *"Osiric, as I have said, I am a Sorcerer. I believe I could heal you—restore your sight. Would you wish me to attempt this thing?"*

The great bird stood deep in thought for what seemed a long time.

"Thaddeus, Sorcerer, know that I thank thee for thy offer, but I must decline it. That day I lost my life-eyes, I also lost my life-mate. To have the

one returned without the other … well, it would not be the same, you see. Nevertheless, I thank thee."

"I believe I understand, Osiric. If you should ever change your mind, however, know that I stand ready. Well, perhaps we should set out. I think we have all we require and there is some distance to travel."

"Wait, Thaddeus, Sorcerer, I already foresee one impediment to our journey. I cannot fly with confidence in a territory strange to me. As you have apparently no other conveyance, how would we proceed? You cannot carry me the entire way, nor would I allow it, in any case."

"Why not perch on my shoulder? Would this not solve the problem?"

"Is your flesh made of iron, then, that my talons—the greatest of all Eagles—will have no effect, leave no mark? This I doubt."

"Your point is telling. Allow me a moment."

For a third time, Thaddeus found inspiration.

"I think I may have a solution. In my pack, I have a leather pouch of tools. The pouch hide is thick enough, I warrant, to withstand those of your talons as will touch me. From it, I'll fashion a type of pauldron, a covering to fit across my shoulders. Then you may stand proudly and sense your Kingdom as we pass by, going from one shoulder to another, as you desire."

"Are you an Artificer, then, with all else? I do not visualize it. I will need a demonstration."

"Very well. Allow me a time, and I will have it."

Thaddeus dug the sturdy leather pouch out of his pack and, with the help of his knife and a length of cord, made a shoulder guard to serve as a perch for the Eagle.

"Osiric, Lord, I am ready with my construct, but you must find a way to achieve my shoulder so you may test it."

"Yes. All right, return to the log on which I stood but moments ago and sit down with it at your back. I will assume the log from the ground and your shoulder from the log. I hope you have trust in your stout hide."

11

The Curse of the Red Dragon
Maledictio Autem Rufus Draco

So saying, the Eagle did as he promised. The great bird was heavy on the boy's shoulder. Thaddeus sagged a bit from the Eagle's weight, even though he was sitting on the ground. Striding along in the open country, though, would be a challenge.

On the other hand, while he now felt the pressure of the Eagle's powerful claws, he had no sense of pain or other discomfort. The device appeared to work.

"You are of passing skill, young Sorcerer. You may even have some small chance of success in your Quest of the Dragon."

"I would rather have more than a small chance, you know," Thaddeus replied.

"Of course. But that is why you seek to take me with you, no?"

Thaddeus laughed lightly. *"Yes. Your point. Well, Osiric, shall we begin our trek?"*

"As you will, Lord Thaddeus."

Thaddeus looked sharply at the filmy-eyed bird. *"I am no Lord, Osiric."*

"Yea, I know it. It is merely a term of respect I lend you pending further adventures and their outcomes. Be aware, the title may be withdrawn as quickly as it has been bestowed."

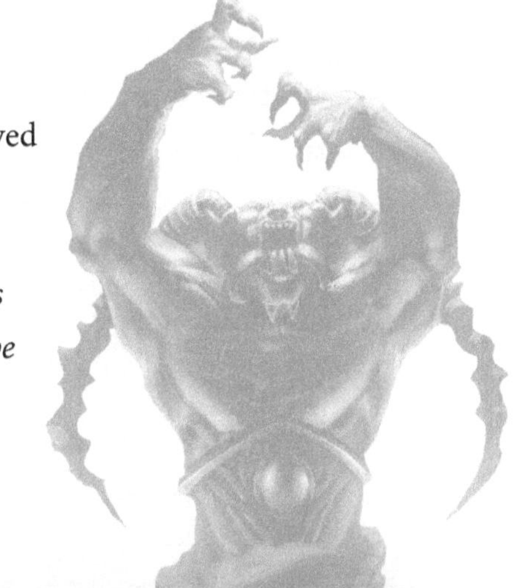

"I shall keep that in my mind."

"As you should."

With effort, Thaddeus stood slowly, trying not to dislodge his passenger. He achieved this practically but not gracefully. Sighting the Sun, the Apprentice regained his direction of travel and set off, slowly attaining a comfortable walking gait.

The trip to the Greater Flatstone River was relatively uneventful. Thaddeus noted the Eagle was not nearly so chatty as his old mule but tended to be more reserved. His habit was to respond to a conversation rather than initiate it. He had a dry sense of humor as well, which the young Apprentice appreciated. As there was no shortage of spring rabbits and fish, the pair never wanted for a meal.

Pursuing another thought, Thaddeus fashioned a hundred-pace tether from leftover rabbit guts. He cured it using a spell learned from Silvestrus, then fastened one end to a clasp of the pauldron and the other to Osiric's leg, having explained his plan in advance to the Eagle.

"This will allow you flight in open country to the distance of the cord and also the ability to find your way back to my shoulder when you are ready without concern of drifting inadvertently away from the course you have chosen. Perhaps, with time, your smell and hearing will sharpen further, and you will no longer need this aide."

Several attempts were necessary before the pair became practiced with the use of the tether, though not without difficulties.

Thaddeus told Osiric to have no care for his ear and neck, as he was sure they would heal well enough. Also, being buffeted by an Eagle coming in at speed tended to provide a measure of discomfort. Eventually, however, their routine smoothed, and they were able to dispense with the tether altogether. Osiric would call as he was coming into land, and Thaddeus would brace himself, issuing a return call which the Eagle used as a final guide.

Thaddeus also found that, once they reached civilization, the Eagle proved effective in preventing him from being jostled, solicited, or pilched. People tended to keep a respectful distance from the great bird. Even the most persistent entrepreneurs turned tail to find business opportunities elsewhere when Osiric flared his wings and skreed.

One night, Thaddeus awoke to a piercing scream, only to see a roughly-dressed man running away down an alleyway, holding his hands to his face, a bloody trail following him. The Apprentice questioned his companion, who threw back his head, swallowing a gobbet of flesh before speaking.

"The intruder sought to lighten your load. He must have been desperate; he ignored my warnings. Now, he and I share a condition." The great bird continued, *"As you predicted, I find that my sense of coordination and reflexes are returning—well, not returning, exactly. It is just that instead of sight, I come more to rely on smell and sound to guide me to my target. It is different but becoming more effective daily."*

"Ah. I have heard of that. My Brother, Anders of Brightfield Manor, has told me bats hunt in this fashion."

"Truly? I have often wondered about that. Perhaps, I should change my name to Vespertiliolis."

It took Thaddeus a moment to realize the Eagle's jest, then he laughed.

The pair of travelers reached the Greater Flatstone River without further incident, and at one of the smaller river landings, Thaddeus purchased passage on a barge going downriver. The vessel was more spacious than the one he'd traveled on coming North. He had redeemed one of Master Silvestrus' Letters of Credit and drew enough from it to pay for his fare and twice again for Osiric. Further, he, his belongings, and the bird were compelled to sit in the middle of the flat deck, well away from the crew and passengers alike, who avoided them.

The weather, however, warmed perceptibly as the barge made its way South into Frantillia. The trees, particularly, seemed less stark and forbidding than those of the North. The flowers showed a riot of colors, and the animals of the forest were busily pursuing each other for a variety of reasons. One morning, Thaddeus was certain he'd spied a satyr pursuing a nymph.

The Apprentice described the lush scenery to Osiric as they drifted lazily downstream. If anyone on the barge thought it odd a young boy should be talking to an Eagle standing guard on his pack, he or she had the wisdom not to mention it.

Finally reaching the mouth of the Greater Flatstone, Thaddeus and the Eagle disembarked, shared provisions, and obtained directions to Vexare, the small coastal fishing town that, according to Master Silvestrus, was their destination.

On the third day overland, the pair achieved the village just before sunset. He imagined he presented an amusing sight to the townspeople: dust head to toe, old staff in one hand, old bird on the opposite shoulder, and him looking young enough to be anyone's grandson. Not much of an imposing figure for a Sorcerer come to save the day.

It took only moments to gain the town square from the village outskirts. And only moments more to perceive the desperation and despair on the faces of the village men talking quietly at tables outside the town's only inn.

Inquiries pointed him toward the house of Chief Magistrate Pontius. A knock on the door and a brief exchange with the housekeeper brought the Magistrate himself to Thaddeus.

"Yes, lad, what can I do for you?" a balding, rotund man of shorter height asked the boy while staring curiously at the Eagle perched on his shoulder.

"Magistrate Pontius, I am Thaddeus of the *Collegium Sorcerorum*. I was sent by my Master, Silvestrus of Somerset, in response to your recent petition."

"Hmm. They sent a boy, then—an Apprentice, I'll warrant." Disappointment tinged the man's voice. "Well, lad, I am glad for a response, but I will be truthful. I was hoping for the Master himself to come, being as how this has to do with Dragons and all."

Silvestrus had gone over this part thoroughly with Thaddeus prior to his departure. "I understand, Magistrate, but do not be disheartened. I come to evaluate the situation and to determine the need."

"Ah, I see. You're here to provide the assessment."

Thaddeus replied, "Yes, Magistrate. Very much like that."

"Well, good. I'm glad we're going along the same road. I hope you can complete your assessment quickly and return with your Master soon. My people suffer, and time is fleeting. Um, that's quite an unusual pet you have there."

Of a sudden, the Eagle spoke to Thaddeus. *"I sense he speaks of me. What does he say?"*

"He asks if you are my pet."

Increased pressure gripped his shoulder as Osiric's talons dug into the leather. Once again, Thaddeus praised the inspiration for the tool pouch.

"Been with you long?"

"No, Magistrate. He and I met only a short while ago in a forest northeast of here. We are traveling together for a time."

"I see. Well, that's remarkable for a bird. They're usually not so smart. Does he do any tricks?"

"What does he say now?"

"It's really not important, Osiric."

"I will not be put off, Sorcerer."

"Very well. He expresses curiosity regarding your level of intellect and wonders if you perform trained maneuvers."

"You mean, whether I have a bird brain and if I perform tricks?"

"Well, yes, but...." The pressure in Thaddeus' shoulder increased to the point where it became painful.

"I shall have his eyes!"

"Osiric! Abate thy fury. He is a mortal man only, and as such, is ignorant. He means no offense, I'm certain."

"Excuse me, lad, but can you speak with that bird?"

"A little, Magistrate. 'Tis a thing they teach us as a part of our training."

"Well, quite amazing. What's wrong with his eyes? Put his head into the suet sack once too often? Heh-heh."

"Tell me, Sorcerer, what does he say now?"

"Very well. He speculates that you have perhaps lost your vision through some mischance of feeding."

"Mean you the old tale of hitting one's head in the feeding pouch due to over-eagerness and lack of thought?"

"Well, yes. 'Tis the gist of it."

"Now I shall have his testicles as well!"

"Osiric, abide! If we slew all those who are ignorant and act foolishly, the world would be empty except for you, me, and seven others I know, and maybe not all of them."

"So you say, but this one had better change his topic."

"He is blind, Magistrate, the result of a terrible fire in the forest last spring. Perhaps, however, we could discuss your need here in the village, and after, mayhap you could direct me to suitable lodging?"

"Oh, yes. Of course, lad, I'm forgetting my manners. Come in and follow me through to the courtyard. Ulina will bring us some cool spring punch. Ulina?"

The town official guided Thaddeus and his companion to an inner courtyard and offered the boy a chair by a table beneath a shade tree. Thaddeus coaxed the Eagle onto a chair back. The weather was gently warm, the beginning of sunset was promising, and the purberry punch the house servant brought was refreshing.

Magistrate Pontius set down his cup. "Well, then, Apprentice Thaddeus—to business. I will tell you of our need. Last year about this time, the seas that surround us began to turn red. In fact, I think it started on this very day one year ago. A tide of crimson water swept in all up and down our shoreline but in that of no other. Soon small fish began to die and were washed up on our beaches—then large fish —then, even larger fish, and so on. Why, early this year, we even had a dead whale wash up on the beach near the cove.

"The pattern is always the same. It starts with the evening tide. Waves and waves of red water, and then a pause before the dead fish appear. And it's not just fish. Crabs, snails, conchs, and sea birds all suffer the same fate. As our village is a village that makes its way by fishing, we are at our wit's end. We have no recourse."

The Magistrate picked up his cup and paused to take a sip of punch.

"Several of the Magistrates in this region come together every so often to discuss common problems and try to solve them, drink a fair amount, and ogle the serving wenches—if you take my meaning. Anyway, late last year at our winter meeting, I was talking over our problem with the Magistrate of South Litus down the coast. He told me that once when he was a lad, they'd had a problem with giant seagulls carrying off the children. So, they'd sent to the College, and one of the Masters came down and set things to rights. He suggested I do the same. And so I did, and that's how you're here."

"I see. Your letter, Magistrate, made reference to a Red Dragon. What can you tell me as to that?"

"Oh, yes. Well, two things, young Thaddeus. One is that around the time of the first red tide last year, one of the old village men was out fishing and swears he saw a huge Red Dragon flying out of a bay cove just down the beach. Never saw one before and never saw one since.

"The second is that there is an old woman who lives down the beach a way. She's called the Old Sea Woman, but her name is Mari. They say

she claims she had a dream that a Red Dragon and a Green Dragon
were fighting. In the end, the Green sent him packing. But the Red
swore he'd wreak his vengeance on her by poison—a red poison—one
meant to kill her."

"A Green Dragon, Magistrate?"

"Well, yes. We have a local legend hereabouts, centuries old, as far
as I can tell. It has to do with a Green Dragon—the Queen of her kind—
who, it is said, has lived in these parts from long ago and brings us
our luck. The legend involves her relationship with a young man she'd
taken a shine to, or something along those lines. Anyway, the gist of it is
that our particular coast is said to be blessed on account of the special
feelings the Green Dragon has for this area and its folk. Now, no one I
know has ever seen this Green Dragon, except maybe Old Mari down
by the beach. She seems to know the most about these legends."

"Do you believe she speaks truly, Magistrate?"

The plump official rubbed his chin. "Well, it's hard to say, lad. I
mean, if she's the only one as has seen it, then how would you know the
truth of it?"

"You have a good point. Well, I think I should begin by speaking
with the old fishing master who saw the dragon and then the old woman,
this Mari. Can you tell me how I may find them?"

"Well, the old fellow won't do you any good. He got so bothered by
nobody believing him about what he saw last year that he up and died
these three months past. As to Mari, I don't exactly know. I can point
you to her home, just an old hovel some ways down the beach. But I
don't know as to what you can get from her. Some say she's a bit daft,
speaking of things as don't make sense, you see. And on top of that,
no one around here has seen her in weeks. She's always been one to
come to town once a month on Venus' Day for her supplies and such.
But she has not been about lately. Very unusual for her. I was just
thinking I ought to be going down and look in on her myself."

"Well, I will be going to talk with her in any case, Magistrate, and I will be glad to let you know if something's amiss."

"Why, thank ye, lad. I'd be in your debt. 'Tis a bit of a trek down to the coast, you see, and time is the enemy of the knee, don't you know."

"Fine, then. I will go first thing in the morning. Now, if you could suggest lodging?"

"I'd say, try the *Locusta Ruber*, just in the square. 'Tis the best inn in the village. Of course, 'tis also the only inn in the village. Speak with Toomus, the innkeep. Tell him it was I as sent you. He'll fix you up with a nice room and some good victuals. Now, the food's liable to be a bit costly, as we've had to cart it in lately because of the tide die-off, but what's there is good. I wish you luck, lad. If we don't find and fix the problem soon, our people will have no recourse but to leave, and our village will die."

Thaddeus nodded. "Thank you for your time and attention, Magistrate. I will report back to you when I have learned something."

The man nodded and stood. Thaddeus, following suit, collected Osiric from his perch. They were shown the door. Magistrate Pontius thanked Thaddeus once again for coming to help the village and pointed him to the inn.

Thaddeus easily found the inn, it being the one he'd noted earlier. After he sought out Toomus, he was put up in a comfortable room and had a good Even-tide, which he enjoyed in his quarters with Osiric. The innkeep was inquisitive, but suddenly remembered other duties once Osiric fanned his wings at Thaddeus' light touch on his left leg, their signal for such occasions.

The pair slept well. Thaddeus had not realized how much he'd missed a real bed these past few weeks on the road. When he first opened his eyes, however, he discovered Osiric was gone. By the time Thaddeus had completed his morning freshening, however, the bird had returned, flying gracefully in through the open window but missing the chair back, his proposed landing place.

As a consequence, the Eagle went head-over-talons onto Thaddeus' bed, coming to a stop with a thump. He struggled to its feet, smoothed his feathers, and assumed as much dignity as he could. *"It was my intention to do that."*

"Of course."

"You know, the Magistrate told you correctly. The Sea Life is dying. I could smell it as I flew over the waters. Death everywhere. It is most unnatural."

"Perhaps we will find its cause."

"And if the cause truly is a Red Dragon?"

"Well, what would you make of our chances, then?"

"No life continues indefinitely."

"Of course."

12

The Old Woman of the Sea I
Anicula Maritima I

Toomus gave directions to Old Mari's home. The trip sounded to be about an hour's journey there and back, so Thaddeus purchased provisions—at heavily inflated prices—as well as a basket to carry it all in. The sun was warm, and the sound of the waves washing up on the beach lent a pleasance to the atmosphere. As he drew near, however, the stench emanating from the structure was overpowering.

The Sea Woman's dwelling lay in a small hidden cove—the only house for several *mille passae* in any direction. The structure itself was made from various debris: driftwood, dried fronds, whalebone, coral, stones, and shells. But that was not the only odd thing about her home.

"Osiric, the doorway is three times a man's height and at least twice in width. I've never known an entranceway to be so constructed. What do you make of that?"

"Perhaps she has large friends."

"Perhaps."

Thaddeus stopped five paces from the entrance.

"Ave! Mistress Mari? I am Thaddeus from the *Collegium Sorcerorum.* They told me in the village you knew of the Red and Green

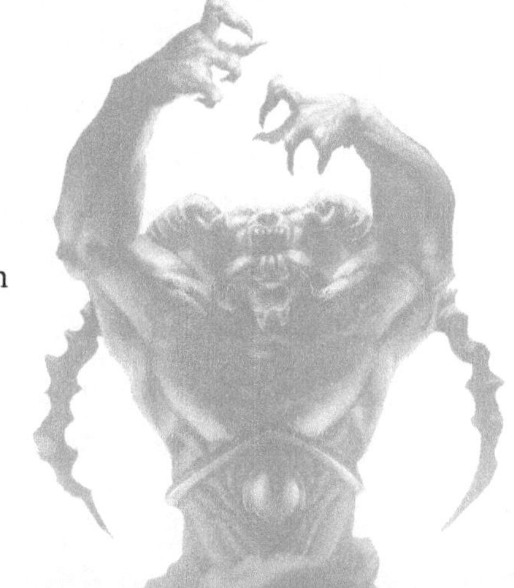

Dragons. I would ask you of these creatures. Have I your permission to approach your home?"

Time passed, and the Apprentice received no reply. He walked slowly forward until he was but a pace from the entrance and called again, but again, there was no answer.

"Osiric, I'm going in," Thaddeus said. *"Should anything untoward befall, make your way to the College and tell Master Silvestrus."*

"I assume you must be somewhat anxious concerning what may now be about to occur in that you list requirements for me that I cannot possibly fulfill. Instead, should something … adverse … happen, I will fly to where I think the Magistrate's house stands and go through some sort of pantomime, hoping the man will be intelligent enough to understand. Failing that, I will then fly out to sea, chasing the sun's warmth. I wonder how far I shall get?"

Carefully, Thaddeus raised his arm till it touched the Eagle's feet. The bird stepped from the boy's shoulder to the long-gloved arm, then to an old weathered gray rickety chair sitting next to the hovel's entrance. Osiric began to preen himself as Thaddeus moved to enter the Sea Woman's home.

"Luck be with you," the Eagle said.

"Aye," Thaddeus responded and went in.

The interior was one great room, appearing much larger than it had from the outside. Several candles had burned down to puddles. Some had been knocked over by force and lay askew, while some appeared to have simply gone out. In one corner of the room was a fire pit, though Thaddeus guessed it was long unused. A sideboard ran from the fire pit to a pantry, likely a food preparation area. The room was littered with the bones and shells of a myriad of sea creatures, some rather large. Several rotting woven mats were strewn across the dirt floor. One wall appeared to have a burn mark with charring over half its surface.

In the seaward corner was a pallet covered with seaweed. On it, Thaddeus found a shriveled, ill-appearing elderly woman who lay on her back, mouth open. It took him a moment to detect the old woman's shallow breathing. She was covered by a soiled blanket.

"Mistress? Mistress?"

Still, the woman did not respond. Thaddeus approached the woman slowly, stopping every other step to repeat his call, but the old woman remained as she was. At last, he stood by the filthy pallet. He carefully reached out a hand and gently touched the lady's shoulder.

"Mistress?"

Suddenly, the woman sat bolt upright—her eyes flashed open, burning bright. *"Dracones Semper Invicti!"* she shrieked.

Then she slowly lay back down again, closed her eyes, and resumed her shallow breathing. A cursory examination, as he had learned to do from Master Celsius, indicated the old woman had been without water and food for some time.

Thaddeus inspected the hut but found none of either. Next, he walked outside and looked for a source of fresh water. He did not find a well, but he did find several old rain pots. Though most were broken or knocked over, two remained upright and full.

Thaddeus shared his findings with the great Eagle.

"…. so I think I'll make a weak seafood soup. From the signs inside, that's what she's been eating. And we need to eat, anyway. She's got a pot or two, though they look like they could use a good scrubbing. And I can get a fire started. It should not take long."

"I see," said the Eagle. *"Verily, you're going to make someone a very good home-mate one day."*

Ignoring his feathered friend, Thaddeus set about his tasks. He didn't begrudge some spell-casting to move the process along and improve the product. Finally, the seafood stew was ready.

Sitting on a cracked stool he'd found and moved over to the pallet, Thaddeus dipped a small spoon into the bowl and carefully let a trickle of broth run down the inside cheek of the old woman's open mouth. After a second application, the woman moved her tongue, smacked her lips, and swallowed. Another bit of the sea broth led to a moment of coughing, which soon subsided.

Over the next hour, she finished about half the bowl, probably enough for now. As he had nothing to do but wait before trying again, Thaddeus dug through his travel bag and produced his flute.

Zoarr had pressed it on him as they were all preparing to set out from the College. "It will help you while away the long lonely hours when you're not with Marsia," the dark youth said with a grin. "Besides," he added, honesty in his tone, "you could use the practice."

Osiric's critique of his playing was more to the point. *"Why was it that my vision was lost rather than my hearing?"*

Thaddeus, however, cheerfully ignored his critic and dutifully ran through his repertoire, tending to repeat those songs Osiric said he liked less than the others.

So passed the afternoon. Thaddeus administered a second feeding to the old woman. She displayed more signs of animation this time and even turned her head to receive the spoon.

Thaddeus noted her color had improved, and he was relieved. To occupy his time, he went over the great room, straightening what few furnishings were there and cleaning what he could. Later, he dug several of Master Silvestrus' scrolls from his pack and began to review them.

The sun set, sinking into the sea with a fiery progression.

With nightfall, the air grew chill, and he started a fire. He then took up his flute again.

Osiric remained outside the house during the cleaning and the playing. *"I normally do not live indoors, you understand,"* the Eagle said in reply to the Apprentice's question after the tall youth had finished one particularly long ditty. *"And there are other reasons."*

The old moon had just fully risen as Thaddeus put down his flute with a thought to offer a third feeding when he looked to see the old woman regarding him.

Dancing flames from the fire pit were reflected in her eyes. "You do not play well," she said in a quavering voice. With that, she closed her eyes again.

Thaddeus thought it was simple sleep rather than a more sinister state, so he put his flute away and resumed his watch. After a time, he arose, and put new wood in the fire pit. He glanced out the vaulted doorway. Osiric continued his guard duty and declined an invitation to spend the evening indoors. He also refused to allow Thaddeus to share the watch.

Thaddeus scanned the cove. The full moon showed on the waves gently lapping not fifty paces away. The beach, as well as the water, was now red-tinged. As the Magistrate had said, the afternoon tide had come in crimson. The stench was powerful, but the beautiful panorama made up for the smell—to a degree.

Thaddeus finished his brief sortie outdoors and went back into the old woman's house. He unpacked his blanket and prepared a place by the occupant's bed and, after a time, fell asleep. He awoke at intervals during the night. At each rousing, he checked to see how his charge was faring. She was sleeping soundly. He then put more wood on the fire and conferred again with Osiric. The stars wheeled in their courses.

The morning light streaming in the window woke Thaddeus with a start, and it took him a moment to regain his bearings. He found the old woman's eyes on him once again, not fearful but curious.

"Mistress, I am Thaddeus of the *Collegium Sorcerorum*. I am come to this village at the request of Magistrate Pontius of Vexare to evaluate what he describes as the Curse of a Red Dragon. In the course of our conversation, he mentioned that you might know of this Red Dragon and also of a Green Dragon said to have its den in this area. When I came to make inquiries, I found you in an ill state. It appeared that you'd not had nourishment in some time. I made you some broth. You seem better today, but I would caution you against exerting yourself for a bit."

The old woman nodded in understanding.

"Mistress, I will make us some porridge now and return to assist you if you need to get up."

The old woman nodded again.

Thaddeus rose and found Osiric outside with nothing to report but complaining of hunger. Thaddeus gave him leftovers from the previous day's provision and set about preparing the porridge. Soon enough, he was spooning the warm, watery Break-fast into the old woman's accepting mouth.

After a somewhat generous portion, she shut her lips and shook her head, refusing more. She spoke. "Thank you … Thaddeus, is it? You have done me a great service this day. I will rest now for yet a little, then we will talk, yes?"

"Yes, Mistress." Thaddeus left his charge napping to explore the beach a *mille passum* in either direction.

Osiric remained behind to continue guard duty, which he appeared to take seriously. *"It is best not to take Dragons for granted. The last knight I heard of who discounted them ended his days as a roast."*

Returning after an hour, Thaddeus found the old woman awake. He assisted her to a commode he'd found overturned out back and had brought in, then rummaged around until he found a reasonably clean linen and a washbasin, which he filled. Placing everything within reach, he excused himself and went out to spend time with the Eagle. Presently, the woman called.

Thaddeus assisted his charge back to bed, which he had freshened as he might, then settled himself in a chair facing the old woman.

"So, Thaddeus, Sorcerer. You have taken your time in coming, and I do not mean just now," she said as the Apprentice began to protest. "All right, lad. You have traveled a far way to ask questions. So, ask them."

Thaddeus saw what the Magistrate meant regarding her manner. A Queen, indeed. "You are the Old Woman of the Sea, known as Mari?"

"Yes."

"Know you of the Red Dragon?"

"Yes."

"I see. How is he called?"

"His name is Attacondros."

"Has he, as is said, placed a curse upon this place?"

"Yes."

"Know you the reason for it?"

"Yes."

"Can you say it?"

"Very well. At one time, he sought the favors of the Green Dragon. She, however, spurned his advances for her own reasons. In his anger, he swore a curse on her. It has taken the form of a red tide that comes each day."

"In what way does the tide affect its curse?"

"It is like unto a poison of the waters. It kills the sea life in its area of influence. The Green Dragon is a sea dragon; she subsists on the sea's bounty. If it is poisoned, she becomes poisoned and will die. That is his plan."

"Why would she not simply move on? The sea, it is said, goes on forever. Surely, he cannot possibly poison it all."

"There are two reasons. First, she has a compact with the folk of this area, whose ancestors befriended her long ago during a time of troubles when no one else would. She feels obliged on that account. And, second … you truly do not know?" The old woman gave the Apprentice a penetrating gaze.

"Nay, Mistress. I do not."

"Very well. She is bound to a saying writ large in the stars. She is to wait here for someone who is to come to her. The outcome of their acquaintance will result in the visitation of a terrible vengeance upon the Red Dragon—for the poisoning and for all the other evil he has spawned over time."

"What of the Green Dragon?"

"She will die."

"Is there naught to be done to confound this curse and thus avoid her death?"

"No. The poison has entered her system already. It now has its hold on her, and its effects are irreversible. There is no cure."

"That is a sad thing you tell me, Mari."

"Think you so?" the old woman asked with an odd light in her eyes.

"Yes, truly."

"Ah. Well, hear this, then. With her death, the curse, having run its course, will dissipate and cease. The sea will be cleansed. Within a short time, sea life will return and restore itself and go on to flourish once again."

"The price is high, though, especially for the Green Dragon."

"Yes."

"Wait! What if he for whom the Dragon waits does not come before—well, before?"

The old woman chuckled drily. "I did not say the Green one waits for a 'he,' did I? Though, in this case, it is true. These matters are, however, determined by the stars, as I have said. What the stars dictate occurs, timing or no."

"I see. And do you foresee the Green Dragon's death in this time?"

"Aye. Within a day or two, I think."

"Ah. Well, I shall relate this sad story to the Magistrate then, so he may tell his people. Perhaps despair will lift and hope return. Oh. One thing yet, Mistress. Know you the name of the Green Dragon?"

The old woman smiled suddenly. "Yes. Of a certainty."

"And will you tell it to me?"

"Yes. To you, yes. It is Mari."

13

The Old Woman of the Sea II
Anicula Maritima II

Thaddeus started in surprise. "The Dragon's name is Mari? The same as yours?"

"Yes. 'Tis a common enough name in these lands."

"Ah, yes. Of course."

"Well, Thaddeus, Sorcerer. Your quest for information is completed, and you may return now to the Magistrate to give him the good news and from there back to your College, I assume."

"Yes. If you feel you are recovered, I thought to set out later this morning. I will leave what remains of the provisions with you, and I will prepare more of the sea stew. That should see you through until you regain the remainder of your strength."

"I should like that. It will help. On a different matter … I have not been quite myself lately, and time has slipped from me. But is the moon full this night?"

"Why, yes, Mistress Mari. It was last night and will be again tonight as well."

"Ah. Good. One thing further, then, young Sorcerer. I know I have had much from you, and I know you must be anxious to leave this place and return to your school … but I have yet a last boon to ask of you."

"What is it, Mistress?" Thaddeus asked, curious.

"There is someone I wish you to meet. It is a personage I judge to be of some importance, but one who travels widely and will be here this night only, for a brief time following the sunset. I deem it of the utmost importance that the two of you meet. Will you return to my home this very night by moonrise and make this person's acquaintance? Afterward, you are free to go on your way with my blessing—no small thing in itself—and I will burden you no longer."

"Mistress, I am under no constraint, but your request is—no disrespect meant—passing odd. Can you tell me something of who it is I am to meet? What would be the purpose of our meeting? Why—"

The old woman raised her hand in an imperious gesture.

"Thaddeus! I understand you have many questions concerning this rather unusual request. I can say only that the stars endorse this meeting. For the rest, you will have to take it on my trust."

Mistress Mari reached out a withered hand and clasped that of the young Sorcerer. "If it has any import to you, know that I greatly desire that you do this, however queer it may seem to you. I swear you will come to no harm from it, and, in fact, I think you will find—"

A loud call from Osiric brought Thaddeus to his feet.

"What is that sound?" the old woman demanded.

"That is Osiric. He's a great Eagle and travels with me. He's blind but has been outside your home standing watch all this time."

"An Eagle, you say?"

"Yes, Mistress. He's rather good company, actually. Quite witty. Would you care to meet him?"

"Um, no. No. I am wary of the great birds from a time in my youth. No, I shall remain here."

"Then excuse me for a moment, Mistress, while I see what he means by his call."

So saying, Thaddeus turned and left the house. He found Osiric sitting on his weathered chair perch as before, but his head was turned down the beach to the West. Thaddeus followed his gaze. A large object lay at the lapping edge of the water. Thaddeus guessed whatever it was must have been washed up recently. He didn't recall seeing it before.

"What is it, Osiric?"

"Amidst all this stench, there is an even more powerful smell. It comes from that area." The bird nodded in the direction of the object on the beach. *"It is disgusting. I have smelled nothing like it before. You have asked that I mark any unusual occurrence, and this counts thusly, I think. How goes it inside, by the way?"*

"It goes well. The woman, Mari, seems to have much of her strength back—surprising in this short a time. I was about to tell her we would be leaving, but she bade me return this evening to meet someone. She said it was important."

"Another mystery. You seem to collect these."

"Truly, do you think it?"

"Aye. I do."

"Hmm. I find myself uncertain. Well, I will go and look at whatever it is that has washed up on the shore. I will call if there's trouble."

"Oh? And what will I then? Fly to where I think you might be—or to where the smell is the worst—and cry 'skree, skree, I am blind, I am blind' until I tire?"

"I will return anon. Have a care not to fall off your perch. Chairs are expensive and difficult to replace."

In a short time, Thaddeus reached what turned out to be the carcass of a merman.

At least, that's what he supposed it might once have been. It was wasted and ravaged, and numerous sea creatures had been at it. Thaddeus thought to drag it over behind a nearby sand hillock, but when he grasped what remained of one arm, it came away in his hand.

Well, there was nothing for it. He covered it with sand where it lay as best he could and returned to the old woman's dwelling. He shared his discovery with Osiric and went back inside.

"Well, Sorcerer, what did you find?" the old woman asked.

Thaddeus described what he had seen and what he did.

"Ah, this cursed red plague scourges everything. If only I had my full strength back…. Well, if *ifs and ands were kettles and pans, we'd never be done with washing them*, eh, boy? So, Thaddeus, what have you decided? Will you humor an old woman and grant me my request?"

"I will, Mistress Mari. It all seems a bit of a mystery to me, but if it's that important to you, I will."

The old woman reached forward and grasped the Apprentice's hand once more. The grip was hard, as was the hand, which surprised the boy.

"Swear it, Thaddeus. Swear that you will!" To his further surprise, her look was commanding, desperate, and anxious.

"Very well, Mistress. I swear it."

The old woman relinquished her grip and lay back with a sigh.

"Thank you, Thaddeus. Thank you. With this act, you will achieve a reward—both now and later—beyond your imagining."

"I swore this for no reward, Mistress," the Apprentice said with a bit of heat.

"Well, I know that, intrepid Thaddeus. That is part of the reason for it, you see." The old woman sighed. "Ah, you put me in mind of someone I once knew long ago. Long, long ago."

"Very well, then, Mistress Mari. I will be leaving now with Osiric, but I will return by moonrise. How shall I know the person I'm to meet, and where shall the meeting take place?"

"Fret not, Sorcerer. Just return here. That person shall find you; never fear. My thanks again, lad, for everything." With that, the old woman closed her eyes, and within moments, Thaddeus detected the heavier breathing of deeper sleep.

It was but a short time later that the sea broth was finished, and he set the kettle to the back of the fireplace. Thaddeus looked around the old woman's home once more and judged that he had done as much as he could. Turning, he nodded to the sleeping form and walked outside where the Eagle awaited him.

"Come, Osiric, let us leave this place."

"…. and then she bade me return to her home tonight to meet someone—she did not say who or why—and made me swear to it. She seemed in her right mind at the time, only weak yet. Otherwise, Magistrate, I have every reason to believe the plague will be ended soon if what old Mari says is true."

The Magistrate, sitting at his desk across from Thaddeus, stopped tapping his jaw with his stylus. "Astounded I am at this adventure, Thaddeus, my lad, and at your part in it. You have done well—no, no, beyond well. You have saved the life of the community."

The Magistrate took a fresh parchment from the shelf behind him and began writing. After a few moments, he finished and signed it with a flourish, then dripped hot wax from a lit candle onto a ribbon he held to the missive and pressed a large seal onto the red puddle.

"Here, lad, a Letter of Credit for two-thousand gold Imperials as promised. Take this back with you to your Master, along with this scroll expressing our undying gratitude." The Magistrate slid the two parchments across the desk to the young Sorcerer.

"My thanks, Magistrate Pontius, but don't you think it might be better to withhold payment until you know for certain the scourge is completely gone?"

"Thaddeus, my boy, when you have been a politician as long as I, you get a certain sense about who tells true and who does not. I find that I would stake much on your words, youth that you are. I hope you take this as a compliment, for it is meant as such."

"Thank you, Magistrate. I will see that my Master receives this letter as soon as I may."

"I do not doubt it a bit, my boy. In the meantime, why not dine with me this eve? Ulina is a wonderful cook—as you likely have surmised—and it would please me to give you this bit of my personal gratitude."

"It would be my honor, Magistrate."

With the contentment of a full belly and still a little heady from the wine, Thaddeus made his way back to Old Mari's home, the light from one of his two torches illuminating his path. He had brought a second for the return. Moon or no, there might be clouds. Osiric did not accompany him, choosing instead to remain on the sill of the open window of their room at the inn.

"I don't like the smell of it," the Eagle had said when invited. *"Besides, by perching here, I can keep a good lookout. That was a bit of humor, Thaddeus."*

The Magistrate had made no jests but had cautioned the Apprentice concerning his upcoming encounter.

"Old Mari is one of a kind, lad. Many there are as say she has powers. Be cautious in your dealings with her, I advise, ill or not. I would keep the meeting, certainly, being as ye've sworn, but I'd keep it with my feet pointing backward if you take my meaning."

At the old woman's dwelling, Thaddeus found her home dark. He called out from just outside the entrance. Being careful of his torch, he entered the house, but of its occupant, he found no sign. Calling several times more brought no response. Puzzled, he went back outside and walked around the dwelling. His search, however, produced no old woman and no new stranger.

The full moon had risen and provided enough light that he doused the torch in the beach sand. Still, he saw no one. Feeling a bit foolish to have promised the old woman this boon, he would have left at once had he not felt obliged to first solve the mystery of Mari's disappearance.

He was debating with himself what course to take when a swooshing sound came from above him, as if something was passing overhead at some speed. It put him in mind of the sound Osiric made in flight, and he looked up to see the bird but to no avail. Whatever it was, however, judging by the sound, was larger than the Eagle. Much larger. The moonlight dimmed suddenly, then brightened again as if a great mass had briefly passed in front of it.

Suddenly Thaddeus froze, his stomach in a knot. What if the Red Dragon had returned? What if he thought Thaddeus was interfering in his plans? He would likely not be pleased. He might even be of a mind to advise an unwelcome intruder as to how he felt.

"Thaddeus! Thaddeus of the *Collegium Sorcerorum.* I am here. Come to me!"

The voice sounded distant, cutting across the soft lapping of the waves. It seemed to be coming from just over the next hillock. But it was not the challenge of an angry adult male. It was a woman's voice, a sultry woman's voice if Thaddeus were any judge. And it was certainly not Mari's voice. It must be the person he was to meet.

He hesitated only a moment, then shrugged and trudged up the sandy dune. Also, this person—a woman, evidently—might know the whereabouts of the Old Sea Woman.

Gaining the crest of the mound, he was unsure what he'd find, but he did not think to find what he saw. A woman dressed in a simple tunic and sandals was gathering driftwood and piling it in a depression in the sand. She caught sight of him at once and stood in a relaxed pose, awaiting the young Sorcerer's approach.

He stopped a pace from her and waited.

The woman was beautiful in an exotic way. She was tall, lithe, and graceful, with thick, dark hair that fell to her waist. Catching the moon's sheen, her long hair seemed to have a green tinge to it. Her eyes were large and lustrous, her cheekbones high and wide, her nostrils flaring.

His mouth was suddenly dry.

The woman let the wood she was holding fall to the sand and addressed the Apprentice.

"Thaddeus? Of the *Collegium Sorcerorum?*"

"Y-yes." It was the only word he could get out. He had never seen a woman like her before.

"I thought it." So saying, she advanced on him, took him in her arms, and embraced him fully. Warm to the touch, her lips pressed firmly against his.

Thaddeus thought he should protest, but before he could take any such action, she released him and stepped back.

"I am Mari."

"How f-fare you, Mistress Mari? D-do many here share that name?"

She smiled, showing teeth. "Yea, they do. In any event, know that I am she of whom the wise woman spoke. I wished to meet you, partly to express my thanks for the care and kindness you have shown toward the Old Sea Woman, and, in part, for other reasons. I have only a short time here this night, but I have food that we may partake of for a late meal. If you will but seek more driftwood, I will kindle a fire."

It did not occur to Thaddeus to question, until much later, why any of what she said or did shouldn't be thought odd. It was almost as if he were in a dream, moving without thought.

"All right, I will look for more."

After a short search, he procured two further armloads for the fire and was trudging back up the hillock when the night brightened suddenly with a flash of intense green light, followed by a low roar coming from just over the sand dune. Thaddeus immediately dropped his burden and ran up the intervening distance. At the crest of the dune, he beheld the driftwood in the sand pit fully ablaze while the woman knelt on one knee close by the fire, rubbing her mouth with the back of her hand.

Thaddeus rushed down the dune.

"Mari, are you injured?" Thaddeus asked, concern in his voice.

"Be not afeared, young Sorcerer. I am well. 'Tis only that, in my preoccupation, I had forgotten my Great-Mother's admonition about standing too near a fire when starting it."

"'Tis good you are unhurt, but, pray tell me, lady, how it was you started this fire? Had you a flint?"

"No," the beautiful woman said mysteriously. "I used an old family trick."

"Ah. I'll go back and fetch the remainder of the wood."

By the time Thaddeus returned, a large blanket had been spread out, and a pig was roasting on a spit with several types of unfamiliar vegetables baking on the hot rocks surrounding the fire. The aroma was compelling though he'd eaten but a few hours earlier.

"Where did you manage to find a pig at this time of night—and these foods?" Thaddeus asked, incredulous.

"Ah. Many feral swine run loose in this place. I prefer the fruits of the sea, but the water here has been tainted of late, so I thought this might do," Mari said, spreading her hands to indicate the feast. "I have also brought us something to drink. It is a special brew my family makes; *Sanguis Draconis,* from the Veins of the Dragon. I think you will like it."

So saying, the woman produced a large sea gourd strung with a leather strap, from which she pulled a cork stopper. "You drink it like this." The woman held up the sea gourd at arms-length and tilted her head back, allowing the liquid to fall into her open mouth. "Umm. That is—pleasant. Here, you try it. Take care to draw only a little at a time, though. It is said to be potent."

Though a small inner voice nagged him that drinking the liquid might not be a good idea, Thaddeus paid no heed and did as he was bid.

The drink burned his lips almost before wetting them. The burning continued all the way down to his stomach. He almost snatched the sea gourd away, but instead, he drank again. The inner voice was now shouting at him … then suddenly, it stopped.

"That's really good," Thaddeus said, grinning.

"I'm glad you like it. Have more, if you wish, but as I say, be sparing. I will tend to our meal."

Thaddeus slaked his thirst and ate all he was offered of the pig and most of the rest. Everything was delicious, even if some parts were unfamiliar. He was thoroughly enjoying himself.

Mari approached him with a steaming linen. "Here, it is scented. Use it to wipe your hands and face. You will find it refreshing."

It was as the woman said.

"Now, Thaddeus, Sorcerer, you have eaten of my warm flesh and drunk of my blood-wine. Do you suspect what comes next?"

"No, Mistress Mari. I do not."

"Ah," said the mysterious woman reaching behind her back to undo her tunic. "I think you will."

14

The Queen of Sea Dragons I
Regina Draconum Marinarum I

Thaddeus awoke slowly, surprised that his head did not hurt as he had feared it might. The Sun was in his eyes, two diameters above the horizon.

He looked around him. The sand pit smoked still, its last embers dying. Of the pig and remainder of the feast, there was no trace. There was also no sign of the Mistress Mari. That is, except for a trail of woman's footprints that led down to the sea into which they vanished.

Thaddeus reviewed the course of the last evening and what had followed after.

The beautiful Mari lay next to him, propped on one elbow. As she gently stroked his hair, she spoke. "Thaddeus, you are a kind and considerate lover for one so young, but I must now give you instruction. Heed me closely, lovely one, else all is lost."

The woman was serious, and Thaddeus listened intently, his earlier drink-induced befuddlement strangely dissipated.

"Tomorrow, when you wake, I will be gone. Do not tarry the morning searching, for you will not find me. Likewise, the Old Sea Woman … she will be gone as well, and neither you nor the village folk will ever see her again. Instead, over the next dune to the East rests a small sea boat. If you hold me at all in your heart, even to the smallest amount for what we shared this night, you will take that boat out to the reef due south and see what it is you may find there. I am constrained from telling you anything further, only to say it is important that you do this. Will you, of your own choice, accomplish this thing I ask? I will not compel you to swear it—but will you?"

"Yes, Mari. If you wish it."

"Ah, my handsome young flute player, come give me another of your sweet songs," the woman said, moving to embrace him. It was only later that it occurred to Thaddeus to wonder how it was she knew he played the flute.

Thaddeus grasped a handful of the warm sand and let it trickle through his fingers, bemused by recent memories. After a time, he rose, drank water from a clay pot left from the previous night, and attended to his other duties.

It was an easy walk over to the next dune to where he discovered the boat—a coracle—small and round, with a ribbed frame over which were stretched cured animal hides. He could not identify the skins, only to know they were neither horse nor cow. A flat stick lying alongside, broad at one end, he assumed to be the paddle.

Within moments, he had dragged the boat to the sea's edge, pushed it out into the water, and climbed in. He sighted the reef and headed toward it, though it took some time to learn how to propel the craft so that it traveled in a straight line rather than simply rotating in a circle.

Half an hour passed before he reached the reef, which, at its highest, rose some thirty paces above water's level. Although he paddled up and down the length of the sea barrier, he found no feature of interest, and he had begun to wonder if Mistress Mari's brew had invented this portion of the story, when it occurred to him to explore the reef's seaward side.

Paddling around to the other side of the atoll, warm sun on his shoulders, he was rewarded with the discovery of a large opening in the reef—similar to a cave entrance—which was visible only from the seaward approach. Clearly, this was what the woman had meant.

Thaddeus paddled to the sparkling white beach surrounding the cavern opening, jumped out, and pulled the coracle up onto the sand far enough that it would not float away. Leaving his paddle in the craft, he cautiously approached the large opening. Immediately, the same oppressive stench he had smelled on the coastal beach greeted him, only stronger.

The Apprentice made his way into the yawning maw of the reef, but within a few paces, it became dark. He wished for his torches, but these had been left behind on the mainland. Well, there was nothing for it. He picked up a sizable branch of driftwood, gestured at one end, and commanded, *"Ignesce!"* The tip of the branch immediately burst into flame.

As he walked further into the cavern, the smell grew stronger until he was nearly overpowered. Then he heard a slow, labored, rhythmic movement of air as if some mighty blacksmith was operating an immense bellows.

Nothing, though, prepared him for what he saw when he turned the last bend in the passageway.

The tunnel opened into a large cavern, which was dominated by an immense form the likes of which Thaddeus had only read of but never seen. He immediately thought of the small black dragon that guarded the *Supremus* hallway but on a much grander scale.

Very much grander.

The recumbent Green Dragon—for it could be nothing else—was clearly ill. The large, plate-sized scales were sickly white and mottled green in color. Flaky patches of bare skin showed through where scales

Mari, Regina

DRACONUM MARINARUM

had already fallen off, and in other areas, gaping sores were weeping a putrid, pale exudate. The smell was terrible beyond enduring.

The beast lay on its side, its breathing slow and labored. Pools of what must be excrement were smeared on its hips and lower legs, and the countless jewels, seashells, and myriad golden coins that formed the bed on which the great serpent lay appeared befouled.

Thaddeus judged the creature at least forty paces from tail to snout. It had four clawed legs and parallel spiked ridges running down its back. The leathery wings—great as sails on the largest craft—protruded from its back but were crumpled at odd angles, torn and ripped in places.

The head sported great back-curved horns and prominent eye ridges. The slack, open mouth showed rows of sharp, brown-stained teeth a hands-length long. The sinuous tongue, slitted at the end, draped from the creature's maw to the cave floor. It appeared lusterless, dry, and cracked.

The eyes were sunken and dull yet burned with a green fire, which pinioned Thaddeus when they opened.

"You've come…."

Thaddeus was unsure how to address a Dragon, recalling no area of his *Collegium* study that touched on this subject, but he forged ahead gamely. "Aye, Great One, as I gave my word."

"That is … good. Hear me, Man most mortal. This is my Dying Day. Mine enemy of old has brought me low at last, as he said he would. But you have given me a gift to right this wrong, and in these hours left to me, I delight in the prospect of Vengeance."

"Is there naught I can do to assist you, Great One?" Thaddeus asked, uncertain as to what she meant but willing to relieve her suffering if he could.

"You have already, boy, though you know it not. Now attend to me most carefully. You must return to this very cave, once past Summer's height, and take that which lies closest to my heart. You may also learn something of import to you…."

The effort of speaking caused the Dragon to fall silent for some time, her breathing irregular. Finally, she opened her eyes again.

"I have lived well and have no regrets—except, perhaps, to wish we had shared more of time, we two…."

"Great One, have you any instructions concerning what to do—after? Do you wish to be burned or…."

"No. I do not think you could prepare a fire hot enough in any case. No. I have lived here; I will die here. And what comes after for this carcass is beyond my caring. I have eaten enough of crabs over time, so I suppose it is only fair for them now to take their turn at me…."

"What would you do regarding your treasure then, Great One?"

"It concerns me not. Do with it as you will. Only do not let Him have it."

"Mean you the Red One, Mistress?"

"Yes. You are quick, Thaddeus, Sorcerer, as I know. Now you must depart, Fair One. Leave me in peace these last hours. I have yet one more task to complete before my spirit may be free to sail the Etheros Sea. Make your way back to the mainland. You will know the signs. Remember, return here after the Summer's height. Farewell, young Sorcerer. Look to see me no more…."

With great effort, the Dragon rose slowly, painfully, and unsteadily halfway to her feet but could not stand. With what might have been a shrug of resignation, she grimaced, then spoke in a voice of thunder that reverberated throughout the cavern.

"I am *Regina Draconum Marinarum.* Know this and remember this day, for here falls one of the Mighty!" With that, the green beast threw back her head and issued forth a great roar, spewing a stream of green fire that lashed the cavern roof with flame.

But for a moment only….

Almost at once, the Dragon collapsed, falling to the cave floor with a force that shook the ground. Thaddeus thought she had died, but the creature breathed yet, though her breath came low and slow. As he watched, she uttered a groan and shifted her weight slightly.

Heeding the Sea Queen's last command, Thaddeus turned and made his way out of the cavern. He could think of nothing further he could do for the Dragon Queen.

The Apprentice returned to the coracle and, shoving off the beach into the water, began paddling back to the Frantillian coast. He was wrestling the boat up the cove beach toward Mari's hut when he became aware of a great silence. No birds called, and nothing stirred. Expectation filled the air. Then, of a sudden, it seemed as if a thousand voices gave rise to a song of rejoicing, though Thaddeus could understand none of what was said nor guess as to the reason or identity of the singers.

The song was captivating, but after a moment, the tone changed, and the melody became sad and melancholy as if those thousand voices were crying out in a great lament. The sea folk, Thaddeus guessed. Their Queen had fallen, and they honored her.

The boy sat down on a driftwood log and gazed out at the reef, his head bowed in respect, remembering all that had happened. After several fingers of the Sun had passed, the dirge of tribute ceased, but he sat unmoving until his musings were interrupted by a familiar voice.

"Aye, Thaddeus, lad!"

The young Sorcerer glanced over his shoulder to see Magistrate Pontius approaching, walking as quickly as he might over the sand. Thaddeus stood. "Magistrate, how did you happen to think to come here?"

"I was concerned for you, my boy, when you did not return last night, so this morning, I determined to make my way to Old Mari's hut, but it was empty. I did see what I assumed to be your footprints leading up over the dune, so I followed them, and here you are—well, and in one piece, I hope?"

"Thank you, Magistrate. Yes, I am well and glad that you came at this sad time."

"Ah, I thought it. As I drew near the water, I heard the Song of the Sea. I recognized it from stories I'd heard when I was half your height. What has befallen, then?"

"'Tis the Green Dragon, Magistrate. She has died."

"Oh. A sad thing, indeed." The Magistrate became thoughtful. "Is there anything to be done?"

"She bade me leave her. She said she had one more task to perform. I believe, though, that whether or not she completed that task, she has now gone on. Before I left, she commanded me to return here after Mid-Summer. She said there was something that I was to find."

"It is probably best to do as she bid, lad. Even in death, there is wisdom in honoring a Dragon's wish."

"Yes, I see it. Oh, and thanks to you for coming all this way to see to my safety, Magistrate."

"Think nothing of it, my boy. When one looks after a village, the people's needs must always be attended to." The older man smiled wanly.

Thaddeus wrestled with himself over the Dragon's treasure. He had already decided it would be foolish to attempt to transport it back to the College. Besides, in any case it was the village's treasure, having been assembled, he surmised, from ships that fell to harm off the coast over the centuries.

But his hesitation lay in what to tell the Magistrate. Would he be the type of man to seek to clasp the entirety of it to himself and thus suffer the fate of all who are overcome by greed? Or would the discovery lead to his own quick demise at the hands of those who would have it for themselves? Thaddeus saw no solution other than to advise the man and allow him to struggle with the outcome himself.

"Magistrate, there is one other thing you should know. The Dragon has left a treasure. I do not know its exact extent, but it covers the cavern floor where she lies. Even though she is no more, I believe that if her remains are disturbed now, a further curse will befall the village.

When I return past Summer's height, I will seek to undo the curse, then relinquish custody of the horde to you for the benefit of your village. But what you will do as trustee then becomes your burden. It will be your decision to make; I see that either great good or great harm could come from this."

The Magistrate looked steadily out to sea for a moment before meeting Thaddeus' gaze once again.

"You are a good lad, Thaddeus, Sorcerer. I take your point. There are many facets to this gem. I think it will be in the best interest of all if I give this matter serious thought during your absence. By the time you return, I hope to have a solution to this complex matter. We have already suffered sufficiently from one curse, and I have no desire to be the cause of a second."

The two of them headed up the beach. The older man hesitated and looked out to sea again. "I think I may have an idea about that, however. Well, we shall see. In the meantime, return with me to the village. A number of people there are anxious to give you their thanks. An equal or greater number of doubters, however, will be eagerly watching for this afternoon's tide to see if it remains red or no."

"Very well, Magistrate. But I know not when the change will occur, only that the Dragon said it would be after her death. If not today, then it must be soon. Otherwise, I believe I will rest at the inn tonight, then leave tomorrow morning for the College to report to my Master."

Thaddeus had begun to wonder whether he still had enough time to meet up with his friends—Marsia in particular. He hoped she would not question him too closely regarding his stay in Vexare. As the Magistrate had said, one curse was enough.

15

The Queen of Sea Dragons II
Regina Draconum Marinarum II

opeful expressions of thanks were given at the village that afternoon, but a few only, that is, until the afternoon tide came in blue-green and proud with no trace of red.

Thaddeus was then the center of a general storm of thanksgiving and showered with all manner of exaggeration. He was even hailed as *Dragonslayer*. The harder he protested such untruths, however, the louder were the paeans of praise.

The food and wine of celebration flowed freely as well. At one point, Thaddeus excused himself, making his way to the Magistrate's home to try to digest all that had occurred. Pontius, who had observed him steal off, joined him.

"Heady stuff, eh, lad? Well, don't think too much on it. These things can change on the instant, and your adoring public can become your worst enemies in the blink of an eye. Always remember the *Coronifer* in the chariot of the Triumph: *Respica te et Memento Mori*." It seemed good advice.

Thaddeus packed his bag the following morning, relating the previous day's events to Osiric. The bird cocked his head to one side.

"You know, Thaddeus, Sorcerer, have you considered that you were not dealing with three separate individuals named Mari, but perhaps one only? Few are more obscure in their purposes, more clever in their design, or have more resources to draw upon than Draco Invictus."

The Apprentice stopped dead as if struck. After a moment, he spoke softly, "The Flower, the Insect, the Serpent, the Beast…."

"That is a rhyme in the Old Speech. I know it not, but I know of it. How does it apply here?" the Eagle asked.

"I don't know, but I think I should discover it." Thaddeus sat down on the edge of the bed and told Osiric what he knew of the phrase and its context.

"Well, you'd think if the verse had any meaning or importance at all, it would have included a bird," was the Eagle's sole comment.

Following Break-fast, Thaddeus bid the Magistrate farewell. The older man had seemed preoccupied, and Thaddeus hoped he was already working on the problem of the Dragon's horde. Others awake at that early hour bade him Godspeed as well. With Osiric on his shoulder, he turned his face toward the warm morning sun and set his course for the great river. The sea breeze brought a fresh smell, one not of death but of rebirth and renewal.

Thaddeus and Osiric made their way overland to the mouth of the Greater Flatstone River, rented space on a barge going north, and settled in for the journey. The Apprentice was so relieved he had fulfilled his Quest and was still in one piece that he did not mind the extra transport fee for the Eagle nor the isolation of the empty patch toward the stern to which he and the great bird were directed.

By the evening of the third day, the Apprentice and his Eagle reached the small landing just below River's Wood and disembarked. Thaddeus wished to avoid the lumber-head port if he could. He remained hopeful his friends were still to be found at their Mid-Summer camp.

Coins from a modest purse Magistrate Pontius had provided out of gratitude, over and beyond the village contract, produced means for a goodly Mid-Day meal at a local inn. Leftovers were appreciated by Osiric, and soon the pair struck out cross-country.

In the late afternoon, Thaddeus set up camp in a small clearing and prepared a large rabbit Osiric had smelled from a distance and had successfully struck, with only minor difficulties. Crusts—the remains of Mid-day—provided the balance of the fare.

The small fire gave warmth, and Thaddeus sat musing with his back to a fallen trunk when it occurred to him that it was his birthday. Osiric offered congratulations, and the Apprentice sang himself the Birth Day's song, even repeating it on the flute after detecting the Eagle did not care greatly for this tune, either.

That night, the moon was bright, though still waning in a cloudless night sky, and all seemed at peace. At his request, Thaddeus guided Osiric to a low-hanging branch of a nearby tree, the Eagle having said he would feel more comfortable out on a limb rather than hopping about on the ground should trouble arise during the night. The young Sorcerer sat down again, soon losing himself in the fire's dancing flames.

"Thaddeus, Sorcerer!"

The youth started from his reverie. *"Yes, Osiric, what is it?"*

"Something approaches from the North. I think it may be—" Here the Eagle sniffed the air repeatedly. *"I think it may be a wolf! It is coming on rapidly."*

Thaddeus jumped up and ran to his pack, tearing out his arrows and bow and cursing himself for not having strung it earlier.

"Lord! It comes now!"

"Stercus!" Thaddeus muttered.

The creature was bounding through the bushes, apparently making no effort to be silent. The Apprentice, his newly-strung bow fitted with a steel-tipped arrow and two more clenched in his teeth, backed up against a sturdy birch tree. He quickly reviewed various spell-castings should the arrows fail.

Suddenly the animal appeared at the edge of the clearing.

Thaddeus could just make out its outline—definitely wolf-sized.

He took aim.

The beast moved forward a pace into the moonlight, which reflected off its golden coat. It then barked twice and bounded across the intervening space, leaping up and pressing the now-useless bow against Thaddeus' chest, all the while licking his face without mercy.

Thaddeus let out a cry of joy. "Bellis! You found me! How are you? Oh, good dog, good dog!"

"I'm thinking you do not need me to try to blindly pounce on this wolf-dog, thus saving you from having your nose tongued off," Osiric observed drily.

"No. No. Osiric, this is Bellis, our dog. I mean, she's a dog we found; well, rescued actually. Wait a moment, and I will sort it out for you."

"Bellis, it's so good to see you! How have you been, girl? I have sorely missed you. Now, down, down. Good dog." Thaddeus spent some time petting and ruffling the golden dog's scruff. Finally, he got down on one knee, eye-level with the golden hound, and spoke to her seriously.

"Bellis, there is someone with me I want you to meet," he began.

If Thaddeus did not know better, he would have sworn the dog drew back and slitted her eyes in suspicion.

"Bellis, he's an Eagle I met. His name is Osiric, and he is blind. He will not hurt you, but you must not harm him in return. I will call him down now."

Bellis now seemed to abandon any air of wariness and appeared merely curious.

"Osiric, come to us. I want you to meet Bellis, my good dog. I have asked her not to hurt you in any way."

"Harrumph! Rather, you should have asked me not to harm it, I should think! Oh, very well. But give me some space. And if I should stumble on landing and you laugh, there will be difficulties between us."

"I understand and I will not laugh, oh, prideful bird. Come down as you may."

"Bellis, Osiric is coming down from his tree, and I will introduce you. All right?"

For his answer, the golden dog stood quietly, her ears pricked in interest.

The next moment, Osiric flew down from his limb, landing flawlessly near the pair. Thaddeus introduced them formally, and they sniffed each other. Bellis looked into the great bird's sightless eyes, and Osiric appeared to return the look with equal concentration. To Thaddeus, it seemed as if they were communicating in some fashion.

As soon as it began, it was finished. Both creatures relaxed. Bellis sat back on her haunches, tongue lolling and tail sweeping an arc on the campsite ground, while Osiric gazed sightlessly at the Apprentice.

"Oh, ho and ho, Thaddeus, Sorcerer."

"And what is that supposed to signify, oh great Osiric?" the boy asked.

"You will see," the bird replied.

"What will I see?"

"You will see."

"What I see is the limited benefit of holding a conversation with a bird," Thaddeus said with some irritation.

"Oh, ho and ho!"

He was sure the Eagle was mocking him, but he clearly was not to be let in on the jest for now.

"Well, Sorcerer, I have met your dog, and she and I have agreed not to seek each other's life, so if you will now return me to a suitable perch, I will try to get some rest for what remains of the night."

"As you wish," Thaddeus said.

The boy got up and retrieved his glove and pauldron. He placed his arm on the ground in front of Osiric's feet, nudging them so the Eagle would know to mount his arm. Thaddeus lifted the bird carefully, and the Eagle made the hop to his shoulder, turning to face front.

"Bellis, I am placing Osiric back in his tree for the night. He feels more comfortable at a height."

The dog cocked her head as if curious as to why the boy was belaboring the obvious.

For some reason, Osiric instructed that he be placed on a tree somewhat farther from the camp than his first perch. Achieving that, he turned and faced away from the camp. *That way, I can guard better this part of the forest and your dog the other. Division of labor, you see.*

Thaddeus shrugged and did as requested, giving the Eagle his farewells for Good Repose.

Returning to camp, Thaddeus offered the dog several treats, which were gladly accepted. Then came petting, followed by a game of fetch and more petting. Finally, weary of play, Thaddeus dug into his pack for more of his Master's scrolls. Though Bellis initially sat quietly, she appeared to grow restless after a time and began nudging him with her nose, demanding more attention. At first, Thaddeus ignored her, but she became more insistent.

"Bellis, stop! I must read these before I return to the College. They're important." The dog snorted and returned to her nudging, becoming even more forceful.

"Bellis! Stop! Bad dog!"

The golden dog looked, by turns, shocked, sorrowful, and irritated.

Thaddeus, exasperated, rose to find a nearby tree against which to relieve himself. When he returned, he found Bellis shredding the last of his scrolls and snarling ferociously.

Thaddeus was dumbstruck and dismayed. He could never replace his Master's scrolls! They must contain much power, as his efforts to repair them came to naught as well.

"Bellis! What have you done? Bad dog! Bad dog!"

The dog sank to its belly and slunk off into the nearby brush when the youth ignored her.

Thaddeus gathered what he could of the tatters of parchment and stuffed them into the pouch, which he put in his backpack. He sat, disconsolate, with his back to the dog for a long while.

Finally, the young Sorcerer put out his bedroll near the recently re-stoked fire and lay down to sleep. His irritation eventually subsided, though he was worried about what the Master would say about his lack of attention and inability to protect his Master's property.

After a time, Bellis came to snuggle beside him in her accustomed place as the boy drifted off into gentle slumber.

Someone was stroking his face and caressing it. The sensation was so pleasant that it took a moment for his mind's critical eye to question who might be doing it. Finally registering that the situation required wakefulness, the young Sorcerer's eyes snapped open to behold himself holding a beautiful woman with long tawny-colored braids. She smiled down at him.

"Yow!" Thaddeus yelled and rolled backward, his heart leaping in his chest.

The woman made no move to attack him but remained in place, smiling still.

Thaddeus eyed the lady warily while deciding his life was in no imminent danger. "Who are you?" he asked, bewildered.

"I am Luperca, of course. Who were you expecting?"

"What do you here?" he demanded, while at the back of his mind, a faint recognition began to form.

"I am here for us to love," the woman replied earnestly.

"Wh-why do you say that?" the boy asked anxiously.

"Because you are my mate." There was a touch of asperity in her tone, suggesting she had become tired of answering silly and irrelevant questions.

"I? I am not your mate. I don't even know who you are. I think you had best leave."

The woman sighed and rose. "All right, if I must do this exercise. I am Luperca. I am a demi-wolf. The Elder Tree Ring predicted long, long ago that you and I would meet, and I have been waiting for you."

Thaddeus wondered wildly what the Fates were on about, filling his life with one strange woman after another. He also wondered how much longer it was likely to continue.

"Well, Mistress, you may think that, and you appear well enough, but I do not know you, and it is not polite to approach strangers in their sleep and begin fondling them."

"Oh, that. I see I must explain everything, then. Very well."

Suddenly, the little girl from Mid-Summer's Night's eve was standing in the woman's place, waving.

"I am Luperca," she said.

Then the Great Golden Pack Leader was there.

"*I am Luperca*," it said in the Language of Those Who Hunt.

Then Bellis stood, tongue lolling and tail wagging.

"*I am Luperca.*"

Thaddeus staggered back, sitting down hard on the soft earth.

The woman reappeared. "You see, I knew you were coming. I looked to see you at River's Wood, but I was waylaid by that madman Corrigan. But then you were there and turned him into the cur that he was. I knew immediately you would be my mate, as had been foretold. The rest has merely been awaiting the right opportunity. And so here we are."

She approached and knelt beside him. She took his hand and kissed it.

He made an attempt to draw it away.

"No, my mate. I have waited too long as it is. You will come to me now."

"But…." He began to protest.

She covered his mouth with her other hand. "Shush, my mate. It will not be terrible."

Although he was at a distance, Osiric's hearing had almost reached the acuity his vision had previously held. Such foolishness, he thought—these humans. For birds, all it took was a little display, a little pecking, and then hop on. How simple and sensible.

On further thought, however, he allowed as how it might not be that much different after all.

Loving I
Amo, Amas, Amat

fter, Thaddeus lay on his back on the bed of grass near his bedroll, stroking Luperca's hair as she rested her head on his chest.

How was he going to explain all this to Marsia, or should he even try?

To simply say, 'Well, I have been with four ladies before you, my dear, but only on account of the Prophecy, you see,' was not the best way to begin. And this one … she gave no indication of wanting to leave him. Not to mention how he was ever going to explain to his Brothers why he had commingled with their beloved pet.

How far would anyone's understanding extend in such circumstances, even for those invested in and accustomed to odd occurrences?

Yes, his life was becoming more than complex.

Suddenly Luperca kissed him, rose to her full height, and grasping his hands, pulled him to his feet.

"That was lovely, my mate, but I must go now and return to my pack. I do not know when we will be together again or not, but in any case, the Elder Tree Ring warns you to 'beware the Great Bear.' Farewell, my mate."

After the briefest of transformations, the Great Golden Wolf Pack Leader stood, proud and serene. She nodded once to Thaddeus, turned, and loped off into the forest.

Thaddeus had difficulty falling back to sleep for any number of reasons. Chief among them, anxiety concerning the potential for future nocturnal ambushes and assaults by Prophecy-driven wild women, all of whom seemed to be in heat.

The morning sun brightened his eyelids, and he eventually awakened. He sat up and scratched, trying not to think about the previous night, but found himself unable to resist mulling over what happened.

The Flower, the Insect, the Serpent, the Beast, he repeated to himself. Perhaps now that he had reached the end of the list, peace would return, and he could proceed with the courting of his own true love, Marsia of Dorset Downs.

And perhaps obtain some rest.

Following ablutions, he called Osiric to his shoulder, where the Eagle landed without difficulty. He greeted the bird Good Morrow, and the bird returned the greeting.

"Oh-ho! Lord Thaddeus!"

Thaddeus suspected the bird might be laughing at him. *"Have you any thought for our Break-fast this day, great Osiric?"*

"Oh-ho! Lord Thaddeus. I have procured several squirrels from the surrounding trees and grounds. Oh-ho!"

Now Thaddeus was certain the bird was laughing at him.

"All right—quite amusing. Now, perhaps we may get on with planning our day."

"Oh-ho! Lord Thaddeus, whatever you say."

"Quite enough! Prepare your own squirrel then, Master Osiric, as you don't require me."

The Eagle responded by hopping over to the first squirrel and eating it raw—as it was, of course, his usual habit.

Somehow, Thaddeus felt he had lost something in the exchange.

Several days of travel brought Thaddeus and the Eagle to within a single night's stay away from the Mid-Summer camp. Rather than push on the remaining leagues in the dark, Thaddeus opted to bed down on the spot so that he'd find his friends fresh and early in the following day.

He set about preparing his Even-tide. They'd chanced by a clear brook earlier, and he and the Eagle had done well for themselves.

Osiric was away from the camp, practicing night flying. He said that, logically, it should make no difference what time of day he flew, though the sounds and smells were different—and the thermals as well. He claimed the most challenging part was getting over the idea that he could now fly at night as safely as at any other time. At first, he tended to undercut the forest canopy by a pace or two, leading to periods of crashing, screeching, and the occasional shower of leaves raining down from above. But now, he seemed to have gained more facility and thus greater confidence.

Thaddeus had just gotten their fire going and was turning to find his cooking pan when a faint green light coming down the forest path toward the campsite caught his attention. It grew steadily brighter, but there was no sound.

What now?

Thaddeus reached again for his bow and arrows.

The light increased until he could make out a form. The being was human, relatively tall, and carrying a green light. It was….

"Marsia!"

"Thaddeus!"

The two rushed to each other and embraced. Thaddeus picked her up and swung her around joyously. She laughed, as did he, and they embraced again. Thaddeus was immediately aware of even stronger feelings for the young Sorceress, but he was uncertain how to proceed. Marsia, however, solved the problem by pulling his head down to hers for a long, lingering kiss.

After a time, they parted but remained holding hands and smiling at each other. Thaddeus drank in the vision of her—tall, fair of face, a few freckles akin to his own—perfect in all details, according to his view. This night, her hair was rolled in a bun at the nape of her neck. She wore a dark brown traveling dress with a leather belt holding several needful items, including a pair of trail knives. She was beautiful.

"Oh, Marsia, it's so good to see you, but how did you find me?"

"Ah, the other half of my family secret, sir. The green stone I gave you was once one larger stone but then was split in two. It has a striving always to find its mate. When the stone is near its other half, it glows. Take yours out; if you still have it, of course."

Thaddeus looked at her sharply.

If he still had it … how could she doubt ….

He was relieved to see the tall girl grinning. Chagrined, he reached into his tunic for his pouch, pulled the thong over his head, and poured the contents onto his open palm. Sure enough, as she had said, his stone was glowing bright green, matching the one she held before her on a delicate golden chain.

"Very well, that explains how you found me, but what decided you to come in the first place, especially at night, when it could be dangerous?"

"Well, Apprentice Thaddeus of Beewicke," she said, replacing the gold-chained green stone in her bodice, "if you don't know why I came, then you are not as bright a flame as I—and your friends—seem to think. Perhaps I should consider turning around and making my way back to Mid-Summer camp. What do you think, hmm?"

Thaddeus turned beet red and was glad it was dark. "No, you don't have to go back."

Marsia laughed, squeezed his hand, and kissed his cheek.

"But coming at night is dangerous," Thaddeus protested again.

In a split second, Marsia snapped into a battle crouch, a dagger suddenly held in each hand. "Not for me, it isn't." Quickly as they appeared, the weapons disappeared.

"But seriously, Marsia, why did you come, leaving your friends?"

"Because I wanted to be with you, Thaddeus. I had thought you might feel the same way, or at least I hoped it."

"Yes. Oh, yes. I am glad, very, very glad." He bent and kissed her again.

"Hmm," she said, her eyes remaining closed for a moment. "You have had some practice at this, I think."

Thaddeus was back to beet red again. He took a deep breath, sighed, and straightened. "Marsia, let's sit down over here. There's something I need to tell you."

The fire burned bright and crackled merrily in front of the couple sitting on the log holding hands.

"…. and so Bellis turned out to be a demi-wolf named Luperca … but was also the little girl, as well as the Great Pack Leader. It is all confusing, and I don't see the purpose in any of it."

"Oh, yes, you do, Thaddeus. But you are so caught up in the feeling of the moment that your *Cogitatio* is clouded. This is how I see it. You are the Great Compass Point; yes, I know of this. And, as was foretold, the secondary points were to come from you. Did you not just say that each of these women sought you out? You did not approach them. Well, then, there was little choice in all that, yes? So, you and your Brothers are the four primary points, and from you are to descend the four secondary points. So, now you have completed your tasks, you see? And so, you need not worry about any other such persons ever again."

"I had been wondering and wondering how to tell you, but it just came out."

"You did it right, Thaddeus. Unless, of course, you'd want to marry any of those women."

"No. I would … I would only want to marry you, Marsia."

"And I, you, Thaddeus. The stones do not lie."

"Um, I was thinking…. When I have done with my training, and you yours, I thought—if you like—we could marry, then move to a quiet village, perhaps one on the coast near Frantillia. We could begin a Sorcerous practice together and help the people there. And, um, have a family … I mean, if you would like it."

The young girl reached up and gently stroked the side of his face. "Yes, Thaddeus, I would like it very much." The couple looked deeply into each other's eyes.

Abruptly, the tall girl stood, took a turn around the campfire, and sat down again, grasping both of Thaddeus' hands in her own.

"Thaddeus, there is something of further importance that we must talk about as well. At least it is important to me."

"Then it is important to both of us," the Apprentice said earnestly.

Marsia nodded a smile, then adopted a serious air. She swallowed. "Thaddeus, I believe you know that no Sorcerer—or Sorceress—can practice Sorcery without having been with someone as an intimate."

"Yes, I know it," the youth replied, trying furiously to act mature while also trying mightily not to blush.

"You have been with … others … and have already begun to express your gift. I … have not. Thaddeus … oh, my, this is hard. Thaddeus, I wish us to have love together." She got it all out in a rush and was silent a moment before continuing. "I want you to know that I desire this most of all because I want it so much for us and not just because I want to be a Sorceress. It is important to me that you believe this. I tell you now as truly as I can, and I will swear it with any oath you wish, I would rather never have a single day as a Sorceress if I could be one only by loving another."

The girl squeezed Thaddeus' hands hard. The look in her eyes was earnest, and he knew her truth. "I believe you, Marsia. I will always believe you."

The tall girl smiled deeply, took a deep breath, and let it out slowly.

Thaddeus was in the Fields of Elysium, so high and bright did his feelings burn. It was time now to take this girl he loved so much, the woman who would become his wife, and prove his love to her. He had no doubt or hesitation. Nothing had ever seemed so right to him before. Now he would—

An Eagle's cry pierced the night.

The young lovers whipped their heads around, facing the direction of the call.

"Marsia, wait here. I will return in a moment."

"I will go with you," the honey-blonde girl said. "We will not be parted, especially if there may be a threat."

"No, it is better if I go alone. It is Osiric, and he is not his best with strangers."

Thaddeus rose swiftly, quickly snatched up his glove and pauldron from his pack, and made his way to a tall yew at the edge of the small clearing.

The Eagle sat preening himself on one of the lower tree limbs, the remains of a large rodent further up the branch.

"*You are with someone. It is another girl. I hear her movements, and I smell her. I smell her on you as well. Tell me, is this something to be expected now each night we travel?*"

"*Hear me, Osiric. I am with Marsia; Marsia of Dorset Downs. I love her, and she will be wife to me one day. I have told her of what has come before, and there will be no others. I would introduce you to her.*"

"*I hear something in your voice I have not heard before. Very well. I am interested in meeting the woman who may become my Mistress.*"

"*As you wish it. Here, I will turn around and back toward you. When you are ready, come to my shoulder.*"

The Eagle assumed the Apprentice's shoulder, and Thaddeus strode back to the campfire where Marsia stood waiting.

"Marsia of Dorset Downs, I present Osiric, Lord of Eagles and King of his Peoples. Osiric, meet Marsia, Sorceress at the *Ludia* and she whom I love." Thaddeus quickly repeated the introduction to the Eagle.

"Hmm. From her movements and the distance from the ground where her breathing is the loudest, I deduce she is of a height for you, and her smell tells me she has good bones. Thus far, she is promising."

"You speak with each other. Anders told me of your talent."

"I don't know much of it. It just seems to happen on occasions. But it's come to good purpose at those times. I believe I could teach it to you sometime if you wish."

Thaddeus glanced at the Eagle, then turned back to his love.

"Marsia, Osiric is blind. He was burned in a fire while trying to save his mate and their offspring. He could not save them and has been locked in despair from that time. But we met, and since then, he has agreed to accompany me as we travel. He was with me in Frantillia. He has developed a keenness of hearing and smelling that compensate, in good part, for the loss of his eyes. He is an honorable companion and has learned to hunt very well using his new gifts, keeping us well-supplied with fish and rabbits." Thaddeus smiled fondly. "He is a touch prideful, though, for one made up of feathers."

"Ah, Thaddeus, he was a Lord to his peoples; he should be proud. Proud of that and proud of what new things he has been able to master. Please tell Osiric, Lord of the Eagles, that I am most favored to meet him and that I grieve for his loss. Tell him also, I would count it an honor to me if I could travel with you two as well." With that, the tall girl bowed to the Eagle, though he saw it not.

Thaddeus turned to the Eagle, who seemed expectant, and repeated Marsia's words verbatim.

The Eagle was silent for a time, then spoke. *"Thaddeus, tell your mate—for I perceive the truth of it now—that I receive her greetings well, and I am moved by her concern. Also, tell her I am now—and forever more—in her service. Those she loves shall I also love. But those who are her enemies shall not long survive in my presence. This vow I, by Aquilla Magna, God of my kind.*" Having finished speaking, the great bird dipped his head to the tall girl.

Thaddeus told Marsia what Osiric had said, and she smiled. The two exchanged a few more pleasantries, but Thaddeus wondered how long he would have to stand there going back and forth between them, especially as other thoughts and feelings were beginning to compete for his attention.

"Thaddeus, Sorcerer, I believe now it is best for me to take my leave. My sense of smell has become quite keen, after all. I think I shall practice furthering my night-flying skills, bat-Eagle that I am. I shall rest at watch nearby, but not too near. Call if I am needed. Fare-thee-well this night, young Sorcerer. You have chosen well—better than you know, perhaps."

Osiric spread his great wings and leaped from the Apprentice's shoulder, beating his way up into the vault of the starry night sky.

Marsia reached out and clasped Thaddeus' hand in hers. She had the look of openness and encouragement she'd had that day so long ago when they'd first met.

Thaddeus squeezed her hand and took a deep breath. "Um, in my village, when two are in love and want all to know they will have none but each other … they stand in the village square and speak the Pledge of Love. Then, at a later time, once they know they will always be together, the marriage takes place. If you like, we could say the Pledge of Love tonight … now, I mean, unless you would not wa—"

"I will say your Pledge with you, my Thaddeus," Marsia gently interrupted him. "Teach it to me."

Thaddeus cleared his throat. "All right. Here, stand by me. Now we hold each other's hands crossed, like this. Now we look into each other's eyes. I say 'Marsia,' and you say 'Thaddeus.' Are you ready?"

"I am ready."

The night grew still and not a sound was heard besides the low murmuring of the loving couple in the midst of a ceremony that was old when humans were young. All creatures held their breaths, for all that might come to be rested on this moment.

After a time that lasted forever but was really no time at all, the tall boy fell silent, and then bent to kiss the girl he loved. Following ten heartbeats, he straightened again and, with stately grace, led her around the circle of the campfire three times. He turned and faced her.

"Now, we have pledged our love to each other. And now, none can ever come between us."

Marsia nodded. Tears glistened in her eyes, but she was smiling. She took a deep breath, then let go of his hand and backed a pace away.

Slowly, she reached up to the nape at the back of her neck and removed the three sticks there. Shaking her head slightly, her hair fell down in a shimmering cascade that glinted in the firelight.

And the Night was filled with their Love—the best, purest, and deepest —shared only with each other. They gave their hearts to one another so there would never again be emptiness, never again be pain, never again be loneliness.

17

Loving II
Amamus, Amatis, Amant II

alk, laugh, eat, drink, tease, play—these placed the group of young people in a high Holiday mood, Sorcerers or not.

Much of the teasing was centered around the old mule. Asullus, however, voiced the opinion that he gave as well as he got, and, as things went, none were able to dispute him.

Toward the afternoon of the second day of the Mid-Summer's Eve's encampment, the girls rode in: Nannsi, Marsia, and Molly o' the Willows. They were hailed warmly and with particularly warm greetings from those to whom they were special, excepting, of course, Marsia.

Her Thaddeus was far away on a Quest, though she hoped he would yet be able to join them before it was time to return to the *Ludia*. Still, she tried to make the best of it, though she felt little satisfaction playing fifth-wheel-on-a-cart.

"But where's Sonnia?" Anders asked, quickly counting the arrivals.

"She and Servilla left us the day before yesterday," Nannsi replied, looking irritated. "She was reluctant to come in the first place, I think, and she was taking out her spleen on all of us, especially our Molly. There were

moments when she was just horrid. Well, after one particularly sour spell, I felt what she said was uncalled for, and I told her how I felt. She did not like that one bit, and the next thing I knew, she and her girl were on their horses heading South. We tried to stop her, but she would not listen. Headstrong she is, at times. So off they rode, and where they are going is nowhere near to getting back to the *Ludia* or even her home, come to that. That girl can be so vexing!"

"Excuse me," Rolland broke in, "but did you say she was heading South?"

"Yes. That is the direction they went when they left. Why do you ask?"

"Well, 'tis fairly rugged country down that way—all dark forest and wild growth. And she picked South for no reason?"

"No. At least no reason as makes good sense. But that's Sonnia. She gets an idea in her head, and off she goes, especially when she's in high dudgeon. Act first; think later." The short girl made a *tsk*-ing sound and shook her head.

"Hmm. That seems a bad idea to me. If she left you the day before yesterday, she still could not have gotten very far—very rugged going. Perhaps I should follow along to make sure she has avoided trouble. Maybe I could convince her to come back and join us."

Nannsi, Marsia, and Molly all exchanged glances.

"But why would you think to do that?" Nannsi asked in a neutral tone.

"Well, I grant you that Thaddeus is the tracker in our class, but he's not here. I know he'd be the first to be concerned for anyone gone missing."

"You would chase after a girl in flight, a girl you have said you don't care for, because you believe Thaddeus might think someone should?" Nannsi persisted.

"Well, someone has to," Rolland said with heat, color springing to his cheeks. "I am the extra tag-along here, and that makes me expendable, I guess."

"Hiking after two people on horses will mean making up a considerable distance and time," Anders said with a calculating expression.

"You can use my horse, Riator, if you'd like," Molly offered.

"You have your own horse, Molly?" Rolland asked, surprised.

The dark-haired girl looked down, a slight flush coming to her features. "It was, um, a gift."

"Apparently, everyone at the *Ludia* is expected to have the means to get about," Zoarr said, joining the conversation. "I heard Molly is cautious with her coin, and the horse was just sitting there in my Father's stables in any case, so I made arrangements for the, um, loan and had him shipped up. 'Tis a common practice in my country; we do it all the time," he added offhandedly.

Nannsi and Marsia hid smiles behind their hands. "Of course."

"Sounds reasonable," Nannsi said.

Rolland flashed a smile of gratitude. "Why, thank you, Molly. Come to think, having a horse would speed the trip up a bit. All right, I accept. Well, no use wasting time. I might as well get my pack together and go on my way. Those girls are probably already knee-deep in it and will need a man to pull them out."

Nannsi bit down on her knuckle-hard. "Yes. That sounds like a good plan. 'Tis certainly getting no earlier," she said as if something were caught in her throat.

"Well, of course. Molly, mayhap you should introduce me to this horse of yours."

"Aye, Rolland, he's just over here."

With Rolland gone, Marsia really did feel like a fifth wheel. But she tried to maintain a cheerful attitude and resolutely assumed many of the day-to-day camp chores to help pass the time.

After Even-tide, Nannsi and Anders strolled off a distance into the woods by themselves, and Zoarr and Molly also went away from the camp but in the opposite direction.

Marsia was thus left to sit and tend the fire, staring at the flaming logs and trying to lose herself in the fluid colors of heat. Every so often, she would reach into her bodice and withdraw her green stone on its fine filigree chain. But it hadn't changed in aspect or attribute from her previous inspection.

She then put it back down her dress, sighed, and returned to her fire-tending fantasies.

"Did you bring the sword, then?" Nannsi asked a touch nervously.

"Yes," Anders said. "It's in the back of the cart, though Rolland wanted to know why I brought it along."

"What did you tell him?"

"I said I wanted to practice my Arms-training, that being my lowest mark at the *Collegium*. But I'm not certain he believed me. He just laughed and turned away."

"Don't you worry about Arms-training," the short girl said fiercely. "I will protect you. No one will bring harm to you while I live!"

"My sweet Nannsi. Was there ever a boy luckier? I think not."

The short girl blushed furiously but seemed pleased, well pleased.

"I have brought the betrothal shifts. I made them myself of the finest material I could find. And I have the laurel wreaths; they are fresh-picked. Do you have the rings, dearest?"

"Yes, my love. Old Balsaamer, our Master Artificer, helped me spell-fashion them. They will never tarnish and are incapable of being destroyed."

"Oh, my clever Anders! I know if you made them, they would be perfect. Now, I have written out our vows." The dark-headed girl produced a scroll with a bright red ribbon tied around it. "Make sure you have the words to heart. I think that is everything. In one week, the moon will be full. That will be our night, then. Hmm … we will need a place of privacy.…"

"I had thought, my love, that gentle sloping hill to the south … where we first kissed."

"Oh, yes, my beautiful lover, that will be the best place. We will spend the week in preparation then. Oh, it will be so hard to wait."

"Yes, dearest," Anders said, placing a protective arm around her. "But think of it. We will be married. How grand!"

"Yes, that will be the good part. Then we will have to live apart for all those years until we are finished with our schooling. Of course, we will be able to meet from time to time like this. So that is something. Then you can teach and share your knowledge with the young ones and I shall help you and tend to our children."

"Speaking of that, my life, how many do you think we should have?"

The short girl blushed again. "I have spoken with Mistress Geanninia concerning this, and she say, given our likely Sorcerous life-span, we may have all that we wish. I think the record reported in the Annals is forty-two."

"Forty-two? My goodness. We'll need a big house—a *very* big house."

"Yes. I thought we could build it next to the school."

"What a wonderful idea, my darling. You are so thoughtful."

"It is easy to be thoughtful when I know I will have you as my husband." The short girl looked away, then back to her love. "Have you … have you told the others?"

"No, my love. You and I agreed that it is best that only we two know. But our parents will want big ceremonies later on, I would imagine: one for Mater and Pater, and one for your family. I think we should oblige everyone, but we two will know that we have always been married, really."

The girl's eyelids fluttered, and it seemed she might swoon. The short scholar leaned forward to kiss her cherry lips, but Nannsi suddenly came to herself, taking a deep breath.

"Oh, no, my love. We must remain pure. This is our last week unjoined, and we must spend it in contemplation and denial as the Scrolls dictate. Oh, this is so hard!"

"It's all right, my sweetest. We will wait the week, then all the greater will be the fulfillment of our joy."

"Yes, my smoothest cucumber. Well, we should probably be getting back to the camp. We don't want to rouse the others' suspicions. 'Tis not their business, really, and all they will do is tell tales. Oh, my love, how wonderful! Think of it! In one week, we will be wed!"

"Yes, dearest Nannsi. And then, after, you will be a complete Sorceress."

"Oh. Well, you know, that's true. How interesting."

Several thoughts bubbled up in the young scholar's consciousness, but he suppressed them, considering them uncharitable.

"Come, sweetest," Anders said, holding out his hand. A gentle breeze sprang up as the couple made their way back to camp.

"Now remember, my Anders, no one is to know our plans. No one. It is our secret."

"Yes, dear Nannsi. None shall know. I do not see how this group could puzzle it out in any case. Only the mule."

"Very well, my dear pumpkin."

"Hmm," said the tall brunette, "if I were to guess, I would say sometime next week. The moon will be full then."

"Yes, I believe you may be right," replied the even taller honey-blonde.

"Where, do you suppose?"

"Probably where they were first together … to the South, over that hillock. That is, if they can wait that long."

"We could put a wager on it if you like."

"Interesting idea. I might consider that."

"My beautiful Molly," the swarthy youth said. "Will you walk with me?"

"I may be beautiful, Prince, if you say it so, but I am not *your* anything. And, yes, I will walk with you."

Somewhat chastened, Zoarr continued. "Have you given thought to my proposal, then? That is, that we marry?"

"What proposal? I heard you make a number of statements and declarations, but I heard no 'proposal' in them, nor even a question to ask leave. You are far too presumptuous, Prince. That will not work well in our relationship."

Zoarr smiled. "Ah, we have, at least, a 'relationship.' It is a step."

The two made their way East, then turned off the traveler's path, moving into the forest.

"Will you hold my hand, Molly?" the Prince said, offering his.

"Aye. I will do that," the dark-haired girl said, grasping his easily.

"So, then, what will work well in, um, our relationship?"

"I do not know. The problem, you see, is that you are spoiled. You have had a lifetime, no doubt, of people jumping up and down at the nod of your head or the snap of your fingers—"

"These would become your people, too, Molly, to snap at," Zoarr interjected quickly.

"Aye, mayhap, whether anyone should have that kind of power or no, but it's not the point now, is it? What is it, do you think, that a woman wants above all things with her man, after his love?"

"Sovereignty," the Prince replied in a heartbeat.

"Why, that's right. Hmm. How did you know that?"

"Oh. I read it in a scroll of romances once, some story about a verdant warrior facing a time dilemma. I memorized it, thinking it might prove to be a handy thing to know one day."

"I see. Well, that helps not at all, then. Let me think. Aye, how about this? Imagine our situations were reversed. Suppose I was the rich and powerful princess, and you were the gutter boy...."

The Prince started to protest, thinking to say she already was a Princess, at least in his eyes, the only eyes that mattered, really. And that, to be with her, he would be in any gutter she chose, along with other things he thought he should say when she cut him off.

"Wait! Aye, let me finish it and then you can speak. So, suppose we were reversed, and I had the high attitude. How easy would it be for you to fit into it, would you say?"

"Molly, if the difference between our stations in life bothers you, you need not be concerned. We shall live wherever you wish it. Sand, sea, air—it matters not to me. If you have no wish to live in a stuffy palace— fine. We can live in a woodcutter's hut. As long as I am with you, the rest is not significant."

"Aye, and how then would you contrive to govern your Father's kingdom from a woodcutter's hut?"

"Well, I—"

"Again, Prince, you have missed the point. What I wish to say is that you need to take my feelings into account." The girl raised her hand to ward off a barrage of protests. "You must know what I mean. A girl likes to be asked, not told as if she were but another servant. If it's a life partner you are after, then we may do business. *May*, I say. But if you are looking only for a no-will bed warmer while your personal maid-ser-vant-trollop fixes you your Break-fast, then we are as far apart as any two lovers can be. That is what I mean."

"Molly, you may find it difficult to believe, but I have loved you since I met you. When I first saw you, something inside me—I have no idea what—said you were for me, and I was for you. I do not mind asking. In fact, I will do it right now. Molly, will you marry me?"

"Mayhap, we shall see. But there is one thing further you should know before counting your unhatched chicks."

"What is it, Molly?"

"I have had little enough in my life. Aye, most of the time, only my wits and the clothes on my back, and sometimes not always those. But one thing I do have and that I have always kept above all else, even in the direst of circumstances, is my honor. I have never lost my honor, though I chose to give it once. But, aye, I have it back now, and I am bound to keep it until I choose to share it with another. So, Prince, if you believe we will be getting all cordial-like with no one watching and with babies to chance, then you have chosen poorly. One person in one piece is what I will be on my wedding day. And if it should never come, then indeed, it will never come, and so much for it. Knowing that, Prince, are you finding yourself so ardent as before?"

"Yes, Molly. Now and tomorrow as well. If our first night together is to be our wedding night, then so be it. I would rather have no future at all than a future without you."

"Do you swear?"

"So I swear."

Suddenly a knife appeared in the tall girl's hand. With a quick motion, she cut her palm and held it out. Without hesitation, the Prince mirrored her action and clasped her bleeding hand with his own.

"Done!"

"Done, then!"

So saying, the Prince withdrew a snowy white linen square from his leather tunic but looked into the crèche girl's eyes before proceeding. "May I?"

"Aye, you may," Molly said.

Zoarr quickly bound the girl's palm, then produced another and, smiling, did the same for himself.

18

Goblins I
Coboli I

The days dragged by for Marsia. Finally, it was the morning of the full moon and followed by the night.

"Are you nervous?" Marsia asked.

"Well, yes, a little."

"Why get married, then? Why not just be together?"

"It is something I want, but also something I promised my Great-mother as she lay dying."

"Do you know what you will do?"

"I have done some reading and talked with some of the Upperclass —and Mistress Liaisonia, of course. But Anders will know. He's been with … others. I know he is a gentle boy. But yes, I am nervous, a little. Fortunately, Asullus will be there to help."

"…. an' by the Gods o' Matrimony, so you swear it."

"…. and by the Gods of Matrimony, so we swear it."

"Aye, an' so, wi' all authority vested in me by Equus, near to being greatest o' the Gods,

do I hereby pronounce ye joined as to man an' to wife. Now, let none seek to sunder ye lest they run afoul o' muledom entire. So sayin', ye may kiss yer bride. Well, now, congratulations to ye both. An' ha' ye yer sword then, young Anders?"

"Yes, Asullus."

"Good lad. So now, I'll be makin' me way back to camp. May ye both ha' a long an' healthy life together wi' all manner o' wee ones an' other blessin's as well. Fare-thee-well, the two o' ye."

Anders strode forward and stroked the old mule's neck. "Thank you, Asullus, for performing the ceremony this day."

"Aye, an' who else would ye ha' chosen as knows what's to do, eh? Been around this same block meself a time or two, don' ye know. But ye're welcome fer me services, an' lookin' forward to the bushel o' apples am I now, entire."

Nannsi, standing by Anders, leaned over and kissed the mule on his forehead.

"Dear Asullus, always our friend, and you will be forever welcome in our home."

"Well, Missus, an' thank ye fer that. Now 'tis time ye two were forgettin' about yer ol' flea-bag here an' gettin' yerselves down to business. *Ave!*"

After the mule left, Anders gave his bride a gentle squeeze. "Dearest Nannsi, I am now your husband, and you are my wife. I have made our bower over here. I hope you will like it."

The young scholar took his bride by the hand and led her to a low place between two trees, heaped with new-cut sweet grass.

"Oh, my Anders, it is perfect."

"Let me get my sword." Anders picked up the heavy weapon and laid it down at the foot of the bower. "Now take my hand, my Nannsi. We must jump over it at the same time. Are you ready?"

"I am ready, my love."

"All right. I will count, and then we will jump. Here we go. One …
two … three …."

The Prince and Molly strolled down by the small lake not far from the
campsite, holding hands as they walked.

"Molly, tell me a thing if you will," the dark youth asked.

"Aye, and what would you like to know?"

"How came you by your name—Molly o' the Willows?"

"Aye. 'Tis a simple enough tale if you wish to hear it."

"I do."

"Very well. As I told you before, I grew up in the Thieves' Guild
crèche in Fountaindale. The building is on the south side of the city in a
used-up district. The authorities rarely patrol there, both by inclination
and by bribery. Near the building housing the Guild headquarters there
is a lake, of all things, right in the middle of town. There's a small river
that carries the water off but 'tis a lazy river, and the current is slow.

"Faran, he was the leader of the younger thieves then, though
Rolland says he heads the entire Guild now, told me once that the
lake was not always there. But there was an explosion or such-like a
long time ago that made the hole—a deep one, so the tale goes—which
filled up with water over the years from an underground well-up."

The girl paused to pluck a stem of grass and suck on the tip.

"Well, over time, willows came to grow along the banks of the river;
willows right there in the center of the city. I was always attracted to
that idle stream and those gentle trees. Every hour I was not needed to
tend the babes in the crèche I was there, walking among the willows.
Faran seemed worried about me at first. That's when he set Groton to
watch over me. After I came along in my training a bit, Faran relaxed
his concern. He felt I could handle myself.

"Anyway, it was Groton as named me Molly o' the Willows. And, for some reason, it stuck. We used to train beneath the willows every day, except in the dead of winter. Afterward, I would sit high up among the branches and think about things."

Molly glanced into the distance, sighed, and looked again at Zoarr. "I miss that lazy stream and those old trees."

"Molly, if you will marry me, I will have a river made to flow right below the window where we sleep, and I will cause it to be lined with willows from that place in your city, as far as your eyes can see. This I vow."

"Just like that, oh Prince?"

"Just like that."

In the dark woods far to the south of the camp, a much darker conversation was taking place.

"Morag's messenger said the children would be coming around this area, so all we have to do is wait," the short Goblin said.

"What's this I hear about them being Sorcerous, though?" asked Cock-Roach.

"It's *children*, as I said—good eating! The girls, he says, ain't popped yet, so they cannot hex anything, and the boys are just Firsties—hardly know how to pee standing up, let alone cause trouble," Dog-Face replied.

A third green creature ran to the two standing near the camp stew bucket.

"Dog-Face! Turd-Open says his lads have spotted two of those we seek coming South. One, he says, is one of the girls, and one is an old lady, probably her servant. Both have horses, just going along leisure-like."

"Just those two? No one else?" the leader asked, incredulous.

"It's what he says—no one else around for leagues."

"Have they seen him?"

"He says not. The two are just coming along."

"Excellent! All right, take twenty of your crew and lie in wait; divide them up, with half ahead and half left behind. As soon as they pass by the first group, jump out and drive them into the arms of the other group. Then, seize them and bring them back to camp. Tell him he and the others can have the horses on the spot, but no one is to touch the females—not once. Bring them back here, both in one piece."

"What then?" asked Cock-Roach.

"Then, the girlie will tell us where her friends are," the Goblin replied.

"And after?"

"Well, after, maybe we can have some fun," Dog-Face said with a grin, his yellowed fangs dripping.

The other two laughed.

"What of the servant?" Split-Eye wondered aloud.

"Why do you think we brought the stew pot?"

The three laughed again while spittle flew from their mouths at the mention of food.

"Once we know where the rest of them are, we can attack at night while they sleep. More fun and more food. Tell the others. But we have been told to save two of the boys and take them to Morag's messenger and turn them over to him. They must be alive, but they do not have to be pretty. As for the rest … all ours!"

It was easy enough for Rolland to follow Sonnia's and Servilla's trail. He'd headed west to where Nannsi said their party had split, and her directions had been without flaw.

Rolland wanted to catch their trace before nightfall—maybe camp, then meet up with them the next day and turn them back to the Mid-Summer's site. If he could talk Sonnia into it, Servilla, he assumed, would go where her Mistress bade. Besides, by then, the Sorceress might already be tired of her little wilderness adventure and would welcome a return to civilization. And if not, so be it. She could find her own damn way home and to the Hells with her snooty stuck-up ways.

Rolland kept his eyes on the track as he followed it South. His own Thieve's arts, plus what Thaddeus had taught him and his training from Sir Eques and Master Chiron, combined to make it no great difficulty. Of course, these two were not trying to hide their passage. They probably had no idea they were being followed.

The redheaded thief camped that night and set out early the next morning. After Mid-day, he was drowsing in his saddle when he entered a particularly dark part of the forest. A bird call—at least he thought it was a bird—brought him out of his reverie. He shook his head to clear it and checked the ground again to regain his bearings.

He found prints from the first horse—Sonnia's, he thought—and then the second, which must be Servilla's. But wait … overriding these were footprints. Only they looked unlike any prints he knew. They were smaller than a man's, five-toed, and clawed….

What could … ah, now he saw it. These looked most like the prints Lilyput made. He examined both sides of the trail. Many such feet. If he had it right, the creatures that made these tracks followed the two horses.

Goblin prints … for they were Goblins without a doubt.

He got down off his horse and looked in the undergrowth on either side of the trail. Ah, these creatures had been waiting in the foliage. Bent and beaten-down branches and straw told the tale. Then the creatures followed after the two horses had passed.

The Hells—an ambush!

Alarms rang in his head.

He was in a dilemma. His first impulse was to gallop headlong after them, but he didn't want to miss critical signs, blundering along and thus losing the track. Neither did he fancy riding into an ambush of his own. Well, he would have to forge ahead, be craft-wise and go as fast as he could without losing concentration.

Suddenly, the hoofprints lengthened in stride, and the earth was churned up. The trap had been sprung! More Goblin prints—the rear group was driving the two horses forward to … where?

Ah, *there* … many, many footprints, maybe fifteen or more Goblins altogether.

Rolland crept forward cautiously, his senses alert. Then, a small clearing and….

Iovis!

Remains of what must have been the two horses lay strewn about: bones, mainly, with tatters of flesh still clinging, alongside bridles and saddles amongst hooves and teeth. But also … yes, several bodies.

A surge of fear shot through him, but he steadied himself and studied the carcasses as best he could. Goblins—four of them, at least—but no humans, thank the Gods!

Well, Sonnia had put up a good fight. Hard to tell how the goblins died, though, as it seemed the buffet was not limited to horseflesh only, as all the bones—horse and Goblin alike—had teeth marks; fang marks, that is.

He made his way quietly back to his horse.

All right, the ladies had been taken alive. That must mean they were safe, at least for now.

Why would they want the two women, though? What were Goblins doing kidnapping travelers? Come to think, why were Goblins here in these lands in the first place?

He had no answers to these questions, including, he suddenly realized, how he was going to slay a company of armed green creatures to save someone whose nose seemed permanently turned upward.

Problems, problems….

After night had fallen, the full moon rose. Rolland moved even more cautiously now. He was getting closer to the main troop and he wanted to remain unseen, if he could help it. If horses and Goblins were on the menu, what was to prevent an Apprentice Sorcerer from being added as a side dish?

Further down the path was a lighter patch. It was … yes, a fire.

He dismounted from Riator and tied his reins to a tree limb. Patting the animal's neck, he gave instructions. "Stay here. Be quiet. Good horse." He had no idea whether his commands would do any good. One ill-timed nicker, and the game would be up, but it made him feel better to have said it.

Slowly and quietly, he edged his way forward. The sound of revelry wafted down the trail toward him. Swells of what must be Goblin laughter filled the night at intervals.

Something was going on … a party, or ….

He did not dare to think beyond that.

His first impulse was to rush in and send bolts of lightning ripping in every direction. But what if the ladies were still living? Would they be struck? What if he needed the Goblins alive to obtain information from them? Who sent them? What did they want?

What if … ah, so many questions. Better to wait.

At least he heard no screams. That was a good sign, hopefully.

One dark thought from his thieving culture intruded itself: What if Sonnia had joined ranks with the Goblins? What then? But he rejected that idea out of hand.

Hmm. Need to get closer….

It was now quite late. The celebrations—if that's what they were— had died away, and now all was still. The campfire had died as well.

Using all his guile, he crept closer to the clearing, which he could see through the branches. He silently parted a curtain of leaves and beheld the Goblins' camp.

They had no tents. All were sleeping on the ground, wrapped in filthy blankets and snoring under the vine-laden trees. Rolland counted thirty-three of the green creatures, one of them upright and sporting a cocked helmet and a big gut, apparently on guard duty. He was strutting around the camp with a vicious-looking short spear resting over one shoulder.

In the middle of the camp were the remains of a fire with a big black pot suspended above it. The smell of stew hung in the air. In front of the pot was a pole, and on top of the pole was a head.

Rolland grimaced, looked away, then forced himself to look back. It was charred, and the hair was all burned off. It had a hooked nose.

As soon as Rolland saw that feature, he let out a breath he hadn't realized he was holding—not Sonnia, then. It must be her serving woman, Servilla. The eyes were absent, and lips crisped, revealing grinning teeth, some missing.

Rolland assumed the rest of her was in the pot.

Or had been.

But where, then, was Sonnia? Anxiously, he looked around the camp.

There, off to the left, a body....

It was spread-eagled on its back over a tree stump, perhaps a pace-high off the ground. Wrists and ankles were bound with rope, running down to stakes that jutted from the ground. Dirty, torn, and stained short clothes were the body's only covering.

Rolland's eyes were riveted on the figure.

Was it alive?

He stared, straining to see ... *yes, there*. Breathing—shallow and slow, but breathing.

He closed his eyes with a quick offering of thanks to the God of Thieves and completed the painful inventory. He assumed the figure was Sonnia. At least the nose was there, and it was upturned like hers. Her hair appeared to have been hacked off and strewn about the stump.

A dark substance—dried blood, probably—ran from her mouth, covering her chin and neck. Her chest was a bloody mess. She made no sound.

Rolland glanced up to a tree next to the stump. Two round pale objects—what Rolland took to be melons—had been nailed to the tree, along with what looked to be a short strip of dark leather.

It took several moments of concentration to realize what he was seeing. His stomach turned, and he bit his knuckle till it bled. He fought valiantly not to vomit.

Anger began to well up inside him then … growing and growing.

As Rolland stared, the lone sentry came into view, pacing his rounds. He would have been comical if not for the situation. Rolland watched him carefully; his eyes narrowed. The guard made his way slowly over to where Sonnia was bound.

Rolland tensed.

The Goblin stopped in front of the stump and tentatively reached toward the roped figure. A taloned finger slowly moved to the edge of the ragged clothing, lifting it up….

Rolland's hands flashed to his belt and back in a blinding instant. Two streaks of silver flew through the air. A knife handle suddenly blossomed from the Goblin's throat, preventing him from calling out, and a second appeared jutting out of the Goblin's ear. The green creature crumpled to the ground without a sound.

His spear, however, clattered as it fell. Rolland cursed.

Several of the sleeping Goblins stirred, and one drowsily half sat up.

"Damn!" the Apprentice muttered.

Well, there was nothing for it now….

"*Vites Vincite!*" he commanded in a furious roar.

Vines from the trees overhanging the recumbent green warriors sprang to life, uncoiling down and fastening onto the small creatures, snatching them back up so they were suspended in air, two to three paces off the ground.

"Cultri Venite!" he barked. Knives and daggers from all the Goblins flew from the ensnared figures and landed in a pile at Rolland's feet.

"You'll not be needing those, you sons of bitches. Hope you all hate heights. Get used to it. You'll be hanging there for a good long time."

By now, the Goblins were awake and yowling in their distress. Soon, cursing and dire threats followed, but Rolland ignored them and rushed over to the body draped over the stump.

It was Sonnia. Tears welled in his eyes as he reached behind and grabbed the grimy cloak from the fallen guard.

The thief cut the ropes binding the girl and covered her with the cloak. He checked the pulse at her neck as he'd learned from Master Celsius. It was weak and thready, but it was a pulse. She made no response to his ministrations.

He bent over, carefully lifted her up, and walked out of the clearing to the Goblins' jeers and catcalls.

"Rest while you can, scum," he called over his shoulder. "We will be back to see you later. And then, for you, things will begin to get difficult."

The green fighters suddenly fell silent.

19

Goblins II
Coboli II

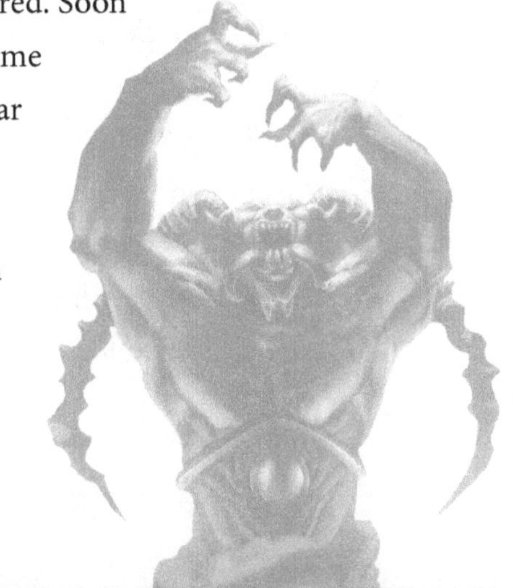

As gently as he could, Rolland carefully positioned Sonnia on Riator's saddle and led the horse back to the path. They soon arrived at the gurgling brook Rolland had noted before. He eased the injured girl down from the horse, laid her gently by the stream, and then cleaned her wounds as best he could.

She made no response.

"All right, Sonnia. I know how this is going to feel to you. It's the only thing I can think of to do. If you can hear me, remember, it will all be over in a minute."

Carefully, Rolland took one of her hands in his own, then raised his free arm, extended it, palm out, and exclaimed, "*Sanum Facite Omnino!*"

Immediately, torn and damaged tissues began to knit together, absent parts regenerated, and healing occurred. Soon enough, Sonnia looked as she had the last time Rolland had seen her—or perhaps a half-year older. She was beautiful, he had to admit.

Sonnia moaned, and Rolland moved to hold her. Her eyes flew open, and she began screaming, thrashing about, and striking at him, clawing and biting.

Rolland could do nothing but hold her and speak what he hoped were soothing and reassuring words, again and again.

Gradually, she stopped fighting. Finally, her eyes came into focus, and she beheld the Apprentice.

"Rolland?" she asked in a small, unsteady voice.

The thief nodded.

"Oh, Rolland!" The girl threw her arms around him and began to cry, great wrenching sobs that went on and on. The redhead held her close, gently stroking her hair, telling her over and over that he was there now, that she was safe and that she would never be hurt again. Eventually, his arms tingled then grew numb, but he did not change his position. Not when he was needed.

After a time, the storm passed, and she slowly relaxed her grip. Finally, the girl drifted off to sleep, and Rolland followed.

The sun called to Rolland, and he eventually heeded it, opening his eyes. He regarded the beautiful one who lay beside him. How fine her features, how lustrous her tousled hair. He shifted his position slightly to view her better still.

The girl's eyes flew open. "Where are they?"

He knew immediately whom she meant.

"Back in the clearing. I left them hanging, bound up in some tree vines."

"All of them?"

"All of them present in the camp."

"Alive?"

"Yes, at least as of last night."

"Good." Sonnia looked away for a moment, then back at Rolland. "Servilla?"

Rolland shook his head, and the girl nodded, her gaze fastened on the ground.

After some moments, she looked up again, tears falling on Rolland's saddle blanket. The girl rose unsteadily with the blanket draped awkwardly around her, then straightened and assumed an imperious pose, thunderclouds and lightning flashing in her eyes. She looked down at herself.

"Have you any spare clothes?"

"I have some in my pack behind Riator's saddle."

The girl nodded and made her way over to the horse. In but a moment, she had taken the pack down from the horse, opened it, and extracted the garments. Clutching them in one arm, she looked pointedly at Rolland.

"Um, I'll turn around and have a look to see if there are any more of the buggers about."

After a few moments, splashing came from the stream. And in a few more moments, a quick glance showed the girl dressed in his spare tunic, rope belt tightened, and sleeves rolled up. She was throwing water on her face. He turned to face her.

"Rolland, may I borrow two of your knives?"

"Yes. Of course." With a flourish, he produced the two daggers he'd retrieved from the dead Goblin guard from his belt.

Sonnia took the weapons and slid one on either side of her belt. She turned and started to walk off.

"Say, where are you going?" Rolland asked.

The girl stopped. "You said the Goblins were all back at the clearing?"

"Yes."

"And it's this way?"

"Yes."

"Then that's where I'm going. I'm going to start with these," she indicated the daggers, "and next call down fire and brim—" The girl stopped, and a dawning realization swept over her countenance. "Um,

Rolland, last night, when you healed me, did you use *Sanum Facite Omnino?*"

"Why, yes. It, uh, seemed like that was the best spell and—"

The girl barked a rueful laugh. "You have healed me better than I thought. I am so stupid and silly. If it were not me that this was happening to, I would laugh at myself. I cannot believe it. No matter how hard I try to run away from it, I keep being drawn back in. All right, then. I will run no longer. I will surrender to and embrace my destiny, or I should say *fate.* Most especially since I appear to have no other choice." The girl let out a long sigh, shook herself, and squared her shoulders.

Stepping off in a march, she headed directly toward Rolland, still sitting by the stream. As the distance shortened, however, the march became a walk, her stiffness began to relent, and as she drew nearer, her hips began to sway. Reaching her destination, she knelt down by the boy.

"Rolland, you must think me an awful person," she began.

"No, I don't. Well, not entirely." He offered a slight grin.

The girl gave him a weak smile, combined with a grimace. "You are right. All of you have been right. The harder I tried to fight it, the worse a person I became."

"What is it you are trying to fight, Sonnia?"

"That which lies ahead, seemingly, whatever I do." She looked deeply into Rolland's eyes. "I—I have behaved badly toward you and worse, thought badly of you, Rolland. You risked your life last night to save me. And you gave of your life-force, in no small measure, to heal me after. And I certainly gave you no good cause to do so."

"Sonnia, that's not tr—"

"No, it is true," the girl interrupted him. "And you know it. You are polite not to say so, but you know it. So, first, I want to thank you for that—and other things." The girl leaned close to the redhead, closed her eyes, and touched her lips to his.

Rolland was surprised and experienced the beginnings of response. Her kiss became deeper, and he returned it. He became aware of ardor. Not the usual feelings he tended to have in such situations, but new feelings—feelings of caring, tenderness, longing—and yearning. They shook him to his roots.

If her kisses told an honest tale, he'd have thought Sonnia might be feeling something of the same toward him.

The girl drew back gently, slowly opening her eyes. She took a deep breath. "And I want to apologize for being the terrible, spoiled, self-indulgent…."

Rolland knew enough of human nature—specifically female human nature—to understand that such self-critical listings tended, once started, to go on and on interminably. Usually, only one sure thing could interrupt them. He leaned forward, put his arms around her, and drew her to him.

It worked like a charm, but that's because it was an old, old charm.

The bright sun beamed down on the treed canopy, filtering through to the branches underneath and onto the myriad green leaves below, dappling the young lovers as they writhed in their passion on the forest floor.

The pair sat beside each other, knees pulled up, arms around knees.

"You caught my eye right away, handsome lad that you are. And I thought to make you jealous by showing attention to Thaddeus." Sonnia flashed Rolland a big smile.

Rolland was dazzled and now understood what the tall boy had meant all those months ago when he had spoken of the girl.

"But then you spoiled it all by announcing yourself as a thief and a scoundrel."

"Wait! I never said I was a scoundrel—no such thing!"

"But thieves are always scoundrels. Everyone knows it. And I knew I could never bring such a person home to my parents. Heavens! What would they say? What would our friends and family think? Not to mention what the townsfolk would gossip about. 'Tisn't done, you see."

She paused, leaned over, kissed Rolland's ear, then leaned back. "Yet, as we spent time together, I became more and more attracted to you."

"You could have fooled me, especially after *Pila Ludere*."

"Oh, yes, that … that was a special circumstance." She smiled again, and the sun beamed forth once more. "Besides, you were so huffed up and overconfident. Then, afterward, it was fun!"

She laughed, and a moment later, Rolland did, too, a bit sheepishly.

"But the final straw was Mid-Summer's Eve's night. All those dreams and visions. I saw us together—married, even! That was a shock. We were in some sort of stately home. You had some high position—"

Rolland interrupted with a laugh. "Unlikely, that."

"I said it was a dream, oh, Rufus!" Again, she grinned. "But I willfully rejected the vision. Whenever I allowed it to happen, a path appeared that took me to that beautiful mansion. But, every time I denied it, the paths took me to all sorts of lonely or unhappy places: a convent, a brothel in some seaport, dead by a robber's hand. They were awful. Not as awful as yesterday, though." A shiver ran through her frame.

"Sonnia, why did you decide to go South when you left the other girls on your way here?"

"It was the only direction I felt I could go. North was River's Wood and wolves, West was back to the *Ludia*, where if I'd come back still a v—I mean if I'd come back early, Mistress Geanninia would have had my hide. And East, of course, was right into your arms. Very beautiful arms, by the way, as it turns out."

"My thanks, Mistress—yours, too."

The couple laughed.

Sonnia put her head on Rolland's shoulder, and they sat in silence for a time, holding hands.

Suddenly, the girl rose gracefully. "All right, my love—for my love you are, and I suppose we must get used to it—I have some Goblins to deal with. But I will not deal with them like this." Here she indicated her lithe but now-unclothed form.

"*Vestimenta Sordida!*" the girl commanded. In a flash, she now stood in full trail garb. She smiled in what seemed satisfaction at both success in spell-casting and the result of her wishes. "It works!" she said, smiling again.

"Do you want me to come with you?" Rolland asked.

The girl frowned while doing her hair in a long braid trailing down her back. "No, Rolland. You have done enough. This is my time for revenge—for Servilla and for me. And I shall mete it out myself."

Judging by his knowledge of the girl and the look in her eye, the thief had no doubt about that whatsoever. The Goblins were in for a bad afternoon.

Suddenly serious, Rolland said, "Well, if you have the chance and inclination, you might try to find out how they happened to come here and what they were about, and...."

"Yes, my love. I already thought of that."

"Oh. Yes, of course. Well, um, I will abide here then, waiting. If you need a hand, send up a green fire."

"I will. *Ave!*"

"You also."

Soon after Sonnia left, sounds drifted back from the clearing down the path.

At first came catcalls, cursing, caterwauling, and other cacophony. Then came a huge roar of many Goblin voices at once.

By sound alone, Rolland could not tell if the voices signaled a victory or merely an anticipated one. He wondered if he should go back to the clearing to ensure Sonnia was in no distress. However, the sky showed no green fire, so he remained at their camp. Several moments later, however, came a mass groan of despair.

Apparently, whatever the crowd had hoped for did not materialize.

Rolland stood and began pacing by the edge of the stream. Sonnia had seemed to place so much importance on attaining her Sorcery that he'd expected to hear thunder and see lightning strikes and fire falling from the sky before this.

A heartbeat later, the day's calm was shattered by thunder, light-ning—and fire really was falling from the sky over the approximate area of the clearing.

Well, once those elements were brought in, things would finish up quickly.

Now the air filled with wailings and screams, interspersed among the booms and crashes—and sometimes over them. Though the display continued for some time, the cries lessened in intensity, shortened in duration, and the intervals between them lengthened. After about an hour, a stillness settled over the clearing, and the smoke dissipated.

Rolland continued pacing. Waiting was never among his strong points. Instead, he relived his wonderful morning with Sonnia and gave thought to the question of what came next.

Rustling sounds indicated someone approaching. He turned to face the intruder, who turned out, happily, to be the young Sorceress.

The girl, however, was a sight. She was disheveled and unkempt, not to mention covered head to toe in green ichor—evidently Goblin blood. *Strange*—he'd seen Lilyput cut her finger once, and before she'd shoved it in her mouth to suck on it, he would have sworn her blood was red.

Sonnia's clothes were cut and torn, and her hair had come undone and was askew in several different directions. Red blood—hers, apparently

—showed through the green and was present in several different places. She had one long gash on her leg that Rolland thought might need sewing—or Spelling. She was walking, crouched over with a wild, feral expression.

To himself, he made a vow to never seriously antagonize this girl.

She stopped abruptly and stared at the stream as if entranced.

"Sonnia?" Rolland prompted gently.

After a moment, the girl shook her head, glanced around as if getting her bearings, and straightened. The maniacal look in her eyes resolved, and *Sana et Prudens* returned.

"Rolland," she said. She then glanced over her shoulder toward the clearing, then turned back to the thief. "It's over."

"Are you … uh, are you all right?"

"Yes. Here," she said, fetching his two knives from her belt and tossing them to him. "Thank you for the loan. They work well—very good knives."

He caught them easily but knew he'd need to clean them soon, along with his hands.

The girl spoke again. "I need … a bath, a long bath." Sonnia held out a hand, looking down at it. "*Sapo!*" she commanded, and a quantity of what seemed to be soapstone appeared. "I will bathe now and come join you later."

"All right. Call out if you need anything."

With a nod of dismissal, the girl walked into the stream seeking its deepest part, ripping off her clothes as she went.

His sixth sense told Rolland Sonnia was not being shy, only that she needed to be alone with her thoughts and feelings for a while.

20

Goblins III
Coboli III

Taking advantage of his dismissal, Rolland rinsed in the creek, then sped down the path to look at the Goblin clearing. He had no reason to believe Sonnia would be in any danger whatsoever during his absence. The peril would be for anyone or anything with the temerity to interrupt her toilette. He was curious, though.

The Goblin campsite was a place of devastation—carnage everywhere. No single Goblin body was intact. Of Servilla or the cooking pot, he found no trace. Holes blasted in the ground pockmarked the area, along with strands of burn marks. Some of the vine-clad trees had been shattered and fired, though most survived.

In the midst of the clearing, he found the only fully recognizable body. From a casual inspection, this Goblin must have been of some importance, as the body sported a variety of bracelets and anklets of copper and silver that the others did not have. He also had several necklaces of different beads and small stones on leather and linen strings lying around his neck. Perhaps he was their leader.

His head showed two knife hilts, one projecting from each eye socket. Upon closer inspection, Rolland thought the knives' design spoke of Goblin manufacture and conjectured they were the chief's own weapons.

Walking around the body, he noted that the Goblin's fangs lay at some distance from the jaws and that all four extremities pointed in odd, non-anatomical directions. Additionally, his genitals were missing.

A tall stone he did not recall seeing the previous night stood off to the side near the sawed-off tree stump. At its base were piled most of the Goblins' heads—those still intact.

The rest of the clearing was spotted with bits and pieces of Goblin flesh, arms, legs, and entrails. Putrid green ichor was splashed everywhere, and the stench was overpowering. The flies were already busy.

With a last look around to fix the scene in his mind, he turned and headed back to the stream.

When he returned, Sonnia was standing bent over, soaping her long hair and, after a moment, splashing stream water on it to rinse out the soap.

"Halloo! Would you like some help?" Rolland called from the bank.

The girl looked up and nodded. The redhead took a gourd cup from his pack and walked down into the stream and over to where the girl stood. He filled the gourd with water and poured it over her hair as she held it out for him. He repeated this process until she seemed satisfied.

"Thank you," she said.

"I saw your handiwork."

"I thought you might have when I looked over and saw you'd gone."

"What—"

"When I first got there, they started in with the gibes. I turned Servilla's pole around, so she could see what would happen to them. After, I dug a grave with Sorcery and placed her in it. I covered her over and said a few words. I vowed to put the heads of all her enemies over her for retribution and as a warning. Then I killed them all; every one of them by myself. Most with Sorcery, but some personally. Their chief … oh, I remembered him."

The Vengeance of Sonnia

The young Sorceress looked away for a moment.

"Him, I killed first. I found him in one of the vines and loosed him down. I offered to fight him, one to the other. At first, he refused, saying there was no honor in fighting a weak woman. He bragged and strutted around, playing to his followers hanging above him, getting them all worked up. So, I insulted him, in a way you might imagine—he'd brought up the gender issue, after all—and told him the alternative was burning alive. To mark my point, I fried the nearest fellow to a crisp right in front of him.

"After that, the chief changed his mind about fighting a woman and started hurling insults, thumping his chest, and so on. He had his crowd crowing. But he, as I knew, was overconfident. He tried lots of tricks—biting, tossing sand in my eyes—what you'd expect. After I'd laid him out, but before I killed him, I broke his arms and legs, one by one, and then his shoulders and hips, one by one. Then I tore his fangs out, one by one. Then I ripped off his penis and testicles, one by one. Then I took his knives and...."

Overcome at last, the girl broke down sobbing. Grasping with desperation, she clung to Rolland, who held her in the middle of the stream, comforting her for as long as it took.

"Marsia, Marsia! Wake up!" Nannsi exclaimed, shaking the girl.

"Wha ... what? What is it?" she said, coming awake.

"You have been dozing, but 'tis early yet. Are you all right?"

"What? Oh, yes. I was just dreaming about ... Thaddeus. You know. But what is it? What occurs?"

"Well, I was just walking by and happened to glance at you, and I saw the fire's colors reflected in your face."

"Nannsi, that is a natural occurrence. How's that of such importance?"

"Well, you will have to determine the answer yourself, seeing as how one of the colors I saw was green."

"What?" The young girl sat bolt upright and, in a trice, had her green stone out by its chain. Indeed, it was glowing green—somewhat faintly but green nevertheless.

"Oh, Nannsi! It's Thaddeus. He is drawing closer. Oh, dear, I must look a sight. Well, no matter. He will just have to have me as I am. I must get busy and pack."

"Dear Marsia," the short girl said, smiling widely. "You look beautiful, just as you always do."

"Oh, sweet Nannsi … one never had a better Sister."

So saying, the girls embraced. Then Nannsi became business-like.

"All right now, I will help you," she said as they strode to the taller girl's tent. "Let's see. What think you of that brown dress? It sets off your color very well…."

Rolland walked into camp, proudly leading Riator, upon whom sat Sonnia, equally proud.

Anders saw them first and called to the others. Soon all had crowded around, everyone asking questions and talking at once.

Rolland helped Sonnia down. The Sorceress, however, had eyes only for one. In a brief moment, she stood before Molly, then went down on one knee, clutching one of the black-haired girl's hands to her cheek.

"Molly o' the Willows. Know that I repent how I have treated you since we met. Where I was vicious, you were ever kind. Where I was sullen, you were ever sweet. I bitterly regret my behavior and all my thoughtless words, and I hope desperately that you will forgive me for uttering them." After her words, she kissed the crèche girl's hand.

"Aye, you were a bit tart at the first; there's no denying," Molly said evenly. "But seeing as how you've come back to us now and brought this handsome knave with you, I see no course but to embrace you. As for the other, I recollect nothing there might be to forgive. Now get up from your kneeling, girl; you will make a mess of your dress." So saying, Molly drew up the Sorceress, and they embraced.

Sonnia stepped back a pace with a petitioner's expression on her face. "Thank you, Molly. I'd … I'd like it very much if you would allow me, then, to call you … Sister."

Nannsi drew in her breath. "Oh, this is wonderful!" she blurted.

"Aye. You know I always wanted to have a Sister, and now, I have three at one time. It is a blessing to me, surely. Come to me, Sister." The two girls hugged, and a moment later, Nannsi was stretching her short arms around both of them.

Anders felt his eyes welling as Zoarr put his arm around his Brother's shoulder. Rolland caught their gazes and winked, smiling broadly and giving the hand sign for *all is well*.

The three couples spent most of the rest of the day sharing portions of their recent lives. More time was taken up with speculation concerning Marsia and Thaddeus.

At Asullus' suggestion—he was, of course, a permanent member of their campfire sittings—nothing of substance was discussed concerning what Sonnia had discovered from the Goblins until the missing couple had returned.

Before retiring, at Sonnia's request, the old mule led the group in the Prayer for the Dead as a memorial for Servilla. Then, all bade each other Good Repose and went to their tents, none having to sleep alone except for Asullus, who tended to take such things philosophically.

The following mid-morning, Thaddeus and Marsia arrived at the camp, leading Marsia's horse. Osiric was perched on Thaddeus' shoulder while Thaddeus smiled and Marsia beamed.

Again, much talk passed before any of it could be sorted out. Most of the rest of the day was taken up preparing for the evening and observing the reaction of Asullus to Osiric and vice versa. Time was also spent learning the Etiquette of the Eagle.

After Even-tide, Rolland announced Sonnia had news of import to share. Silence fell among the other humans, one mule, and two birds.

"I have learned that Goblin troops have been dispatched in this area to look specifically for us. We were to be captured and turned over to an agent representing one Morag. In turn, I believe Morag may be a Daemon."

The others gasped in surprise—all except for Rolland, who added, "And I think this Daemon may be closer to us than we know. I think he may live in the Tower at the College itself. Further … I think he may be under the control of Master Perditus."

21

A Daemon Speaks
Daemon Dicit

"What?" said the collection of voices, their tones incredulous.

"Wait," Anders cautioned. "We should hear their reasoning."

"Yes," Zoarr added in the tone he adopted when discussing things political. "Let us hear the reasoning."

"Very well, Rolland, Sonnia—tell us," Thaddeus said, then wondering again who had made him the Agenda Reeve.

"Sonnia can tell it better than I," Rolland said. "Best to ask her."

The girl flashed a smile at the thief. "After Rolland rescued me, I went back to the Goblin clearing. Before … before I killed them, I asked them questions. I started with their chief, but he proved very stubborn and gave me less information than I'd hoped: curses, mainly. Once I finished with him, his second-in-command—the fellow with the second-most jewelry—had more to say after he saw the fate of his chief, and the third even more. And so it went."

The *Physica Maritima* paused to collect her thoughts before proceeding.

"What all of them generally agreed on was that someone named Morag had recruited an agent to contact their group of Goblin freebooters. These warriors were conscripted to intercept us and kill all excepting two; two of the boys, he said. I'm not sure why they wanted only you males. Perhaps because you would look more inconspicuous at the *Collegium*."

"How do you know he was from the *Collegium?*" Anders asked.

"Because we were described to him—all of us. They knew who we were and where we would be."

"It might have been someone from the *Ludia*. Would they not have the same information?" Anders asked.

"Well, yes, except two of the higher Goblins mentioned that this agent was from the East. That would be you fellows and not us," the girl answered.

Sonnia took a deep breath and continued. "The Goblin chief's assistant relinquished his silence toward the end and said the agent was to meet the Goblin leaders in one week near *Arx Montium*. For the prisoner transfer, I assume, and their reward."

"Is the agent human?" Zoarr asked.

"So far as I could deduce. The Goblins who spoke of him referred to him in that way."

Anders leaned forward. "What about this Morag? A Daemon, you say? How do you know that?"

"Again, it was the way they spoke of him. When his name was mentioned, they all flinched and looked away as if they were afraid. Very different than how they spoke of the agent or any of the other humans."

Anders looked thoughtful. "I see. But how do you get from there to Master Perditus?"

Rolland snorted. "A human agent working for a Daemon? In the East? Daemons cannot just go out and set up a Will-Work-For-Sulfur tent, you know. Much less hire Goblins to kill people. It's from that, we get to the likelihood of Master Perditus' involvement,"

"Likelihood?" Anders said. "Hmm. Perhaps more a possibility. For example, what would move someone to act so?"

"Power or control over power. Old Pox-Face is a left-out sort, I'm wagering. That sort of power could be quite an intoxicant for him," Rolland answered.

"I wonder how would he have gotten in contact with a Daemon in the first place?" Thaddeus said.

"The old Tower of the Cin. It sounds like it may have been Daemons who helped the Eastern Mages in the first place against the old Tyrannus Superbus. Maybe some Daemon was left over in the Tower from that time. Or, maybe just a way to get in touch with them—you know, knock three times, and they appear—and Perditus ciphered it out. He's supposed to be so damn clever."

"Hmm," the short scholar said thoughtfully. "I have always heard Daemons don't care to submit to humans all that much. They tend to favor it the other way around."

"Maybe Perditus was offered the prospect of becoming a Lord as a part of some bargain: 'You help us out, you get to be *Dominus*,'" Rolland said.

"Possibly. For a time, perhaps," Zoarr added.

Anders snapped his fingers. "That could explain how we happened that time to see Perditus in the Tower, and a moment later, he appeared right behind us. It was the Daemon in the Tower posing in Perditus' likeness as a deception. His voice seemed like it could be a Daemon's, now that I think on it."

"Well, he must not be a very great Daemon if he has to skulk about in a Tower. Why is he not out and about eating everybody up?" Rolland said.

"I don't know."

"And who is this agent?" Zoarr asked.

Anders answered, "It must be someone who could come and go in, not only the College but through Mountaingaard as well. Only the Masters can do that with impunity."

"Modus," Sonnia said.

"What?" Thaddeus exclaimed.

"Modus. That was the name one of the Goblins used when he was talking about the Daemon's agent."

"Modus? The porter? That hardly seems possible," Anders said.

"Nevertheless, that was the name."

"Well, this is still all just conjecture. There is not an iota of evidence for any of it. And these would be serious—not to mention dangerous—charges to bring."

Zoarr looked thoughtful. "I must add that torture—or even constraint—is often an unreliable method of obtaining accurate information. No offense."

Rolland jumped in hotly. "I'd say the little orffers had it coming, whatever happened to them!"

"Of course, Brother. I am with you," the Prince responded.

"Aye. I have a thought," Thaddeus said. "Asullus. Didn't you tell me once that being around the Daemon Charles makes your nose burn?"

"Aye. 'Tis true. I did, an' it do. What's yer point, laddie?"

"And didn't you also say that the Tower made your nose burn as well, and that is why you stayed distant from it?"

"Aye. Aye! Well, right ye are, young Sorcerer. I ha' no' put the two together, but there ye be."

"Ah, Thaddeus. That would certainly tie the Tower to a Daemon, but that does not mean it was a particular Daemon here in the present. It's still pretty much thin soup," Anders complained.

"Well, I may be able to thicken this soup up a bit. Hmm. I think you all should move away to the outer ring of the campfire now."

"I will not move away from your side, Thaddeus of Beewicke. You pledged. I remain here," the tall girl said.

"Pledged? Who pledged what, Thaddeus?" Anders asked, confused.

"Why do you want us to move to the outside of the fire ring?" Zoarr queried.

Rolland looked skeptical. "What are you on about, Thaddeus?"

"Why…." Molly began.

"Because I am about to summon a Daemon. I may be able to find out something from him directly."

"Oh. Yes. Good idea. Let's just stand over there, dearest," Anders said to his bride.

"Do not look at me like that. I am not going anywhere," Marsia replied to his raised eyebrow.

"Well, all right. Here, I'll try." Thaddeus held his arm straight up, fingers spread apart as if reaching for the sky. *"Carlus, veni!"*

At first, nothing happened, then came a loud boom accompanied by a cloud of acrid crimson smoke.

In the middle of the campfire stood a hulking, muscled brown figure, horns and fangs glinting in the firelight.

"New Master! New Master summons Charles. What want, New Master? Eat these others bothering New Master?" The creature looked about, a hopeful expression on its face.

"Not tonight, Charles."

The *Daemon Minor's* face fell.

"I need you to answer some questions for us."

"Answer questions? Not kill anyone? Not eat anyone?"

"Not tonight. My companions and I are going to pose certain questions to you. You are to answer them as truthfully as you can. Do you understand my command?"

"Yes, New Master."

"Charles, do you know of Morag?"

Silent, the Daemon flinched and bit his tongue.

"Charles, what is the matter?"

The tall brown Daemon looked extremely uncomfortable. "New Master! Name a task otherwise for Charles! Any otherwise."

"Charles, tell me—what troubles you?"

"Um, Charles not talk now, if New Master not mind."

"Charles, New Master does mind. Now tell New Master or face the displeasure of *Septentrionis.*"

The Daemon began to sweat tiny droplets that produced a little *poof* of flame when they touched the earth.

"What you ask … it is forbidden. Morag find out, Charles end up in Morag's belly, then, later, out."

"He's constrained from answering, Thaddeus," Anders offered. "And he's torn because of the compulsion he has to do your bidding, yet the doing of it would place him in direct jeopardy. Is that right, Charles?"

The short boy held out his hand and snapped his fingers. "Oh, wait, I have it! Charles, if what any of us asks you is true, do not move: stand stock still. If what we suppose is incorrect in our question, then nod your head as if you agree. That way you can tell anyone who might ask that you answered no question *yes* for us, and that you answered *yes* to our questions when we were wrong. What say you?"

Charles remained stock still.

"Ah, yes. All right, Thaddeus, proceed with your interrogation."

The tall boy closed his eyes in concentration, then opened them, seeming decided. Beside him, Marsia squeezed his arm, giving him a look of encouragement.

"Charles, is Morag a Daemon?"

Charles was still.

"Is he a powerful Daemon?"

Still.

"More powerful than you?"

Still.

"Are you obliged to obey him as you do me?"

Charles rocked back and forth on his taloned feet. Fiery beads struck the earth again.

Anders broke in. "Charles, is that a complex question that is difficult to answer *yes* or *no* to?"

Charles was still. Nannsi beamed at Anders.

"Charles, do you obey Morag out of fear rather than from the compulsion of a bond?"

Still.

"Does Morag live in the Tower?" Rolland interjected.

The Daemon looked constrained again.

"Charles," Anders offered, "if you hear one of those complex *yes/no* questions, don't say anything. Just rock your hand back and forth like this." The short scholar demonstrated.

Charles rocked his hand.

"Does Morag live any other place in the College?"

Charles nodded his head.

"We have seen someone in the Tower who resembles Master Perditus but speaks in a deep voice and laughs coarsely. Might that be Morag?"

Still.

"So, he is in the Tower, but he does not live in the Tower?"

Still.

"How can that be? That makes no sense. If he does not live in the Tower or any place else, then where can he come from?" Rolland asked in exasperation.

Charles rocked his hand.

"Ask *yes* or *no* questions, Rolland. Remember the rules."

"Oh, well, let me tell you about your rules...."

Sonnia, standing beside Rolland, her hand in his, stood on tiptoe and whispered in the thief's ear.

"Well, get on about your questioning, then. Time is slipping here," the redhead said, chastened.

"Is it possible, Charles, that Morag comes from a different place—a different place entirely—and just visits the Tower?" Thaddeus asked.

Charles was still.

"What made you think of that, Thaddeus?" Zoarr asked.

"Well, I was thinking about the Great Ring—how it can be a different time and place, but you can travel back and forth, as through a portal. Then I thought of the Cauldron of Creation—that terrible scene I witnessed Mid-Summer's Night's Eve this year past. And I, uh, put them together."

Zoarr nodded. "Yes, I see it."

"Charles, does Master Perditus control Morag?"

Rock.

The humans looked at each other with puzzled expressions.

Anders snapped his fingers again. "Hah! Charles! Does Master Perditus *think* he controls Morag, but in reality, he does not?"

Still.

"Oh-ho. Interesting," Zoarr said, his eyes narrowing in concentration.

"Morag," Sonnia's voice said suddenly. "Why does Morag come now?"

The Daemon began to put forth his hand.

"No. I mean, is there a reason Morag comes now?"

Still.

Sonnia's lips tightened. "Does Morag seek food?"

Still.

"Human food?"

Still.

"Hmm," Thaddeus said. "I do not believe that to be the only reason." The tall Apprentice thought back to his vision. "Charles, do Morag—and the other Daemons as well—is it their freedom they seek?"

Still.

Zoarr rubbed his chin. "Does Master Perditus help Morag come here?"

Still.

"Does Perditus want something from Morag in return for his assistance?"

Still.

"Hmm," Rolland said. "What could he want?"

"Well, let's try the obvious. Charles, does Perditus seek power from Morag?"

Still.

"Power over the College?"

Charles nodded his head.

"Wait … that is not…."

"Hold. Charles, does Perditus want power over more than the College?"

Still.

"Power over the Westlands?" Marsia asked.

Nod.

"Power over the entire World?" Anders whispered.

Still.

"*Iovis!*"

"Charles! What is…."

"Charles is summoned," the Daemon interrupted. "Must go now. Farewell, New Master."

With that, the Daemon vanished.

In seconds, one mulish and eight human voices were all speaking excitedly, with a shrill bird's voice trying to override the others, wanting to know what in the Hells was going on. It took some time to sort most of it out.

"….and that is why we can't go to Master Silvestrus right away. We need something more substantial."

"Aye. I think I have your substantial for you; leastwise, it's what I'd do," Molly o' the Willows offered.

"What is that, Molly?"

"Go pinch this Modus fellow. He's bound to have something to say. If not, I am sure you can persuade him. Besides, he's on your way home."

The others fell silent, looking at their non-Sorcerous companion with new eyes. Zoarr puffed up with pride.

"Excellent, Molly! Simply excellent. Good for you," Thaddeus said admiringly.

"Well," Rolland said reluctantly, "the week the agent has had to wait will be up in a few days. I suppose we should get started packing."

Faces fell around the fire.

"One more night, Rolland," Sonnia said. "One more night for all of us, don't you think?"

Rolland looked to Thaddeus. "What say you then, Master Beekeeper?"

Thaddeus smiled. "Like Sonnia said—one more night. For all of us."

And so it was.

22

A Traitor Is Uncovered
Reus Laesae Majestatis Reveletur

The morning dawned too early and passed too quickly, with everyone moving too slowly. It seemed no one was anxious to depart or even to acknowledge the end of their time together.

Camp was broken, and tearful, heartfelt farewells were universal. The boys, at least, had little concern for the girls' safety since three of them could now use Sorcery.

The group in the cart was quiet. All were absorbed in their losses and had little interest in the trail songs they had sung on the way West. Eventually, Zoarr's tenor called out plaintively with the likes of "What Say You Now, Fair Jenny?" and "My Heart in Your Eyes, My Lass," and all joined in.

Asullus tolerated an hour of this before breaking in. "Aye, ye four. Now the bird here an' I ha' been of good sport, allowin' ye to wallow in yer maudlin songs an' yer pity o' yerselves fer some time apace, but ev'ry thing has its limit, don' ye know. So go on now wi' yer dirges, should ye wish—or ye could be plannin' wha' t' do aboot Porter Modus an' all tha' might be followin' him after."

"Um. Good point, Asullus," Anders said, his tone reflective. "What do you think we should do, Thaddeus?"

The tall Apprentice fell silent for a moment. "We need to catch him out and take him to Master Silvestrus and Master Beatus. They will know what to make of it all and what to do."

"Sound idea," Zoarr said. "But, however will we find him? According to Sonnia, the Goblins said only that the agent—assuming that's Modus —was going to meet them just outside Mountaingaard. That could be any of a thousand places or more up and down the entire range. A grain of sand in the desert."

"I have an idea as to that. Hold a moment." Thaddeus turned in his seat and looked at the Great Golden Crested Eagle, whose clutched talons anchored him to the side of the pitching cart.

"*Osiric, we seek a man who acts on behalf of a Daemon named Morag. We have been told he will be waiting to meet with the Goblin chief who sought to kill several of us this week past. Their place of meeting will be outside the mountain range known as Mountaingaard. We can place it no finer than that. Can you help us find this man, so we may question him closely regarding this dire plot?*"

"*Find him? I assume you mean me to fly up and down this range, smelling and listening for one man, then advise you of it? That is a grain of sand in a desert.*"

"*Yes, that's what Prince Zoarr said. Well, can you do it? Will you do it?*"

"*I will attempt it. No love of Daemons have I.*"

"*My thanks. I owe you a great boon for this act.*"

"*You speak truly.*"

"Osiric will locate Modus for us once we get close to the range. Then, when we have him, we can go to Master Silvestrus ... no, that will not work. We cannot drag Modus around through the College and expect to go unnoticed."

The tall lad sat for a moment in thought. "Oh, I have it! We will collect our agent and ask Non-Dar to hold him in the forest until we can notify Master Silvestrus. Then our Master can come and have a conversation with the man, undisturbed."

"Hmm. That is indeed a solid plan," Rolland said, then asked in his most impudent tone, "who helped you with it?"

Thaddeus responded appropriately.

Arriving in the early afternoon, the boys set up camp near the foot of the rise to Mountaingaard and sent Osiric on his way. The great Eagle returned within the hour.

"There is only one human scent I can detect in the area, about a league east of here and a half-league off the path into the forest, at my estimate. The human is male. He smells old, and he smells … anxious."

The boys looked at each other after Thaddeus had finished translating.

"Well, then," Rolland said, "let's be about it."

"Thaddeus, if I may?" Zoarr asked. "Psittaca, we have a small task for you. Are you in good voice these days?"

"Ho, there, Modus," the voice called from the bush.

"Aye, Master Perditus, here I be," Modus answered.

A cowled figure came from behind a large tree. It was prodding along two of the Apprentices, bound at the wrists. *Ah, yes, the little know-it-all and the tall bee-head….*

Good. Now he'd get his reward!

But wait…. The Goblins were supposed to be bringing the two boys … and he was to take them to Master Perditus.

Something … something ain't right about….

And wasn't Master Perditus a bit shorter than—damn! Time to go!

"Hold, Modus," the dark-skinned Upperclass said as he pinned one of the old man's arms behind him. The boy appeared out of nowhere as the porter turned to flee. "We would have conversation with you."

Got to get away…. The old man moved with surprising swiftness.

Nasty bugger of a Solaris! Knocks me knife away, then picks it up and puts it against me throat, all in the blink of an eye! How did he do that?

"I said, hold! Now my Brothers and I wish to speak with you, but you can still talk, even if a fair amount of you suddenly goes missing—if you take my meaning."

"Aye, young Master, I takes your meaning. But what do ye with old Modus? Ne'er harm did I you, Prince, nor your Brothers as it comes to that. Ye surely have the wrong fellow, and I must be getting about me business at the College."

"Talk first, Modus. We will talk about the College later."

The other three figures approached. The prisoner's bindings came off easily enough, and there was that ill-mannered redheaded knockabout under that robe, grinning to beat all.

A bleedin' setup it was. Hope they forget who it was I hailed.

"Ah, Modus, we're curious to know why it is you'd be thinking to meet Master Perditus out here past Mountaingaard at this time?" Rolland looked over to where the porter had parked the College wagon. "And why you thought you might need a wagon on a non-market day?"

The old man did his best to spin a story, but the infernal, oh-too-clever brats kept poking holes in it.

Then things got difficult.

"Well, Modus, you have not been all that forthcoming, I think, and, therefore, we do not have much use for you. I believe we should tie you to one of these trees and tell Master Perditus we met you out here. Perhaps he will send Morag along to free you up."

Rolland grinned when he saw the old man flinch.

Ah! He knows. At least he knows somewhat.

What a ditter. The school's own porter up to his elbows in it, and no one knowing.

"Oh, young Master, I beg ye to ha' mercy on me! Do not be leaving me to … to the likes o' him." Sweat popped out on the porter's brow.

"Why, what would be wrong with that, Modus?" Rolland asked. "Do you think you have anything to worry about from a Daemon you have disappointed, do you?"

The rest of the conversation went much more quickly after that.

Getting by Captain Geoffrey was accomplished by using a simple sleeping spell on Modus and curling him up in the back of the wagon. Rolland and Zoarr—the two fast talkers of the group—went through first in the cart with airy ease, followed by Thaddeus and Anders in the wagon.

The story they spun was simple: apparently, they'd all met up on the way back, and they'd found Modus indisposed over some bad fish he'd eaten, so the boys had offered to drive him back to the College.

"You know boys, the last several times you came through here, I have had the uneasiest feeling. And now, Modus, too, with his increased number of comings and goings. If I were in a position to say it, I would say something was afoot. However, I am not, so think carefully about what it is you're up to, lads."

Good advice. For another time.

Before turning away, the Captain marked the Eagle on Thaddeus' shoulder. "What a handsome bird, lad. Reminds me of the falcons back home, though none there were near as beautiful."

"What does he say, Thaddeus, Sorcerer?" Osiric asked.

"He says you are a magnificent bird," Thaddeus replied.

"At last—someone with intelligence."

An idea began to form in Thaddeus' mind. "Captain Geoffrey, you may not have noticed, but this Eagle is blind. If you have but a moment, it is, I believe, a compelling story."

Quickly, Thaddeus sketched Osiric's history as he knew it.

The Captain seemed captivated by the tale. "What a moving piece you tell, Apprentice. You say his smell and hearing, then, have made up for the loss of his vision?"

"Aye, Captain. He's as good as he was, or better. My problem lies in the fact that a bird this grand should have the free sky, tall trees, and open forests and brooks; not be cooped up all day in some dingy, drafty dormitory room."

"Hmm. I think I see where this is heading. All right, I might consider keeping him here for you while you're at school, but have you asked His Highness how he might feel about it?"

"Um, I was just about to, actually."

Thaddeus turned his head to the bird. *"Osiric, Captain Geoffrey has taken quite a fancy to you and wonders if you should like to abide with him during the times I am at the Collegium? He said he would take over your care and see you get your fill of flying and hunting—a surfeit of which is here for you in this mountain range."*

"Hmm. That is a rather tempting offer, but my oath is to you and your mate alone, and I will give it to no other."

"Perhaps if it could be on the basis of a temporary loan, renewable at intervals?"

"Well, on that basis, we might be able to do business. He seems nice enough, though I suppose I cannot speak with him directly."

"Not directly, no."

"Ah, well, not every nest can be made of cedar buds. Very well, I accept."

"Excellent. I will tell the Captain. I do not know how I will summon you, though, should there be a need or to let you know I am coming."

"I have it. Should you need me, Thaddeus, Sorcerer, simply stroke the ancient Great Golden Crested Eagle feather you have. I will know, and I will come."

"Done."

"Done."

"Lord Geoffrey, he has agreed and, in fact, is very pleased."

"My thanks, then, lad. I will treasure this loan and care well for your bird."

"Nay, Lord, the thanks are mine. Farewell."

They were almost to the College, having met none of the *Aelvae,* and were becoming considerably anxious about it when their luck changed. They chanced across the half-*Aelvae* twins, who were also returning to the College from a family weekend. A number of questions were posed first, then followed the heart of the matter.

"I think there's something sinister to do with Porter Modus here, and it may involve Master Perditus," Thaddeus explained to Argentus and Platinus. "We are on our way to inform Master Silvestrus, but we have no wish to drag Modus through the school and create a commotion. Would the two of you be willing to watch guard over the porter while we fetch the Master? I think it will take all four of us to convince him to come."

"Aye, Thaddeus, we will aid you. But you must agree to tell us the tale when you are done. It must be a strange one indeed, and we want to hear it. Of course, if this takes a great deal of time, we will need to get word to Non-Dar as well. 'Tis his forest, after all."

"Very well. We are in your debt, and a story you are owed. Many thanks!"

Waving goodbye, the boys headed east in the cart, leaving the wagon, the old porter, and the twin half-*Aelvae* Apprentices behind.

Achieving the College, they deliberately took their time, appearing in no hurry. Asullus was stabled, brushed, fed, and bade Good Repose.

The four boys made their trip around to the east entrance and were met, as usual, by Lilyput, who seemed a bit subdued this night.

"Ah-heee! Back, are you? But safe and sound, are you? That is a question, is it not? No talk tonight. The Master has said you are to come to his study immediately." The green Goblin paused, dry-washing her hands. "I hear the wind blowing. I see a storm coming. And you four at the middle of it. How will it end, eh? That no one living knows. Go now; see the Master."

The Apprentices arrived at Master Silvestrus' study as the old man opened the door, surveyed the group, and pointed to Thaddeus.

"You, come with me. The rest of you, wait here for your turn."

23

The Loss of Three
Tres Pueri Perditi

haddeus spoke openly, leaving out nothing, however small the detail, from start to finish. Occasionally, the old Sorcerer interrupted him with a specific question.

"You say the dog ate your homework?" Silvestrus asked, incredulous.

"Um, yes, Master. But I have all the pieces."

"What a remarkable excuse. Very well, continue."

Daemon Morag's foot was planted squarely on Daemon Minor Charles' neck. Smoke rose from the contact. Waves of tremors ran over the smaller Daemon.

Master Perditus sat on a nearby stool, twirling his wispy beard, occasionally looking out of the top Tower windows at the blackening sky.

"Think you, Morag, he tells true?"

"I believe so, but whoever knows for certain with these scum. I detect no outward lie, but he is a sneaky sort and thinks a ziggurat represents a straight line."

"He knows the penalty if he plays false with you?"

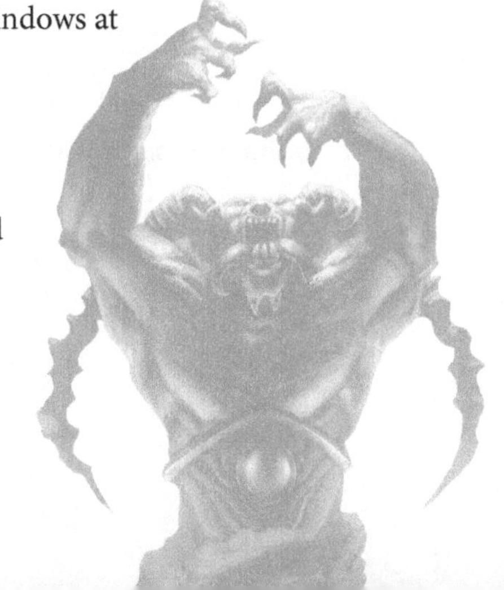

"Oh, yes, of a certainty." The larger Daemon grinned, fangs gleaming in the moonlight. "You want I should kill him now?"

"No. I think not. Old Silvestrus still may try to call upon him from time to time and will wonder what is afoot if he does not appear. The young one, though…."

Perditus left his stool and walked to one of the windows, gazing out for a time.

"Morag, let us do this. If you are able, compel this one to hide himself from the boy's summons. Perhaps he could abide for a time on the Ninth level, somewhere he could not be easily reached by the usual measures. Then, instruct him to avoid relating to Silvestrus what has just transpired with us. Can you do this?"

"It is a thing done already."

A half hour later, Charles knew his fate for certain if he should transgress, and a tangle of terrible spells and imprecations had been heaped upon him. Any perfidy would immediately transport him into the presence of an unhappy Morag. Charles would not be returning from that meeting.

Morag stepped back from his conjuring. "All is completed, Perditus."

The Sorcerer nodded, and Morag clapped his hands once. Charles disappeared in a puff of smoke. "Now, perhaps we should see if we have any better luck with our porter. You're certain you can safely leave the Tower?"

"Yes. At night, and only for short periods of time. My powers will be diminished but not absent. And I am constrained from appearing in my true form."

"Come, then, let us be gone."

The watch on duty at Mountaingaard decided he would not report seeing a man in Sorceror robes riding a winged goat streaking across the face of the half-moon.

Nor was Osiric able to recall the next morning why his sleep had been troubled and interrupted for a short period during the previous night.

Deep inside the forest, Silvestrus walked the gore-spattered ground, hands behind his back, lost in thought and concern.

Thaddeus and Rolland returned from their look-about and reported to Silvestrus. "We found nothing of the twins and no tracks leading in or out."

"Well, I must assume these remains are those of Modus," the old man said with a sigh. "That is the old cloak brooch he used to wear. A sad end for this servitor. I wonder what it was … a threat if he didn't or a reward if he did? We shall likely never know. Ah, well. The questions now are what is the fate of the twins, and what is the plan of the Sorcerer?"

Silvestrus continued to pace, speaking aloud as if marshaling his thoughts.

"I cannot, with success, approach Master Perditus privately or even with Master Beatus. He will be wary, perhaps even expecting something of the sort. It would result only in denials. He has grown too strong to bully, beguile, or bespell so easily. Aside from this, he may already have a rather powerful Daemon to call upon, even though it appears it is not yet fully in the moment with us. And I see nothing good coming from an all-out Sorcerous battle in the halls of the *Collegium* itself."

The pacing continued.

"Nor can I go to the Council at this time with nothing in my hands. Clever he is, and sorry am I for plucking him out of that pigsty village of his. If Hadrout and I hadn't been disagreeing with each other about whether a Centaur would condescend to give a ride, I might have been able to pay more attention to the warning signs I noted but did not attend to. *Harrumph!* But who can say? Was this meant to be? Prophecy versus random acts? *Pfah!* It makes my head ache. Ah, Gennie, where are ye, lass, when it would feel most good?" He sighed.

The boys listened with wonder at this candid and self-revealing rhetorical criticism. It was assuredly an uncommon event in their lives.

"Well, there's nothing for it but to go back to the College and watch and wait. This is becoming a game of dice. Move too quickly, and we expose ourselves and warn the perpetrator off. Move too slowly, and we have a band of Daemons running loose within our walls."

The old Sorcerer bent to pick up Modus' broach, then straightened, squaring his shoulders. "All right, lads, let us be off. There's much to do and a tightrope to walk. First, we will find Non-Dar to see what he knows of the twins, and then … well, we shall see."

Master Perditus sneered at the two *Tirones* secured before him on the floor of the Tower.

"Now, you two, here are some things for you to consider. First, there is no escape. I have warded this place, as has the Daemon beside me in his own fashion, specifically to prevent you from leaving this tower and forestalling anyone from coming here to rescue you. Of course, that would be unlikely in any case, as none there are who know you are missing, let alone would think to look to this Tower for you.

"Second, you should know you will die here. Three Sorcerous lives are required to accomplish a task this Daemon and I share. We have one already—that *Supremus Pila Ludere* fool. He should have remained disinterested in matters that did not concern him. That responsibility was his. Granted, you two simply happened to be in the wrong place at the wrong time. So, the responsibility for your fate is mine. Perhaps that knowledge will sustain you for a time. We shall see."

Master Perditus sneered a cruel smile and continued.

"Third. You will give us the information we desire. Now I know of the legendary courage and natural resistance of the *Aelvae* to coercion. Who does not know of it? It is described in tedious detail in all those tiresome epic fantastical tales. However, consider that you face a Master of the *Collegium Sorcerorum* and a genuine Daemon of the Inner Circle, Third Level. Against this, do not think to pit your negligible *Tirones* skills or *Aelvae* inheritance—half an *Aelvae* inheritance, to be precise. Be assured that the outcome is a foregone conclusion.

"Now, to save time, I will list what it is I want. That list includes you telling me what your fellow students and Porter Modus said to you earlier. Next, whatever the Apprentice, Thaddeus, and his colleagues have said to you concerning this Tower and me. And, lastly, anything of interest in these areas you may have heard from old Silvestrus."

Perditus waited for the twins to digest his demands.

"Provide this information freely and completely, and I will promise you both a quick death before hungry Morag here has his way with you. Resist or even hesitate, and … well, it will be more difficult. Morag, a small demonstration, if you please?"

The Daemon, grinning, strode forward, grasped the hand of Argentus, the half-*Aelvae,* and, spreading the boy's fingers by force, leaned over and bit off the smallest and began chewing it, making smacking noises of enjoyment.

Argentus tensed, looked straight ahead, and made no sound.

"Ah. Strong-hearted you are but let us see how much your strength will serve you against your love, one for the other. Allow me to explain. I will ask one of you a question. Any failure of response and Morag will feast on the other, a painful and bloody portion at a time. Let me think —how to know with whom to start? Ah, I have it—*Papyrus, Forfices, Saxum.*"

The ill-featured Sorcerer made a series of gestures with his hands.

"Very well, Apprentice Argentus, we will begin with you. Tell me what it is I wish to know. Now."

Dismissed at last from Master Silvestrus' study, the weary Apprentices trod back to their rooms, on the way bidding Good Repose to Zoarr.

Non-Dar had not been able to offer any information; he had not seen the twins that evening. But he told the old Sorcerer he would have his folk looking for any sign of them.

As Thaddeus approached his door, he found a surprise waiting. Curled up and sleeping in his doorway was a small white creature who looked familiar.

"Atreus?"

The small griffin started up, becoming instantly alert. "Ah, Apprentice Thaddeus. I have been waiting for you."

"Why are you here, Atreus? And what would you have of me?"

"I am here seeking employment, as we spoke of the other day. You see, my Master, the Captain … well, he left and has not been back. I-I no longer feel his life force. I fear he may be … may be … gone."

The griffin buried its head between its legs for several moments. Finally, it raised a tear-streaked visage. "He was a good Master, Captain, my Captain. He took me rabbit hunting and always saw to my needs."

"Atreus, what happened to him?"

"I do not know. I was hoping you would. After you came and spoke to him that time, he was quiet and never mentioned your visit for the longest span. Then one day, he came out. He said he was going to the Library and afterward to pay a call on an old acquaintance. And that was the last I saw of him. He never came back."

"Did he say who the acquaintance was?"

"No. He did not."

"Did you tell anyone?"

"Oh, yes. First, I told my fellow guardian colleagues, but they knew nothing of it. Then, finally, House-Mistress Lilyput came by, and I told her. Moments after that, Master Silvestrus was here, and I told him everything. He took it all in, then turned on his heel and stalked off. Then I just kept waiting—as guardians do—but my Captain never returned. And, after a while, I began to grow hungry, and lonely. And then I thought of you and our talk." The griffin sighed.

"Well, his room has been empty for many weeks now, and I have nowhere else to go. I am a guardian griffin, you know. It is what I do. But I have no one to guard, and I feel … I feel without a purpose. I am empty. I was hoping, perhaps…."

Thaddeus broke in. "Of course, Atreus. I would be honored to have you here. I will try to find you something to eat, and we will hunt rabbits as we can. I am not sure there will be much to guard here. I—and my Class, of course—are *Advenae* only and have little importance."

The griffin sat back on its haunches, cocked his head, and regarded the tall youth solemnly. "I think you have no idea. Anyone else, I would have said *false pride*. But you, my New Captain, I think you have no idea."

"Um, how is it, then, you do your guarding, Atreus?"

"You tell me whom you want in and whom you do not, and I sort them all out."

"Not to be personal, but if it were an intruder … a bigger person, or several at once, perhaps … how do you…?"

"Oh, that. Step back a five-pace." The griffin threw back its head and barked, *"Extende!"*

Immediately, a goodly portion of the hallway was filled with the great white bulk of a now-mighty and formidable griffin. Hands-length long talons and teeth gleamed in the torchlight, his mane and eyes

burned brightly with green fire, and hot breath bathed Thaddeus' face.
A deep bellowing roar raised the hackles on the boy's neck.

Up and down the *Tirones*' corridor, doors flew open, stayed so for
the briefest of moments, then slammed shut again—excepting Anders'
and Rolland's, which remained open but a crack.

"Thaddeus, are you all right?" came the two voices simultaneously.

"Yes. I am well."

"Oh. Very good," Anders said.

"Speak with you later, then," Rolland said hurriedly.

The pair of doors closed quickly.

"I take your point," Thaddeus said.

"Contrahe." The griffin rapidly returned to the size of a large cat.

"All right, Atreus. Come in with me. Let me see what I can find for
your Even-tide."

Anders stood in thought with his hand on the door lever. Thaddeus led a
most interesting life. He did not sound in distress. Indeed, he acted as if
huge white monsters in the hallway were everyday fare.

Anders reckoned he should check in on his Brother, but as long as
there was no sound of mayhem, he thought it wise to wait a bit.

He sat back down on his bed, trying to sort out recent events
and their meaning. All the humbly-jumbly going on was somewhat
upsetting, and he did not care for it. He preferred his course of events
to come in sequence, one at a time, with the leisure to digest each in
between. However, it seemed to him life rarely offered this option.

As he sat musing, waiting for whatever it was in front of Thaddeus'
door to go away, he regarded the mirror again. His efforts to plumb its
depths were beginning to yield fruit. He had even succeeded in conduct-
ing his reflecting glass research in such a way that did not automatically
trigger a visit from the green House-Mistress.

To accomplish this required not only a deft touch, as it were, but single-minded concentration. It was much as Rolland had described his method; an intense focus on the emanations to the exclusion of all else.

Well, no reason not to try now. It would be something to pass the time on the moon dial.

Now, look not at the mirror but into the mirror into the depths of the mirror. Let it absorb your complete attention, occupy all of your consciousness, squeezing all else aside.

Look deeper, deeper....

24

Into the Mirror I
Per Speculum I

nders began to feel there was little difference between himself and the mirror. They were as one.

He reached out his hand … *slowly, slowly….*

The surface of the glass seemed to ripple. *Like water….*

His finger touched, then went on through. Entranced, he extended his finger, then the other fingers, his hand, his wrist, his arm…. It was cold at first, then just cool.

Carefully he stood and moved forward. The surface yielded to his presence, thumbs-breadth by thumbs-breadth. Footstep by footstep, he crept into the mirror. *Slowly, slowly….*

Then he was through.

The light was dim, coming only from behind him. He turned and beheld the bright, albeit blurry rectangle of his room. Turning back, he stood still as his eyes adjusted slowly to the gloom. Passageways ran off to his right and left. In a flash of insight, he knew they flowed by the other Apprentices' rooms.

The floor of the passageway was made of stone, worn smooth with time and travel. The walls were great stone blocks as well, and the ceiling was an arch reaching twice Anders'

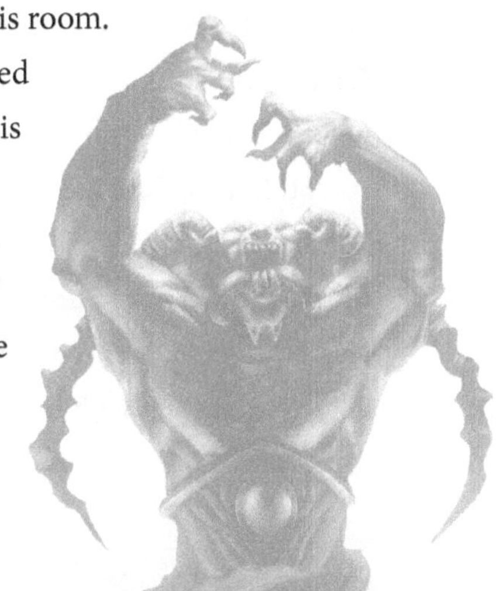

height. Sconces for torches stood out from the wall every twenty paces but were uniformly empty.

Most of the upper reaches of the ceiling were lost to cobwebs, though Anders could not imagine what fare the inhabitants dined on in this cold and dry-worked stone tunnel. His question answered itself, however, as a centipede scurried past on some business of its own, and farther down the passage lay a rat's skeleton.

Of greater interest, however, was the pattern of use, as described by the dust. Anders squatted down, peering at the floor. There were footprints in the dust, all of a uniform size. One individual, it seemed, splitting the middle of the passage. Occasionally, the steps would lead off to one of the lighted rooms and return.

He looked back over his shoulder. There, dimly, he could make out … a path going to his mirror! Chills ran down his back as a terrible suspicion began to form in the young scholar's mind.

Anders rose slowly and gazed around him. The passageway was deathly quiet. Summoning courage he was unsure he possessed, he started forward … *oh, so carefully … one soft footfall after another.*

He came abreast of the next lighted rectangle. He moved closer to the glass and peered through the bright, wavy outline. He gazed intently and made out details … furniture and figures.

Thaddeus was feeding a small white creature sitting on its haunches at his feet. Suddenly, both his tall friend and the beast looked at him. Or, at least, it seemed they had….

Probably just looking at the mirror.

Still, he backed away rapidly and turned from his Brother's room.

It was a decidedly odd feeling to be gazing into another's personal life. He knew it was rude, yet he was aware of a … curiosity. A chance to learn things. A chance to *know* things.

He struggled with himself, attempting to reason out his various impulses.

Finally, he decided he would not look. It was not his business, and he knew he would not wish to be watched by others. Once free of the internal struggle, he turned his energy to exploring the corridor in more detail, taking in all he could.

After a time, he came to a widening of the passageway, corresponding to the end of the *Advenae's* corridor. There, he discovered a skeleton lying on the floor.

This, however, was no rat but a full-bodied adult. Male, Anders thought, judging by the shape of the pelvis and the robust long bones.

It lay sprawled on its back, a small quarrel protruding from the skull's forehead. Only wisps of rotted cloth hinted that the figure had been clothed. A rich, strangely engraved ring holding a large crimson jewel adorned one skeletal finger. Anders could surmise nothing further from the remains other than they had been there for a long, long time.

A sudden thought stopped him. Would he be able to get back? He'd gone through the mirror without that much difficulty. But what if….

His ruminations were abruptly interrupted.

"Whooo-ooaaah-oooo...."

The hair on the back of his neck stood straight up. The call had come from down the wider hallway, followed then by a shuffling sound.

Something was moving in his direction....

Panic blanked his mind. Turning on his heels, he pounded back the way he'd come.

He skidded to a halt in front of his mirror, pushing forcefully on the unyielding surface with his finger, then harder, using his hand. Finally, he struck at it with his fist.

"Whoaahh-oooaahhh-aahhh...."

He looked to his left up the corridor.

There! A tall, thin, swaying shape dragging a foot that scraped on the stone was making its way toward him. The dim light from his room made it difficult to see with greater detail.

"Wooahh-ooo...."

The sound was coming closer.

"Open up, Gods-be-damned!" he cried out, striking the brightness with all his might. The result was unchanged.

The figure was now passing by the next light over, headed directly toward him. He yelped and ran further down the passageway for all his worth.

With a start, he banged his head smartly against the end of the corridor. Bright spots orbited his vision. He whirled around, his hand going frantically to his belt, fumbling out his knife, which slipped through his fingers and clattered to the cold stone somewhere at his feet.

The tall form was now just three paces away and coming on, then two....

He could see it clearly now. It was skeletal-thin with one long, bony arm outstretched before it. Its clothes were ragged, its hair matted, its beard was wispy, mouth gaping, eyes filmy, nose rotted....

A desperate idea darted into his mind.

"B-Brother Longbone! Lilyput has sent me!"

The twitching, filthy, clawed hand stopped a thumbs-breadth from his sweat-swathed face. Slow, raspy breaths blew a chill wind across his face, accompanied by the stench of decay.

The silence stretched out.

"Brother Longbone?"

An eternity passed. Anders' heart pounded in his chest.

"Whooooarreyoouuu...?"

"A-Anders of Brightfield. I'm an Apprentice. A *Tironis*."

The gaunt man's filmed-over eyes seemed to slowly focus on the trembling boy.

"Whaatdooyou here?"

"I have been trying to solve the mystery of the mirror. It's taken months. I had a feeling it was more than just a reflecting surface."

Slowly, slowly, the arm fell to the man's side.

Anders studied his face. Parchment-thin skin yielded to patches of bare bone on the forehead and cheekbones. The eyes were sunken and the ears were shriveled nubs.

"What of Lilyput?"

"She is our House-Mistress. She has told us often of Brother Longbone. She said if we misbehaved, he would come for us in the night."

What sounded like a dry chuckle rasped through the figure's cracked and shrunken lips.

"Yess. She would."

Anders relaxed a pinch. Perhaps he would not be summarily throttled by a ghoul in a magical labyrinth after all, at least not immediately.

"The way she talked of Brother Longbone coming … well, it was odd. It was never as if it was through the door but by some other means. After a while, I began to wonder if she meant he would come by the mirror."

"Clever boy." A dusty tongue swept over the thin-stripped lips.

"Pardon, and meaning no offense, but you are Brother Longbone, then?" Anders was prepared to bet "the house, but not my privates," as Rolland often said, that this was the very personage himself.

"Yes. Now. Not always…."

The apparition raised its hands for a moment, startling Anders, but only gazed at them before letting them fall again. He stared at the boy before him.

"You are the first in a long time. Maybe hundreds of years. I forget. How is Lilyput?" A tender note of regard had crept into the spectre's voice.

"She is well. She is very intelligent for a Goblin and very caring. In fact, we…."

"She's not, you know. Not really, that is."

"I am sorry. I do not understand your meaning. You say she is not really a Goblin? I thought—"

BROTHER LONGBONE'S TALE

Anders fell silent as the figure raised its hand again.

"Ah. I have not spoken of this in … in centuries … if truth be known." The creature seemed to be debating with himself, then arrived at a decision.

"All right. It is a long story and an old story. I will tell it to you if you wish to hear it. But you are, oh, so very young. And the patience of the young is like the stillness of a battle—there is none. I will understand if you do not want—"

"Oh, yes. Please. I would very much like to hear it."

"Very well … Anders, is it? Then come with me. It cannot be comfortable for you to stand where you stand and behold me as I am. Up the corridor a bit is a bench. It is stone and without cushions, but at least we may sit while we talk. I regret I have no refreshment to offer you, but I do not receive company so often, you see."

Anders blinked. One corner of the man's mouth twitched a hair. He thought the fellow might just have made a jest. He smiled. "I will follow you, then."

The figure turned and shuffled off. Anders trailed behind with rising excitement. He had begun to have an idea about what he was going to hear, and he was looking forward to seeing if any of his logical, though wild, speculations would prove to be true.

The old man passed by the arrowed skeleton without glancing at it and shuffled slowly on. Several paces further down the broader corridor brought them to an open area where two stone benches stood facing each other across the width of the atrium.

Brother Longbone gestured Anders to sit, and the boy did so.

The tall figure—scarcely a thumbs-breadth over Thaddeus in height—paced up and down while he spoke.

His speech was that of the old days. The very old days.

25

Into the Mirror II
Per Speculum II

The ancient, decaying figure gazed for a time at Anders before speaking. At first, his voice was raspy, as if long unused. But as he spoke, it became stronger, with more inflection, with memory, with feeling, with passion.

"I was once as you are now—an Apprentice newly come to the *Collegium.* But much was different in those days. All was new. There was no Mountaingaard. There was, however, the Empire and Sextus Arrius, the son of the Admiral of the Imperial Fleet, its Emperor. He ruled all the land from the Imperial Palace in Fornia. The *Pax Imperia* held sway throughout the various kingdoms and domains, and the Legions kept the peace. An unaccompanied virgin could walk from one end of the Empire to another without care or concern. I know this because my mother did it once and told me of it.

"In those days, there were fewer Sorcerers, but they walked more freely up and down the country, seeking students of talent—girls as well as boys. All became Apprentices, and all came here.

"There was no *Ludia,* then—no separate *Collegium.* Boys and girls learned together.

Relationships of lifelong duration were formed. A girl in my class—Lillia by name—caught my eye immediately. She was pert, spirited, and very beautiful. I despaired of ever attracting her attention, however. She was pursued by all the *Indigenae,* the Upperclass. But love has no reason, no rhyme, no logic. Over time, she came to seek me out, and I could not believe my good fortune. We talked and eventually shared our love, vowing to marry, and my happiness was complete.

"However, also at the *Collegium* at that time, came to power a new *Princeps Academiae*: Iusti Mores. He was the youngest Master yet elevated to that Chair. It was after the first year that he began to display an interest in my Lillia. In the beginning, she paid him no heed—the gestures, the extra conversations, the requests, the familiarity. I was confused. I did not think one in his position should behave in such a way.

"As the year wore on, he became bolder, and hints became requests. Expectations became demands. We did not know what to do. We felt we could not approach the members of the Council, who we thought would surely take his part and discount our testimony. So, we began to make plans to leave the *Academiae*—training or not.

"Around that time, I made an amazing discovery regarding the mirrors. The one you yourself have just made. I discovered their secret. I could go through them. I was very excited about this. I studied the phenomenon day and night. Finally, I made the breach and passed through.

"I began to explore up and down these very same corridors. And one night, not too far into our final year, I found Lillia's mirror. I passed through. She was surprised at first, then pleased. We spent the night together and then other nights as well, whenever our studies would permit—without detection.

"For some reason, she was never able to pass through the mirrors herself. On the other hand, there were many things she could do that I could not.

"One night, I was making my way to her mirror when I beheld a presence in front of her light. I recognized him at once. It was *Princeps* Iusti Mores. He was standing outside my Lillia's room staring through her mirror—just standing there and gazing into her quarters. Confused and in a rage, I fled back to my room.

"In those days, I had a gift for ingenuity, and I had crafted many simple tools with my hands through invention. One of these was a small hand-held cross-set bow that could shoot projectiles. It amused me to use it on the ravens and rats that have always populated this school.

"Upon reaching my room, I was angry, disoriented. I grabbed up the weapon, not knowing what I might intend, and headed back through the mirror. I came upon the *Princeps* still standing there, his aspect fixed. I had thought to surprise him and force him to leave, but, alas, he had known I was there from the beginning.

"Ah, Apprentice Longius," he said. "I see you have returned—to gaze at your lady, no doubt. Or … perhaps to offer me chastisement for my own indiscretion here? Well, no matter. You will, I think, be able to gaze all you want … *ha* … for some time to come."

"I flung imprecations and curses at him; all I could summon. But he was not *Princeps* for no reason. 'Silence!' he said, and it was so. He bound me where I stood, arms to my body, leg to leg. But I managed to keep a grip on my invention, though it seemed of little use at the moment.

"Then, he bade me 'watch and learn.' And putting first his hand, followed by the remainder of himself forward, he passed through into my darling's apartment. I could hear nothing in my ears, but I heard her scream in my mind. Next, I saw a flash of green light.

"Soon enough, his hand preceded the rest of him back through the glass, and he returned to me in the corridors behind the mirrors. He was alone. He stood looking at me with an odd expression on his face.

"He laughed for a moment and then spoke. 'Your lady said if I spared you, she would be mine. How heroic. How tiresome. I think, though, that I have a more interesting solution. She told me she had wished to marry you and to have children—many children. Well, now she will have all the children she could wish for, for a long, long time. Ha! It is, after all, our substance that is most important, yes? More so than our form, so superficial it is. Now your Lillia will stay put where she is. Perhaps a new name for her, yes? So, I have granted her wish.'

"He paused, I think, to gauge the effect of his words on me, then continued. 'Now to you. It would not be politic for me to have you telling tales concerning your *Princeps*. But I am no taker of life. So, what to do, what to do…. Ah, I have it. I see that you have taken a fancy to these dim halls? Your discovery, yes? Well, if you like them so much, you shall be able to have your fill of them. They will be like a family to you, and you their brother. They shall now be your home for a very long time, Apprentice Longius.'

"Then began his Sorcerous spell-weaving. This went on for what seemed the better part of an hour. I felt myself … changing. 'Now attend to me,' he bade me. 'You will roam these halls as you are now. You will require neither meat nor drink, nor rest or relief. You will draw what strength you need from those same mirrors you seem to cherish so. True, if others come to find you someday, they may be surprised at what they see. Ha! Old bones long before your time, they might say.'

"He laughed again. 'Oh, you will still be able to go into the mirrors, but not entirely through. You will never be able to touch anything in any of these rooms again—only through a glass skin if you please, which will stretch to cover you but never yield. You will be able to enter a room but never pass through the door—always encased in your crystal coating. You will be able to see everything, including her. And she will be able to see you—through a glass, darkly. But you will never touch each other again nor be free of this curse; unless, of course, I should decide to use my Talisman. And I do not foresee that happening in my lifetime.'

"He continued. 'But I am merciful, am I not? You will both live long lives—very long lives. Also, you will be free to roam these halls forever. And your lady … ah, she will roam her halls forever as well. But these halls shall never meet. Ah, this is delicious…. So, *Liberate!* You may go forth unimpeded. Begin your new life, Apprentice. And choose more wisely in the future. Ha!'

"He turned to go, but I called to him in my already raspy voice. 'Master!' I said. He turned around, a smile on his face, expecting pleading and groveling, I imagine. Instead, I held up my invention and pulled the trip pin. The bolt flew true and took him in the middle of his forehead."

"The skeleton in the corridor—just over there!" Anders exclaimed.

"Just so. 'Twas there he fell, and there he rotted. But it changed nothing. I am in here and cannot leave. She is out there and cannot change. Well, he was a powerful Sorcerer, to give him his due. Sometimes we gaze at each other through the mirrors."

"Has no one been able to give you succor?"

"None. Some few who have known of us have tried, but all have failed, even your Master Silvestrus. For a time, we believed he might free us, but all his efforts came to naught. We must always wait to be discovered; we cannot tell others of our plight or situation. And we know of no cure."

"What of the Talisman of which *Princeps Academiae* spoke?" Anders asked.

"None there are who can say what it may be. After *Princeps* Iusti Mores did not return, his study and rooms were searched, but nothing of it was ever found. So, I was reduced to frightening *Advenae* into getting to their cots on time and Lillia—Lilyput to you—to making beds and scrubbing chamber pots. Eventually, I think the Council began to understand what he had done, for it was afterward that the girls were sent West to found their own school. Perhaps it really was safer in that way."

"Um, Brother Longbone, if you were Apprenticed during the reign of Sextus Arrius, that would be…."

"Yes, a good long time. We had been already five hundred years under this curse when the cream of our legions went off to invade the East following the narcissist, Tyrannus Superbus.

"Later, a certain Ephemerus—one of the first Apprentices to attend the *Collegium* following the great Eastern disaster—authored a Prophecy that appeared to concern us during a brain fever he sustained. He said eventually one would come who would set us free; one of the yellow and black, though I know not the significance of it. But we have seen nothing of him for more than a millennium."

"How is it you keep your sanity, then? I cannot imagine the toll of such a curse."

"Oh, our *Princeps* was a crafty sort. He—among other things—caused it to be that we should both always remain sane; we can never retreat into the bliss of a lost mind. We can only survive and suffer."

"That is … that is *monstrous!* I cannot imagine how you can stand the pain."

"You are a kind and thoughtful lad, Anders of Brightfield. I suppose the answer is that one becomes accustomed to anything, given enough time. But it is my curse and my burden. So, I have told you a tale, a sad and dreary one, to be certain. Had I a wish, I would hear something of better cheer. Pray, tell me of yourself."

Anders spoke of his past, his present, his future, his dreams. And of his Brothers and their task.

"Ah, the *Circuitus Octipes Magnus.* That … that sounds of something I should know. Almost … almost…."

They spoke together for many hours until Anders' eyelids began to droop, and he was having trouble staying upright on the bench.

"I see I am keeping you from your bed. Forgive me. Fresh news and willing ears are a powerful narcotic against which I have little resistance.

Get you back to your room, Apprentice, and take your rest. And know you have the friendship of Brother Longbone."

Anders gratefully made his way back to his room, retrieving his knife from the stone floor where it had earlier fallen from his grip. Using his new technique, he passed through.

His excitement at his discovery almost succeeded in driving him to rouse his friends, but he knew he must rest. The hour was late, and the news could wait. It had, after all, been waiting for fifteen hundred years already. One more night should make no difference.

Later in the day, in the Tower, Master Perditus shifted in his seat regarding the broken table and empty, blood-spattered chairs. "Clearly, the others know, or soon will, then they will go to that meddler Silvestrus and the old fool, Beatus. Next, the Council will be raised against us."

"Those pups can be dealt with. I will go to them tonight in their rooms, and they will trouble us no more," the Daemon said, caressing his fangs with his long red tongue, drops of spittle falling on his gray-mottled chest.

"You present the same solution to every problem, Morag. Those rooms are warded. Such a presence as yours at their doors would alert everyone in the College, should you attempt this. No, I think, rather a different approach is required. At last, I think it is time we assay the Portal."

"And I have explained to you that the timing for that enterprise does not favor us. The moon is only half, not full. If we begin tonight, it will take longer and be much more difficult. Our best chance of success is to wait two weeks further. At that time, we will have the advantage— the moon full, my powers waxing. More of my tribe will be able to come through and sooner. Then all the Councils in the world will avail them nothing."

"I understand your words, but the situation will not wait. We must strike now—else all is lost. Send your signal to your warrior vassals to come forth. We will have use for them in the sacking of the *Collegium*. Next, come aid me, and we will begin."

"Very well, Perditus. It shall be as you say." As the Sorcerer turned to take several of his scrolls down from a locked cabinet, the Daemon regarded him with slitted eyes and spoke under his breath. "For now."

The diminutive green figure awaited the scholar's return.

"Ah-heee! You have discovered the secret of the mirrors, have you —that which I before told you to forego. And you return alive." The Goblin peered intently at the startled Apprentice.

"Lilyput! I have seen him, spoken with him; Brother Longbone! He-he told me everything. I-I am so sorry. I had no knowledge...."

"My wise, foolish boy ... oh, Anders. How was it any would know? Yet you ... wait!" Lilyput held up a restraining hand, cocking her head and sniffing the air.

"Ai-eee! It starts! Oh! Oh! Oh! Quick! Come with me now! You four ... you must be saved!" So saying, the House-Mistress grabbed Anders' hand and yanked him out of his room into the hall. She was amazingly strong.

In the corridor, Rolland and Zoarr stood, rubbing their eyes and yawning.

"What is it, Lilyput? Why have you awakened me and brought me here?" Zoarr asked, sounding more alert.

"Lilyput! You needn't have jerked my arm so hard, you know," Rolland complained, massaging his shoulder.

"Pssst! Put your words aside, all of you. To your Brother's room now!" With surprising ease, the Goblin shoved and dragged the three boys to stand in front of the small white creature curled up in front of the Beewickean's dormitory room.

"Atreus!" the Goblin commanded.

Immediately, the griffin sprang up, baring fangs and claws, looking about for enemies. "Yes, House-Mistress! What befalls?"

"There is no time for explanation! Pass these three into your Captain, then guard you the door against all comers. To the death. Understand you?"

"Yes, House-Mistress! To the death!" The door to Thaddeus' room banged open, revealing dark shadows and a form just sitting up, looking startled.

"You three—in there! Stay together. There's something ... *something*. I must go to the Masters. Oh, oh, oh! Too soon, too soon! Guard each one another. If the door starts to change...."

The Goblin paused with her hand on the old oak and looked over her shoulder. "I must go. Stay here! Be safe, my babes!"

With that, she slammed the door and was gone.

A muffled *"Extende!"* came from the hallway, then all was still.

"What in the Hells...," Rolland's voice whispered in the dark.

"Wait," Thaddeus' voice came. "I have my flint."

Sparks sputtered in the darkness, matched by sounds of stone striking stone. Then, a tiny glow, a gentle blowing, and a small flame revealing Thaddeus' face and his hand holding a candle sideways wick to fire. Once the candle lit, the tall Apprentice made his way around the room to the other candles, holding his hand in front of the wavering flame, lighting them one by one.

The boys took their accustomed seats and began to talk in hushed voices.

Abruptly, their speech was cut off by a high-pitched wailing sound, which seemed to come from everywhere at once, rising and falling in tone and intensity.

"What is happening now?" Rolland asked exasperatedly.

Zoarr moved to the door, placing his ear against it, then motioned Rolland to join him. "Lilyput said not to open the door, but let's see what we can hear."

Anders turned excitedly to Thaddeus. "I have seen Brother Longbone! I went through the mirror tonight. He and Lilyput—" The short scholar stopped, his jaw dropping open.

The door had begun to change, turning gray with a sheen to it, hardening.

It was—turning to stone!

Zoarr yelled. One side of his face was turning the same gray as the door.

The keening sound intensified.

Anders' eyes bulged. "Zoarr!" The ceiling nearest the door and the walls began to take on the same grayish sheen as well. The effect was spreading into the rest of the room.

Now Zoarr was half-stone.

Rolland cried out in alarm as he grabbed his Brother to pull him back from the threat. The hand he held on Zoarr's arm began to turn as well.

By this time, Zoarr was petrified. "Help!" the thief yelled, desperately attempting to tug away his hand.

Thaddeus immediately started forward, only to find Anders dragging on his arm.

"No, Thaddeus! Do not do it; 'tis a curse. I will help him. You— go through the mirror! Use the emanations! Find Brother Longbone. I know he will aid us! Leave now!"

"Anders!"

"Don't talk! Just go through the mirror. You are North. You must stay free!"

Saying this, the short boy threw himself at his half-stoned Brother, but as soon as he touched his arm, Anders, too, began to show the gray sheen, spreading quickly up to his shoulder.

"Go, Thaddeus! Through the mirror. Just concentrate on the emanations. Block all else from your mind. *Go!*"

Thaddeus turned away from his friends. It was the hardest thing he'd ever done, to leave his Brothers in peril. But Anders was Anders.

And Anders was never wrong.

26

Choices
Electiones

On impulse, he grabbed his backpack as if he was going on a journey and faced the mirror. He stared at it, concentrating, concentrating. After a moment, he saw the emanations. The surface of the mirror wavered as he reached out a trembling hand. The surface was cold to the touch. He pushed, and his finger went into the mirror, then his hand....

In a moment, he was in a dusty corridor, faintly illuminated by evenly spaced receding rectangles of light. He looked back and stared, astounded. All his Brothers were frozen, and the gray sheen was spreading toward the mirror's surface. Candles turned to stone and shelving, rugs, his cot.

He began running to his right down the hall. "Brother Longbone! Brother Longbone! Help us! Help us!"

Rounding a corner sharply, the tall Apprentice skidded to a halt in front of a living skeleton. Thaddeus jumped back with a yell.

"*I heard you coming,*" the gaunt figure said.

It took some moments for Thaddeus to get over the shock and speak. "Y-you heard me?"

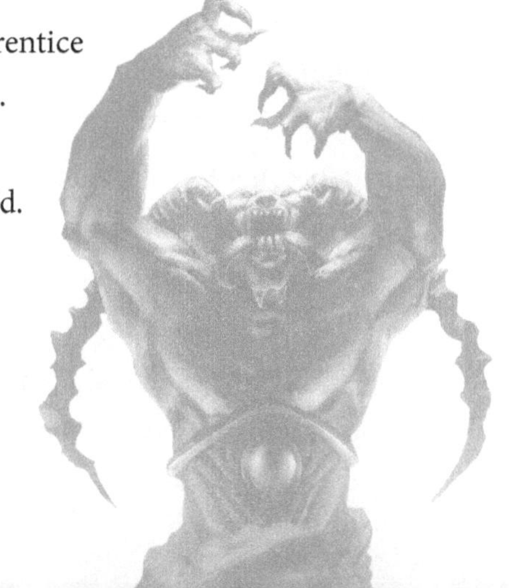

"Yes. I'm half dead, not half deaf." The creature grimaced with what Thaddeus took to be a smile.

"You are Brother Longbone?"

The head nodded slowly.

"I have been sent by Anders of Brightfield!"

"Yes," the man said. *"I thought you might be. Fifteen hundred years, nothing—then two at once. Interesting. What is the help you require?"*

"It's the room and my Brothers … they are turning to stone! You see, Lilyput shut us in our room and ran off, then…." Quickly, Thaddeus sketched the recent events.

"The room was turning to stone?"

"Yes."

"Just a moment." Brother Longbone cocked his head to one side and closed his sunken eyes. Abruptly his lids flew open. *"Ye Gods! All right, Thaddeus, come with me and do not get lost. Your life will depend upon it."*

The figure could not move very rapidly, but it moved determinedly. They trekked down several corridors, making a number of turns when Thaddeus noted the right-hand wall was taking on the grayish sheen. It was hard to make out in the dim light, not to mention that the walls were already made of stone. But the texture now was different. Different enough to notice.

Brother Longbone looked up to see the change as well. He spun around to face the boy.

"Thaddeus, listen to me! The cursed hourglass is our enemy! You must run. Run until your throat burns. Go up this corridor to the left until its end, then right, then left again. In time, you will see the passageway change to a small square opening, a pace on a side. Go into it. You will have to crawl on your hands and knees. Go to the end. You will have no light, but you will know when it ends; you will strike your head. It will seem like a dead end, but there is a way out. Simply…."

The figure looked up, then cocked its head again as if listening to something unseen. *"Go now! Fly! Go! I will do what I can."*

Thaddeus was off in a trice as if in a race against time, which he was. He followed the directions he'd been given and soon came to the small square opening. He dropped to his hands and knees and crawled along as fast as he could.

His arms and legs were screaming their displeasure at the abuse when he suddenly bumped his head. He had come to the end of the passageway, just as promised. He felt around. The tunnel ended, sealed off. He could not go forward, and he certainly did not wish to go back.

He thought to pound on the plate blocking his progress. It had a vibration to it as if it was not solid. He struck it with more force. It seemed to give a little. He hit it with all the strength he could summon in that awkward position. The barrier flew down, and fresh air flooded into the tunnel.

He crawled out. After a moment's disorientation, he realized he was outside. Stars shone in the night sky. He stood up, easing his cramped muscles.

Then came a familiar murmuring. He concentrated.

"….*in the Hells does he think he's doing breaking open the base of my pedestal? Why, I've a good mind to….*"

"*Alistair, hush! Terrible things are transpiring. Thaddeus! Thaddeus! Do you hear us?*"

"*Yes. Yes, I hear you.*"

"*What is happening to the school?*"

"*I don't know. The House-Mistress shooed us into our room. She seemed more than a little worried, almost frightened. Then the room started to turn to stone, and my friends as well.*"

"*Stone? Good! Nothing wrong with that.*"

"*Alistair! The boy's in trouble. Thaddeus, can you see what is happening now?*"

Thaddeus turned to gaze at the College by the light of the half-moon. The now silver-gray sheen was spreading out in all directions from the quadrangle.

"It's turning. It's all turning to stone!"

"Thaddeus, listen! You must get to a place of refuge—a magical place—lest you end as your friends!"

"But where? I don't…. Wait! I think…."

The tall boy knelt down quickly and undid his pack. He rummaged through its contents and exclaimed with relief when he found what he sought. He drew out the large brown-gold feather.

Silently he grasped it and closed his eyes tight in concentration.

I must get away. I must get away.

The world suddenly turned upside-down.

Once the wave of dizziness had passed, he opened his eyes.

Yes. It had worked!

Before him stood the sentinel *Orbis Magnus* with its imposing ring of stones, all fresh and gleaming. He stood and moved forward toward the inner circle.

He had not gone far into the second ring when a familiar voice called out behind him.

"Welcome, Traveler."

He turned.

Iam's peaceful countenance beamed up at him. "You have not, by chance, brought my orange blanket along, have you, now?" he asked. "I must admit I have been missing it."

Following the boy's greeting, Iam led the youth to a stone bench and bade him sit. Thaddeus declined refreshment and could hardly contain his impatience. At last, he was invited to speak, and he launched into his narrative of the night's strange and awful events. Iam allowed him to talk until he ran out of words.

"….and so I must return and help my friends and overcome the evil magic, and—"

"Forgive me, lad, but to cast a spell of that intensity in a place of such potent Sorcery would require rather significant power. It would almost have to be a power of Daemon-strength."

"Daemon-strength?"

"Yes. And, if that is so, charging back in a rush will only end with you becoming a Daemon's dinner. Let me think. You will need a plan and some rest."

"I cannot take a day for that, Iam. I must return immediately. There is no time!"

"Peace, Thaddeus, peace. You will have time. You will have all the time you need."

The false dawn began in the East as Thaddeus made his way away from the tumbled down, vine-invaded, ancient, and broken Ring. He had his day's rest, compliments of his kind host, but had returned to his own time in what seemed only hours after he'd left.

The forest and everything around him had transformed into gray-sheening stone. He made his way over the now rock-hard paths. It was deathly quiet.

A league into his journey, he passed a frozen faun, his hand only a thumbs-breadth from the figure of a fleeing nymph, her mouth open, though whether in a scream of pain or pleasure, he could not tell.

A short time later, the stillness was shattered by a shrill *skree!*

Thaddeus jerked his head up. There, a dot that became a speck that became a bird that became an Eagle—his Eagle.

Thaddeus called to the great predator.

"Osiric! I am here. Come to me. But have a care when you land. Everywhere is jagged stone." The Apprentice knelt and dug around in his pack until he found his shoulder leather, then put it on. In a moment,

the Eagle came gliding in and landing smoothly, a mere pace away from his Master.

"*Greetings, Thaddeus, Sorcerer. I felt your summons and have been looking for you since. Strange things transpire. Everything smells of dust. There is no sound. All feels hard.*"

"*A terrible curse has been laid on the Collegium, Osiric, and all is turned to stone.*"

Thaddeus quickly related his recent experiences, ending with their reunion.

"*Aye. This matches my experience. I was sleeping on my usual perch in a high cove of Arx Montium when I heard your call. I flew to the Collegium, but you were not there. I circled the area for a time, then flew back to the fortress to wait. As I passed over the forest, I heard wails rising up from below, then silence. It was all very odd.*

"*I had just regained my perch when the watch called out and sounded the bell of alarm. The men came rushing out of their barracks. I recognized Captain Geoffrey's voice organizing his troops. They spoke of the spread of a steely-gray sheen, stone-like, coming through the forest toward them. Within minutes, he had his men on the other side of the great gate and quick-marching down the hill. At a deafening, cracking sound, Geoffrey halted his men. The mighty gates were turning to stone. But there, the stone change stopped and spread no further. After a time, he went back to inspect the portus, then called the rest of the men to join him.*

"*Of a sudden, I felt your presence again and have now come to you as I said I would.*"

An idea that had been simmering in Thaddeus' mind for a time surfaced.

"*Osiric, I think Master Perditus has caused this curse to further some scheme of his. And I think he has the aid of the Daemon Morag.*"

"*Why consider you that?*" the bird asked.

Thaddeus outlined his thinking and waited for the Eagle's response.

"A fascinating tale. Perhaps he has chosen to act now before your reports would uncover him. If he has indeed turned all to stone, then he will have a free hand to work his will on the school and all its inhabitants as he wishes."

"Yes. That is why I must return and do what I can to disrupt his misdeeds."

"Very well. I will accompany you. Let us see what a blind Eagle and a fifteen-year-old Apprentice may do against the likes of a Master Sorcerer and a full-grown Daemon. Perhaps I shall fulfill my first wish after all."

"Your first wish?"

"Yes, to die quickly and join my mate. Either way...."

"Osiric!"

"Oh, very well. You proceed, and I will follow, scouting the forest from above."

Thaddeus resumed his march. Nothing had changed. All were stone. He passed two of the *Aelvae* on the path, both transformed into stone with looks of surprise writ large upon their faces.

The tall Apprentice was but a half-league from the meadow when his Eagle glided down smoothly to land several paces in front of him.

"There is a company of Goblins emerging from what I take to be a series of caves southwest from here."

"Goblins? How many, think you?"

"I would guess five hundred in all."

"How is it they are not stone themselves?"

"Perhaps they are in league with the Sorcerer and Daemon and thus protected in some way."

"Well, we will have to increase our pace then. If we can disrupt Perditus' plans, mayhap that troop will come to naught."

"Brave words but little sense, I think."

"My thanks for your support. Fly on."

"As you command, Lord Sorcerer."

Thaddeus reached the meadow clearing, skirting the forest's edge around to the southeast, farthest away from the Tower. He crept to the Gargoyle-guarded stairs as stealthily as he could manage, using what cover there was.

He swiveled around in his crouched position and sat down, putting his back to Alistair's pedestal. He opened his mind.

"...enough noise for twelve clumsy humans and all in plain sight. The boy has not a wit about him, Thra-gora."

"Alistair, some days you are simply impossible! Most days, actually. But hush, he is here. Thaddeus?"

"I am here. What has occurred since I left?"

"Not much. A lot of flashes, bangs, and bad smells coming from that tall red and yellow eyesore over there. Otherwise, quiet. Except for you."

"Thaddeus, have you seen anything?"

"Nothing different than here. The stone curse extends all the way to Mountaingaard, though not beyond. It has overcome the Aelvae and some of the Iron Company garrison. Oh, and Osiric, my Eagle, said some five hundred Goblins are making their way here from the Southwest."

"Goblins, eh? Perfect. Let them come. I have just the cure for Goblin infestations."

"Alistair. All know your prowess. Now be silent. What will you do now, Thaddeus?"

"I must achieve entry to the Tower, but I cannot simply walk up to it."

"Yes, you are correct. Thaddeus, go back in the tunnel the way you came. At its end, if you keep bearing to the left, you will find a passage that leads to the cellar under the Tower. There are stairs. Brother Longbone—"

"Thra-gora! We are forbidden from mention—"

"Alistair! There are times during which you almost subdue my patience. This is the gravest of emergencies! Brother Longbone will assist you, Thaddeus. So there, Alistair, I have said it. Fear you that we will be turned to rock?"

"Oh, ha. How amusing. Stupid pea—"

"Shush! Now, Thaddeus, be on your way. If a summoning is taking place in the Tower, then time flies indeed."

With a hurried thanks-be-to-you, Thaddeus crawled back into the tunnel and made his way toward the central passageway. As he struggled, doubled over, he thought furiously about what he would do when he arrived. Nothing occurred to him.

At the end, he scrambled out and found a tall skeletal figure awaiting him.

"Brother Longbone! You have not turned to stone. Are you well?"

"That is a relative question, Thaddeus, but no mind. As curses go, Mores' curse was one of the more complete sort. I am not sure I can be killed, at least not by ordinary Sorcerous means."

Thaddeus again detected a slight smile.

"What transpires above?"

Thaddeus reported on all he'd seen and heard.

"Ah, yes, the passageway under the Tower. Very well. I can guide you to that tunnel if you wish it, though I cannot enter it myself. It will be very perilous for you, lad. Are you certain you wish to try this?"

"I know of no other choice, Brother Longbone," the youth replied softly.

"No, I suppose no other choice would occur to you. Very well. Follow me."

The pair navigated the long-dead tunnels until Brother Longbone indicated a corridor on the left that did not seem to branch.

"There is your path if you choose it, lad."

"I will go, then. My thanks to you, Brother Longbone."

"Fortune and the Gods be with you, Thaddeus. I will await your return here."

27

The Loss of Belief
Fides Concidit

With a last wave, the youth turned and made his way up the dusty passageway. Turning a corner, he beheld a small antechamber and, directly opposite, stairs going up.

Climbing the stairs cautiously, he arrived at the main floor. The entrance door was to his left, with the stairs leading to the higher levels carved from the nearer wall. Against the far wall stood a decorative pedestal on top of which sat a severed head with drying black blood dripping down from the neck's stump to the pillar's base.

The head was green.

Emotionally numb, Thaddeus stumbled over to look at it.

"Oh, Lilyput, no…." Tears rose unbidden to his eyes, and he dashed them away with his hand. "No, no…."

The eyes flew open, and the mouth grinned a fearsome grin.

"Ah-heee! Young Apprentice making enough noise so those upstairs will come down and see him, then he can join Lilyput up here at her new post, eh?"

Thaddeus jumped back a pace. "Wha-what has happened to you? How is it you live?"

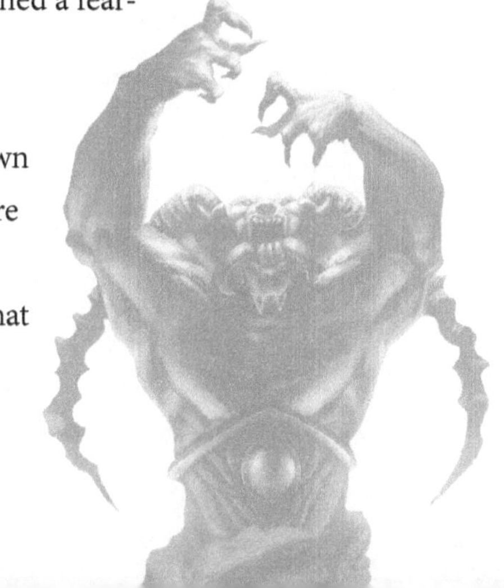

"Hah! I should think even slow-witted Apprentice can figure out what happened to Lilyput. Obvious, yes? How am I alive? Well, in usual way. Stupid Daemon thinks a simple talon swipe will snuff out life suffering under millennium-and-a-half curse? Poot! Daemon has no idea. To be safe, I play dead. Will wager the rest of Lilyput discarded out back window of Tower on refuse heap—probably in one piece. Daemon does not eat Goblin; he does not care for stringy meat. Lucky for Lilyput. After you do whatever you plan, just retrieve Lilyput carcass and fasten silly noggin to it, and House-Mistress should be once again ready to deal with fool Apprentices and all the rest."

"Oh, Lilyput … I am so glad you are alive!" the tall boy said, still awash with relief.

"Ah, sweet Thaddeus. You are the tender one. Apprenticiatrix Marsia has the luck of seven in having you, but this works in other direction as well, does it not? So, what is your plan?"

"Um…."

"Ah-heee! Why is Lilyput not a surprised Goblin? All right. Know you what they do upstairs?"

"No."

"So, beginning with basic things. Two are there at top. Lilyput has seen. Master Perditus—if were not head stuck on pedestal, would spit at his mention—and foul Daemon."

"Morag?"

"Ah. Yes. That was name Perditus addressed him with. How do you know that? Never minding now. All right. Know you what occurs above?"

"No."

"Ah-heee! Of course, why should you know … you are Apprentice only. All right. They are, together, opening Portal to other realm—Daemon realm. So they can…."

"…let the rest of the Daemons through to conquer and enslave the world," Thaddeus finished grimly.

"Hmm. Very good. Apprentice head useful for something other than separating ears or, like now, topping off pedestal. So, as even Apprentice can imagine, all Daemons running around world not a good idea, interfering with studies here at school and eating everyone. Now, question is: How to stop these two from opening Portal? Know you that, Apprentice?"

"No. No, I don't."

"Poot! Lilyput was hoping you would. Hmm, not so much advice to give, then." The old Goblin's eyes flicked first one way, then another. "Thaddeus, you do not have to go up. It may not be so bad. If you were to take Marsia and move far, far away…."

"No! I will not have Daemons here running about in our world. Not if I can do anything about it."

"Ah-heee! My brave boy. All right, then. Best be about whatever you're to be about. They are on the top floor, just the twain. A lot of smoke and arm waving and evil speaking. Hope you have better luck than Lilyput. I tried to stop them, but, alas, *Adversa Fortuna.*"

"I will do what I may, Lilyput."

"I know you will, sweet boy, though so far from home and alone and all is weighing on his shoulders … and so very young. But I know you will. Remember, as Masters say, all depends on Belief! Best go now, Thaddeus. Sooner better than another time."

"Farewell, Lilyput. I will be back for you."

"I will await you here. Ah-heee! Not going anywhere else is Lilyput in any case, eh?"

Breathing heavily, at last Thaddeus achieved the uppermost level. He'd encountered no hindrance on the way up the several flights of stairs.

Perhaps the pair of them at the top were comfortable in their power. Good. Sir Eques always said unwarranted overconfidence in an enemy was one's best ally.

The door to the top level was ajar. Lilyput was right. Lots of loud noises: explosions, wails, screams, and a fearsome wind blowing. Terrible smells, too, worse than rotten eggs. Lightning flashes, colors, and smoke.

And above it all, Thaddeus could hear a shrill chanting, high and piercing.

Thaddeus carefully and quietly pushed open the door just enough to admit himself.

Huge mirrors and prisms stood at every angle in the room, all turned to focus on a single point at the far end. A creature stood slouched in front of a section of curved tower wall, which was worked with several arcane symbols.

Thaddeus realized that the creature must be the Daemon, Morag.

He was taller than Charles by half, and his piggish eyes were all that was small about him. He was gray where Charles was brown, but, unlike Charles, he was winged. The Daemon had spikes, like oversized thorns, growing out of his shoulders, elbows, and knees. Unlike Charles, however, his feet were cloven rather than taloned. And he had four horns on his head rather than two.

The collected rays of the mirrors and prisms merged at the Daemon's chest and appeared to pass through and exit behind, striking an upside-down five-pointed figure, its center painted in what looked like blood. The light intensified and dimmed in a cycle, and the Daemon's body seemed to be doing the same in lockstep. One moment it appeared to be solid; the next, almost transparent. The Daemon, himself, was otherwise motionless as if transfixed.

Kneeling beside him, waving his arms, was Master Perditus. His whole attention seemed riveted on the wall, which now began to glow and dull in the same rhythm.

Thaddeus was entranced by the spectacle. It took him some effort to come to himself and recall the urgency of his task. He advanced, one hesitant step at a time, drawing closer, closer.

The Daemon's eyes stared straight ahead, unfocused.

Perditus appeared to concentrate solely on his Sorcerous task; the opening of a Portal to the world of Daemons.

Five paces … four … three.…

Master Perditus stopped his gesturing and chanting and let out a deep sigh. "Damnation! Must I be interrupted every five minutes? I shall surely have to start over again. What do you want, Thaddeus? Why do you come here?" he asked without turning around.

Startled, the tall Apprentice stopped abruptly and swallowed hard. "To … to convince you to stop, Master Perditus. This is an evil thing that you do this day. No one wants a world overrun with Daemons. Think of the horror, the destruction, the death. Why do you do this?"

"No system of rule is perfect, Apprentice. Some must suffer so that others of greater worth survive and thrive. This is the Rule of Merit, a part of Mother Nature's Law, not my own. As for the Daemons … well, they are a means to an end only and are easily controlled by those with the knowledge to do so."

"Master Perditus, I have spoken with another Daemon. He tells me your—Morag, is it?—flatters and beguiles you only to achieve that which he himself wishes. Then he will dispose of you."

"Oh, you must mean your little pet, Brown. Well, I shall deal with him later. I understand what you say, Thaddeus. And it is a reasonable concern for those less well steeped in Daemon lore than I. But you see, I have made this subject the center of all my waking energies for the past two decades, and I feel confident in what I know, never fear. In a short time, I shall rule the world with the aid of these, my obedient servants."

Master Perditus' eyes seemed to be losing some of their focus. A touch of foam flecked the Sorcerer's lips.

"Then I must oppose you, Perditus. You do not know what you do." With that, Thaddeus advanced yet another pace.

"I know more than you, *Septentrio*—Great Compass or not. Still, I cannot have you interfering with my plans further. So…."

With a dismissive flick of his hand and a clearly spoken *"Ligate!"* Thaddeus was caught, tied in bindings that slapped him hard against the wall behind. He could breathe and barely move his head but could make no other movement.

"You can make no Sorcery here, Apprentice, so do not frustrate yourself in the effort. Also, as I am sure you realize by now, with all turned to stone, calling out would be equally futile. Therefore, take what ease you may, and I shall open my mind to you. Speaking aloud helps organize my thoughts—that and the chance of an appreciative audience, captive or not. You see, vanity drives most things, Apprentice. The self is, after all, at the center of everything. Else why strive?

"Also, and perhaps not insignificantly, I am aware of the opportunity my genius—if you will—has afforded me. This is reality, and I know what I am about. Therefore, there will be a different outcome for me than for the *Cibus* in the stories.

"Let's see, where to begin? Ah, with motivation, of course. Mine is simple. I find little pleasure in human relationships. To me, they are unfulfilling and tend to end in frustration. My accomplishments, however—based on my rather significant intellect—provide me with much pleasure. The conceptualization of a goal—the organization, the journey toward that goal, and its achievement—is almost anticlimactic, as it were. These provide the sweet taste of life for me. But then, why not? Surely not everyone is meant to be a loyal comrade, loving husband, or patient father. Just as all are not meant to be judges, teachers, or Sorcerers, eh? Some must till the land, else none will eat, and some must cleanse the chamber pots, else plague will take us all. You see?

"Well, what of the means? A good question. Practicalities, after all, must overarch all theory; else everything is but an exercise. One might as well spend afternoons hypothesizing about the inconstancy of time and space. A thing that cannot be, after all.

"So, having completed my student studies in the main, I turned my attention to this Tower. Over time, I learned to reach out farther and farther. Then, one day … *contact*. I could hardly contain myself. I began to realize the power that could be available to me—the power to create, bend, or destroy—all the things one would generally think of, given these circumstances.

"Morag, of course, has his own agenda. He and his tribe have their appetites, and they wish to indulge them. They'd rather be free to eat us than each other. I gather they regard us much in the same way as we regard sheep or pigs. So, the promise of a change in diet was compelling, and, after a period of negotiation, we reached an accommodation.

"Now, do not be alarmed. I am fully aware that as soon as the Portal is open, he and his minions believe they will have us all for their larder, starting with me, I imagine. But I know something that he does not. Shall I share it with you? Ah, perhaps not. Who knows who may be listening, eh?

"Suffice it to say, I do not intend to end my days in the role of a wrapped item from a butcher's shop. True, the Daemons must have sustenance. Fortunately, the world is full of people. Some will have to be sacrificed, but there are some who we can spare. It will be no great task to decide who will have such honor. I have given it much thought over time, have made a list, and checked it over, not once but twice. I am content.

"So, my alliance with the Daemon horde has produced the means. I have learned much of their Magicks. They are, in their way, most compelling. It is amazing, is it not, the truly magnificent tasks one can complete with Belief? If you Believe it, it will occur. That old chestnut is still a wonder after all these years. More so now than ever before, in fact."

The Sorcerer paused and smiled to himself.

"Well, this has, believe it or not, been pleasant, Thaddeus. It is not so often I get the chance for this sort of self-indulgence. However, all good things do come to their end. I must now return to the task I was about when you interrupted me. Oh, I shall try to put in a good word for you with the Daemon horde. Hopefully, they will listen."

Perditus turned back to the wall, which had again become solid, and started speaking his incantations. Thaddeus thought he recognized some words, phrases of what was said. They made the hair on the back of his neck stand straight up.

Hours passed. By now, the wall was cycling back and forth—pulsating. With time, an image began to form on the wall. It became clearer and clearer. A smoking, burning land—yellow and red flames everywhere. Millions of Daemons striving, cursing, fighting, struggling.

Thaddeus recognized it—the Cauldron of Creation!

The Portal was opening. He must act!

He began to yell out phrases for the spells he knew and had read about. But all to no avail. It seemed as if the Daemon wind laughed at him.

Frantic, he sought to free himself, but his struggles led to the same result. Nothing changed. He pleaded with the Sorcerer's back, then threatened, cursed. But Master Perditus ignored him.

There … the Daemons in the Cauldron seemed to be aware of the Tower, of the opening Portal. They were crowding forward now, ever more insistent, eager. Soon they would begin to come through.

It was something Perditus had said: *Belief is the key. If you Believe it, it will occur.*

The First Principle he had ever learned. A desperate idea began to form in his mind. If that was so, then … yes, it must be! But what if … no time for doubts!

He began to concentrate, to order, to flog his will. If … then…. If … then….

If … then!

A scorching pain passed through his mind, searing his soul. He felt a great wrenching—it was splitting him in two! He yelled out in agony; the searing pain was intense, beyond mortal endurance.

He screamed the words aloud: ***"Mea ... Fides ... Concidit! I—Do—Not—Believe!"***

Never had he experienced burning like this before. The agonizing pain seared him to his soul.

He was losing, losing, losing—a last, ragged scream, and it was gone … ripped away from him entirely.

The Agony

28

Death of a Daemon
Mors Daemonis

Half-conscious, he panted, leaning against the wall for support, every extremity shaking.

He opened his eyes slowly. He was in a wide, circular room with many windows. A number of mirrors and framed panes of glass were scattered about, standing off the floor at random intervals.

A skinny, pockmarked man in a tattered robe was kneeling in front of a wall, waving his arms and speaking strange-sounding words. *Per … per … oh, yes, Perditus.*

Ah … it was he whose actions must be stopped from whatever he was doing.

With care, Thaddeus stepped away from the wall and looked about him. There—a broken table canted wildly to one side. Thaddeus walked over to it, bent, and picked up one of the solid oaken legs. Holding it firmly in his hand, he advanced purposefully on the kneeling figure.

The wall the skinny man faced had been painted in odd markings—glyphs that made no sense. Thaddeus reached the kneeling man's side, brandishing his improvised cudgel.

At the last minute, the figure whirled around to regard the boy. He looked surprised, startled … almost frightened. "No!" he shouted.

But it was too late. Thaddeus' arms came down in a high arc, and he smote the figure with a mighty strike to the side of the head. The man was lifted off the ground by the force of the blow and flew sideways, landing crumpled more than a pace away.

Thaddeus walked over to the prone figure and hit him once again for good measure.

There. That was better.

Then he dropped the table leg and walked slowly to one of the windows. Once there, he regarded the painfully brilliant blue sky.

It must be noon, he thought. He realized how tired he was—and how hungry as well. The sun shone brightly over the meadow.

It was a beautiful day.

The Daemon Morag jarred awake as if torn loose from a trance. Confused, he looked about himself.

Why was the fool, Perditus, lying unconscious with a broken piece from a table close by his head?

He glanced over his shoulder and wailed in despair. The Portal was closing!

"No!" he bellowed.

This was all the Sorcerer's fault….

He had warned him to wait for the proper auspices, and now he would rend the fool from nose to rectum. He would drown him in lakes of blood. He would … *wait.*

There, by the window….

The boy—the one they called North! Perhaps, somehow, this was his doing—impossible as it seemed.

"Ho, boy! Is this your work, worm? If so, you shall die horribly for it!"

But the youth did not respond.

Was he deaf? How dare he ignore a Daemon!

"Respond to me when I speak thus to you, Mortal!" Again, no acknowledgment.

This was preposterous! Did the boy not recognize his peril?

Well, there was only one thing for it.

He strode toward the youth. This would be over soon enough.

Outside the window, the stone curse was abating, streaming in an ever-accelerating wave, flowing away from the *Collegium* in all directions.

All the work! All the effort! These puny Sorcerers would pay dearly for this affront....

Morag raised his arm to strike. Still, the boy did not pay him a jot's worth of notice. It was almost as if the youth believed he wasn't there at all....

Morag swung his sharp-taloned hand down to rip open the boy's back. That would get his attention. But his hand passed through the Apprentice as if he were smoke.

Astounded, Morag staggered back. What sort of the blackest magic was this? He tried a second strike, and again, the boy paid no mind. It was as if the Daemon did not even exist for him.

The door burst open with great force, banging against the wall and splintering off its hinges. Morag turned in surprise to behold a mule, a small albino griffin, and another Daemon.

Oh, the pitiful Brown. This odd assortment had come to ... what? Save the boy? Save the day? Hah! This would be amusing indeed.

He grinned and licked his fangs. He'd deal with this lot, then return later to the problem of the boy.

"Hold, Daemon! Touch ye not yonder lad wi' yer filthy claws, lest ye regret yer birthin' day on the shat pile!"

"Ho! A mule with a wreath of weeds about its neck, a pale birth deviant, and a poor excuse for a minion of evil. Ha! Are you, then, the entertainment sent over from the carnival? Let me see, what shall I eat first? I think I shall start with the being that calls itself a Daemon and end with the bastard horse spawn for dessert." Cracking his knuckles, muscles rippling underneath his mottled skin, he moved purposefully toward the three.

Asullus nudged Charles before him with his head. The smaller Daemon seemed reluctant in the extreme. "Do no' forget yer oath, ye big, brown scaresome! Have at him, there! We're here wi' ye!" So saying, the mule threw back his head and called out, *"Commuta!"*

The white garland encircling Asullus' neck blazed forth brightly.

There no longer stood a mule but a large coal-black, horse-like creature with crimson eyes, great ragged bat-like wings, claws for hoofs, and saber-like pointed fangs. Roaring, the fire-horse expelled a train of yellow-orange flame, engulfing the Daemon, who flinched but came steadily on.

"Extende!" Suddenly the griffin seemed to fill the room, roaring and bellowing. "Oh Captain, my Captain, your succor is here!" Muscled claws and slavering fangs leaped at the stalking gray figure.

Charles flexed his muscles and tried to stand taller. Fiery beads of sweat stood out on his brow. He swallowed the lump in his throat. He hoped this would turn out well, but he was not altogether certasin, no, not certain at all.

It was all over rather quickly. Morag crouched down and stripped more of the remaining meat from the smaller Daemon's bones, collected in a heap on the floor before him. Chuckling, he gazed at the white griffin's broken body, neck at an odd angle, tongue ripped out, and throat torn open.

The old mule/ex-fire-horse lay moaning over against the wall. Morag had torn the silly flowers from around its neck and backhanded the beast into a wall. He would keep his word and eat him last. He always kept his word … when it was useful to do so.

After that, he would finish with that irritating boy, who still stood looking out the window.

Truly, what was that lad all about? Well, no matter.…

His ears pricked up as he heard a rush of feet up the stairs.

In the name of A, couldn't he finish a meal in peace.…

Several old men burst into the room, their brilliant robes shimmering with what must be Sorcerous work, and suddenly, flashes of lightning and entanglements were everywhere. Morag hardly had a chance to stand up again before one of the older men danced in front of him, weaving back and forth a glittering silver sword, chased with brightly burning, intricate markings. He recognized him.

"Silvestrus! Welcome to your dying time, Sorcerer. It is my lucky day at last!"

"I do not believe so, Morag! In fact.…" In a blur of speed, the old Sorcerer whirled, his sword extended before him. A thick *schiss*ing sound sliced through the room, and the Daemon's head flew from its shoulders, bouncing and skittering across the floor.

Morag's hands grabbed at his neck, which was spewing forth vast gouts of bloody black ichor. The Daemon remained upright for only a moment before toppling over backward, crashing onto the cold stone floor. It twitched for a moment, then lay still.

"….I think your luck has just come to its end."

Master Beatus limped over to the Daemon's head, carefully picked it up by one of the horns and took from his belt what appeared to be a long silver dagger, chased with many of the same symbols as were etched on the sword. He pierced the head's eyes, severed the tongue, and punctured the ears. "Can't be too careful," he announced to his colleagues.

Assuring himself the Daemon was no more, Silvestrus rushed over to where Thaddeus stood at the window, appearing bemused.

"Thaddeus, my boy! Are you all right?"

This was certainly an interesting place. He'd never seen a mule come indoors before, yet here the animal was. It looked familiar. Then it had stood up on its hind legs but eventually settled down against the far wall. Thaddeus supposed it must be sleeping.

Moments later, several old men came into the room from the stairwell. Their robes were old, faded, spotted, and soiled like those of that Perditus fellow he'd laid out a few minutes ago. The group of them appeared disheveled and unkempt—and in sore need of a bath.

He wrinkled his nose. His mother would never have allowed such vagabonds into the house.

They danced around in the middle of the room for a few moments. The tallest one had an old, tarnished sword that he waved to and fro for a time.

After a bit, the fellow put the sword down and approached him. He seemed familiar, too. *Oh, yes.* His name was Silvestrus. He was one of the leaders here at this place. The old man seemed concerned and called out to him.

"I-I am all right … um, Silvestrus? Yes, I am fine. But I am not sure what I am doing here. Can you tell me?"

The other old men had started to join the two, but the man named Silvestrus waved them off, staring at Thaddeus for a long moment.

"I see. Well, lad, I think I can explain. Why don't you walk with me outside? It is a sunny day, and I can tell you what I know."

"All right." Thaddeus followed the old man across the floor toward the stairs going down.

As he passed the mule, one of the other old men got up from where he'd knelt beside the animal and patted it. At once, the mule clambered to its feet. It looked at Thaddeus. In fact, its gaze followed him across the floor. That was remarkable—a barn animal inside a building who watched him. Perhaps it belonged to some traveling troupe and could do tricks.

Some fifty or sixty people were milling about the first floor as he and the old man made the last turn of the spiral stair. Some of the younger ones seemed to know him and called out as soon as they saw him, waving their arms. But Silvestrus raised his hands and ordered silence.

He then told the assembly that all was well but that Thaddeus had been through a strain and was not to be bothered for a time until they'd had a chance to talk. The crowd grew silent. The young boys looked concerned.

Silvestrus led him to the door leading out of the Tower but stopped and spoke to a marble pedestal on the near wall. Thaddeus thought this odd, but perhaps it was some sort of ritual one did in this place on entering or leaving a building. He could not catch the words the old man murmured exactly, but his tone seemed reassuring.

Silvestrus turned and motioned Thaddeus to accompany him outside. The afternoon was fair, and the boy felt his spirits lifting. The old man steered Thaddeus over to a park-like area he called the Commons and invited him to sit beneath a birdless cherry tree. Silvestrus plucked several of the fruit and offered them to the youth.

"Thaddeus, can you tell me what happened in that Tower this morning?"

"I-I am not sure. I remember walking up the steps looking for someone … that Perditus fellow, yes, that's it. I found him, and I knew he was doing something to try to hurt me and, I think, um, others and he had to be stopped. I remember standing in front of a wall. I saw the thin man kneeling there, waving his arms and shouting something. So, I walked up to him and hit him with a table leg—"

"Excuse me? You … hit him? With a table leg?"

"Yes. It was there and at hand. I remember feeling … angry. He said he was going to … hurt people. I feel a bit badly about it now. He is a smaller man, and perhaps it was not fair of me, my being bigger and all."

"Did anything go through your mind before you struck him?"

"I think … I don't remember. I-I feel, I feel that I … lost something."

"You lost something?"

"Yes. It feels like it was important, but I cannot remember what it was I lost."

The old man fell silent. After a moment, Thaddeus, who'd been gazing at the green forest beyond the meadow, looked back at him. Tears gleamed in the old man's eyes.

"I'm sorry, Ma—uh, sir. Did I say something wrong?"

"No, lad. It is I who am sorry—sorry for your loss."

"Can you tell me what it is I have lost?"

"Your Belief, Thaddeus. Your Belief in what you can do. Do you know the word *Sorcerer*?"

"Only from the stories my mother used to tell me."

"Well, to some, the stories are true. You, yourself, were a Sorcerer."

"Me? A Sorcerer? That does not seem possible."

"That, my boy, is what you have lost. Belief."

"I do not understand…."

"I believe I do. Thaddeus, as an Apprentice Sorcerer—one able to perform Sorcery—you went into the Tower to challenge a Master Sorcerer and a Major Daemon, who were working their Evil together. That upon which they worked was an attempt to open a Portal to the Daemon's world so that those *Inferni* might come into this world to work their havoc. You walked up the stairs to that Tower to interrupt them—and you did! And I think I know how you accomplished that. I think you ceased to Believe. You denied it. You gave it up. You sacrificed a part of yourself by denying your Belief in it.

"The pain must have been intense, beyond enduring. Therefore, you could no longer practice Sorcery, but, as a result—and, likely, the reason it occurred to a part of you to do it—you were no longer subject to any Sorcery, either the Sorcerer's or the Daemon's. In order to be affected by Sorcery, one apparently has to Believe that it exists. Otherwise, *sine qua nihil.* I once read a scroll about a somewhat similar situation that happened a long, long time ago. Not to the extent of yours, but in that direction."

The old man looked down, sighed deeply, and shook his head. When he raised his head, his eyes were shining, and he smiled at the boy with pride and affection.

"My dear Thaddeus, a terrible deed, undone by a terrible decision, freely given at a terrible cost…. By selflessly surrendering that living part of yourself—akin to ripping out your own heart—you have just saved the entire world!"

Outside the fortress at Mountaingaard, Geoffrey spoke to his soldier. "What make you of the gate, Sergeant Grunius?"

The grizzled veteran took down the spyglass and handed it back to his Captain.

"Aye, 'tis changed, Lord Geoffrey, as you said. It's lost that stony color and now looks as it always did."

"All right, Grunius. You remain here with the men. I intend to go inspect it. If all's well, I will wave my neck scarf, and you bring the men up."

"Aye, sir." The older man fisted his chest in salute.

The blond Captain cantered back up the winding trail to the great gate.

The Sergeant had it right. It looked as it always had. He assayed the sally port. It opened without difficulty. He gazed out over the forest to the *Collegium.* All the fires and fumes that had been shooting up in the air above the school had stopped, and the pall that had overlain all seemed to be dissipating.

The Captain took the steps up to the watchtower two at a time. Once there, he removed and then waved his red neckcloth. A short time later, his troops returned to the post, and his subalterns joined him atop the construct.

His hands on his hips as he surveyed the skies, Lord Geoffrey noted the Eagle's return. It had taken flight sometime earlier and was only now coming back to Mountaingaard. As it grew larger and larger, it cried out repeatedly, *skree*ing shrilly in a rhythmic beat.

That was unusual. The great bird flew down to just over his head, then swerved off and flew back in the direction of the *Collegium*. After only a moment, however, it turned, and came back, swooping low over his head again, still giving its insistent cry. It did this twice more before the garrison commander spoke.

"Sergeant!"

"Aye, Captain!"

"I believe Lord Osiric is telling us we should be on our way to the *Collegium*. Assemble all the men able to ride and get them on their horses. The rest will remain to guard the gate. We leave in five minutes. Full battle dress."

"Aye, sir! Best be prepared in case there's a row."

The Captain nodded and headed down the stairs. At the post, he swung onto his bay and cantered over to the assembly yard.

Sergeant Grunius called over his shoulder to his young second-in-command. "Corporal Marius! You heard the Captain … get all the men in their gear and mounted. We're leaving for the *Collegium*. Now!"

"What is it we're doing then, Sergeant? Helping the lads with their Headmaster?"

"Nay, Corporal. We are riding to the rescue!"

Cleansing the Land
Terra Purgata

ord Geoffrey's saddle creaked as he turned to observe Osiric's flight. Once again, the Eagle came winging in from the southwest with an insistent call.

"All right, Grunius," the Captain called over his shoulder. "It seems our Eagle's feathers are ruffled again. Send Renditius to check in that direction and report back."

"Aye, Captain." The Sergeant signaled the man. "He's on his way, sir."

The company was almost a league from the meadow, and the Captain expected answers soon. A few moments later, the thud of galloping hooves announced the scout's return, interrupting his train of thought.

"Cap'n," the man said breathlessly, "it's Goblins, sir! Shot at me, they did, with their little black barbed arrows. Got one stuck in my behinder, I think—or at least, it feels like it."

"How many and how far away?" Lord Geoffrey barked.

"As near as I can count, sir, close to half a thousand or so. Coming on quick, they are, straight for us. Be here in less than half an hour. Must have gotten wind of us somehow."

"Five hundred Goblins? Well, that'll be ten for each of us. We cannot draw them to the school, as we don't know the situation there. We must needs make a stand here. Very well, Renditius, good report. Get someone to tend your wound."

The Captain turned and gestured. "Sergeant Grunius, have the men dismount and get the horses back into those trees behind us with two or three men to guard them. Have everyone else deploy in two squads, each forming the wing of a chevron, facing in. I will take the right-hand group, you the left. The little Greenies will want to get at us, three or four of them to one of ours. They especially like to get behind, come at us from the rear, and will try to hamstring us with their axes. Have the men watch each other's backs and swat them off as they come on. Spread the word."

"Aye, Captain! All right, troops, dismount! We've got us some buggers coming hard, wanting us to end their lives, and we're going to oblige them! Follow, on my command!" the older man said, bawling out the orders to his charges.

The Iron Company assumed battle formation and had not long to wait before hundreds of small green Goblins poured out of the forest, rushing toward the men and voicing their eerie, high-pitched ululating call. Each green warrior bore a small round shield with a sigil on it and a piece of totem animal skin. Most wielded hand axes, though some had short swords, and a few, to their rear, fired cropped black arrows from short bows. The men tensed, holding their swords more tightly and gripping their shields more firmly.

The Goblin charge broke on the Iron Company's shield wall, and the hewing began in earnest. It was as Lord Geoffrey had said. The Goblins sought to work around behind the men to get at their legs while the men attempted to fend them off with arcing sword swipes. Although a man would go down from time to time—followed by a Goblin cheer— mostly the Goblins took the brunt of the battle, green heads and limbs flying off in all directions.

Time, however, favored the smaller, quicker, and more numerous green fighters. The Goblins could not overcome the lesser force as a mass, but, by sheer numbers, they could wear down the men forming the mass.

"Captain," Corporal Marius called out. "The men are tiring, but I see no end to the little bastards."

"Keep at your work, Corporal," Lord Geoffrey said, gutting his current adversary as another swarmed in to take its place. "We've no place to fall back to, and we cannot let them get to the *Collegium*. So, we will have to earn our pay today, however dearly it comes. Pass the word."

"Aye, Captain! We'll do our best, long as limb and heart allow."

The Captain himself had the same thought. No matter how much damage the men did, more Goblins joined the fray. The Goblin archers had drawn closer and began to take a toll. Mostly, the arrows bounced off the men's armor, but not always—and another soldier would go down, accompanied by the screeching Goblin cheers.

The men guarding the horses had their bows out as well, but they were only three in number, and after a time, they had expended their arrows. Lord Geoffrey began to consider the odd notion that he might not leave this clearing alive.

There! A nick on his calf—one of them had gotten through his guard. He was starting to tire. "Corporal! Signal Sergeant Grunius. Unite the two squads, and we'll make our stand with those oak trees to our back!"

"Aye, Captain! I will relay it. Captain, sir—just wanted to say it has been an honor, sir."

"You as well, Corporal, and the rest of the men. Now, let's be about it."

At that moment, above the clash of swords on axes and the crash of the blows to shields, came a high silvery note that wafted over the battlefield, sounding so pure and sweet that the fighters held their weapons still for several heartbeats and did not strike before beginning the melee again.

Now the horn—for Lord Geoffrey recognized its music—sounded again, much nearer. The next he knew, dozens of silver arrows flew from the trees skirting the battle glade to the North and fell among the enemy. Another volley arced up, over, and down among the green ranks. The Goblins fell in numbers. Then another volley. Now, fewer than half their number stood.

The Goblin leader, who had been encouraging his troop from the rear, screamed curses in frustration, so intent had he been on over-whelming the men.

Another volley flew, and then still another.

The Goblin leader shrieked again, and the remaining Goblins broke ranks and ran back the way they'd come, with more volleys whistling after them.

At the same moment, an invisible wave, flowing outward from the College toward *Arx Montium* past the troops, turned the stone foliage back to its original green lushness.

At that moment, the archers emerged from the forest, advancing, drawing, and shooting their arrows as they came.

One of the silver-haired forces, slightly taller than the rest, detached himself from his ranks and sought out the Captain.

Lord Geoffrey strode forward to greet the ear-pointed *Aelvae*, clasping the newcomer's arm with enthusiasm. "Ha! Well timed, Lord Non-Dar, and well done! We were beginning to feel a bit stretched. How did you manage to drive off the Goblins and change the scenery simultaneously?"

"*Ave*, Lord Geoffrey of the Broom! We thought only to be of assistance in clearing the land of these pests. The remainder of what has occurred is beyond us. But know you where these Goblins are headed? For I'm of a mind to pursue and let none escape. I have taken it as a personal insult that they have come and sullied our woods."

"They go Southwest, I believe, toward the caves from whence they emerged, I wager. Though I am most curious as to how they came to be there at the first."

"It is Evil Sorcery for certain, Captain. Know you anything of events at the *Collegium?*"

"Nay, I do not. I am somewhat torn as to whether to make all haste there and see to setting things aright if needs be. Yet, I share your thought and am especially reluctant to leave even the remains of this troop to our rear. Since some have come, others may come. And I have no wish to either lead the beasties to the *Collegium* or have a new batch of them fall upon us from behind."

"Then we are in accord, Lord. Let us join forces and see these few into the earth, leaving their masters to pause and wonder."

"Agreed. If you wish to set out after their host now, I will see to our wounded. Once mounted up, we will rejoin you shortly."

Each acknowledged the other with a nod of respect and set to their separate tasks. Soon enough, the Iron Company had caught up with the fleet-footed *Aelvae* in pursuit of the Goblin remainder, which Lord Geoffrey estimated as, perhaps, a third of the original number.

However, the Goblins were the fleetest of all two-footed beings, and within a short time, had outpaced their pursuers. As the men and *Aelvae* approached the Southwest caves, the sky ahead of them erupted with great bursts of light—reds, oranges, yellows—followed within seconds by great roars, booms, and crashes. In moments, dark clouds formed, and bolts of lightning blazed and flashed, followed by earsplitting, thunderous detonations.

The party halted at the crest of a low rise to survey the scene before them.

"Sergeant Gruntius, the glass," Lord Geoffrey said, extending his hand.

"Aye, Captain." The old soldier retrieved a worn brown leather cylinder from his saddle pouch. He opened the case and passed the scratched brass tube to his commander.

Lord Geoffrey stood in his stirrups and focused the spyglass on the area of greatest meteorologic activity. He was silent a moment,

COMPANY STANDS

then a dry chuckle escaped his lips. He handed the glass down to Lord Non-Dar, who put his eye to the lens and gazed at the not-too-distant mayhem. After a moment, the *Aelvae* smiled and passed the glass back to the human Lord.

"What is it, Captain? What occurs?" the Sergeant asked.

"Here, look for yourself, Grunius," Lord Geoffrey said, passing the glass back to the older man. "And tell us what it is you see, Sergeant."

The grizzled veteran took a long turn at the glass. Finally, he put the brass tube down.

"Well, Captain, to put words to it, as you ordered, I do see a company of those little Greenies—a hundred or two, I'd say—milling about down in the hollow. Each one of them not already on fire is either exploding before my eyes or being torn in two by unseen forces. But most interesting of all is that—in the very middle of all the commotion—there appear to be four very pissed-orff Sorceresses."

Having wended his way down from the school, Silvestrus sat on the old cart seat, smoking his pipe and patiently awaiting whomever—or whatever—the path from the forest would bring.

He'd noted the sky display in the direction of the Southwest caves and considered it likely to be yet another interesting event in an already interesting day. He had a suspicion about what had occurred, but....

Asullus' ears pricked up. "Aye, Master, we're aboot to be receivin' company is me guess." The old mule sniffed the air. "Friends it is, an' welcome they be."

Within moments, the jingle of horses' bridles and the soft thud of hoofbeats on the mossy forest floor sounded clearly. Soon enough, a diverse party emerged from the surrounding green.

Lord Geoffrey, straight and tall in his saddle, an Eagle circling overhead, and beside him, Geannie rode easily with three—no, four—of her girls. The Four Girls, actually.

Little surprise there....

Perhaps thirty men-at-arms of the Iron Company accompanied the Captain, and to the side were Non-Dar and an equal number of *Aelvae.*

For certain, this day was going to be a Remembering Day.

In the Tower, Master Celsius carefully examined the positioning of the torso. Finally satisfied, he nodded to Master Beatus, who signaled the healer to apply the head to the body. The Master aligned the severed parts of the neck, with Lilyput giving advice and commentary throughout the procedure. At last, he rose and stood back.

As soon as the fleshy parts were in proximity, tendrils began to extend from each stump toward the other, and the neck and torso quickly knitted themselves together. Within moments, no evidence of injury was visible. Soon after, the Goblin rose carefully to all fours and shook her head.

"At least it didn't fall off," Rolland commented to his short scholarly friend.

"Ah-heee! That I heard, poor excuse for an Apprentice with room always messy! Wait you a moment longer until Lilyput is stitched whole again, and we shall see what it is will fall off then, eh?"

Slowly, the Goblin straightened and moved to push herself to a standing position. Zoarr strode forward and took her elbow to assist.

Lilyput's head came up with her usual hideous smile. "Fair manners, oh Prince. Something to teach backward barbarian Brothers, I think. My thanks."

Zoarr stepped back a pace, leaving Lilyput standing easily. A rousing cheer issued from the assembled Apprentices and Faculty. Master Beatus came forward, looked her over, and gave her a wink while Master Celsius pronounced her whole and hale as ever.

More cheering.

The Goblin House-Mistress gave a girlish curtsy, obviously pleased.

"Ah-heee! Grateful it is I am for these old bones and these new friends. You will not say it, I wager, but Lilyput has lived long enough of time to know love when it swims around her, nipping at her toes. Wanting all to know, feeling is returned to each and every one.

"Now, Lilyput is certain her recent indisposition has left all in disarray, which means more work for House-Mistress, of course. So, if Apprentices will make way, Lilyput will return to her duties, working all day, never resting—as always."

30

The Secret of the Mirror
Speculum Arcanum

The House-Mistress went about greeting those who had gathered, nodding and bobbing her head, partly in gratitude, Anders thought, but partly also to make sure of its sturdy connections.

"Anders," Rolland said, "come on. Zoarr and I are going to try—again—to talk some sense into Thaddeus. Maybe he has a brain fever or is otherwise ill."

"No. You two go on ahead. I will join you anon."

Rolland looked skeptically at his short friend, but Zoarr gently drew the redhead away, leaving their Brother to his own devices.

After the others had finally dispersed, Lilyput approached the young scholar.

"Ah-heee! Clever Anders does little without purpose, Lilyput knows. What do you wish to say to this green Goblin, young Apprentice?"

"Um, that may be the point, House-Mistress—your Goblin-hood, I mean. That is to say, I have been thinking about some things, and … I have an idea. I would like to try an experiment. But I need you to come to my room for a moment if you are willing."

"Hmm, young scholar leaves out many details concerning his intentions, yet would Lilyput trust him with her life? Actually, she has, as a matter of fact. All right, *Occidus*, you have roused Lilyput's curiosity, so let us see where it will lead, eh?"

The odd pair made its way from the back of the Tower to the *Collegium* entrance and up to the *Tirones* quarters and thence down the hall to Anders' room.

The boy set his palm to the brass door plate, and the old oak portal swung open. Anders gestured Lilyput in, and he followed. The room was dark, and Anders was searching for his flint kit when the House-Mistress clapped her hands sharply, and all the candles sprang to life.

"Um, thank you, House-Mistress."

"Welcome be you, Apprentice. Now what have you in store for Lilyput she has not seen before, for I am thinking this is something special with a mysterious part to it, eh?"

"I hope it will be special, Lilyput. Now wait here, please. I must get something, and it may take some moments."

"I will await you," Lilyput replied serenely.

Anders approached his mirror, let out a deep sigh, and then focused his attention, concentrating on the glass's surface … looking at it, looking into it, looking through it. He put out his hand and slowly extended his finger. Closer, closer … contact … and then through.

Behind him, Lilyput gasped.

Within a moment, he was once again in the dusty corridor, gazing up and down the passageway, waiting for his eyes to adjust to the gloom.

"Brother Longbone? Brother Longbone?" Anders strode forward in the direction of the stone bench he'd previously shared with the spectre.

As he came to the hallway skeleton, he knelt down, looking for what he sought. He hoped the idea that had earlier occurred to him would bear the right fruit. Standing up a moment later, he proceeded around the outer ring of the corridor, calling Brother Longbone's name every ten paces.

He was nearing the area he thought must lead to the Daemon Tower when, at last, he heard a response.

"I am here, Anders of Brightfield," a raspy voice called.

"Brother Longbone! I did not expect to see you at this place."

"I was waiting for your colleague, Thaddeus, but he has not come. Know you of his fate?" The skeletal figure lowered his voice. "Did the Daemon have the advantage of him, then?"

"No, Brother Longbone. After Thaddeus left you, he went into the Tower and confronted Master Perditus and the Daemon Morag." Anders didn't think there was any point in telling the skeletal form of Lilyput's decapitation, however briefly it had lasted. "He defeated the Sorcerer, after which the curse on the *Collegium* was lifted. Then Master Silvestrus was able to overcome the Daemon."

"How was it Thaddeus could vanquish such a powerful Sorcerer?"

"Perditus had bound him, but Thaddeus freed himself and hit the Master on the head with a table leg."

"A table leg? Truly? Ha! Good. But wait—how did he free himself from the Master's spell? To do such is no small feat."

"Silvestrus explained that … he, um … gave up his Belief." Anders glanced away before speaking again. "He gave up his Sorcery. He stopped Believing. Then he was free. He saw no Sorcery and was, therefore, subject to no Sorcery. He cannot see, hear, or touch any Sorcerous creatures or objects, and the same, them to him. To him, Asullus is a mule only, and Osiric a bird only. He could not detect the Daemon, and, in turn, he was not affected by anything it did or said. Very little memory of his Sorcerous life remains. He even had trouble remembering us at first. He discounts all our spell-work and anything 'superstitious,' he calls it. He cannot even see Lilyput. It's as if he has surrendered his Faith."

"Ah. I wonder if he realized beforehand that he would be fated thus?"

"I do not know. But I think it would have made no difference."

"No, I suppose it would not have. Have any of his Masters said whether his condition might be reversed?"

"They seem unsure of what to do. Before Master Silvestrus left to investigate some trouble in the wood, he thought it might be an issue to be addressed by the Council."

"I see. Well, you live in interesting times, scholar. But that does not explain why you have come seeking me, young Anders."

"Brother Longbone. I-I think I may have a way to make things, um, better for you. But to test my idea, I must have you accompany me. If you are willing, of course."

A flicker of curiosity stirred across the rotted visage.

"You lads have turned my life—such as it is—upside down in this short space. I am not sure to what account, but I am game. Lay on, Anders of Brightfield. I shall follow apace."

Anders led the spectral figure back to the pale rectangle of his mirror.

"Abide here yet a moment, Brother Longbone."

"Hold, Anders. Is that Lilyput I see through the glass? I know not what you intend but be aware that many diverse remedies have been applied to us in the past and none with any success."

"I understand. But please be patient if you will, sir. I have a feeling…." With that, the distiller's son put out his hand and eased back through the surface of the mirror with a practiced motion.

"Ah-heee! Clever Anders returns after a protracted absence, serving only to deepen this mystery. What occurs, then?" Lilyput sounded curious.

"Lilyput, please trust me. I am about to assay a task with which I have no experience and many doubts. It may all come to naught and serve only to have wasted a portion of your afternoon."

"Who it is could resist such an encouraging prologue? What need you of me?"

"House-Mistress, if you will but stand here close to the mirror…."

"Ah-heee! These old eyes see a form through the glass. There is only one that could be. What do you mean to do here, Anders?" Her eyes narrowed in suspicion.

"Please, let me but continue." So saying, Anders reached into his pocket and donned the object in which he'd recently come to place such desperate hope, which had long ago belonged to a high *Princeps* of the school.

"Now, Lilyput, I must needs hold your hand, if you will allow it."

The Goblin extended her bony extremity, and Anders grasped it carefully. It was shriveled and cold to the touch.

"Now, please wait but a moment longer. I must go a way into the mirror."

"That strategy has been tried before, boy, with no...."

"Please, House-Mistress. Just a moment longer," he interrupted.

With his free hand, he reached toward the mirror, concentrating. After a second, his finger, followed by his hand, slid into the glass and through it.

However, he stopped halfway, one foot in either world. He turned his face to Brother Longbone. The skeletal form regarded him carefully.

"What transpires now, Anders of Brightfield?"

"Much, I hope, Brother Longbone, though I am uncertain. Please, grasp my free hand."

As Anders extended his arm toward the walking skeleton, a faint pale light glinted off a red jewel affixed to the boy's finger.

Brother Longbone's hand slowly reached to clasp the young scholar's. The sensation in Anders' hand was even stranger than that of holding the Goblin's—and not the least bit pleasant. The touch sent shivers up his spine.

"I see you wear old Iusti Mores' ring, lad. Have you taken to fashion, then?"

"It is an idea—a premonition if you wish. Now face about here, please."

As soon as Anders' hand made contact with Brother Longbone's, the Sorcerer's ring on the boy's finger began to glow with a rapidly intensifying ruby brilliance—brighter and brighter.

"Do not let go!" Anders called to the spectral man. He turned his head to the left, and his face broke the plane of the mirror in his room.

"What happens, Anders? What is that red light?" the Goblin asked.

"Do not let go, Lilyput!"

The glow became brighter and brighter, almost painful to look at. It started to pulsate, and a low thrumming noise began to issue from Anders' hand.

"Hold fast! Do not release me!" Anders called to the twain.

Pressure began to build, and the light and noise increased.

Anders pressed his face back through the mirror to the dusty corridor. "Now, Brother Longbone, come you to me!" Anders commanded as he began to move through the mirror, becoming sweaty with the effort, attaining his room gradually, pulling the tall spirit behind him.

The mirrored surface clung to Brother Longbone, stubbornly refusing to surrender its hold on him. The pressure increased, but Anders pulled steadfastly, gaining a bit at a time.

Now some of the glass coating relented, and Brother Longbone's thumb and index finger, still grasping Anders' hand, pulled free of their silver casing. Very slowly, his other fingers shed their shiny encasement, like sticky swamp mud reluctantly surrendering its catch.

Then a hand … an arm … followed by the rest of him….

Without warning, the glass released him, and the three flew off-balance, almost falling yet still managing to maintain their desperate grasp on Anders and his on them.

Suddenly the Goblin and Skeleton were regarding each other directly for the first time in a thousand and a half years.

"Longius!"

"Lillia!"

"Wait…." cried Anders. The ring's brightness filled the room, and the pulsing sound was almost deafening. "There is more! Wait! Join hands—*now!*"

Each figure reached forth a trembling hand that closed one on the other.

"Now!" Anders cried and suddenly let loose his grip on the pair.

A great flash of ruby-red fire burst forth in the room and just as suddenly died away. The noise ceased, as did the pulsing and pressure.

However, further changes were taking place.

Brother Longbone's face and frame began to fill out, his matted hair and beard retracted, flesh covered his bones, and signs of unthinkable age reversed. Soon a tall, young man with dark brown hair and light brown eyes of fair mien and aspect stood in front of Anders, his eyes full of the creature in front of him.

And that creature, too, was changing. Though not gaining height, the green skin gave way to a milk-toned complexion, eyes of brightest green, and light brown hair with the most numerous curls Anders had ever seen. Her lips were full, and her smile warm and radiant.

The couple's other hands joined and they stood rooted, staring at each other. Suddenly, Longius picked up his Lillia and swept her around, placing her gently down again. He let out a rich, deep laugh, and she laughed in return. Tears sprang to her eyes, then to his, and they wept and they laughed, and wept and laughed, holding and looking at each other.

Tears were coursing unashamedly down Anders' cheeks as well, and he let them flow unchecked. After a time, once he was able, he managed to speak.

"Well, I-I have something I should see to … I will leave you tw—"

Two heads snapped to look at the boy as if seeing him for the first time. Both Lillia and Longius held out their arms, and Anders was engulfed in their joint embrace. And all three laughed and cried and laughed and cried for a long, long time.

A pounding came at the door, accompanied by a muffled call. "Anders! Open! Are you well, Anders? Open!"

Anders came to himself, went to the door, and opened it a handsbreadth.

Rolland peered intently at his Brother. "What passes? Your eyes are full of tears. Have you been injured?" His voice held concern.

"No, no. I am well. I just put some pepper in my eye, and it stings."

"Well, of course it stings, Anders. Why would you do that? That was ill-considered. Are you certain you are all right?"

"Yes, yes. It was just an experiment. Why do you come?"

"Oh. There's a big commotion. Afarius said there's some sort of parade coming out of the woods, and we should see it. Zoarr's already gone on with Thaddeus."

"All right. I will join you shortly. Give me a moment to wash my face." So saying, he shut the door. He disliked lying to his Brother but thought it was not yet time for the College to learn the secret of Brother Longbone and the Goblin Lilyput. There would be more than enough opportunity for that later.

"Um, Longius, Lillia, I must go now. If I do not, it will only draw curious eyes here. I advise you to remain in the room this little while. You have need of some private time. Stay here as long as you wish. None will disturb you. I … well … 'tis glad I am to see you as you are. I must go now." Anders turned to leave.

Lillia plucked at his sleeve. "Dear Anders. You have saved us … and saved us well. I do not know what—"

"Anders of Brightfield," Longius broke in, bending a knee before the youth. "Hear me now. I pledge my service to you, in all things, for as long as I shall live. This do I swear gladly and with no constraint."

Lillia looked at Longius, smiled, and knelt before the young scholar, speaking the same oath.

His face flushed a brilliant crimson. Anders did not know what to make of the double oaths of fealty so freely given.

"Lillia, Longius … please, please, rise. I will accept no such oaths. I am *Tironis* only. You were *Supremi* when you were cursed. You have lived longer and suffered more than any. 'Tis I who should be kneeling to you."

"These oaths are not yours to take, Anders," Longius said, smiling. "They are ours to give. And they are given already; so therefore, they are binding."

"Aye, 'tis so, sweet Master. What will you have of us, then?"

"Um … to live long in peace and happiness together. Oh, and be sure to finish your schooling. It is important, you know. Now, I really must go. Stay here. Fare-thee-well."

Anders entered the hallway, carefully shutting the sturdy door behind him.

"What are you grinning at, bookworm?"

"Oh, a secret to share later, thief. And that will be a double pleasure. But come, tell me what know you of this parade."

"Well, Afarius has said it began with stars shooting skyward from the forest, accompanied by blaring trumpets and the booming of deep drums."

Word of the strange happenings had spread rapidly throughout the *Collegium.* The death of a Daemon and the relief of a threat to the school left the Apprentices and Faculty in the highest of Holiday moods. The entire student body was arrayed in front of the main entrance where they had been celebrating.

As soon as Zoarr and Thaddeus appeared, a great "Huzzah!" went up from every throat.

Thaddeus had been told what was understood of his actions several times by now. But he remembered little and thought it all a puzzle. The seemingly grateful response of all these people made him uncomfortable, however. So, he bobbed his head in acknowledgment, waving to the few faces he remembered. It was all very strange.

And while those who spoke with him seemed sincere in what they said, he could not give credence to something so patently absurd. The possibility that he'd fallen in with an Order of Madmen had occurred to him, but that did not seem correct, either. He needed to think further on it.

Other ruminations were cut short by a commotion coming from the nearby woods. He gazed around him. All eyes were fixed on the people just emerging from a dirt path leading out of the forest. It looked to be an old man … yes, Silvestrus … sitting in a cart pulled by the old gray mule Thaddeus had seen earlier. Next to the old man was a mature woman with raven locks, glaringly white at the temples, who sat straight and proud, her arm placed lightly on his. Trailing behind the cart was a dark chestnut stallion.

Other riders were emerging—some girls and soldiers—all in all, quite an assemblage.

"Thaddeus," the dark youth beside him said, drawing his attention. "See you the procession?"

The tall boy related what he observed.

"Oh, my Brother … so much is lost, lost! Here, I will be your eyes, my poor tongue a palate, and I will try to paint you a canvas. Attend to me…."

31

Reunion and Explanations
Reunion et Explicationes

The scene put Zoarr in mind of the description he'd heard from his Brother concerning their activities on Mid-Summer's Eve this year past, only more so.

Six emerald green fire-drakes bellowed and roared, swinging their great heads from side to side and sending gobs of red-orange fire to the skies. They were tethered by massive silver chains to a great ivory chariot, layered with gold filigree.

The passengers of the conveyance were a tall, black-haired man and his stately lady. Creatures of all sorts gyred and gamboled, playing instruments of silver and singing with such sweet voices that no one could listen without being moved.

Then, on two sides, led by a handsome blond man, a large bird on his armored shoulder, and sitting astride a noble chestnut stallion, mounted arms-men on proud horses filed out of the forest, accompanied by a troop of woodland elves in bright green garb, their silver hair glinting in the yellow sunlight.

But Zoarr had no further eyes for these as soon as he espied four maidens on beautifully groomed horses that pranced and tossed their heads. He knew one of the horses immediately—and its rider.

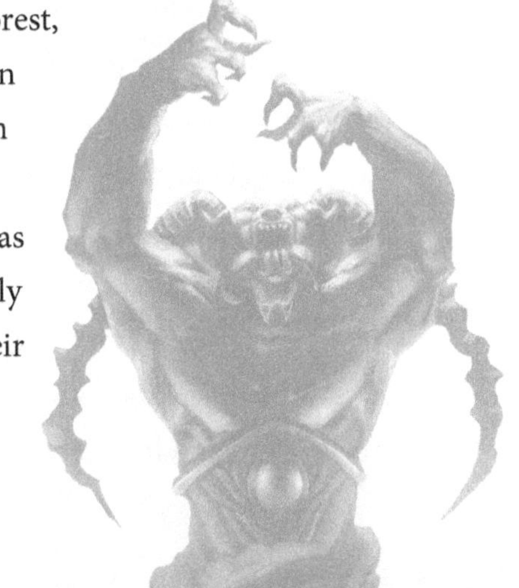

"Thaddeus, look! The girls have come! There's my Molly—and look, there's Marsia!"

The name had an immediate effect on Thaddeus. Yes, he could make out the tall girl, long hair in a flowered plait resting over her shoulder. The beautiful girl was busily scanning the faces of the crowd. Was she searching for him? Memories came flooding back to him. Yes! This was his true love.

Before he could think, he was leaping down the stairs three at a time, past two statues, and down the Lannon stone path leading to the meadow. He was vaguely aware of the swarthy lad just behind him, keeping pace, his brilliant saffron robes flying in the wind.

"Marsia! Marsia!" Thaddeus waved his arm as he ran, shouting her name.

The girl's head snapped toward him in an instant, and she kicked her horse in the ribs, sending it surging through the line of soldiers, who scattered, trying to control their own mounts. A black-haired girl followed immediately behind her, pounding up the gentle slope on a black-coated stallion.

The distance between them diminished rapidly, and the girls reined in their horses not five paces from the boys.

Marsia slid easily down from her mare and, covering the remaining ground in an instant, was wrapped in Thaddeus' arms a second after that.

They spoke each other's names and laughed. Thaddeus was dimly aware of Zoarr and the girl he called Molly doing the same.

Other shouts sounded in the background, and two other boys and two more girls on horses joined their group in the meadow.

After the first greeting frenzy, Marsia stood back from her lover and raised her hand to gently stroke the side of his face. "Master Silvestrus said you sacrificed your power to save us all." She looked deeply into the boy's eyes, concern writ large on her features.

"I remember nothing of it, actually. But people tell me of things I cannot see and deeds I cannot believe."

"Oh, Thaddeus," the girl said, a catch in her voice. "You have lost your Sorcery." She gazed at him intensely, then let out a great sigh and straightened her shoulders. "It matters not. I have enough for the both of us. 'Tis not your Sorcery that's important in any case but that we have each other."

"Yes," he said, smiling down at her. It was all he needed to say.

"And, let none forget, it was you who has saved our world!" she said, a fierce note of pride springing to her voice and a dash of fire shining in her eye.

Marsia stepped back two paces, made a fist, and began striking her chest rhythmically above her heart. "All honor to Thaddeus! All honor to Thaddeus!" she cried in a clear, clarion voice.

"Psst! Marsia! Please! No!" the boy urged, reddening to the roots.

Immediately, six other voices took up the call, then the old man and the woman standing beside him in the cart, and next the blond Captain and his troops, banging on their shields in unison. The exultant clamor took some time to die down.

Caught up in the moment, Zoarr barely noticed the creatures in the parade singing his tall friend's praises or the *Aelvae* doffing their forest caps in salute. It was impressive, and Zoarr idly wondered if he could arrange for such a display at his funeral, whenever that might occur.

But, glancing sideways at Molly, he hoped fervently it would be a long time coming.

Soon those in the meadow were joined by the students and teachers who'd been watching from the *Collegium's* entrance. So much commotion— and all so unnecessary and embarrassing.

Thaddeus fervently hoped his parents would never hear of such fuss being made over him for knocking a smaller, unarmed man—one of his teachers—senseless with a piece of furniture.

"See there, all the commotion. What a waste of time. And for what? He probably only succeeded because he fell over his own two feet in his clumsiness."

"Alistair! You are impossible! The boy is a hero and deserves our heartfelt thanks. We should celebrate his victory."

"Oh, rat turds. But, speaking of celebrating, if you are not otherwise occupied tonight, I was thinking we could get together, you know, like last time, and…."

"No! Most definitely not! Next time—if there is a next time—I shall be the one who decides what I wear, not you! Honestly, where do you come up with those ideas of yours?"

The guests were escorted to the *Collegium* amidst much cheering and celebration. Master Silvestrus and Mistress Geanninia conferred for several moments before deciding to gather the principals together in the Star Chamber, where the Council often met for its most secret deliberations. Several considerations recommended this action, including, but not limited to, the fact that it held the most comfortable chairs in the building.

The small group followed Master Silvestrus down the twisted corridor to an ornate door carved with symbols and layered with gold plate—the portal to the Star Chamber. Master Silvestrus held up his blue stone, and its vibrant glow reflected over both the hallway and the visitors.

"Recludite!"

The great door opened inward, swinging soundlessly.

Silvestrus clapped his hands, spoke a word of command, and the candles in the room all burst into flame.

As Thaddeus entered the room, he saw plush rugs, far richer than those he saw in Faran's tent, covering the floor. A massive, darkly polished table of wood Thaddeus could not identify dominated the room. Leather-bound oak chairs with cushioned seats surrounded it. A marble fireplace filled one end of the room but remained unlit. Silken tapestries, chiefly in colors of burgundy and dark blue, lined the walls.

A glance revealed Rolland's lips moving silently, performing his habitual summing of the room's contents. He looked up to find Thaddeus' gaze on him, then glanced to both sides, whistling softly and shaking his head. Thaddeus had never seen the thief do that before. It must be an expensive room as those things go.

The mood was somber, and Thaddeus felt intimidated.

Several of the other Faculty had been turned away from the meeting by Master Beatus, who had followed the group into the chamber. The Master Cook sent refreshments, and the rest of the afternoon was spent in discussion. Once everyone was seated, Silvestrus cleared his throat and began the conclave.

"You are saying, Master Silvestrus, that Thaddeus does not see me even as I sit here, nor hear me, even as I speak?"

"That appears to be the truth, Lord Non-Dar." Turning toward Thaddeus, Silvestrus asked, "You are certain, lad, you do not in any way experience the Chief of the *Aelvae?*"

"No, Master Silvestrus. I see only an empty chair and hear only moments of silence during which I note that others appear to respond to someone they believe is there."

"But, Master Silvestrus, how is this possible?" the astonished *Aelvae* asked.

"We do not yet know. However, Mistress Geanninia and I have spoken together regarding this phenomenon. We believe Thaddeus has been able to surrender this part of himself from our world yet remain in it. He can detect nothing Sorcerous, nor, on the other hand, can he be affected by anything Sorcerous. It is that which allowed him to prevail over Perditus, despite the protections conjured by the Daemon, Morag."

Mistress Geanninia regarded the *Aelvae*. "I believe he now lives simultaneously in two worlds that might be considered side-by-side, the one to the other. It is as if he has a foot in each of two camps at the same time, so to speak, but in neither one entirely."

"Can he then return fully to this present or the other, or is he doomed to be forever twain?" Non-Dar asked.

"This remains a mystery. Who knows what will come of it?" Silvestrus said. "In the meantime, he experiences only the most ordinary and humdrum of existences."

The tall blond Captain shifted in his seat. "If I may be permitted to speak, Master Silvestrus?"

"Of course, Lord Geoffrey. Proceed as you will."

"I have little cogent to contribute to these high-minded discussions, being but a simple soldier. However, it occurs to me that, in some ways, our lad here has an advantage now that the rest of us do not possess, which has the potential to be put to possibly dangerous purposes anon."

"How do you mean that?" Rolland asked a bit sharply, ready to jump to the defense of his Brother at the slightest hint of any perceived threat or criticism. At the same moment, hands were placed lightly on his wrists —one from Zoarr on one side and from Sonnia on the other.

"Um, apologies," the thief said, reddening. "Just curious."

Lord Geoffrey smiled and winked at Thaddeus. "What I mean, young Rolland, is that our lad Thaddeus is no longer subject to any Sorcery. He could now, if he wished, cause any manner of mischief in this building, including murder, subject only to physical restraint by other humans, but with no other penalty."

"He would never do any such thing!" Marsia's voice rang out hotly.

"Of course he would not," the Captain replied. "And luckily so. But it is an important point to consider. He could become, in that way, a most formidable weapon, and his destiny must now, it seems to me, be a matter of serious debate."

"You speak truly, Lord Geoffrey," the old Sorcerer said. "And thank you for that pearl of wisdom. We have been discussing so much what we consider him to have lost, it has taken you to point out that we must also be discussing is what he may have gained. Perditus certainly experienced the consequences of it."

"Master, if I may?" Anders asked diffidently.

The old man nodded at the boy in assent.

"Ah ... where is Master Perditus now? Has he been...."

"Disposed of?" Silvestrus finished for the youth. "No. He is confined in the bowels of this building under multiple Sorcerous constraints. Once all concerning this affair and his part in it can be discovered, the Council will determine his fate."

"He should be put to the sword!" Mistress Geanninia said, color rising to her cheeks. "Immediately."

"Yes. Well, some few have supported that judgment, yet I feel there is much to be learned from this ... adventure. Also, consider, if one can do what Perditus has done, cannot another do so as well? Time, however, is necessary to sort this matter out—though," the old man added, glancing at his lady, "that was certainly my first feeling as well."

"Master Silvestrus?" Zoarr's Solarian drawl interjected itself into the silence.

"Yes, Prince?"

"I am curious to know—if I may look to a different point—how was it these lovely ladies knew to come and join us in our struggle at the time they did? It begs much of coincidence, leaving it all to chance."

"My stone told me," Marsia offered, drawing out her green stone on its chain. "It has the virtue, presently, of flashing when one is in peril."

"I assume we might all guess as to whom that one would be?" Zoarr asked, smiling.

"Just so," Marsia said without a trace of embarrassment in her public acknowledgment.

"Hmm," Zoarr hesitated. "Even so, you are—and no disrespect intended, dear Marsia—Apprenticiatrix only. How was it you were able to persuade your Sisters—and more importantly, your Head-Mistress—of the gravity of the situation and, further, the need for timely intervention?"

"I am able to answer that for you, Prince," Mistress Geanninia answered, smiling. Reaching into her bodice, she withdrew a delicate golden chain from which was suspended an even larger blue stone. "There was additional evidence, you see."

"Ah," said the Mauretesian. "Many matters are clearer now. My thanks, Mistress."

The stately brunette nodded in acknowledgment.

"Um, Mistress, if I may?"

"Of course, gentle Anders," the lady replied.

"Granted, you had the means of knowing there was danger here, yet how was it you contrived to respond so quickly, covering distances that generally require weeks to traverse?"

Intrigued, the other boys leaned forward attentively.

The Head-Mistress smiled mysteriously. "I used an old family trick."

Thaddeus started at that revelation. The words sounded familiar, as if he should know it, but he could bring nothing to mind.

"I have a question," Rolland interjected. "If that's all right, of course."

The Silence of Assent followed.

"Five of you came to our aid—and of those, only four were Sorcerous. Not that the fifth wasn't death-on-the-hoof herself," Rolland added hastily at a look from Zoarr. "But here was the entire *Collegium* at peril with some fifty Sorcerers at hand, give or take. Yet with the resources available to you, you thought to bring just these few?"

"I can answer you that, Friend Rolland," Sonnia said with a malicious grin. "It took no time at all to calculate that we five would be equivalent to your entire *Collegium* in terms of talent and competence and that any others would only be in excess and unnecessary."

While the other ladies grinned openly, Rolland blinked, looked steadily at his love for a moment, and then smiled unabashedly. "Um, well spoken, Sonnia. I take your point."

Zoarr leaned toward Anders, speaking in a loud whisper, "Our Brother continues to gain in wisdom with the passage of time."

"Truly," Anders replied while clasping Nannsi's hand in his own.

"Master Silvestrus," Lord Geoffrey spoke up, "I should like to corroborate the effectiveness of the Sorceresses' timely intervention. I rode down to the caves to greet the ladies at the conclusion of their battle and found not one surviving Goblin. All—numbering close to two hundred of their warrior class—lay slain, destroyed in ways most terrible. It is a sight I shall not forget."

Mistress Geanninia shrugged and spoke quietly again to Master Silvestrus.

Despite straining to hear, Thaddeus could make out only the words *vermin* and *extermination*.

He shuddered at the description but could not acknowledge the trueness of the beings involved nor the means encompassing their destruction. Yet, he knew that he would take the word of any here on any such matter.

He was thrust onto the horns of a dilemma and saw no way to resolve it.

32

A Judgement Rendered
Iudicum Factum

"I would like to know what is being done to help Thaddeus," Marsia said, looking steadily from one to the other.

Thaddeus tried the hand-on-the-wrist technique he'd seen work so effectively on Rolland, but his true love was having none of it and shook her arm free in an instant.

"For without him, we would not be sitting here enjoying this tea and these sweet cakes."

"Hear, hear," joined his classmates and their ladies.

"We must first understand the problem before we can provide a solution," Silvestrus intoned. "If, indeed, it *is* a problem."

"Excuse me, Master?" Anders said.

"My dear children, we have not yet heard from Thaddeus as to whether or not he even considers this state of affairs a problem."

"Of course it is a probl—" Again, the magic wrist maneuver performed its Sorcery, and Rolland fell silent a moment before speaking again. "I mean, anyone would consider it a problem."

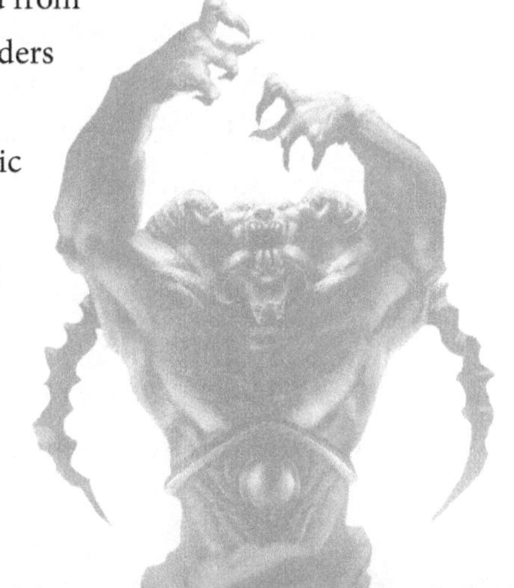

"Hmm. Perhaps. Perhaps not. In order to suffer from a loss, one must first acknowledge it as a loss."

"Very well. Thaddeus, do you feel you have sustained a grievous blow?" Zoarr asked.

"Nay, I do not."

The room fell silent for a moment.

"Um, Thaddeus?"

"Yes, Anders?"

"If a means could be found to restore to you the ability to perform Sorcery, would you seek it?"

Thaddeus considered the question. "I don't know. I feel fine now." He cast a glance at Marsia. "Most especially fine. Your question, though, strikes me as if I were to be asked, would I wish to have a pig that could fly. It might be a marvelous thing indeed, but where would I keep it?"

Lord Geoffrey laughed aloud, as did Rolland, but both fell silent when the others did not join in.

Master Silvestrus cleared his throat. "That is the crucial point. Thaddeus does not experience an injury, so he detects no sorrow for the wound. And, we must remember, he gave up his power voluntarily—by force of will alone. This is a peculiar and fascinating dilemma.

"I believe Captain Geoffrey has the right of it. We must be about studying the problem with all our resources. But this falls in the purview of deliberations of talkative old men—and, of course, the wisdom of beautiful mature ladies."

He sketched a bow to Mistress Geanninia. "Geannie, perhaps it would be wise to convene an emergent meeting of the Council with you as our Special Representative from the *Ludia* if you are willing. In the meantime, unless there is need elsewise, perhaps our guests might have the freedom to stroll the grounds and enjoy each other's company?"

"Your pardon, Master Silvestrus," Captain Geoffrey broke in, "but I should look to getting my men back to *Arx Montium*. I believe all is well now, and our presence no longer required."

"My people and I must also leave, Silvestrus," Non-Dar said. "The matters to be addressed go beyond any contributions the *Aelvae* might make."

"Nonsense to both of you. You must remain at least one more night. We would do you honor for delivering us from the Goblin Horde and, therefore, have planned a celebratory feast that Master Specus is even now preparing. Much effort has gone into it already, and to have our steadfast Guard and our erstwhile and honored allies depart, showing so small an inclination to share themselves, would be a grievous blow."

The tall blond soldier looked at his *Aelvae* counterpart, who shrugged.

"All right then, Master Silvestrus. You have persuaded us. We would not willingly insult your generosity while at the same time taking great advantage of it."

"Excellent. Then let us be about our diverse tasks. Gentlemen—and ladies as well, of course—consider the *Collegium* your home and treat it in a likewise manner. Thank you all. Oh, Anders … a word, please, if you will."

Startled, the short boy jumped up and made his way to his Master as the others got up to leave and filed out of the room, speaking softly to one another.

Beckoning him closer, Silvestrus leaned to Anders' ear. "My boy, run you quick as a rabbit to the Master Cook and tell him to prepare a feast the likes of which we have never seen for tomorrow's eve. Um … and you need not mention the timing of this request to anyone, I think."

"Yes, Master. Of course. Right away."

Anders hurried back to his Nannsi. "I must go about some business of the Master's, but I shall be only moments away."

"Of course, my Anders, you must go. Return when you can."

As her young lover left her side, Nannsi puffed with pride. "My Anders is often called upon to accomplish such critical tasks," she announced to no one in particular. "He writes to me of these frequently but is too modest, himself, to mention them to others."

Later in the day, the girls had been shown the boys' rooms—all but Anders'. The scholar had given the others the impression he wished for some private time with Nannsi, and they all respected his wish.

As he put his hand to the door plate, he leaned over and spoke in Nannsi's ear. "Dearest, do not be alarmed, but I have, um, guests in my room. They are a fine, well-intentioned couple with a bit of a story about them. But I think it better for us not to tell the others for now. You will see."

Silvestrus had arranged for tents to be erected in the meadow for Lord Geoffrey's troop and sleeping silks just inside the forest for Non-Dar and his tribe. Specus had sent over victuals for each group.

Mistress Geanninia's tent miraculously appeared, just as it had been on Mid-Summer's Eve. The girls' tents had appeared, though everyone understood why Nannsi's tent was set over to one side. Technically, the boys were to bid the girls Good Repose and remain in their own rooms during the night....

Thaddeus and Marsia strolled hand-in-hand around the Commons, then settled down beneath the cherry tree. Over time, this had become Thaddeus' reflecting place. The night was cool, the air clear, and the stars out in vast numbers, though some few streaked across the sky from time to time. The couple sat side-by-side, then lay on the soft grass facing each other, their heads resting on hands supported by their elbows.

After satisfying herself that Thaddeus had no pain or discomfort from his loss and—as Thaddeus suspected—that he'd suffered no significant brain palsy, Marsia slipped back to being the thoughtful lover she recollected from the Spring.

"—and so you see, there would be no problem. You could pursue any trade you wished, and I would do the Sorcery." She looked earnestly into his eyes. "That is, if you still wish to be married to a Sorceress. You are, of course, under no obligation to do so, and I would underst—"

This seemed to Thaddeus as good a time as any to kiss his true love fully on the lips. And so he did.

"I have written to my parents about us. Initially, they were quite upset and threatened to come to collect me and take me home from the *Ludia,* but I have convinced them not to do so."

"How did you do that?" Rolland asked.

"I told them any attempt on their part to separate me from school— or from you—would compel us to run off together. I reminded them that we were now fully active in our Sorcery and, therefore, in any case, they could do little about it. Mother came around rather quickly after that. She was always the more sensible of the two. Father has taken longer but now seems more reconciled to the situation than before. They want to meet you, though, and judge for themselves. I will not insist that you do, but—"

"It might make it go better?" Rolland finished.

Sonnia smiled her brilliant smile. "Oh, my, yes. Perhaps you could come to stay with us over the Summer for a time if you wish it."

"I would like that very much. But will your parents not balk at having a thief as a house guest for the season?"

"Ah, but I have already told them that you are no ordinary thief. As I'm sure you could guess, no ordinary thief could have ever stolen my heart."

Near a quiet stream that ran through the forest, Molly sat on a high branch of an old willow tree while Zoarr perched astride one of the limbs closer to the ground. It had taken some research to obtain a description of the type of willow tree that flourished in Fountaindale, and then more effort to locate one in the nearby woods. He often stopped there at odd moments as it conjured up the image of Molly, and he could think of no better way to pass the occasional idle hour.

He had brought his lute strapped to his back up into the tree with him. Finding a comfortable playing position, he tuned his instrument and accompanied himself, strumming the sweet lays of sorrow he remembered from the palace bards. The effort to maintain his balance in such an awkward pose while simultaneously singing and playing was difficult. Still, he didn't mind, especially when he witnessed the effect this effort wrought on his lady love.

In the sweltering *Collegium* kitchen, Specus looked around, checking off items in his mind. He'd pushed the kitchen crew, supplemented by various *volunteers*—"….you, boy, come with me. Now!"—fairly hard, but he wanted everything to be perfect.

It was not every day one of his lads, as he thought of them, was able to put a Daemon to rights. Also, it was not every day he was called on to prepare a Feast of Feasts, where ladies were to be present. He was sure his work would receive extra scrutiny and all must pass muster and more.

His thoughts returned to the Beewicke boy. What a courageous act! Of course, the price had been high, to be sure. He'd always felt himself to be least of all at the *Collegium*, as his own talents were modest in the extreme. But to be without any skill at all? He shook his head.

And would the Masters ever be able to heal the boy? Specus had heard that even Master Celsius had been baffled. He shook his head again. *Well, things would be as they would be.*

The Master Cook paused in his reflection to redirect two of his impressed scullions: "No! You two go there and do that. Now!" before returning to his train of thought.

The boy was a good lad—best of the lot, it seemed to him—and would do well wherever he lighted. He, himself, was not getting any younger. Perhaps the tall boy would like to take over the kitchen when he, Specus, was ready to leave his position. No Sorcery was necessary to bake biscuits, and he could maintain a connection to the *Collegium*.

Specus considered this. No, it would probably be more difficult to remain here without Sorcery than to be elsewhere. He sighed. He would need to continue his search for a successor.

Not Faran, certainly. He had tasted his son's cooking that week they spent fishing up North. No, Faran taking his Pa-ap's position was not an option.

Well, he would have to toil a while longer before he could get back to that small cottage by the stream he still owned. Where his Coqua rested yet … awaiting him.

In the stable, the eight friends sat in pairs on piles of hay spread about. It was cooler in the shed, and Thaddeus always liked the smell.

More importantly, it was one of the few places they could all talk without people—mostly well-intentioned—troubling Thaddeus with unanswerable questions, unrealistic demands, or unfounded remedies. His Brothers and Sisters had, by instinct, formed a wall of defense around their leader that few could breach.

In addition to the Apprentices, the group's retinue numbered among them one mule, one parrot, and one hard-used Eagle.

"It is my impression," Zoarr said thoughtfully, "that we are all dancing around a possibility that we should discuss, however painful it may be in the mentioning."

"What's that, Brother mine?" Rolland asked.

"The possibility that Thaddeus may not ever recover his Sorcery. Far and aside from the question of whether or not he would wish to."

An uncomfortable silence followed, broken by the tall youth himself. "Zoarr has a point. I may not be able to become a Sorcerer again. If I could, anyway." He continued in a softer voice, "If there is such a thing...."

Sitting beside him, Marsia grasped his arm and squeezed.

"It's true, Thaddeus, I swear it by the All-Mother!" Rolland said with passion.

"I know you say it, and you believe it." Thaddeus spread his hands. "But I don't. I-I can't."

"The mule verifies his assertion," Psittaca interjected. While the others could hear the speech of Asullus, Zoarr's companion understood Thaddeus could not. Also, the fact the tall boy could hear the parrot speak—but not Asullus nor Osiric—had been the topic of an earlier discussion.

"I hear what you say, parrot, but...."

"I believe I see the thread of Zoarr's concern," Anders broke in. "If what we have come to understand is true, then we four Apprentices have some sort of part to play in a future described in a Prophecy. I assume that our Brother's recent defeat of the aberrant Master Perditus' scheme was not that which was indicated by those foreshadowing words.

"We are the designated Cardinal points of some symbolic—or, perhaps more correctly, mystic—eight-sided Compass, and Thaddeus' chil- ... uh, that is, there are others who represent the Ordinal points. Apparently, if any of this is true, we all have certain important roles in whatever future catastrophe is rushing with all haste toward us. I have no evidence to suggest that has changed; therefore, our contributions— whatever they are fated to be—are still expected. The question is: Does the change in Thaddeus' status alter any expectations of us in successfully playing the parts we're to be assigned?"

"Well, Short and Sweet, does it?" Rolland asked.

"I don't know. But I would certainly like to."

Marsia looked deeply into Thaddeus' eyes. "There may be even more to it than that, Anders," the tall girl said.

"What?"

"I believe I know it, but it's upon Thaddeus to share if he wishes it."

Thaddeus looked down. When he raised his eyes, the pain present in them was evident to all.

"I-I do not believe I can stay here. Not as I am. If the Masters cannot help me, I will have to leave this place. Forever."

The thin, sallow-complexioned, pockmarked figure stood before the nine men seated on a raised dais at the back of the great room. All nine were elderly and dressed in robes of colors specific to their *Gens*.

The thin man before them was the youngest of those present, and his robes were tattered and torn. Also, he was bound in shackles at the neck, wrists, waist, and ankles. The metallic restraints gleamed silver, glowing palely in the flickering candlelight of the Star Chamber.

Master Beatus presided at the center of the long table.

"Do not think to Spell in this chamber. As you know, it is warded against such activity. Additionally, the nature of your confinement serves to prohibit this."

Perditus smiled sardonically. "Do I represent such a threat to you that you believe this action necessary?"

"It is our custom to proceed in this manner on such occasions, rare though they be—so we enforce it now. Do you wish to make a statement as we consider these debates?"

"It is not needful. My deeds are my speech."

"Yes, but that is the issue then, is it not? Very well. Master Perditus of Skara-Brae, know that the accusations that stand against you involve the following: that you conjured an Arch-Daemon with the intention of using that being to fashion a Sorcerous Portal through which others of his ilk could travel to our plane of existence where they would work their will. In exchange for this assistance, you sought to receive power over your fellow man so as to rule him as you saw fit. Also, that you were instrumental in the disappearance and subsequent deaths of at least three of the Apprentices of this school—*Supremus* Wil Rathboneson and *Advenae* Argentus, and Platinus Silverfoot. And further, that you conspired with said Daemon to attempt the same end with *Tironis* Thaddeus of Beewicke. What say you to these charges? Do you deny them?"

"Yes, of course. The lot of them. My studies these past twenty years have been directed solely toward the further understanding of the properties of the Tower of the East. Communications with sentient beings connected with the Tower have been helpful in addressing these concerns but incidental only to my research. What any such individuals may have believed would occur at some future time was purely their own fancy and had nothing to do with me. As to the possible disappearance of those you have listed, I know no more than you. Perhaps they have run off to return home or seek their fortune elsewhere. It has been known to happen, even here."

"Hmm, well, yes. We, of course, have made effort to consider all possibilities, and so, as a part of our study, we called on Master Celsius to examine the remains of the *Daemon,* Morag. He has written out his findings in much detail on a scroll."

Here the *Princeps Academia* indicated the rolled parchment at his elbow. "However, the essence of his investigation is that remains of the *Platinae* were indeed found in the Daemon's stomach, along with those of another smaller Daemon, Charles by name. Master Celsius assures me no uncertainty exists regarding the identity of these individuals. In addition, though no trace of the older boy has yet been discovered, we believe he suffered the same fate."

"I do not see how that affects me. I have no control over the diets of others."

"I agree. You likely did not force the Daemon to eat those boys, but we believe you did not attempt to prevent that action, either."

Master Perditus smiled wanly again. "I also have no control over what you choose to believe. As for Thaddeus of Beewicke, I attempted no such assault, although I yet bear the evidence of his violence to my person. As I understand he still lives, why not ask him yourself to recall the events of this afternoon past if you remain so uncertain?"

"He has, as I believe you are aware, Master Perditus, suffered a great trauma as a result of these acts, which has affected his memory, among other things."

"Well, then. It appears to me that I stand here subject to judgments for no proven misdeeds. Therefore, I eagerly anticipate my immediate release from this constraint so that I may return to my studies forthwith, for they are the mainstay of my intellectual life at this time and are extremely important to me."

"You are clever and well-spoken, Master Perditus, yet you do not convince. We here of the Council deem that you have indeed transgressed as we have described. Therefore, we render the following judgment. At the conclusion of this hearing, you will be conducted to the lowest level of this building, where you will be housed in a cell especially constructed to keep you. There you will be maintained in the restraints you presently wear and be confined in that place for the rest of your natural life. I should add, for the sake of completeness, that, given you have been accused and found guilty of crimes capital, you yet live only because of the intervention of one of our members—Master Silvestrus of Somerset —who, for his own reasons, has interceded effectively on your behalf. Have you a wish to make any further statement?"

The thin figure shook his head, bearing the expression of a person who has decided to bide his time until some future date should generate different circumstances.

"Very well. Masters Rastius, Caecus, if you would be so good as to escort Master Perditus to his new domicile, he may begin serving his sentence. Hopefully, the time provided here will aid him in reflection and the attainment of insight concerning the enormity of these heinous crimes he has perpetrated upon this, our school, and its students.

"These proceedings are closed."

33

Women Warriors
Amazones

"…. and it was very dark in the caves. In the winter, we call them the ice caves, as some of the girls like to go exploring there when the lake by the *Ludia* freezes over. But none of us had been there in Spring before."

"Mistress Geanninia actually guided the boat?" Rolland asked, moving a piece on the game board that rested on their blanket, then took another bite from a roll, followed by a swig of punch.

Sonnia glanced at the board for only a moment before making her own move.

"No, she just pointed in the direction we were to go, and we rowed. She is Head-Mistress, as you know, and life is easier if we accomplish those tasks she sets for us. Once there, we used candles going in. It was quite a twisty path; every time a wave rolled in, our feet got wet all over again. Mistress Geanninia's stone—and Marsia's, too—kept flashing, so Nannsi, Molly, and I just kept following them."

Sonnia watched closely as Rolland made another move, then smiled briefly.

"We found some stairs carved into the moss-patch rock floor that went down a distance. The dampness made it slippery, so we had to be careful. Then we came to an old, weather-beaten door that opened at the Head-Mistress' command. The room was dank and clammy.

"Carved into the middle of the floor was an odd symbol in the shape of a sea-horse-shoe. The Mistress bade us stand around it in a circle, holding hands. She spoke another word, and we were in a different room. It was not damp but dry and smelled more of the earth than sea."

"So you'd somehow traveled to the caves in the forest?"

"Yes, but we had no notion where we were at first. The symbol on the floor was different; a clawed-toad print. She told us to stay together and remain alert. We had no idea what we would find. We walked out through an archway and followed a path leading up and—we hoped— out. After some moments, she signaled us to be silent, and we could hear voices. I knew in an instant what they were: Goblins. I will always know those voices." She shuddered as her visage became grim and distant.

Rolland reached over and gently stroked her arm.

The girl gave a little shake, seeming to come back to herself, then smiled at the thief.

"From there, we went forward most carefully. When we began to see flickering torchlight, Mistress Geanninia and Marsia tucked their stones back in their bodices to hide the light. We came to a branching of the corridor, and Mistress looked cautiously around the corner. Then she drew her head back…."

The tall raven-haired woman known as Mistress raised her left hand to her mouth and pointed the first two fingers of her right hand downward.

Goblins!

Sonnia gasped. Marsia reached forward and patted her shoulder.

The older woman held up seven fingers to the girls behind her. They all nodded. She signaled the sign of the Half-Circle, then two hand thrusts. Her charges nodded again.

Molly quietly drew two knives from her belt, and the others raised their hands in front of them. At a nod from the Mistress, they strode around the corner as a group.

Five Goblins in leather harnesses lounged on the cave floor next to a heap of baggage and equipment. Some chewed hide, while others sharpened their weapons and spoke to each other. Two stood further on, each with bow and arrow, looking out toward a brightening source of light, which, Sonnia supposed, must be the cave opening.

The two nearest Goblins jerked their heads up as soon as the women appeared, calling out. They raised their weapons while the others jumped to their feet. It was the last thing they did. Two exploded into gobs of green pudding, while three others were instantly charred to a crisp with fireballs. One of the corridor guards who had started to rush toward the girls was cut in half by an invisible blade. The other Goblin guard turned to flee but fell a pace later with two knife handles protruding from his back.

Mistress Geanninia held up her hand, and the girls froze, each casting about for signs of any additional green creatures. None appeared. After a moment, the Head-Mistress signaled the girls to follow as she led them toward the light.

No others were detected as Molly retrieved her knives, and they emerged from the cave mouth into the noonday sun.

The Sorceresses cast their gazes over what appeared to be a campsite, noting several other caves. A large central fire pit with a flame was burning over a collection of logs and several pots. Seeing this, Sonnia clenched her hands tightly.

Weapons and other supplies were collected in various piles, which was as expected. What was not expected was that every tree, bush, and blade of grass had somehow become shimmering gray rock.

As the girls stood surveying the scene where the entire world had been turned to stone, Mistress Geanninia began swearing, thunderclouds gathering on her brows.

The Sorceresses' curiosity, however, was interrupted by sounds of conversation issuing from one of the other cave openings.

Shortly, two Goblins sauntered out of the cavernous entrance, each carrying armfuls of what must be victuals. They were overloaded to the point of appearing comical, but as soon as they saw the women, they screamed, dropped their encumbrances, and ran off in opposite directions. It did them no good, however, and in a trice, the campsite was again silent, though an aroma of charred flesh hung in the air.

Finding no others of the green tribe, the Sorceresses set their course for the *Collegium*. They'd not gone far when a *skreeing* sound pierced the air above them.

Marsia narrowed her eyes and rapidly searched the sky. *There....*

"Mistress, Sisters, wait! I believe that's Osiric, Thaddeus' Eagle!"

A moment later, the bird descended, landing close to the group and hopping over to greet his Mistress. Marsia looked into the Eagle's face and focused her attention as Thaddeus had earlier instructed her.

"Lord Osiric?"

"Mistress! It is well I have found you! I did not expect you here and only just discovered your scent in the air. I am scouting the area for Lord Geoffrey of the Iron Company, who is in pursuit of a remnant of a Goblin force that attacked his command. The soldiers were riding to aid the Collegium, which is under some sort of Daemon siege and is all turned to stone.

"It was then I first detected the Goblins heading toward the troops— the green ones having issued from these very caves sometime earlier in the day, though how they chanced here, I know not. Lord Geoffrey, with whom I have been abiding, formed his men and met the Goblins just near the forest boundary. It was a close thing until Lord Non-Dar and his Aelvae arrived to even matters. It was then that the surviving Goblins took flight, and I have been following them to find whither they flee. Mistress! They number at least ten score and are running full out toward these caves and

will be here in moments only. You would do best to hide. They have not yet detected you, but their sense of smell is keen. Not as keen as mine, mind you, but keen, nevertheless."

"Osiric! I thank thee for thy timely warning. But have you … have you news of your Lord?"

"Nay, Mistress, none. But he is a hardy lad, and I am certain is even now preparing to vanquish the evil Sorcerer and his treacherous minion, the Daemon!"

"Yes, of a surety. Osiric, abide here yet a moment while I relay to my Mistress and Sisters the news you have borne us."

Within minutes, the other women learned of the Eagle's report and fashioned a plan for the Goblins' reception—simple yet effective.

"All right, ladies, this is where your training pays out. Stand in formation as we have practiced. Remember, let none escape!" Mistress Geanninia straightened her skirts one last time and assumed the position.

Marsia addressed her Eagle.

"Osiric! Fly with all speed back to Lord Geoffrey and alert him as best you can to our situation. Take care for thyself, Lord of the Skies."

"Take care of yourself, Mistress, or else your Lord will breathe his last upon hearing such evil news. I go now!" So saying, the great Eagle leaped into the air, powerful wings propelling his rapid ascent.

Moments later came the first of the ululations.

Sonnia reached toward the board, moving her piece forward and thereby capturing Rolland's Ruler. She found herself of two minds concerning the ploy.

On the one hand, she thought to gently chastise her future husband for getting so caught up in her story—however well told—that he lost his concentration for the game. Yet, on the other, had he not, she would have cause to doubt the power of her charms to distract her lover with her smile and other attributes.

After careful consideration, she believed she favored the second of these posits.

Anders took a sip of tea, set down the mug, and continued.

"So, when Longius said someone would come from the black and yellow, it set me to thinking. Then I reasoned that it could mean bees. It was the first thing that came to my mind, and Primus always said that was the thought that held the greatest truth.

"Thus, I reasoned if black and yellow referred to bees, then that meant Thaddeus, or one of us who are linked to him might be the ones who could help."

"Well, done, Anders," Longius said. "But what turned your attention to Iusti Mores' ring as the Talisman?"

"Your description of the event. You said he indicated he could reverse the curse with a Talisman if he chose. I thought that must mean it was something simple and near at hand. You went on to say his room and laboratory were searched following his disappearance, and nothing of the sort was ever found. And I considered it might be that it was never found because *he* was never found, having died in the corridor behind the mirrors. So it occurred to me that the Talisman might be something he had with him, or on him, at the time of his death. When I examined the skeleton, there was only one object present: the ring. And so...." Anders spread his hands.

"Ah-ha!" Lillia said. "Clever Anders, as I have always said."

Longius raised his mug. "To clever Anders!"

"Clever Anders!" the other two in the room echoed, raising their mugs as well.

Anders blushed and bobbed his head in embarrassed acknowledgment while Nannsi looked on with a smile of pride.

Anxious to change the subject, the young scholar addressed his two guests. "What will you do now, Longius and Lillia? You have the whole world before you."

The tall *Supremus* looked to his promised one, who nodded, then to their savior.

"We have said already, Anders. We are pledged to you in all things. Having lived fifteen hundred years, we are unlikely to change our minds after a few hours. No, we gave our oaths, and we are content to keep them. If you will have us, we will go where you go. Your work, our joyful burden. Your lady, our Mistress," the tall man said, with a seated bow to Nannsi, who smiled and nodded in return.

"Longius and Lillia, please know we accept your pledge with all humility and hope you will come, over time, to look on us as friends— not oath-holders," the dark-headed girl said earnestly.

"Yes. Of a certainty," Anders endorsed. "But, to return to the question, what will you do now? A few hours ago, Lillia, you were House-Mistress to the *Collegium Sorcerorum,* and you, Longius, a ghostly legend. Now all is different. And while undeniably better, it is a great change for you both. So, the question."

"I must be honest. I have given it no thought, having been entirely caught up in the events of this day. What think you, dearest?"

"I have no idea, my love. Like you, I am in the moment. I care not what even the next minute brings, as long as I am with you now in this minute," the short, curly-haired girl replied.

Nannsi tilted her head thoughtfully. "They cannot go back to their former callings, Anders, whatever the future may bring. The question is how to capture the hearts of the others, for they also have a say in what will be. The ruling Council is made up of old men. And old men, Sorcerous or not, are reluctant with change and tend to oppose loss, perceived or actual. They will not, with good cheer, surrender their housekeeper willingly. We must capture their fancy to gain their support. But how best to accomplish this?"

"My love," Anders replied, "let me share with you even an additional concern. You have seen how hard all this has been on Thaddeus. I fear for him at the feast tonight; certainly, all eyes will be on him. You know how he always seeks to avoid being the one to whom attention turns. I wonder if we might strive to relieve Thaddeus' discomfort and find a useful direction for Longius and Lillia—all at once."

Anders furrowed his brow and stared hard at his hands for some moments before looking up with a trace of a smile on his face. "Ah, my sweet, I think I may have a way to sharpen the razor so it cuts both coming and going. See what you make of this…."

"Tonight at the feast, Thaddeus will sit in the position of honor at the raised table with the Elders. He will be uncomfortable and anxious. Perhaps that would be the time to introduce our new *Supremi,* along with the tale of their undying love and centuries of suffering. It would rally all around our couple and take the light of the Bright Candle from our Thaddeus."

Nannsi gasped in delight and clapped her hands together. "Oh, my brilliant boy! That is wonderful! But wait. This asks much of Longius and Lillia. After all these centuries, to be thrust into such scrutiny … they may wish this least of any."

"Anders, Nannsi," Lillia said. "Consider us not. Our joy could not be dampened by a thousand things worse. And we would do this and more for Thaddeus in any case, even without your request."

"This is true," Longius added. "Simply tell us your wishes in this matter."

Anders paused in thought. When he looked up, he was smiling.

"I have an idea, then. Pray tell me what think you of this…."

That night, the dining hall buzzed with heightened activity. All manner of decoration had been applied, with draping ribbons, blazing candles, and sweetly scented boughs in abundance. Tables on one side of the hall held Captain Geoffrey's troop, and on the other, Lord Non-Dar's *Aelvae.*

The *Tirones* ringed the back of the hall with the *Indigenae* closer and the Faculty closest of all to the two raised head tables. The lesser table held Zoarr and Molly o' the Willows, Anders and Nannsi, and Rolland and Sonnia. An empty chair sat nearest the greater table that had initially held Marsia—until Thaddeus rose from his chair and fetched her to sit beside him. Some eyebrows raised at this, but none moved to hinder him.

Also seated at the high table were Master Beatus, Master Silvestrus, Mistress Geanninia, Master Celsius with his foot-cloud tucked beneath his chair, and Lords Geoffrey and Non-Dar, taking their ease in compatible discourse. Master Specus himself served those on the dais while keeping a close eye on all his helpers—this meal being table-served, rather than line-served, in honor of the occasion.

Thaddeus spent most of the dinner in quiet conversation with Marsia, except for those times when a question was directed at him, or when Marsia persuaded him to address others at the table. His eyes, when not fixed on his true love, strayed to his Brothers' table where waves and hand signals passed back and forth, and Rolland did his best to attempt to break his tall companion's composure with a variety of faces and gestures whenever he thought he could evade Sonnia's gaze.

After seven courses of the Master Cook's wondrous creations, the participants sat back, comfortably full.

At last, Master Beatus rose, and a hush fell over the assembly. He gave greetings to all, thanked them for coming, and introduced the guests and those to be honored. He outlined in general terms the history and dangers faced and summed up the deeds that had recently transpired as far as they were known.

To Thaddeus, such a speech was new and compelling—as much as it was intimidating and embarrassing—especially those parts concerning himself, which he still could not accept.

To Zoarr, however, it was a speech in the manner of a thousand such he had heard delivered over the years at his Father's court. They seemed always to carry a certain similar comfort of rhythm and familiarity. This predictability allowed his attention to stray with great regularity to the dark-locked lady sitting to his left.

Next came words of wonder from Master Silvestrus.

Following that, praise mixed with thoughtfulness from Mistress Geanninia. Lord Geoffrey and Lord Non-Dar were acknowledged, and each spoke briefly.

Anders realized this was all leading up to Thaddeus being singled out and perhaps required to address the hall. Anders knew his tall Brother would rather sacrifice an arm than be subjected to such scrutiny and expectation.

Fortunately, there was an alternative.

34

Thaddeus Decides
Thaddeus Iudicat

At a natural pause in the presentations, while Master Silvestrus was in a brief whispered conference with Master Beatus, Anders stood and clambered up onto his chair, calling out for the room's attention by expeditiously beating his flatware against his tableware.

It took a moment for the crowd to understand what was happening and who was speaking. Most at the head table looked puzzled, though Master Silvestrus appeared bemused after a moment and stroked his beard in anticipation.

"Masters, guests, students—your ears for a moment! Much praise has been given here this eve—and rightly so—to those brave and hearty souls who had a hand in the defeat of a Great Evil to which we were all witnesses this day past. And not least among them, to our very own Thaddeus of Beewicke!"

At this, the assemblage broke into loud shouts, and many stood to lend emphasis to their cheering. Thaddeus turned red and gave Anders an *I-thought-you-were-my-friend* look.

Zoarr leaned over to Rolland. "What is it our Brother points at with this pageantry?"

"I have no idea," the redhead replied, casting a glance at Nannsi, who sat still and smiling, her gaze never leaving her beloved's countenance, "but I'm sure it's going to be good."

Anders continued. "However, we have, unfortunately—and inadvertently, I'm certain—overlooked two others whose own roles have been pivotal in providing the outcome that we celebrate this night. I refer, of course, to the two *Supremi* whose part in this drama was over a thousand years in the making."

Master Silvestrus' brows knitted together in concentration for a moment before dawning insight flooded his face, followed by a chortle of delight. He leaned over and whispered into his lady's ear. Mistress Geanninia turned to gaze at him, her lips forming a perfect *O*, then she smiled in understanding and clasped her hands together in anticipatory pleasure.

"This couple has worked tirelessly over the centuries, constantly guarding our school and keeping all within it orderly and safe. They labored thusly, without complaint, in the face of a most terrible curse placed on them by a long-ago Master of the *Collegium*."

At this, a loud buzz of surprise and speculation swept through the hall. Anders lifted his hands for silence.

"Then, when all was in jeopardy this day past, these two willingly sacrificed themselves to thwart Evil's plan. Let me call upon you to give great honor to *Suprema* Lillia of Falling Stone and *Supremus* Longius of Adventitia."

At that moment, the doors at the end of the dining hall opened, and a young couple walked into the room holding hands: a tall, dark-haired young man and a short, curly-headed young woman.

No cheering greeted the couple, however, as they strode silently up the table-lined aisle to where Anders, who had gotten down from his chair, met them on the dais, turning to face the crowd.

"See you these two, my love?" Marsia asked.

"I do, but I do not recognize them. Do you?"

Marsia shook her head in response.

The assembly murmured with curiosity and confusion, understanding neither the persons nor the intent of their introduction into the evening's festivities.

Once again, Anders called for quiet.

"I understand your hesitation in bestowing loud huzzahs. I believe it is because you are at a loss to recognize this man and this woman as they now stand before you. That may be because you know them otherwise. They have changed forms, you see, forms they have each held for a millennium and a half.

"The woman who stands before you was, until yesterday, a Goblin, green and wrinkled, and the man, a spectre, a haunt of the mirrors. Faculty, guests, and students, may I introduce to you the former House-Mistress Lilyput and her spectrous companion, Brother Longbone!"

A moment of stunned silence was followed by a rolling uproar and noisy pandemonium that went on and on. A quick glance showed a look of relief—and gratitude—on his tall Brother's face.

Standing in front of such an audience in the center of things with so much attendant drama was one of the hardest things Anders had ever endured. But it was for a good cause.

Only briefly did he allow himself to wonder if what he did was right. He was quickly reassured, however, when he noted the proud expression on Nannsi's face. It was quite satisfying.

Thaddeus gazed around his Master's study. The room seemed like a cross between an apothecary and a bookseller's establishment, though more random. That tarnished sword Silvestrus had been waving around the other day was now sitting in the giant lizard's foot. Speaking of lizards, the one named Antigonis that his Master kept in this room lay dozing atop a corner bookcase.

The old man sat behind his desk with his fingers tented and regarded his former Apprentice. After a time, he spoke.

"Thaddeus, I have had deliberations with all the Council members. I have examined cases dating back to the founding of the *Collegium*. I have conferred at length with our resident Physician, Master Celsius, and he has conferred with his professional colleagues elsewhere. I have had conversations with the Head-Mistress of our companion school, the *Ludia*. I have even had communication with more arcane and rarefied sources. None of us have been able to formulate an intervention, Thaddeus, that would serve to restore to you your Belief and, therefore, your Sorcery. I am sorry. Sorrier than you know, I expect." The old man's face was at once troubled and grieved.

"It is all right, Master. I have no hurt and am content. But, Master, I have been giving this much thought, and … well … I have come to the conclusion that I must leave. My parents could use my help at home, no doubt. And I should be about training for a trade or a craft so that I may make my way in the world."

"Ah, yes. Thank you for sparing my having to say it, lad. You were always quick to know a situation. Had you decided to stay, we would have obliged you, certainly. It should go without saying that you have the highest regard of all here, and we are in your debt for not only our way of life but for our very lives. All realize this. But, as you suggest, what life would you have here? Never seeing what others see, never feeling what others feel? That would be hard; hard on your friends and those who love you and hardest of all on you."

The old man gazed at his hands a moment, then raised his head. "That is not to say, however, that there is not the possibility of a remedy for your condition."

"A remedy, Master?"

"Yes. When I said there was nothing we could do here, that did not mean there is nothing that can be done anywhere. I have given the matter much thought, and if you truly wish that part of you that was lost to be restored, there may be a way to accomplish this. But the cost would be high and the risk great."

Curiosity began to intrude upon resignation. "Please, Master, tell me if you will."

"Thaddeus, you should look to the East—to the land of the Cin. As I have told you before, their magicks are ancient and different from ours. It is in this difference that I feel you may entertain hope."

"How is that, Master?"

"I believe it may be possible for them to approach your situation in a way that we cannot here in the Westlands. In so doing, they may know how to correct it, to heal that which has been damaged, to restore that which has been sundered. But as I have said, the way is difficult in the extreme, and the outcome is unknowable."

Thaddeus' eyes lit up, his interest pricked for the first time in days. "How would I accomplish this, Master?"

"You must make a journey, Thaddeus, to the East—beyond the Golden Range, beyond the Graecolian peninsula, beyond the Lands of Sand, even beyond the Indas. It is there that the Cin dwell. Once in that land, you must find an Ancient One who will agree to instruct you in the healing. Then all you can do is hope; hope there is a way to recover what was lost. When you are whole once again, you can return to us, complete your training and take your rightful place as a Master Sorcerer of the Westlands."

"It is far, Master?"

"Yes, Thaddeus, very far. And hazards will abound at every step. You could be injured or killed at any moment. As a stranger, many eyes will turn from you. The culture of those you seek is—different. Perhaps so different as to prohibit any commerce whatsoever."

Thaddeus frowned. "The Cin were our enemies, Master."

"Yes. Once, long ago. But because their hands were set against us once does not mean it is to be so always."

"I will need to know the way. Perhaps in the Library…."

"Brother Cartographus will assist you."

"I fear I do not have the money with which to purchase food and secure shelter."

"The Council has considered this as well and has agreed to make available to you certain funds that, if frugally and thoughtfully applied, should go well toward providing you most of the required necessities. For the rest, you are young, intelligent, and strong. You will, no doubt, be able to work for whatever extra you will need."

Thaddeus stopped his considerations as a look of bleak sadness crossed his face. "None can accompany me. I must go alone, mustn't I, Master?"

"Yes, Thaddeus. Your friends—your Marsia and the others—will remain behind. Though I believe any would gladly accompany you to wherever you journeyed if you but asked them."

"I cannot ask that of any of them, Master. They are Sorcerers. They have the gift. They must complete their studies and make what they can of it."

The old man simply nodded.

"I-I think I should leave right away. There is really nothing to be gained by staying, and the year is going on. How long might my journey be, Master?"

"I presume here you are not speaking philosophically but, rather, geographically. I would estimate six months, perhaps as much as a year, depending on how things fall out. In Graecolia, it should be possible for you to purchase passage with a caravan going East. That, at least, would relieve you of some of the burdens of travel and provide for a measure of safety. Understand, my boy, this journey will be perilous in the extreme. You may not even get safely beyond the Westlands. However, you will have a guide with you if you choose—at least a guide of sorts."

"A guide, Master? I thought I must go alone."

"You will not have the advantage of human companionship, true enough, but there is one who said he would accompany you. Actually, he rather insisted on it."

"Who, or what is it, Master?"

"Ah, Thaddeus, can you not imagine who it must be?"

"The mule, Master?"

"Yes. The very same."

"But it must know I can no longer speak with it."

"He does and says it matters not. As it turns out, he was offended that any considered you would undertake the journey without him."

"But Master, this is your mule; it belongs to the College. You need its services. I cannot simply take such a valuable animal with me at a whim."

"I know it is difficult for you to accept this now, my lad, but know that Asullus truly is aware and his own person, so to speak. He is not mine to give, take, or command. To negotiate with, yes, when he is not being so damn stubborn, but not the other. He said—in fact, with some heat—that if we try to constrain him, he will simply kick down his stall and set out to join you in any case."

"Well, a mule would be welcome. I could carry more that I might require and ride when I tire. But I will, of course, care for him and see to his needs."

"Yes. He said the same of you."

"As you say, the mule 'knows.' Do the others?"

"By now, almost certainly. In addition to your packing, you will have several goodbyes to make. Mistress Geanninia said she would delay the Sorceresses' return to the *Ludia* to help with this. I do not envy you these tasks, though, my boy."

"Well, then, Master, I should probably be about it."

"Yes, Thaddeus. I think you have the right of it. I will see you before you leave, but I want you to know I will sorely miss you, lad, and you

The Intelligentiae

will be in my thoughts often. You are a good man, Thaddeus, a very good man."

Smiling, Silvestrus rose and grasped Thaddeus' arm as his former Apprentice turned to exit the room. He squeezed it, then let his arm fall to his side as the boy left.

After the door shut, Silvestrus emitted a great sigh.

Antigonis, awakening at the noise, looked up briefly to see if anything were amiss. Detecting nothing untoward, he lowered his head to finish his evening's Repose.

Outside the old Sorcerer's mid-air window, it began to rain.

Later, at midnight, Silvestrus made his way slowly up to the Western tower and out the stairwell door onto the cold stone parapet. He walked over to the tower wall and rested his hand on the cool gray granite while surveying the meadow and forest beyond.

He looked up. The sky was clear and full of stars. *How many*, he wondered again. He did not think he could count them all, even if he had a hundred lifetimes.

Sensing a change in his surroundings, he turned to behold four very tall glowing female forms standing on the walkway and silently regarding him. He moved to meet them, looking up into indistinct, almost hazy faces.

"He will go."

The four figures nodded as one in understanding, then faded and were gone.

Silvestrus waited a few moments more before making his way back into the *Collegium* and down the stairs and corridors to his chambers.

His thoughts and feelings were so entangled by events and fatigue that he could make no sense of any of them. He hoped the morning would bring clarity.

It was going to be hard enough as it was.

35

The Pain of Farewell I
Abitus Dolorosus I

haddeus had very little to pack. Still, it seemed he could never make it out of his room due to the endless stream of visitors and well-wishers. First came the Upperclass, most representing those against whom he had played Pila Ludere. Others of his own class soon followed. These visits were interspersed with various Faculty members.

Master Beatus congratulated him on behalf of the *Collegium*, presented him with words of wisdom gathered over a long lifetime, a fat purse that jingled, and, finally, a Blessing.

Master Specus arrived carrying a bulging basket containing, "Just a few things for the road, lad, should a hunger take you unawares." He appeared red-faced and uncomfortable and left as quickly as he could. From the hall came a loud honk, the kind which tended to require a large handkerchief.

Then two of the *Advenae* came to pay their respects. One asked if he might have his room afterward.

Next, Knight-Master, Sir Eques, knocked on the door. Zoarr said later that it was widely known the stout knight had not visited the Underclass floor since he had lived there himself. He walked in carrying a large parcel wrapped in canvas. It appeared to be heavy and clinked.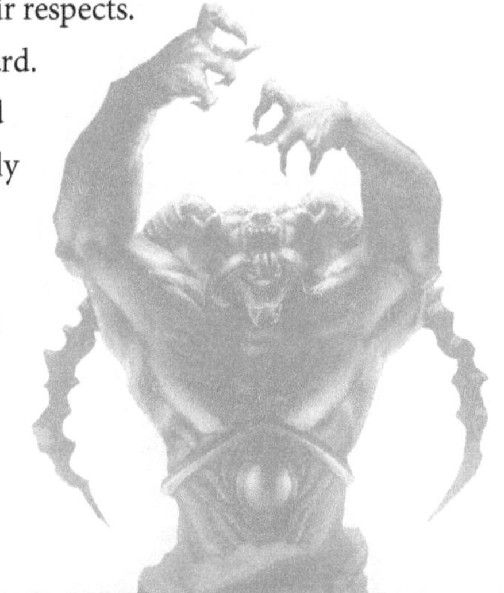

"It's a long journey you'll be taking, Apprentice Thaddeus, with danger at every turn. It is best you have protection if needed and a way to make your point. The other Battle-Masters and I have put together some goods we think you might find useful. I imagine you will be able to puzzle out what came from whom."

With that, the Knight laid his burden on Thaddeus' cot and invited him to unwrap the gifts. The ex-Apprentice undid the ties and laid back the canvas cover, revealing a variety of keen-edged weapons, all polished until they shone.

First, he found a well-used double-curved bow of dark lustrous wood with a leather quiver and thirty-three silver-hued arrows. Thaddeus remembered the day the Bow Master had demonstrated this oddly-shaped weapon to his class. He claimed the design was uncommon in the Westlands, and he had handled the bow with great respect.

"Master Arch-Iten has told me that where you're going, this is the bow to use. No great open plains but rocks and crags and out-of-the-way places where a good shot around the corner can make a difference."

Next, Thaddeus picked up a small hand axe, the handle of which was carved with numerous runes.

"Master Pumilus has asked me to inform you that this tool will be as good for chopping firewood or a chicken's neck as it will a Goblin or even a Hob-Goblin. Oh, and he says you should know there will be little need to sharpen that blade any time soon."

Lastly, a sword in a leather scabbard nestled in a shield, face down on the cot, that had cradled all the other weapons. Thaddeus slid the blade slowly and carefully out of its glove. The sword, marked only with an 'Λ' on the blade, was heavy but well-balanced. The shield face was marked with the same device.

Thaddeus took the shield up in his right hand. The straps were well-used but fit comfortably. He was immediately taken with the pair—almost as much as he had been with his own first tools.

"I gave those two a lot of thought, lad. I had originally considered giving you my own set from my Apprentice days, but I use them still, and I doubt they'd fit you so well. Then I thought of this pair. They belonged to Callidus of Agilitium, the most accomplished Apprentice Swordsman of the Imperium, who grew to become a Sword-Master in his own right and, eventually, Knight-Master. He perished with Tyrannus' Army of the Invasion, but his squire—one of the very few who survived—was able to bring his weapons back to the *Collegium.* Oh, and perhaps more importantly to you, he was left-handed. These weapons were made especially for him by Master-Smith Fabricus. I hoped they might bring you luck."

Lastly, the Knight-Master reached into a leather pouch at his belt and withdrew a long golden chain from which hung a circular disk the size of a hen's egg. He held it out.

"Here, lad, a gift from Master Luctarus, who has asked me to remind you that if you understand and use this tool as it is meant, you will have no need of these other—as he puts it—trinkets." The Knight-Master smiled.

At once, Thaddeus saw the symbol of the *One unto the Other* sign, which Master Luctarus habitually referred to during his instruction. He had often seen the Master wear this same piece to and from field practice, during which time it spent most afternoons on a tree limb, moving to and fro in the breeze.

Thaddeus was speechless. He did not need Rolland to tell him that this collection of brilliant arms was worth thousands of gold Imperials, perhaps tens of thousands. Consequently, he stood there gulping air, thinking he must look brain-struck.

"Nay, lad, speak not. I've a notion I know what is going through your noggin. I ask only that you bring it all back, along with yourself, in one piece. I'll not demand the usual 'show us no dishonor,' as I do not believe that is even a possibility. Well, my boy…," the old Knight-Master said, clasping Thaddeus' hand firmly, "fare-thee-well, and may the Gods watch over you—with more than their usual indifference." He gave the youth a wink and strode out.

It was some time before Thaddeus came to himself. He could not believe his good fortune nor fathom what had befallen him.

With great reluctance, he rewrapped his treasures carefully and placed them under his cot. He could not wait for the time to come when he would be alone and could let his eyes drink in the sight of these magnificent gifts and touch these brilliant jewels of destruction.

At a knock, Thaddeus raised his head to greet Rolland and Sonnia.

"May we come in, Brother mine?"

Thaddeus grinned. "Since when did you begin asking, thief?"

The redhead held back, allowing his love to enter the room first. "Since I have found civilization, I mean, since civilization has deigned to find me," he replied wryly.

Sonnia smiled her bright smile.

"Hello, Thaddeus. We've come to say hail and farewell. And Rolland has a little something for you." The beautiful girl turned her head to acknowledge the red-haired youth, who withdrew a scroll of parchment from his tunic and handed it to his tall Brother.

"What is this?"

"Open it and see," the thief replied with a grin of his own.

Thaddeus chivvied open the ribbon and seal on the parchment and read quickly.

"Sonnia helped me with the wording, and Zoarr handled the transfer of funds."

Thaddeus was astounded. "Rolland, this is a Letter of Credit for three hundred and thirty-three gold Imperials. What is this?"

"You just said it, big oaf. It's a third of my earnings from my tuition from Faran. I talked it over with Sonnia, and we thought this would be the most useful of gifts. To be fair, we were going to split it into fourths, but Zoarr would have none of it. Anders tried to refuse as well, but I bullied him into accepting it. Now I admit, it's not actually a third; I kept the extra Imperial for myself." He grinned and shrugged.

"Are you moon-addled? I can't take this. These are your earnings!"

"Of course you can. And besides, they are not my earnings; they are Zoarr's extortion. But that's all right. You'll need this more than I. Not to mention that if I ever really need any gold, once I am done here, I can always st—" The boy stopped suddenly at a sharp look from Sonnia, then coughed. "I mean, I could always go to a finance factor and apply for a tradesman's loan."

Thaddeus was immediately reminded of the flying pig illustration. The two images seemed to him equally likely.

The three friends talked for a time, reminiscing and laughing, then the couple embraced the tall boy and left.

It was but moments later that Master Celsius strolled in to check on his patient's health and pronounce him fit for his journey.

"Now, my boy, and most importantly, remember to let no week go by without a good physic. If the innards are not functioning as they should, neither will the outards. Ha!"

The green-trimmed figure barked a laugh at his own jest. "Oh, and by the way, your Master Silvestrus has made arrangement with me to broker the cost of any emergent treatment you might require during the time of your absence from the *Collegium*. I think that is quite generous of him, and in fact…." here the Healer adopted a reflective pose, "… that might be an interesting concept for the awareness of others. Hmm, if one could assure payment in advance from, let us say, a group of like-minded, foresighted patients to cover the expense of the treatment for whatever medical mishap might befall them throughout a year's time, then…." The Physician left the boy's room deep in thought, green leather sandals slapping on the cold stone.

Next came a forlorn-looking Anders and his solemn-countenanced Nannsi, who carried a parcel under a cloth.

"Ah, Anders, what transpires? You do not look yourself."

"Well, it's your departure, you see. You and I … well, that is, we have been together since the beginning; you trying to think up ways to get us into trouble, and me trying to think up ways to get us out. I am not sure how this is all going to work without you." The short boy looked miserably unhappy while Nannsi stroked his arm, murmuring reassurances.

"It's all right, Anders. It will probably be only a year or so, and then I will be back with lots of stories to tell you of the exciting things I have seen, and you can tell me all about what has transpired here during that time. And we can always correspond."

It took some time to cheer up the glum scholar, but Thaddeus had a year's practice soothing the clever boy's vacillating worries.

"Well, all right. I … that is, we wished you to have a gift—a remembrance if you like—from the two of us. I had thought to give you Iusti Mores' ring, but I cannot get it off my finger for some reason. Nannsi believes that is because it was meant to be so."

"Not even pig grease has worked, Thaddeus," the red-cheeked brunette said. "And Anders thought of everything else to try. It's not natural."

"But we did want you to have something from us, so we got you this. I hope you like it. Nannsi?"

The short girl stepped forward and handed Thaddeus the parcel she'd been holding.

Expressing thanks, he took the gift from her, but as he hefted it, he began to have a sinking feeling concerning its identity. He pulled off the covering cloth gingerly.

Ah, as he'd feared.…

"Why, it's a crock of honey," he said, wishing he could still perform the Sorcery they all said he used to have. Then he could spell his friends so they would believe he really liked it or, perhaps more expediently, cause the whole damn thing to disappear in a puff of smoke.

"Not just any honey, Thaddeus. See the label? It's Beewicke's own!"

"Yes, you should have seen what my clever Anders went through just to lay hands on some. It's not an everyday commodity, you know," Nannsi added wisely.

"Yes, I can imagine," the tall youth said with the best grace he could manage.

The boys spoke at length of the old times, carefully avoiding recitation of events associated with vintner's mistresses, blue butterflies, and governesses' nieces—of which Anders had told Thaddeus earlier, Nannsi disapproved.

It was during a quiet pause that Anders snapped his fingers. "Oh, Thaddeus, I almost forgot. Lord Non-Dar of the *Aelvae* … wait," Anders said, holding up a hand to ward off the tall youth's protests, "I know you don't now believe in these people, but accept that I do and just listen to the message."

The tall youth nodded.

"Taddy, he asked me to let you know that he and his people have sent word of their Blessings for you on ahead throughout the domains of their far-flung tribes. Should you be in need in any lands where the *Aelvae* dwell, you have only to contact one of them, and they shall aid you as they can."

Thaddeus sighed. "I thank you for carrying the message and bringing it to me, Anders, but I am not sure how that might be helpful. I mean, if I cannot see *Aelvae*—even if such exist—how can I call upon them for help?"

"Well, that thought crossed my mind also, but it seemed impolite to point it out at the time."

"Besides, which, Thaddeus," Nannsi added, "this affliction of brain humors you have may be only temporary. Who knows? A quick, random thump on the head, and you might be right as rain again in no time."

Thaddeus nodded, not trusting to speech when he was uncertain as to what response to make to such an assessment.

Finally, the three ran out of words. They stood, embraced, and then they, too, were gone.

Once again, Thaddeus had but a few moments to himself before his peace was interrupted by another knock at the door frame … soft and gentle this time. Thaddeus turned to see a dark figure in crimson robes, surmounted by a turban of whitest silk with a centered blood-red jewel the size of Thaddeus' thumb. At his side was a tall brunette vision, also in silks, who looked slightly less assured.

"Molly, Zoarr, welcome. Come in, come in."

"Do you tire of this endless line of well-wishers, Brother?"

Thaddeus sighed, then chuckled. "No, not really. It's been hard, though. I hate saying goodbye. And this has gone on all day; I feel no higher than a mite of dust."

"Perhaps, then, it would be better if we left," the Prince said.

"No, no, please come in. Sit wherever you like."

"You mean on the cot," Zoarr said, grinning.

Thaddeus grinned back, nodding. "You both look ready for the Lords' and Ladies' dance at the Shire Faire."

Molly blushed, then pirouetted. "Do you like it?"

"Very much, Molly. It suits you, I think."

"I am hoping she will not only get used to it but come to wish it on a regular basis," Zoarr said, still smiling.

"Mayhap. We shall see."

The three laughed.

Zoarr turned serious. "In Mauretesia, Thaddeus, we say *goodbye* when we are glad someone is going who we really have little wish to see again. But when we are with someone who matters, we say *when Mother is ready*. It means when that which rules over us—Goddess, destiny, the Fates, randomness, you choose—is ready for us to be reunited, it will happen. Neither before nor after, but then only. Until then, we must wait. So it is with us, Brother. Until Mother is ready, we wait. However, in the meantime, we have some things for you."

Molly stood and advanced on the Beewickean. She drew two daggers from her belt and handed them to Thaddeus, hilts first.

"Here, Thaddeus. These are the best throwing knives I have ever had. Though a little heavy for me, they are in all other ways perfect. They will keep you safe. Now, please, do not argue with me. I know what I give you, and I am content." Having spoken, she resumed her seat.

Thaddeus hefted the blades. They were perfectly balanced. He thanked the girl profusely and set them down beside him.

Next, Zoarr rose and withdrew several small scrolls from inside his robes, handing them to his taller Brother. "Here are some pieces of parchment you may find useful. No—do not open them now. Wait until a different time. I had thought of giving you my flute as well—for your practice—but there is another who has taken a fancy to it." Here, the Prince's eyes flicked to his lady. "I hope you understand. It is just that she and I—that is, our music together...."

"Have no care, Brother. I understand."

Zoarr smiled gratefully. "Thank you." The Prince rose, as did the tall ex-Apprentice. "Well, Thaddeus...." The dark lad embraced the Beewickean warmly and stepped back. "When Mother is ready."

"Yes, when Mother is ready." Thaddeus was finding it difficult to make out their features clearly. It was late in the day, and recent events had been demanding. Also, it seemed as if something was in his eyes.

Molly rose as well, then leaned forward and kissed Thaddeus on the cheek, whispering in his ear. "I am bidden to tell you that if you are not yet overdone with saying farewell at the end of the day, there is one who would meet you down a path in the forest when first the moon rises. Thus, my message. When Mother is ready, Thaddeus."

"Thank you, Molly. When Mother is ready."

He watched the two as they moved smoothly from the room in their silks and heaved a great sigh.

This had been an emotionally draining day, and it was not over yet, apparently.

He was sure he knew who Molly meant. Now all he needed to do was to wait for the moon.

At last, he closed his door.

He'd had enough of goodbyes for one day.

36

The Pain of Farewell II
Abitus Dolorosus II

haking off his melancholy for the moment, he crossed the room swiftly, excitement building as he knelt down and pulled his weapons cache from under his cot. Within a moment, he was fingering the various instruments of death with a keen eye and an appreciation he'd not possessed a year earlier.

He was still going over his hoard with an oiled cloth when the first light from the moon shone into his room. With a start, he came to himself and collected, wrapped, and shoved the trove back under his cot. He was out the door in a trice.

Thaddeus pounded down the stairs, around and through the halls, out the *portus,* and down the steps in less than an eye-blink. He was halfway across the meadow when he realized he'd neglected to ask which path he was to take. No matter, he'd let instinct guide him. His Brothers had told him that the pathways constantly changed. He had never confirmed that was true, but he did trust his instinct.

The pale stretch of path beckoned him into the forest, and he followed it willingly. After some minutes, he came to a branch in the trail, chose the left path, and walked rapidly.

Soon, however, the path narrowed and faded away, ending at the base of an ancient oak.

A figure emerged from behind the old tree and moved to meet him.

"Thaddeus."

"Marsia."

"I have brought meat and drink. And a blanket."

"I find myself not really that hungry. Or thirsty."

"I see. Then come; tell me of your day."

"I would rather not. It hurt."

The girl moved closer and wrapped her arms around him. "We can share our hurts, Thaddeus. That is one of the things Love does."

"It's not that, really. I cannot think of any other place I'd rather be, nor anyone else I'd rather be with. But the fact that you and I are here at all is only because we are now going to be parted for such a long, long time, else we would not be meeting like this. So, I am mixed about it all, and I—"

Thaddeus never got the opportunity to complete his sentence.

The three-quarter moon was overhead by the time Thaddeus slowly made his way back to the *Collegium*. He had thought he might spend some time under his cherry tree and try to sort out his feelings, but as he approached, he saw it was occupied. A couple sat beneath it, side by side.

He was surprised and so delayed a moment before retreating back the way he'd come. By that time, however, one of the two had stood and was facing him.

"Thaddeus?"

"Yes?"

"'Tis I, Longius. I am here with Lillia."

"How did y—"

"Not many have your height, *Tironis*. Also, you have special importance to us and are thus more highly placed in our memory."

"You have just come from your lady love, then?" Lillia asked.

"Yes. How did—"

"What other reason would a boy be out on a night like this? You were coming from the wood and moving slowly. Now, if you were on your way to your rendezvous, you would be moving impatiently and full of energy. Anyone with eyes knows this. But that is not what we wish to talk about. We wish to talk of farewell. You are going tomorrow, yes?"

"Yes."

"And you have been spending all day saying painful goodbyes?"

"Yes."

"Ah. It is hard. But it must be. You would do no good for yourself to remain here, as you know. Perhaps out there somewhere is the chance to put things right. Or to come to accept what is. The choice will be yours, but it's coming to terms with the choice that will be difficult. That aside for the moment, we want you to know that we regret you will be absent from our wedding."

"You two are to marry? How wonderful! Congratulations! When, if I might ask?"

"As soon as may be. We've asked Master Beatus to officiate. We both knew him … from before."

"Well, again, congratulations. I shall certainly be sorry to miss your celebration."

A moment of quiet persisted until Longius cleared his throat. "Thaddeus, have you those things needful to you and your journey?"

"Yes. I want for nothing."

"Nothing tangible, he means, my love," Lillia added.

"Forgive her, Thaddeus. Naught escapes her, but she must always have the last word."

"Aye. True it is."

"See you what I mean?"

"Aye. True it is."

"Well, I must get some rest. I will depart the *Collegium* on the morrow. Take care of each other; I will see you when I return."

"Fare-thee-well, Thaddeus. Know that we love thee."

"I love you both also. Fare-thee-well, and best to you both."

Thaddeus' last view of the couple was to see them, arms around each other's waists, waving to him.

After that, a short stop at the privy, then his cot, then blackness.

The parrot walked herself down the top board of the stall to be closer to the mule. "So, you are going with him?"

"Aye. He canno' be makin' such a journey wi'out his faithful old servitor."

"But he can no longer speak with you."

"Well, that be the situation now. Howe'er, who can tell what will be in the days to come? He is goin' East, after all, to correct this situation. An' when all is said an' done, I'll be there to once again instruct him in what it is he's to know."

"What of you, Osiric?"

The Eagle, talons anchoring him to the opposing top stall board while he preened under his wings, raised his head. "I see no purpose to be served by traveling with the boy who cannot hear me and whom I cannot see. Instead, I will accompany my Mistress on her journey back to her school. Of course, should she decide to leave me at Mountaingaard with Captain Geoffrey to keep an eye open—so to speak—for my Lord's return from the East, I shall acquiesce. But to go with him? No. That is practical for neither of us."

A moment lapsed. "I would ask, however, Asullus, that you do take care of your charge. He is likable, for a Human, and seems to make somewhat fewer errors in most things than others of his kind."

"Aye, that I will. He do seem to ha' that effect on a being. E'eryone is always aboot askin' me t' take care o' him. Interestin', don' ye know. On another topic, Lord Osiric … ha' I heard ye correctly say our Thaddeus was wi' the Serpent an' the Beast durin' yer recent travels?"

"Yes. He was. I was there, and he did."

"Well, then, that's the last o' 'em. Whee-oosh! Prophecy unfoldin' it is, right here in front o' our eyes. Who'd ha' ever thought it so?"

"All the more reason for the lad to regain his Sorcerous abilities," Psittaca said. "Now, the Writ of Mauretesia will hold for some of the lands you will be traveling through, so that should help. My Master has given papers of assist toward those ends. For the rest, we will simply have to hope. Your wreath is no more?"

"Aye, 'tis shredded to nothingness, thanks to that black-hearted, cloven-hoofed, manure-spawn o' a Daemon. 'Course, he's dead and writhin' in the flames by now, I'll wager, while I be standin' here and conversin' wi' me friends. So, I'd say I ha' the best o' it so far. But poor old Charles. I am goin' ta miss 'im. He was always a handy one to ha' wi' ye when push came to shove."

"Well, then … we have to trust to luck and the Mother's Graces. I can think of nothing else for it."

"Nor I."

"Nor meself, neither, don' ye know."

The air was cool, and dew lay heavily over the wide expanse of meadow, slicking the stairs so that the tall boy had to take care as he made his descent. Ground-hugging fog lay here and there in great patches in the steely gray, pre-dawn sky. No one else was about—not even the kitchen help was up yet—so the quiet was undisturbed.

Getting his possessions, particularly his gifts, down the stairs without alerting the entire *Collegium* with his clattering was a feat in itself and required more than one trip. But, at last, he'd built up a pile in the stable.

He'd fashioned himself a leather knapsack with a long belt which he hung over his shoulder. In it, he placed the *Collegium's* Letter of Credit, Rolland's Letter of Credit, a change of short clothes, stockings, extra jerkin, tunic, a traveler's robe for heavy weather, and the three small scrolls Zoarr had given him. He planned to open those at his camp later that night and review them at his leisure.

Thaddeus fed, watered, and groomed the mule, walked it around a bit, then fitted the straw panniers onto it, one on either side, which he filled with his weapons, clothes, camp supplies, Specus' basket, and his few personal items. He found himself wishing for Zoarr's flute but did not begrudge the Prince his duet. Perhaps he'd come upon a fallen branch or some other material he could fashion into a flute of his own. Molly's knives looked like they could carve a stick of kindling as slickly as a cutpurse's best blade.

The mule stood patiently while Thaddeus readjusted the contents of the panniers until their weight was balanced. He was grateful Master Silvestrus had allowed him to take the carrying baskets. Otherwise, he and the mule would have looked like a traveling peddler's show with items sticking out in all directions.

He finished, looked at the mule, and sighed. "Well, I suppose we should be on our way, mule." The beast of burden returned his look and moved its mouth, which Thaddeus took to mean it was working yet on the last of its Break-fast.

He'd turned to lead the mule into the stable yard when he suddenly stopped.

Master Silvestrus stood at the door, lighting his pipe. "Good morrow, Thaddeus. Ready to begin your journey?"

"Yes, Master. I suppose so. I don't think there's anything else left here for me now."

"Yes, I take your point. Here, let me walk for a bit with you and Asullus."

Thaddeus led the mule out of the yard, then around to the front of the quadrangle, heading down the meadow toward the forest. His steps were heavy even though he knew he'd made the better choice.

"I believe the ladies will be leaving today. Have you said all the goodbyes you intended?"

"Yes, Master."

"Good. It is important, you know, even if painful."

The three walked on in silence. Oddly, Thaddeus was as glad for the quiet as for the companionship. Something about it struck him well, though he could not have said what.

They were nearing the edge of the forest when Silvestrus stopped and faced his ex-Apprentice. "Thaddeus, I will take my leave of you now. Know that I have been very proud of all you have accomplished this year, and I expect there is more we will hear from you in the future.

"I think, though, that you will face great challenges in the months to come in your search for that which will come to replace what you have lost—the loss of your Belief. Indeed, the loss of your Faith. If you have no objection, I should like to give you my Blessing now. I know you may think it of little value, but, pray, humor an old man and his fancies."

"Of course, Master."

Silvestrus raised his arm and touched his palm to Thaddeus' forehead.

"To those who listen and attend to such things, know that this gentle warrior and seeker-for-truth now sets forth on a great journey. To mark this, I say he shall no longer be known as Thaddeus of Beewicke but henceforth be called Thaddeus the Faithless. Let all who hear this Blessing know by this name that he who is called thus faces one of the greatest struggles of mankind—the coming of age to know oneself. In this task, though he shall be alone, know that those who cherish him strive for his eventual victory, just as he does—even if by a different path.

"To those who may meet him on this journey, I pray you give him what aid and succor you may. But to those who would seek to hinder him or harm his flesh, know that you will feel my wrath and that of … others.

"Therefore, go now in peace, Thaddeus the Faithless, and know our Love goes with you for all the steps you take until you return once again to those who await you."

Having finished speaking, the old man withdrew his hand and stepped back.

"Thank you, Master," the boy said.

The old man nodded but remained silent, gazing after the tall youth until he was lost to sight in the great wood.

"Well, there he goes. Maybe he'll make something of himself yet."

"Oh, Alistair, it's all so sad. If I were not made of stone, I believe I would cry."

"What? And wash away all the lime? Then what? Have your tits fall off?"

"Alistair!"

The small figure sat in the tree, dashing tears from her eyes as rapidly as they formed. Thaddeus had not even seen her! It was just as they said—he'd lost his Sorcery.

Well, there was nothing for it now.…

Drying her eyes after his passage, she sighed, then leaped off the limb of the old crimson maple, with sunbeams dancing off her purple form and wings fanning out to propel her ascent.

37

A Purchase
Mercatura

The oddly shaped wagon drove slowly up to the stately manor and came to a halt at the entranceway.

"*Domina!* There are strange men who come to the manor on a great conveyance pulled by horrid beasts! Adrocles says it is near to the work of Daemons!" the older woman finished breathlessly.

"Peace, Catria. Fetch my robe—the yellow one if you please—and have Sennacis join me in the antrum. Then we shall see what we shall see."

By the time Sophia of Brightfield Manor had reached the entranceway, a small army of curious household staff had congregated in the foyer, craning their necks for a view of the Outlanders and whispering among themselves.

For Outlanders these surely were—as strange in their appearance as was the wagon in which they traveled.

Their wagon, a tall, humped affair, was covered in garishly striped canvas. Its huge wheels were the height of a man. The wicked steel points and edges looked sharp enough to saw a person in two, and the rims and spokes were painted blood red.

The Mistress had never seen such a strange conveyance, nor had she ever seen animals such as these that pulled the great cart. They seemed most like bulls but were much larger, each with magnificent horns flaring out to either side of the head, fully a pace and a half in length with bright brass balls on the tip of each. Additionally, every beast had a great brass ring in its nose, and its steamy breath blew hot from its nostrils.

But most amazing of all were those who accompanied the strange wagon.

As Sophia walked out to the head of the steps leading to the bricked pull-up, an extraordinarily tall black-skinned man swung down from the driver's seat and moved to take a stand in front of the wagon. He was by far the largest man Sophia had ever seen with gold hoop earrings big around as duck eggs that bounced on his massive shoulders as he walked. He was dressed head to toe in a white silken robe, his feet shod in black leather sandals. Over his left breast was embroidered a red dove. A long curved, serrated blade was thrust through the wide sash at his waist.

A second companion, less gaudy, remained seated on the wagon, holding the reins. Two other men with leather harnesses and panta-loons—and wearing little else save weapons—stood alert at the rear of the wagon. The pair of them sported the mark of a red dove on their left cheeks. She at first thought the designs must be tattoos but later realized they were scars.

The lady surmised these must be guards—else why the fierce mustachios and even fiercer cutlery?

At her signal, Sennacis glided to his mistress' side.

"What make you of this ensemble, Steward?" the lady asked, *sotto voce*.

"I think, *Domina*," the man whispered back, "that they are sent here in connection with our former houseguest, the Prince. That is his sigil on their clothes and skin. As to their purpose here, I can surmise nothing."

The Mistress of Brightfield stood forth. "Come then, let us greet these Outlanders and thus end the mystery."

The impossibly tall man approached her, halted two paces away, and pressed his palms together. He bowed deeply as his men performed the same gesture.

"Fair Lady, do I address Mistress Sophia of Brightfield Manor?" The man had a strange accent but a deep and resonant voice. He remained bowed.

It was but a moment only before Anders' mother understood. "Yes, you do. Please rise and take your ease, men of the House of Abdomoolano."

The tall man stood his full height, eyebrows raised in surprise, then nodded his respect.

"You have seen it correctly, Mistress. We are of Abdomoolano. I am called Sanadar and am Captain of the House to his Highness, Zauda, King of Mauretesia."

The woman nodded. "And to what purpose have you, Sanadar of Mauretesia, come this long way to Brightfield Manor?"

"I am bidden to speak to you the following, Mistress." The House Captain tilted back his head and spoke in a deep yet sonorous voice as if reciting poetry.

"Know all who dwell in this land that a report of the unselfish hospitality of the Master and Mistress of Brightfield Manor, shown toward Zoarr, Prince of Mauretesia, on the occasion of this *Saturnalia* past, has not gone unnoticed but has, indeed, reached the ears of his father, the King. Know, in addition, that his Highness, King Zauda, is grateful beyond words for the kindnesses and generosity you have demonstrated toward his son and sole heir to the Leopard throne, who came to you as a stranger in a strange land.

"Know ye further that he now regards you and those who dwell with you as 'of the Family of Mauretesia.' Let all with ears hear this claim and know that those who show favor toward Brightfield Manor will receive favor from our King, Zauda … yea, until his last breath. Those, however, who would show disfavor to the House of Brightfield shall be judged the enemy of our great King and shall entertain a fate which will bring trembling and fear for generations yet to come to any who shall hear of it."

The tall man and his retinue quickly covered their eyes with their hands at this pronouncement of doom before continuing.

"As a small—and regrettably inadequate—token of his regard for the Blessings given his son under your roof, receive now these negligent porcelain works, which his Highness hopes shall find some small merit in your eyes. Please know that the King is aware these trifles are as nothing to ones as noble-hearted as yourselves, though he dares to hope they may yet please."

At this, the tall man snapped his fingers, and the two guards at the rear of the wagon swept back the canvas cover partway to expose two long wooden boxes nailed tightly closed.

At first, Sophia thought they must be coffins by their shape and size.

The two men, however, slid the boxes down from the wagon bed with great care, lowering them gently to the ground. They then took out long metal bars, angled at one end and curved at the other, and applied them to the boxes, slowly prying the pair open.

Soon enough, the nailed lids were off and revealed that each box was filled to the brim with wood shavings that brought the scent of cedar. Sophia wondered to what porcelains Sanadar was referring.

In a moment, both men knelt and began carefully scooping out handfuls of wood chips. Soon, in each box, the outline of a great man-sized vase began to form. With continued effort, the vases themselves appeared.

Sophia was aware of Sennacis' sharp intake of breath. He saw it, too. Her hand went to her mouth in surprise. These were indeed porcelain— the finest she'd ever seen. They were magnificent and must be priceless.

Ever so slowly, the men swept away the last of the packing. Sanadar strode to the back of the wagon, and at his signal, the guards elevated the head of each box to an angle for better display. Now a collective gasp went around the entire household assembly.

With the greatest care, each vase was gently taken from its protection and set to stand alone in the sun's full gaze. The porcelain was of the clearest white, reminiscent of Sanadar's dress, and displayed a rim and base chased with a delicate filet of gold. Tiny, brightly colored mosaic designs and figures covered the urns from top to bottom and were visible under a pale, age-yellowed glaze. These pieces were obviously quite old and, therefore, beyond the worth of a small kingdom.

The Manor's mistress started forward involuntarily, caught herself, then moved with decorum to inspect the gifts more closely. As she walked around the magnificent works, each of the great urns seemed to tell a story that started, continued, and finished back at its beginning.

One story involved a boy pitted against perhaps, thirty-five to forty-five base antagonists who appeared to live in a cave with a hidden entrance, while the other vase detailed the adventures of another boy attempting to gain control of great magicks imprisoned in a common household lighting appliance.

They were beautiful beyond description. She would not let this Sanadar leave the manor until she obtained the complete history of these vases—insofar as he might know it, and she suspected he did.

If only Astonius were back from his business with the Fermentor's Factor in Fountaindale, he would indeed be surprised. But he'd see the pieces soon enough.

After her inspection, she straightened and faced the royal House Captain.

"Sanadar, please convey to his Highness that we, here at Brightfield, are quite overwhelmed by these most wondrous gifts. There are neither words sufficient to describe the beauty of these works of art nor to express our heartfelt thanks for King Zauda's generosity."

She paused a moment before continuing. "And please add that, having had the occasion to meet the Prince and see for ourselves the quality of man he is and the glimpse we have had of the wise and worthy ruler he is sure to become, we know full well that such a wondrous son could only have come from the greatest of royal sires and the most lovely of queens."

Sanadar smiled broadly, displaying an alternating pattern of ivory and gold. "I have your message to heart already, great Mistress, and I assure you it will be most warmly received back at the Court Royal."

"I thank you, House Captain. Now, in the excitement of the moment, I have almost forgotten my manners. Please let me offer you refreshment following such a long and perilous journey. Come, name a preparative; we have a great variety here and, if I may claim, some local reputation for quality. Also, please tell your men to name their desire, and we will surely find it for them as well."

"Ah, Mistress, you are more than kind, as the Prince has instructed us already. For myself, I am given to understand you have a peach brandy here of passing excellence. The same will be true for my porters. As they do not speak, I will say for them."

"Oh, I am sorry. They are dumb?"

"Nay, Mistress—tongueless. But it was long ago, and they are used to it. To tell you truly, their silence does lengthen the miles over time. On the other hand, they never complain."

Sophia was unsure whether this was meant as an inside jest fashioned by Sanadar or merely a simple truth-saying. "I see. Well, will you be able to spend the night with us, House Captain? We are in your debt and would show our gratitude, and I know my husband would count it a boon to be able to meet and converse with you."

"Ah, Mistress, were I my own man, I would grasp your gifting at the moment. Alas, I have been given a date, and I must already hurry to meet it. I am instructed to be at the Frantillian docks at a particular time, there to meet the royal sloop, else I am stranded forever. Should that happen, however, perhaps I might make so bold as to return here and inquire concerning a like position in your household?"

Sennacis coughed while Sanadar smiled before continuing. "If I may be permitted, Mistress … we do, however, have one item of business yet to address that I am bidden to bring forward by my master, the King. I did not mention the fame of your peach brandy entirely from chance. Even in far-off Mauretesia, we know of this luxury and count it next only to that of the fabled ambrosia of which the poets sing. Therefore, my Highness has decreed that, as I am here at its source, he should like to make a purchase of this sweet elixir, so he may become the envy of all his brother monarchs by having achieved this bounty."

"Your King flatters us beyond our due, Sanadar. However, given that, it shall be our pleasure to send back with you some few kegs of our finest as our return gift."

"Oh, Mistress, again, you surpass your reputation. But please be aware that I am under the strictest of orders to purchase—at the current market price—several lots of your exquisite liquor. And it is worth my head that it be so."

"I see. Very well, how many lots would your majesty require, then, House Captain?"

"Twelve, Mistress."

"Yes. Well, that is no difficulty. Twelve kegs of our peach brandy, special reserve, will be brought to you immediately as you seem anxious to return to your lands."

"Ah, Mistress. Forgive me, but I fear I did not make myself clear. The King does not wish to purchase twelve kegs of your finest peach brandy. Our Highness, the King, wishes to purchase twelve *hogsheads* of your finest peach brandy."

The mistress blinked, then swallowed. "Twelve hogsheads. That is … a fair amount, worthy Sanadar."

"Hence the wagon, Mistress."

"Of course. Very well. Sennacis! See immediately to his Highness, King Zauda's order."

"At once, Mistress." The man disappeared.

"I-I shall need a moment to compute the total, Sanadar. We do not usually receive an order for such amounts. His Highness will, I assume, and at his leisure, wish to forward a Letter of Credit for the sum?"

"Nay, Mistress," the tall man said, grinning, while he clapped his hands.

The two guards rushed forward and drew back the rest of the canvas from the wagon, revealing two large oaken chests resting on the cart bed. Quickly, they leaped to the cart, produced large iron keys and applied them to the chests' great brass locks, throwing back the heavy lids to expose more gold coin than Sophia of Brightfield had ever before seen in one place at one time.

"His Highness, the King, is at heart, I fear, a provincial and tends to distrust parchments covered with ink scratches. He hopes, instead, you would not be averse to this more direct method of payment."

Astonius was going to be surprised, indeed.

Eyes widening and mouth drying quickly, Sophia managed to get out, "No, Sanadar. We would not be averse. Not in the least."

Thaddeus' trek to Mountaingaard was uneventful.

He camped that night in the forest with none to intrude upon his thoughts. After finishing Even-tide, marked by the excellent victuals Master Specus had sent along, he withdrew from his scrip the three scrolls Prince Zoarr had given him and opened each in turn.

First, the largest:

My Dear Brother,

Please know that you will never be far from our thoughts during this year of your absence. It will certainly not be the same here without your wisdom and commanding presence to see that all goes as it should. In a way, I envy you your journey. What interesting things you will see, and what exciting things you will do! On the other hand, being away from here would also mean being away from my lady, and that I cannot now imagine. Yet, the poets say Love will abide, whatever faith you choose to place in their wisdom.

On now to business. Of the other scrolls you have in your possession, the smaller will ensure you are advanced funds at a time and place of your choosing in any amount you deem necessary. Simply contact the Mauretesian Financial Ministry at any of the larger cities in the path of your travel, and arrangements will be made for you. If there is any doubt or hesitation, mention my name and The Red Dove.

The second of the smaller scrolls calls upon any Mauretesian fortification to assist you with arms-men or other similar force, should it be needful. If you wish such assistance, go to any marketplace large enough to hold a beggar missing his left leg above the knee and drop a piece of parchment into his bowl along with a few coins. The parchment must contain the phrase The Red Dove, and a location where someone can come to you. The rest will be taken care of.

Be safe in your travels, Brother, and come back to us alive, wiser and stronger.

When Mother is ready.

Z.

Astounded, Thaddeus stared at his Brother's letter. With such gifts, he could foresee no unhappy circumstance that could not be corrected. He was overwhelmed by the Prince's generosity and thoughtfulness and vowed to write him a letter of gratitude when next he was in a position to do so.

After musing over his good fortune in Brothers, he fed and watered the mule before making preparation for sleep. Once settled, he entered a dark, soft, and dreamless realm, unaware of the multiple pairs of eyes of varying heights and shapes that regarded him throughout the night from the limits of his dying campfire.

The following night he spent in Mountaingaard. Lord Geoffrey, having arrived ahead of him by a half day, welcomed him with good cheer, insisting that he join the Iron Company in the mess for Even-tide.

Thaddeus found it odd—many of the men who'd been on the forest campaign looked at him with the respect they'd reserve for their own brave warriors. Others looked at him as if he were first among the fool-hardy. The younger ones tended to make up the first group; the older, the second.

"So, your plan, then, Thaddeus?" the blond Captain asked.

"I will go west—first to Beewicke. I should say farewell to my parents. Then south to Frantillia and on to Vexare. I made a promise I'm bound to keep, though it all seems a bit unbelievable now."

Thaddeus took a deep draw from his cup and set it down carefully. "Captain, I believe I heard Sergeant Grunius say you were also making preparations for a journey?"

"Ah, yes. As it happens, I will be leaving the Command soon. I've received word that one of the newer officers—a Lieutenant Labienus— is making his way to this station to be my replacement. I understand he brings a few dozen recruits with him to not only replace those we have lost lately but to increase the size of the garrison. I gather the Council has decided a greater number is better since the fiasco with Perditus and his pet Boogus.

"Once he's arrived and tucked in, I'm off to the South to discover some comely lord's daughter with a golden voice, a golden braid, and a golden purse. In the meantime, let me offer you a new vintage, just up from the Southlands. If its quality is any indication, then Raugauld has, at last, made a good choice."

So saying, the Captain poured his young guest a small cup.

Thaddeus took a sip, savoring it. It was very good, though he'd little enough experience with wine.

After a time, he was given a larger cup. Soon enough, the troop became rather merry, and Thaddeus was called upon to share some of the songs he'd learned from Rolland. These were greatly appreciated, and he was given an even larger cup.

After that, the party became merry indeed....

38

Dragon Legacy I
Draconis Legatum I

Thaddeus gazed with a kind of bucolic torpor at the landscape slowly gliding by. In another, more alert part of his mind, he was reviewing the events of the past weeks, trying to digest them as he might a banquet of new and unfamiliar foods.

He'd heard from one of the Iron Company that the Eagle, Osiric, who many there had assumed was his bird, was accompanying Marsia through the forest, but might eventually winter over at the garrison. Thaddeus was unsure what would happen after Lord Geoffrey left. Would the Eagle fly to the *Ludia?* How would it find Marsia, in all that distance, especially when it was blind? And why would a bird behave in such a way in the first place?

It was the same as his experiences with other things lately. People made fantastic claims regarding this or that person, animal, object, or event, then insist he take it as whole cloth. It was beyond him to do so, though he tried to be polite about it.

Certainly, many he cared for were fervent in their beliefs. Perhaps he should consider it as he might some new form of religion.

His visit to Beewicke had been difficult, and even now, it raised a lump in his throat.

True enough, his parents had been thrilled to see him and full of talk about the Saturnalia just past, but they had seemed uneasy as well. The villagers—people he'd known all his life—were obviously uncomfortable around him.

Old chums would either fall silent at his greeting or avoid him altogether. One of the village residents even waggled his fingers at Thaddeus, perhaps thinking that was what Sorcerers did. After the third attempt, he gave up trying to explain that he was no longer involved in that line of study.

"Why do you have to go East, then?" his mother had asked. It was a pointed question, and one he'd been asking himself and one for which he had no good answer.

Another surprise was the attitude of his father. Thaddeus had expected him to try to convince him to return to beekeeping, but nothing of the sort happened. Their new Apprentice, Barcus, was apparently working out quite well. And Thaddeus did not have to be told there was only work enough for one new apprentice at a time in the village.

Then there was his parents' odd, mixed view of him. They seemed to be proud that he'd become something of an important figure in the hamlet, yet they appeared hesitant regarding his particular path to that same fame. It was as if he'd been appointed chief headsmen by the Crown: a distinction, yet a distinction of a particular sort only.

He had great difficulty explaining what had happened to him, especially when trying to tell them about such things as the necessity of physically assaulting one of his Masters in order to thwart an invisible menace. It stretched the bounds of his parents' credulity beyond their means to follow. After a time, he gave up trying.

Slowly, he came to a strengthening of the realization that had begun with the Saturnalia. Whatever he once had here was gone and gone forever. It was time to move on. He had no joy in this work—and no choice.

Soon thereafter, he packed his few possessions, embraced his parents in farewell, and set his footsteps toward the South. In the end, he'd had a feeling they were almost as glad of his decision to leave as he was sorrowful in making it. But it had released a certain tension that had been building during his stay, and that in itself was a relief.

He did not believe he would ever return.

The Dockmaster at the river port remembered him from when he'd traveled with Osiric and thus raised no objection when he negotiated for the mule to ride on the downriver barge rather than pull it from the shoreline. In fact, the word had spread on board that he provided wild animals for a broker dealing in carnival entertainments.

He shrugged. As long as he could do as he intended with the least resistance to his plans, let others make of them what they would.

Thaddeus' travels finally brought him to Vexare on Mid-Summer's Eve. The date held much significance for the young ex-Apprentice, and his mind returned to it during odd moments.

As soon as he entered the small village, he began to gather a following, with many calling out his name and small children running ahead in the nature of a parade. It was all very embarrassing, yet he was glad to see the townspeople again, and he even remembered several of them, though he could not recall exactly why that should be.

The procession wound its way to the Magistrate's abode, where Pontius stood waiting to greet him, having heard the commotion and the news simultaneously. He shook the youth's hand warmly, then leaned forward to speak to him in a low voice.

"Ah, Thaddeus, my lad. Good it is to see you again. Come along just as you said you would, though never had I a doubt of it. Here, abide for a moment, and I will purchase us some privacy."

Turning to the crowd, the Magistrate assumed his official persona and began to speak.

"My fellow citizens. Here before you, as I had foretold, stands our savior, Thaddeus, Sorcerer. He it was who delivered us all a mere year ago from the Plague of the Red Dragon's Breath. He has returned to bring to us intelligence on further matters of import concerning the health and happiness of our town and our people. Give him the gift of your greetings and plaudits of joy and gratitude!"

The assembled crowd immediately broke into loud cries and applause, calling the youth's name. It was even more embarrassing to Thaddeus than the procession had been. Finally, the Magistrate held up his hands, and the townspeople quieted.

"I go now to closet separately with Thaddeus, Sorcerer, so that he may divulge his mind to me regarding diverse matters of import. It shall be following this that I will have the leisure to share these tidings with you that we may all take value and profit from his message. Until that time, I pray you all abide for a while and give us these moments of peace to discuss such news. Disperse now, good people and friends. I will join with you anon. Thank you. Thank you!"

Thaddeus had to admit Magistrate Pontius knew his business and knew his fellow townspeople. In moments, the people had drifted away in twos and threes, and he and his host were free to proceed inside. It was but a short time after that Ulina left him and Pontius alone on the patio with a sweating pitcher of purberry punch, two cups, and a plate of fresh pastries.

"So tell me, my young friend, how fares it with you? And where is that well-appointed Eagle of yours?"

Thaddeus had given much thought to this very topic on the way downriver and decided to be forthright with the Magistrate. He had already told him much, and Thaddeus either trusted him by this time or he didn't. So, the boy revealed to his host that he'd lost his power but spared him the tedious details.

"So you see, Magistrate, I am no longer a Sorcerer. Hopefully, I may regain this ability on my journey East. But now, it is a power I no longer possess."

Pontius gazed at him for some time before speaking.

Resisting the urge to squirm, Thaddeus had the feeling he was being weighed on a fine balance.

"You know, lad, you continue to be a fellow of surprises. With what's at stake—a fortune that entire countries would fight to the death for, with possibly only the threat of Sorcery to fend them off—you admit to me you have lost that power. Yet, I also find that it is exactly what I would expect you to say. I take pride in making good judgments regarding people and I am equally proud that I am seldom wrong. And here you go and confirm it all for me. You are a treasure, to be sure."

The Magistrate let out a sigh, then smiled. "Aside from which, my boy, it's not your craft I was counting on to help out at this point so much as your sinew and endurance.

"Let me share with you how I see it all falling out and what plans I have made to date. The problem, as I came to view it, was how to work the Dragon's treasure for the greatest good. If I'd gone and announced it outright, each of my friends would have killed the other just to get to the cave where it lies with old Mari's bones.

"If I'd said naught about it and gone after it myself, then I'd have been found out sooner or later. Well, who around here could fill up a storeroom full of gold and jewels with no one the wiser? Even keeping it there or hiding it in another place would not do. There'd soon enough be questions about where is it the Magistrate goes and why does he always come back with his pants dragging the ground? Then one day certain, some clever lad or his friends would be following along to learn the secret, and they'd either have to be cut in, and others would still find out, or I'd be cut out, either of my share or of my neck. Probably the latter.

"So, you see, it's been an interesting problem and kept me up many a night: How to keep the trove intact until such time as it could be distributed to our folk on some equal basis? As for myself, I'd always thought of sharing it out. I mean to say, how much can a man spend in a year before he becomes ridiculous?

"Well, all this did give me a headache until I happened to recall a cousin of mine on my late wife's side. Always got along well, we did. And I thought he might be one who could handle such a delicate task well enough and be willing to do so on my account alone. Plus, he has the advantage of being the owner of a small school of skiffs manned by members of the family."

The older man paused to take a long pull from his cup.

"So, this summer past, I hied myself up to Port Stellatus where he lives and spoke with him at some length. I started with a simple sounding-out, then a brief possibility, and at last, an outlined plan. I told him each of us gets an equal share with the town's portion coming out of my own."

"But, Magistrate," Thaddeus protested, "that hardly seems fair to you."

"Ah, well, lad, as I've said … how much can a man eat before he chokes? If there be in that cave as much as you described, I will not suffer. Besides, I did not want to conjure up the God of Greed in the core of his heart, and it seemed to be the best way to do it.

"It will be his men and boats; after all, he does share risk and thus deserves a proportionate reward. I could not haul it all out myself, neither by the bend of my back nor for other reasons, as I've said. Besides, if someone is going to get a knife in his chest on a dark night over the subject of unhappy distributions, better him than me."

Displaying a slight grin at the man's logic, Thaddeus nodded, approving his host's plan and giving even more respect to the man.

"How may I help, then, Magistrate?"

"Well, if all goes as expected, my cousin and his boys should be pulling up on the shoreline any day now and seeking us out. I have told him of your skills and your part in all this. So, he probably has enough information about you already. And he has no need to be burdened with this new knowledge of your current situation, eh, lad? It will not hurt him to think you still have those resources to draw on, will it now?

"In any event, some nice dark night, this week or next, I'm thinking, when the moon is new and too embarrassed to show her face, we will all of us traipse down to those boats with a bale or two of gunny sacks that I have been gradually setting aside over the past several months. Then we will course around to that reef where old Mari lived and go into that cavern to pay our respects."

The Magistrate suddenly looked up. "Now, wait, lad. You said you'd have to perform some rites to free up the old Queen's spirit before we could start helping ourselves. Does your change in status make that a problem?"

Thaddeus thought quickly. "No, Magistrate. It should not change what I have to do." He hoped this was true.

"Very well, then. After you do what you need to do, just give us the sign, and we will get busy loading our sacks with whatever we find there, along with a box or two of light-wood for each bag so we can tow them behind on rope-bound light-wood rafts. That way, we don't overload and sink any of our transport.

"With luck, the lot of us will make it over and down to Port Ostia. There's another of my cousins there, and he is a banker. He gets a small fee from the Captain's share for converting the hard metal and whatnot into scrip. In this, he'll have the assistance of another cousin who's a barrister. And so, with a fortune to be made, everyone should be happy enough to lend us their skills."

The older man rubbed his chin. "Truth be told, with what I reckon we'll find, we could likely buy the bank, itself, outright, and most of the town, too.

"So, once we have the treasure nice and secure, our banking friends will issue us Letters of Credit for each of our good citizens here, all in equal shares. Some won't like it, complaining they should be getting a dole according to need, and others will just drink up their portion till it's gone, but I can't help that. Most, I hope, will use their credits to improve their fishing boats or mayhap buy new ones. Perhaps we can start a school or even open a sick house. One thing's certain, all our lives will be different, and that is a certainty. And for that, Thaddeus, my friend, we have you to bless or blame, as the case may be."

"I hope 'tis the former, Magistrate, and not the latter."

"Only time will tell, lad. In the meanwhile, you're to be my guest here at the house. Ulina! Come see to Master Thaddeus' needs, won't you? Rest you here, lad, while I go prattle to the mob about the possibility of good fortune that may be coming our way … the news of which you have just delivered to me, eh?"

39

Dragon Legacy II
Draconis Legatum II

Two nights later, Magistrate Pontius and his young guest were taking their ease on the patio after sundown and observing the stars in their courses.

"….and on an especially clear night, you can see a fifth star there in Uria's Chair. I understand, though, it's only seen here toward the Southern climes. In fact, my eldest brother once said—" The Magistrate cut off abruptly, raising his arm for Thaddeus' silence.

An instant later, he'd sprung into a crouch, a long dagger appearing in one hand.

Thaddeus imitated his actions, quickly scanning the area.

A rustling sound came from nearby, and a moment later, a cloth-covered head appeared above the retaining wall. Then a male figure hoisted itself over the wall and stood grinning in the candlelight.

"Carthago!" the Magistrate called. "Do you fear invoking a curse for knocking at the front door like other people?"

"But, cousin, as I have told you repeatedly, I am not like other people. Besides, doors and knocking are all so formal, especially among family. This is the lad?" the slender, dark-hued figure asked. "Hmm, I thought he would be older."

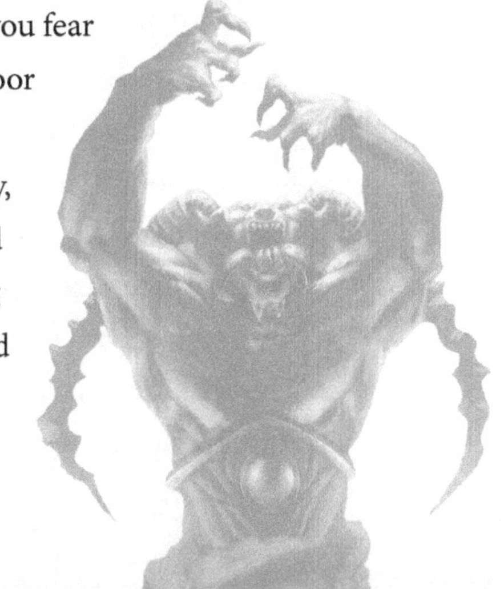

Thaddeus had been caught off guard by the sudden and unorthodox appearance of this mysterious cousin. An intricate red and white-striped head covering was knotted at the back. A swarthy complexion similar to Zoarr's, a gold hoop earring, sweeping black mustaches, and ebony curls that escaped the edge of the headscarf gave him a decidedly rakish appearance. His striking countenance was marred only by a wide pale scar that ran down his left cheek from ear to chin. He had to be Thaddeus' senior by at least twenty years, but he had a straightforward manner and ready grin, and Thaddeus found himself taking to him easily.

"This is the lad, cousin. Thaddeus, Sorcerer, may I present my cousin, Carthago of Zama. Cousin, here is Thaddeus of the College of Sorcerers. Meet and be friends."

The two strangers advanced and shook hands. The cousin had a sure and confident grip.

"Pleasure."

"Likewise."

"Good. Enough of formalities—now down to business. When do we go?" Carthago said, addressing the Magistrate.

"Patience, cousin. All good things come to those who … so on and so on. Let us sit first. I do my best planning when astride a chair. Oh, and help yourself to some punch." At the Magistrate's gesture, the other two sat down at the table where Pontius joined them, his arms crossed on the chair back.

"First of all, how many boats did you bring?" Pontius asked.

"Four, with a crew of three each. Do not worry." The man raised his hand, forestalling the Magistrate's sudden alarm. "All are family—more or less—and sworn to me with blood ties. Someone talks and they end up with two smiles. All know this."

"Well, if you're sure. There's much riding on this, cousin."

"You have my oath on it."

"Very well. Now have you cork, shark bladders, and light-wood rafts in sufficient numbers?"

"Yes to all, though the bladders were the harder to come by. I also brought barrels of the light-wood. It ought to be enough for our purposes."

"Good. Thaddeus, are there any additional preparations you require?"

"None, Magistrate. I stand ready."

"Excellent. Then I propose we move tomorrow night. Carthago, you will need to keep your men and your boats out of sight after dawn tomorrow. Then, when the Dog-Star shines its brightest, expect us down by Black Cove. Have you a manner of navigating at night in these waters without being seen from shore?"

"Of course, cousin. We will string out shielded lanterns fore and aft. None will note our passage."

"Right, then. Tomorrow night."

"Tomorrow night it is, cousin, and rich men we will be. Sorcerer," he addressed Thaddeus, nodding, "Pleasure, twice over. *Ave!*" In the blink of an eye, the fellow disappeared over the patio's wall with only a faint rustling of vines to mark his passage.

"Well, I know, lad. You're thinking he may be a bit dramatic, but his word is his bond. Best to get some rest now, my boy. Tomorrow night will be a full one. Ah, to be young again. But…." the Magistrate added, grinning, "….rich comes fairly close to the mark."

Sleep proved elusive for Thaddeus, as excitement and anticipation came and danced on his heart and did not leave for a long, long time.

The following day seemed interminable and full of meaningless activity—and mounting tension—until, at last, the sun fired the western sky with a brilliant display of colors before sinking beneath the horizon's lapping waves.

Pontius had advised his charge to wear clothing both dark and rugged. Thaddeus was ready immediately after Even-tide. Finally, the Magistrate came to the room where the boy had been pacing and signaled to him.

"It's time," he said from the hallway. "Here, you will likely need these." The older man tossed him a pair of worn leather workman's gloves.

The two made their way to the patio balcony, swung over, and climbed down trestle and vine, hand over hand. Thaddeus was impressed by the Magistrate's agility.

Noting the boy's silent homage, the older man said, "'Tis merely the legacy from a misspent youth, lad."

Quietly and quickly as possible, Thaddeus followed on Pontius' heels as he wound his way down by back paths to the farther of the two coves bracketing Vexare.

Near the water's edge, the Magistrate squatted among several of the larger rocks and whispered, "Now, we wait."

Soon, a hoarse whisper cut through the silence. "*Ssst!* Cousin?"

"Yes. Here, Carthago."

In a moment, the swarthy man joined them.

"We're ready. Come, follow me."

Thaddeus' pulse pounded in his neck. This was exciting! He hoped the men would be as good as their word and allow him the time he needed in the cave. Being in the same surroundings again did seem to stir some memories, but only of being here before, not of any of the fantastic events his Brothers said he'd told them.

The boy followed the two men down to the beach. In the darkness, the four boats were barely visible, lying cocked on the sand with sails furled. Several groups of men, who'd been standing around, became immediately alert as the trio from the residence approached them.

Carthago made hurried introductions, then directed Thaddeus to the second boat. The Magistrate and Carthago took their places in the first boat, where Pontius, the more familiar with these waters, would act as a pilot until they were safely beyond the cove. Thaddeus soaked his boots reaching the craft and clambered aboard with little grace. But then, he never was a sailor.

The crew pushed off, and soon the small triangular sails were unfurled, putting them underway. Thaddeus noted the lanterns cast light only seaward. He spent the journey looking about him in wonder and trying to stay out of the way as the sailors went about their appointed tasks.

A half-hour later, all four boats snugged up on Mari's beach, fronting the entrance to the great cavern. Thaddeus hopped out, re-soaking his boots, and strode ashore.

Carthago had, by that time, lit a torch, and the other men started theirs from his. He held out one to the youth.

"Here you be, Thaddeus, Sorcerer. Go on inside and do what needs to be done. But as is possible, be aware of the time. We have only this one night to complete our task."

Thaddeus nodded, took the torch, and walked into the tunnel open-ing. There was a pungent stench in the air. He followed a twisty path and soon came to the base of the cavern said to have been Mari's home.

In front of him lay a giant skeleton, picked clean and shining palely in the dim light. It was poised on top of a massive mound of treasure: gold, jewels, and precious artifacts. The creature must have been a whale or great fish, he reasoned, though how it had gotten in here, he couldn't say. He moved forward to examine the beast. As his gaze swept down the skeleton's rib cage, he noted that one of the ribs on the left seemed a slightly darker color than its neighbors; almost pure ivory, as opposed to the bleached white of the others.

As he stood staring at it, a phrase rose from his mind. *"Take that which lies nearest the heart."*

Hardly understanding what compelled him, he reached forward a hand and grasped the oddly colored bone, almost a forearm's length long. It came away easily in his hand, all in a single piece. Then another thought intruded: a flute. Quickly both visions faded.

Thaddeus was curious about what had just occurred. It was unlike him to have such fancies. Perhaps this is what his Brothers meant in their descriptions of impossible dreams.

Abruptly the remainder of the skeleton collapsed into a powder, outlining its former shape on the treasure. Thaddeus stepped back a pace, watching closely, though nothing else untoward occurred.

Finally, he had a sense that he'd done all he could, but as he was turning to leave, his eye fell on a collection of what seemed to be pottery shards strewn over a smooth bed of sand, lying to the sea creature's side.

The tall youth went to investigate. Securing the rib bone in his belt, he squatted to get a better look at what lay before him. He reached out and took one of the pieces of white, porcelain-like material in his hand. It was clearly neither bone nor in any way obviously related to the nearby skeleton. Instead, it was smooth and shiny, though closer inspection revealed a surface pockmarked by numerous small pits.

The shards were uniform in thickness, approximately half a thumbs-width. The vision of an improbably large chicken crossed his mind. Thaddeus wished for Anders; he would know what this was and what it might mean. Deciding nothing further was to be gained, he rose and turned to go. Considering the mass of treasure glinting in the torchlight, he wondered how long it would take them to clear the chamber.

It was but a brief walk back through the tunnel before he rejoined the others. As he exited, Pontius approached him.

"Well, Thaddeus, Sorcerer, is it propitious for us to be about our appointed tasks?"

"Indeed, Magistrate, proceed as you will."

"Right you are, my boy. Here is a sack. Just lead us in when you're ready. We're all right to go, then, Carthago."

The darker man nodded and barked orders to his men. In moments, the group was wending its way into the tunnel with looks combined of equal parts apprehension and anticipation.

For the remainder of the night, the men toiled at their work, each one entering the tunnel with an empty sack and emerging with one heavily laden, which they deposited down by the boats before returning for more. It reminded Thaddeus of a line of ants.

As false dawn approached, Carthago urged his men to increase their tempo. The initial sense of apprehension had vanished, and that of wonder soon after. In short order, the adventure became just plain toil; the full sacks were heavy.

Finally, the cavern was looted to the swarthy sailor's satisfaction: every last coin, ingot, and jewel removed. Then the second part of the work began: attaching the shark bladders and buoys of cork to the heavy sacks in their barrels fitted under the light-wood rafts. Carthago did not expect the rafts to ride high on the surface, as that would draw too much attention. He only wanted them not to sink.

Soon enough, a string of swamped rafts stretched out behind each of the skiffs, and the boats set off with the tide, just in time to race the dawning sun. As the last boat left the atoll, the men raised their fists in a silent cheer and set their course for Port Ostia.

As they sailed, Thaddeus saw the wisdom of Carthago's strategies. Trailing the submerged gold kept prying eyes away. Also, having the men on the boat and the treasure off the boat kept temptation a healthy distance removed.

The small flotilla made port by late afternoon and anchored just north of the sheltered bay, out of the way of prying eyes. Carthago sent his second-in-command swimming to shore to notify the banker of their arrival. He, in turn, was to inform the barrister, whose duty it was to create the correct parchment-work, which, Thaddeus was told, meant taking care of the Customs officers, as well.

Within the hour, a collection of wagons pulled up to the dock across from where the boats were anchored. Burly teamsters drove the wagons, and burlier men—tavern brawlers, Thaddeus assumed—wielding stout cudgels and projecting a menacing presence, stood in each wagon bed.

Now came the part that seemed to worry Pontius and Carthago the most: docking the boats and transferring the cargo. The timing was critical. Pontius did not wish so much time to lapse that it drew an interested crowd. The transfer had to be completed quickly. The distance to the finance factor's office was short, but all needed to remain on high alert: Ambushes, double-crosses, and out-and-out mayhem were always possible once gold was involved.

Thaddeus formed part of the train, heaving bags hand-over-hand to the next in line. In a surprisingly short time, the clearing was completed. The cargo, minus the portion for Carthago and his men, which remained behind with the boats as pre-arranged, was soon loaded onto the wagons.

Pontius thanked his cousin and bade him farewell. Carthago said his goodbyes to Thaddeus as well, then reboarded the lead boat. With a final wave, he cast off, his waterborne retinue trailing after him.

"He might make it out of this alive," Pontius observed to the tall youth. "Always possible. But after his men get over the initial part of things and begin to cipher up what a third of that trove totals, well.... " The Magistrate let out a sigh. "Still, he is a grown man and has been in tight corners before. It's up to him now. In the meantime, lad, let's hope our own teamsters will not be forgetting their manners. This is no time for loyalty to play the strumpet with us."

With a word to the chief hauler, the Magistrate and the boy swung up and took their places on the lead wagon, and the procession creaked off, taking certain byways to the office of the finance factor. The small crowd that had gathered dispersed while the mercenaries hired to protect the wagons kept a sharp lookout.

If any wondered what the heavy, sodden sacks and soaked barrels held, they kept their curiosity to themselves.

By the time the wagons pulled up to the finance factor's, the banker and barrister were there to greet them. A new squad of guards took their places around the wagons and the entrance to the establishment, looking threatening, while the wagons were off-loaded by a team of porters, who transferred the sacks and barrels to the factor's interior. Once their burden was secured in a large storeroom, the teamsters were paid by the banker and drove away, undoubtedly curious as to what their cargo might have been.

Pontius kept Thaddeus by his side throughout the process. While the Magistrate had been careful to make no comment about the treasure itself, he'd been careless enough to mention to several of the men along the way that his young colleague was a representative of the *Collegium Sorcerorum* and a bit hot-tempered, as far as that went. As a consequence, the workers tended to avoid the youth, who, at his host's behest, often posed with a frown of disapproval and a snap of impatience throughout the late morning.

While Pontius and Thaddeus looked on with interest, the banker, his assistant, and the barrister began opening sacks and barrels and ordering their contents. Several scrolls were necessary to itemize the entire inventory.

Thaddeus marked the looks in the eyes of the two gentlemen managing the affair and decided Pontius was right about the power some allowed wealth to assume in their lives. He fervently hoped he would never fall prey to such a hold. The glare of greed on their countenances was both alarming and ill-advised.

40

Leaving the Westlands
Praeterirns Occidentem

By late afternoon, the treasure had been sorted, counted, recounted, counted once again, and sums tallied and totaled. The captain of the bank guards and his lieutenant assisted the banker in moving the trove to the most secure area of the building, while others of the guard closely patrolled the premises. The banker mentioned more than once that the building would likely need to be enlarged to accommodate not only their new assets but also the additional business these assets were certain to accrue. A great deal of anticipatory hand-rubbing accompanied his pronouncement.

Once the sums were transcribed, the banker, the barrister, and the Magistrate worked over the papers and wording of the Letters of Credit until all were satisfied.

By First Star, all was complete. Pontius' scrip was full of the requisite number of officially stamped and sealed scrolls for his constituents, plus an additional parchment with a red ribbon encircling it. The Magistrate accepted the bundle from the barrister, shook hands all around, and ushered Thaddeus out of the bank.

At the entrance, the Magistrate spoke a few words to the chief bank guard, and in

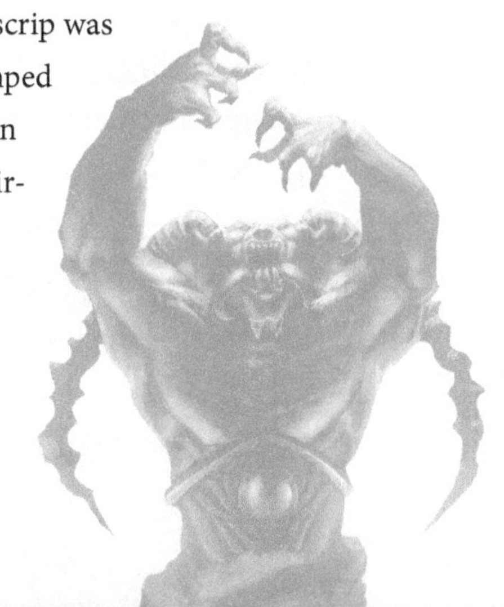

moments, a small detachment of his crew escorted Pontius and the boy back to the docks, torches held aloft by the guards lighting the way in the gathering darkness. At the wharf, Pontius thanked the detail and gave each a small purse. His action brought nods and smiles from the men, who, in short order, pivoted and marched back in the direction from which they'd come.

"Where do we go now, Magistrate?" Thaddeus asked, exhaustion tugging at his eyes.

"Home, my boy. But abide here a moment."

So saying, Pontius walked to the end of the dock and called out, "Piscellus?"

"Aye, Magistrate, here I be."

An old, hunched-over weather-beaten man in fisherman's garb appeared out of the shadows.

The Magistrate spoke in low tones to the man, who nodded once and gestured for them to follow. The three clambered down a bleached and swaying hemp ladder at the end of the dock, taking seats in a small dinghy.

The old man set a pair of oars and rowed the small craft toward a point of light out in the pristine bay. Thaddeus saw that a wide estuary had been formed at the mouth of the river that flowed by the port city.

Soon, a small, undistinguished fishing boat with a pole lantern providing the dim illumination he'd seen from the dock became visible.

When the dinghy reached the fishing boat, the old man tied up to the larger craft. Pontius beckoned Thaddeus, and they, somewhat awkwardly in the bouncing waves, achieved the deck of the boat. Thaddeus cast a quick glance out to the outer bay and detected a string of small, bobbing lights he deduced must be Carthago's flotilla, though there was a larger, flickering light from the third boat in line. Thaddeus instantly intuited the skiff to be afire.

Well, no plan was perfect in its execution.

As his eyes swept the horizon, he was aware of how they stung. He'd been without sleep for a day and a half, and his body was becoming insistent in calling his attention to the fact.

Once the fishing boat had been made fast, the old Captain directed his two guests below decks where they discovered two hammocks strung high in the tight quarters.

"All right, Thaddeus. We're over the main hump, I think. The captain of this vessel turns out to be another cousin of mine…."

"You have a large and well-placed family, Magistrate," Thaddeus commented with a smile.

The older man grinned. "Truly. In any case, I thought it prudent to make separate arrangements for our departure. Simply because we have banked our gold does not mean we are out of danger yet, but it'd be a curious fellow indeed who'd be marking our progress to this point."

The Magistrate looked around the snug quarters, then back at Thaddeus.

"We'll sleep on board the boat tonight … an insignificant cork on this teeming ocean … not worthy of any notice. Then we set sail, off to Vexare with the morning tide. After that, things will really become interesting." Pontius smiled. "You did well today, my boy. Now get some rest. Morning will be on us soon enough. And, oh, you'll be wanting this." The Magistrate reached into his bag and withdrew the large scroll with the red ribbon, which he handed to Thaddeus.

"What's this, Magistrate?"

"Why a Letter of Credit for your share of the Dragon's treasure, of course. One-third, by our banker's reckoning."

Thaddeus stood stunned for several moments, then started to protest, but the older man cut him off. "You have done well to this point, lad. Now don't go and ruin it all. You did your part and more, and these are your just desserts. Also, do not think to turn this over to the *Collegium*. As you have said, you're no longer a Sorcerer and so have no obligation to them. Besides, they were already paid for their services. I advise you to keep ahold of the greater part of this and tend it wisely. Over time you will be able to live comfortably for the rest of your life and even build yourself a feathered nest of your own for you and your family when the time comes."

"I-I don't know what to say," Thaddeus stammered. "But thank you, Magistrate."

Thaddeus thought furiously, then nodded at the decision to which he'd come in that instant. "I have no head for business, though. Would you be willing to help me with the investing of these funds, Magistrate? As you know, I plan to travel East and will have no fixed home for a time. I have enough with me to see me through, I believe, until I return. Of course, take from it the charges necessary to cover the expenses of your work." Thaddeus proffered the ribboned scroll to the older man.

Pontius gazed at the parchment a moment before speaking.

"Ah, yet another time I have amazement when I should not, having come to know you as I do, lad. Yes, I'd be willing. Vexare should prosper mightily now, and all manner of profits are likely to be there for the making, with the boom I'm expecting to see in the near years. But are you sure you want to be leaving such monies in the hands of another, my boy? This is more than a mere tidy sum, Thaddeus."

"I am, Magistrate. Please put it to good use as you may, and when I have a need, I will come back by the village for it." Thaddeus smiled. "And then you can show me all the changes our gold has wrought."

The Magistrate shook his head but smiled broadly and accepted the parchment from the youth. He held out his hand.

"Done, then!"

"Done!" Thaddeus said, taking the man's hand.

Later, as the youth was drifting off to sleep, his mind returned to the wealth he'd briefly held in his hands and had relinquished so easily.

Still, he was glad. He certainly had enough burdens to carry as it was, and he was pleased to have avoided adding another.

Each night as Thaddeus sat at his campfire, he worked on the Dragon's bone with one or the other of Molly's knives. He had thought to fashion it into a flute, and he carved it carefully, taking his time and working the material with great care. It seemed almost as if some agency were guiding his hands, though he dismissed the idea as nonsense.

After some weeks of effort, he'd completed his work—the carving and polishing finally completed. Tentatively, he lifted the instrument to his pursed lips and blew softly.

A delicate, silvery tone sounded throughout the glade where he was camped for the night. He assayed a few runs and trills, then added several lines of a graceful tune concerning remorse and redemption. The forest, which had moments before been alive with sounds of busy insects, birds, and small, scurrying animals, suddenly became silent for no reason Thaddeus could determine.

Pausing before continuing to play, he realized he must be more tired than he thought. For a moment, he imagined he'd tasted the tang of the salt sea on his tongue.

Shrugging, he spun through his repertoire. He had to admit this was the best he'd ever sounded. The tones were clear, almost other-worldly in their quality—if such a thing were possible.

When he, at last, put the flute down, he was startled to see a collection of animals just at the edge of his firelight sitting still as if listening. He considered this another fancy, however, and supposed he must have inadvertently left out some scraps of food around the campsite.

It was some moments after he stopped playing before the animals dispersed. They seemed … disappointed.

But that, of course, was not possible.

"Mistress," the shadowy figure called to the girl from back in the alleyway.

Lallie peered down the narrow and dark cobblestone wynd. Typically, she would have ignored such a summons and walked on hurriedly. But something in the voice was compelling—something of import, urgency, command….

She turned to behold a tall man, his head and body shrouded in a cloak. He walked forward slowly. She stood transfixed as she realized he was no man at all but a man-horse! She'd heard of such creatures but had never thought to meet one. And what was he doing here, talking to her—in this city, this alleyway?

"Y-Yes?" she stammered.

"You are called Lallie, daughter of Morella?" His tone suggested he already knew the answer but sought only her acknowledgment.

"Yes. I am."

"Good. I am called Chiron. I am … or was, rather, Horse-Master at the *Collegium Sorcerorum*. I have come for the babe, Akireu."

Ah, so this was the gentleman they'd been awaiting. A Centaur, of all things…. What would he want with the boy, anyway? And the babe's name: Where had that come from? Perhaps a test would be in order. It would not do to give away their prize to just anyone … or anything.

"And know you, Horse-man, the parentage of the boy you seek?"

"Ethne of Tarandon was the mother and Thaddeus of Beewicke, the father, Mistress."

Ah, so it was true, as her mother had suspected. What a peculiar situation.

"Very well. Follow me, and I will take you to him."

The Centaur appeared hesitant. "Perhaps it would be better, Mistress, were you to bring the boy to me here."

At the girl's pause, he quickly added, "I have gold."

Gold? Well, that changed things.

It had been harder to start their seamstress shop than her mother had at first thought. A little extra would be welcome—more than welcome, as it turned out. Yet, she was going to miss the little one. He always smiled and cooed and never fussed; he was such a good and happy baby. But always hungry … oh, my! And he was so strong. She was going to miss him, even though she had her own Somada.

Still, gold….

"Very well. Wait here. I shall return shortly."

"I will abide, Mistress."

Thaddeus carefully unrolled the scroll from its case and laid it down on the table, having first taken the precaution of wiping off the puddles of cheap beer left by the prior patron with his sleeve. The parchment itself was holding up well, given the number of times it had gone through this exercise. Still, it was a link to those he loved and therefore worthy of revisiting.

Anders had, thoughtfully, sent it straight to Vexare, and so Thaddeus had been able to retrieve it from the post-runner. Luckily, it had come on the morning of his departure; it seemed there was timing to these things.

He was wished well on his journey by his Brothers—and Sisters. Apparently, several of them had decided to Summer over at Brightfield —all except Marsia, who again had no desire to be an extra member in Thaddeus' absence. Therefore, she had decided to go home to Northfast for the interval.

Also absent from Brightfield were Rolland and Sonnia. She was taking the thief home to meet her parents.

The others agreed to join Anders for differing reasons. Zoarr still could not safely return to his own home at this time, and Molly—with no other place to go—was apparently reluctant to be parted from him.

Anders and Nannsi had decided to announce their marriage once they arrived. Thaddeus suspected, however, that Anders' Mater and Pater would consider it an engagement only until such time as the local priest could be summoned.

Osiric was to spend the months at Mountaingaard. It was uncertain where he would go afterward, especially once Lord Geoffrey was relieved. And none of them knew the whereabouts of Bellis.

At the *Collegium,* much talk and many secret meetings were ongoing over the Perditus-Daemon business. Several of the Masters were seen daily combing through the Tower, searching for … who knew what? They shared little, if anything, of what they'd found, leaving rumor, hearsay, and conjecture to fill the empty spots in their knowledge.

Anders inquired how the honey was holding out, but he needn't have bothered. Thaddeus' new blankets were warm, if some hand-breadths short, and he supposed the one-eyed man in the woolens stall in town thought he'd had the better of their bargain.

Anders had also set his formidable intellect toward understanding the function of the ring he'd obtained from the old *Princeps.* Thaddeus expected he'd be hearing more about that in the not-so-distant future.

He sighed as he rerolled the scroll and returned it to its worn leather case just as the assistant to the tavernkeeper placed a bowl of bear stew and a spoon in front of the ex-Apprentice, along with a cup of the same watery brew that likely doubled as table rinse.

Thaddeus wolfed down the Mid-day rapidly, now eager to be through the Scralia Pass before dusk. The tavern windows faced one of the Golden Range's two known passes and presented a spectacular view. Asullus was hitched outside, and the youth kept careful watch on him while flicking his eyes—every other moment—to his trail-pack. He had learned on this trek East to be observant and ready with an instant response to difficulties of diverse sorts.

SCRALIA PASS

But now, his journey would start in earnest. He'd be leaving the Westlands soon and entering Graecolia. He'd been warned about travel there a dozen times over in conversations he'd struck up while on the road.

It was wisest, he'd found, to place himself in or close to a traveling group of some kind. Pilgrims were best. They tended not to be at you all the time seeking coins for this or that misfortune; most of which, he'd learned, were apparently invented. Also, they usually did not try to get into your belongings while you were otherwise occupied, or—even more inconvenient—attempt to slit your throat while you slept.

He had found it necessary to discourage several potential appropriators since his journey had begun. He'd even had to break a man's leg once. Such language—as if the attempt at robbery were Thaddeus' fault. Unbidden, Asullus had even helped, kicking the stuffing out of two of the accompanying ruffians while Thaddeus dealt with the remaining two. All in all, traveling had turned out to be broadening; just as he'd been told.

He'd written Marsia another scroll last night and would make certain to post it in town before he entered the pass itself. The timing might be a little tight if he wanted to tag along with that spice merchant's caravan heading back to Oasia this evening, but he thought he could manage it. The old merchant's guard captain had even offered him good wages to join the caravan's crew. He'd declined at first but was now thinking it over. Thaddeus did have weapons and some skills. Perhaps a little additional experience would be useful.

He started as he looked out the tavern window to see the caravan animals being roused and prepared to resume their trek. It was time to be gone, especially if he wanted to post his missive this side of the mountain range. Who knew when his next opportunity might come?

He wondered idly whether any of his letters would ever reach his true love and hoped at least some would. If he were very, very lucky, he might even receive a reply from Marsia once he could give her a more permanent place to send a scroll.

The sadness at the thought of leaving his true love leached from him with the onset of activity and was replaced by anticipation and growing interest. It was really all rather exciting—at least so far; and he hoped it would remain so.

This was one adventure he'd like to be continued.

Epilogue

Proud and erect, the woman sat astride her horse—a magnificent chestnut stallion—and with a gentle draw on the reins, guided her mount's head to follow the trail leading away from the main road. A heavy forest cloak of the finest velvet, colored a deep, dark green and hooded against the chill, clung to her statuesque frame. The gold clasp securing her cloak was an intricately fashioned design portraying, in turn, a flower, an insect, a serpent, and a beast. Her ensemble was completed by dark riding boots and a matching saddlebag.

She had been traveling these few days to the south, staying at local inns along the way and arriving in Topian early this very afternoon. The woman had set out for Dorset Downs just after taking Even-tide at the University's hostel.

With the start of the spring courses a week off, few were venturing out, and she reached the turn-off to the Master's home without difficulty. Just as well, too, for twilight was beginning to dusk give way to. Five moments more of easy riding brought her to what must at one time have been a well-appointed manor house, though now those parts not swallowed by ivy showed the need for some attention and repair.

The lady pulled her horse to a stop near a weathered hitching post, dismounted gracefully, patting the horse's flank, and then laid her head affectionately on its neck. "Ah, my beautiful Bucephalus, you are the best of horses. Stay here, brave one. I may be some time."

The horse snorted in response and gave his reins a shake. The woman did not tether the horse to the post. There was no need.

As soon as her feet touched the ground, a dog began barking from inside the dark house. She walked slowly up the Lannon stone path leading to the entrance; there was no reason to cause alarm. The dog's bark was quite distinct now. He must be just on the other side of the heavy oaken door.

The woman threw back her hood, revealing classic features of mature beauty. A carefully constructed pile of raven tresses dressed her head, marked at the temples by splashes of brilliant white. The lady reached forward, rapped the brass knocker ring twice against its receiving plate, and waited.

Moments passed, and still, the dog barked. Nothing more. She reached forward again and, with greater force, applied the ring to the door twice more. She was not used to waiting, and her lips bent into a frown of impatience.

She was on the point of alerting those who dwelt within of her presence in a more dramatic fashion when the peep door opened behind a small grating. The dog's bark was louder now, and a flickering of candlelight made its way into the night.

A rheumy eye topped by a silver brow regarded her. "Who are ye an what d'yer want at this time o' the night, m'lady?"

"I am Head-Mistress Geanninia of the *Ludia* and I have come to see Professor Smythe."

"So ye say, Mistress. And what, if I may ask, be the nature o' yer business wi' the Master at such an hour so that I may inform him directly an' see to his wishes in the matter, should he be in residence at this time?"

The old housekeeper—as the Head-Mistress of the *Ludia* judged her to be—was pert but to the point and was clearly a loyal family servitor, protective of her employer. Well and good, then.

"Please tell the good professor that I have come to see him regarding his daughter."

"An' which daughter might that be now, Mistress? The Master do ha' several, ye know."

"The youngest. Marsia, by name, I believe."

"Oh, the Master's heart. Well, then, ye seem to be o' the upstandin' sort. Please come into the residence, good Mistress, an' avail yersel' o' our hospitality, though it be less than what ye're used to, by me lights, while I go an' inform the Master o' yer presence an' yer business. Oh, an' gi' no mind to our Daisy here. She poses no threat to ye whatsoever unless ye ha' an aversion to bein' licked to death or accosted fer a treat."

At once, the evening became darker with the shutting of the peep door. This was followed by the clanking of the bolt-works and the painful complaint of the great oaken door's hinges as it was compelled to open.

Shortly, a generous entranceway, partially illuminated by light from a hanging chain iron chandelier, was revealed along with its occupants: an older woman, bent with years of care yet still spry, and a great golden dog, who had ceased barking once she decided this guest provided no immediate threat. The light from the guttering candle held by the house servant bobbed in time with the old woman's head-nodding greeting.

This one was skilled, Geanninia thought. How many could, at such an age, simultaneously force open a thumbs-length thick door, hold a lit candle perfectly upright, and restrain a lunging hound?

The tall lady bent down to ruffle the dog's neck, making friends at once.

"Ah, Mistress, as I'm sure ye've now surely concluded, our Daisy here poses no concern unless ye be constructed o' sweetmeats. She's a good-hearted hound an' will love to death anyone as'll give her that chance."

"Yes. I can see the truth of your saying." Geanninia resumed standing and began to doff her robe, but the older woman was instantly behind her.

"Here now, Mistress, you'll no' be needin' to do such things for yerself, not while old Janeiva is still walkin' and breathin'. Let me get that fer ye."

So saying, the servant captured the taller woman's traveling cloak and hung it carefully on a nearby wall peg, brushing stray bits away before being satisfied with its placement. She then turned to her visitor.

"I hope ye ha' taken no offense at me brevity wi' ye earlier, but the Master teaches at the school, an' o'er the years, the students ha' been known to push a prank or two. 'Tis their nature, as most o' them is young, ye know."

Geanninia smiled. "Give it no thought, Janeiva. It is never unwise to be wary of strangers at the first, especially in times such as these. Who can know when and from where the next bedevilment will come?"

"Ah, Mistress, ye have the right o' it and are well-spoken, ye are. Now, if ye'll but follow me to the guest parlor, I'll see about summonin' the Master. It will be but a quick minute."

The old woman led her guest down a short hallway to a larger room with a beamed ceiling, tiled floors covered with ancient carpets and tapestried walls.

"Wait here, Mistress, and take your ease. The Master'll be wi' ye presently."

The old woman left the room by a far door, Daisy trailing behind, tail wagging.

Geanninia took the time to examine several of the tapestries. Exquisite workmanship: These pieces were of an age and had great value.

The Mistress of the *Ludia* recognized one of the works. She had known the artist who had directed the creation of the tapestry, but that had been long ago and far away.

A baritone "Harrumph" interrupted her musing, and she turned to behold a tall man with a trimmed beard and full head of hair—all white as snow—dressed in loose work garb. He was somewhat stooped but held himself well. A powerful man at one time, the Head-Mistress surmised. An elevated forehead indicated a man of careful thought as well.

"Janeiva said you wished to see me in regard to my Marsia. What do you want of her?" he said somewhat imperiously.

"Well, Professor Smythe, I am Head-Mistress Geanninia of the *Ludia* and—"

"I know who you are. What do you have to do with my daughter?" he said in a demanding tone.

"—it is a pleasure to meet you as well." Here the woman smiled. "And yes, I would favor some refreshment after a long ride from Topian, and I would very much enjoy sitting down with you to discuss your Marsia's future. If, that is, you have no objection."

The man stared at the Head-Mistress in a hard way for a moment, then looked down at the floor.

"Um, I am sorry, Head-Mistress. I grow old and grumpy with time —as my Marsia often remarks—and I forget my manners. Forgive me; you are weary and thirsty. Come, please give me the blessing of sharing what we can offer while we discuss whatever topic you wish. This way, please. Janeiva! Some of the Port and a small slab. In the sitting room."

Geanninia swirled the contents of the goblet, inhaled, then tasted. This was an excellent vintage indeed. After another sip, she set the glass down and looked up to find her host examining her closely.

"I am here, sir, to speak with your daughter, Marsia, about the possibility of her becoming a student at the *Ludia* this fall. I believe she has aptitude for the training, and I think she would do well there."

"You'd have her to be a Sorceress? My Marsia? No! She is ... she is too young. And that is that."

"She is of an age, Doctor. And I do believe she would do well." Here the raven-haired woman reached into her bodice and withdrew a large blue stone on a fine gold chain hanging from her neck.

"I understand how you might find it difficult, especially at this time, to lose your youngest, leaving you alone in this great house, but the girl has, I feel, great potential for the training. Perhaps she and I could discuss it yet this evening while you give the matter further thought." As the woman spoke, the room was bathed in a soft blue light that became brighter and brighter.

The girl was tall, of serious demeanor, with long, honey-blonde hair kept in a braid that trailed down to her waist. She was a beauty, though not one to invite attention drawn to herself. In addition, she was respectful and seemed to understand the core of a concern quickly. Oh, she would do well....

"Janeiva said you'd be staying the night, Mistress, so I took the liberty of grooming your horse and have seen to his feeding and watering. I hope you find no fault with this, but the hour was getting late and...."

"That is quite all right, Marsia. I had thought to be gone from Dorset Downs already, but your father has extended me his hospitality for the night. And you were correct; the hour was drawing on. My thanks to you for this service. But I am curious. How did you persuade Bucephalus to allow you to minister to him? He has, until now, allowed only me this ... hmm, honor."

The girl had the sensitivity to blush and looked down at the small well-used table in the buttery where the two of them sat across from each other. The Head-Mistress cut herself another slim slice of cheese and awaited a response.

"I cannot say exactly, Mistress. But I have always had a way with animals. And your mount—oh, truly, he is magnificent—did not seem to mind. And he appeared to enjoy the apples." Here the girl smiled.

"Ah, apples. Yes, he does favor them. All right, then, what do you think of my proposal?"

"I am of two directions on it, Head-Mistress Geanninia. Although I see nothing in myself that suggests developing such powers as you mention, I admit to being game for the testing. But I feel I cannot abandon my father. His years weigh heavily on him and have done so, actually, since my mother died. Every year there seems to be more pain and less strength. I do not believe he will do well without me to care for him."

"You cannot halt the march of time, Marsia. Time will have its way with him as it does with us all, sooner or later. So, consider. The *Ludia* is a relatively short distance from the University here in Topian, as such things go. You could come home to see him on those weekends you wished and over the summer recess. And I will be pleased to assist in providing him with some small additional help if it will make your acceptance easier. What say you?"

The girl turned to gaze at the casks lining the far wall. "The future is so uncertain, Mistress. I feel badly for even considering to leave him for something which may not be, in any case."

"Well, let us see if we can make up a bit for that uncertainty. How would you like to view the image of the man you will marry one day?"

The girl's head whipped around. Initial incredulity became mixed with extreme interest and an undeniable portion of excitement. She blushed again. "Yes, Mistress. I would see this one."

"Very well. Fix your gaze here." The older woman indicated a place midway on the tabletop between them. She placed her right hand, palm down, over the spot, yet two foot-lengths above it. Her hand began to flex and extend in a rhythmic pattern while she spoke some phrase the girl could not make out.

Slowly the air under her hand became turgid, then a mist began to form, and a figure was in the midst of it. It was the image of a boy near Marsia's age. He stood next to a shed and appeared of a goodly height and sturdily built, with sandy hair and a handsome countenance. An old hound dog was next to him and, in the background, what appeared to be a collection of beehives. After a time, the image faded and soon was gone.

Mistress Geanninia looked up to find the girl once again blushing.

"And do you believe that I, with necessary effort, may learn to do such works, Head-Mistress Geanninia?" she asked.

"Of a certainty, Marsia," the older woman replied.

The girl was silent for a long moment, then nodded. "I will go with you, Head-Mistress. I wish to become a Sorceress, if I can, in a manner similar to yourself. But I must speak with my father first."

"Well said, my dear. Then you'd best go and take some time with him. I promise you that his great love for you, as well as his wish that you succeed in life and the pride he will soon come to feel regarding your accomplishments, will win out in the end over his sense of anxiety and loss at your leaving."

The girl nodded again.

"Afterward, gather together those things you will need. It will be a journey of some length, so we must leave at first light."

"Yes, Head-Mistress Geanninia. But, pardon my saying so, 'tis only but a quarter-week's journey to the *Ludia*." The girl blushed yet again, looking down. "I have looked at it, from time to time, on maps we have here."

Geanninia smiled. This girl was going to be *very* good. "You are correct, Marsia. The distance to the *Ludia* is indeed a rather short piece in direct travel. However, our path is not direct. We are to embark on a far greater journey than that. First to Frantillia, and then all the way to Graecolia."

Marsia's eyes grew large. "To Graecolia?" The paleness in her face lasted only a moment before serious resolve returned to her countenance. "Very well, then. To Graecolia. I shall not tell that part to Father, however. He would only worry."

The Head-Mistress smiled again. This girl was a treasure, to be sure. Silvestrus was usually right about this sort of thing; bloodlines do often tell out, she thought, with some pride. "Yes, I think that would be best. Our extended journey is in search of two others to complete our group. I think you three will all get along quite nicely."

"There will be three of us, then? All right."

"Hmm. With, perhaps, a fourth later on, but we shall see."

"Mistress Geanninia, it is not my business, but I am closest in distance to the *Ludia,* yet you have come for me first rather than on the return journey…." The girl's voice trailed off.

"I wished to have a little extra time to get to know you better, Marsia. Why that is important will perhaps become clearer later. By the way, have you ever considered teaching others as an interest in your life?"

It was but a short time later that the two bade Good Repose, with the girl going off to talk to her father and Geanninia following Janeiva's flickering candlelight to her host's guest bedroom—once the master bedroom, according to the servant.

Following the soothing bath, it was only a moment or two before the Head-Mistress of the *Ludia* was able to luxuriate in the Scholar's full-size bed with goose-down mattress and quilted comforters. She had the thought, before drifting into a deep sleep, that this must have been his wife's favorite place in the house.

Just before first light, House-Mistress Janeiva bustled down the upstairs corridor, lit candle in one hand and folded blankets in the other. The door to young Marsia's room stood open, and the candle stand was alight, but the girl sat motionless on the side of her bed staring out the window, her belongings but half-packed.

"Darlin' girl, should ye no' be in a bit o' a hurry here? I did ha' the impression that Head-Mistress Geanninia intended to leave wi'in the hour or so."

The Professor's youngest daughter turned a tear-streaked face toward the House-Mistress. "Oh, Janeiva, I cannot leave him. We both know Father cannot manage so much as he used to. And it should not rest on you alone to provide for this manor and my father's needs—and his fancies. I must stay to his tending. 'Tis my duty."

Janeiva marched into the girl's room, carefully set the candle on the bedside stand, placed the blankets on the lid of the traveling trunk, and sat down next to her charge, taking Marsia's hands in her own.

"Now listen to me, my little sweetie, an' listen well. In that yer blessed Mother is no' here to do it herself, leave it to yer ol' House-Mistress to tell ye well what yer duty be in this matter. As all children do, who grow to a certain age, yer duty is to leave yer birth-home an' spread yer wings, tastin' o' the sun an' the sky as ye go. How else will ye learn who ye're to be? This yer lovin' father knows verra well. He did it himself, in his young days, as did his father before him, as do they all. Ye be no different from him in this. O' course, the tearin' away at first be painful but necessary it is. An' he'd be the first to say so."

Janeiva brushed back the girl's free-flowing locks. "An', o' course, we both know there's another reason yer father's likely to ha' a bit o' a time lettin' ye go—it's that ye'r yer Mother all come back. Just like her, ye are —a tall beauty, kind, thoughtful, loving, but wi' a steely determination an' the brains to go wi'. Ye do resemble her mightily, yet, ye are yer own one as well, an' let none say it different."

The House-Mistress raised her hand and placed it tenderly against the side of the girl's face in a fond caress. "An' never mind ye abou' yer father's welfare while ol' Janeiva's still breathin' and movin' from here to there. We will manage, the two o' us—an' our dear Daisy, o' course— just as well as can be. Ye go on, now, an' get yer trainin' an' become the finest o' the ladies at yer school an' then in yer trade. That'll puff up yer father's chest more than any other thing ye can think. Mark me words: Hard it'll be at the first, but 'tis biscuits ye'll get at the last. An' that's the sure o' things."

The girl looked down at her lap for a long moment, then finally up again. "Thank you, Janeiva. You have always been so kind to me. And now you help me to leave all that I know for that which is unknowable. Thank you." Marsia threw her arms around the House-Mistress and did not release her hold for some time.

Deciding what to pack took a scant moment, in that there was not all that much she possessed, in any case. Marsia sorted through her meager possessions quickly. She left for last the specially wrapped item shoved far back in the bottom of her bureau drawer. She pulled out a pair of old worn woolen stockings and carefully undid them, revealing a yellowed lace kerchief tied with a faded green ribbon.

She slowly worked the knot out of the ribbon and soon enough gazed upon the pouch's contents. Two green stones shone dully in the palm of her right hand. Each stone was half of an ovoid and about a third the size of a robin's egg. Judging by their shapes, they had been conjoined at one time.

Marsia did not know their purpose, but she vividly recalled what her Great-mother had told her on the day she had given them to her. The elderly lady—always a bit of a mystery in the family—lay dying. She had declined from the very day she received the news that her only daughter—Marsia's mother—had fallen ill and passed.

Although her frame was shrunken, her eyes burned with their usual fire. "Listen to me, Marsia. This is important." The woman closed her eyes for a moment, grimaced, swallowed, and went on. "Reach under my pillow, and you will find a lace kerchief tied with a green ribbon. Bring it out. Well, go on!"

The young girl did as she was told. It was never a good idea to keep Great-mother waiting when she had given an instruction.

"Now undo the ribbon. Do you see those two green stones? Yes. Well, they once were one, but that is not important. What is important is that I am giving these to you. Think of them as a bequest, if you will. I do this because I see in you something that I do not see in any of your sisters—something I fancy we two share.

"Now, you must keep these hidden and never, ever show them to anyone. Do you understand me, girl? Never, ever—not your father, not your family—no one. The only one who will see these stones is the one who shall be the one for you. And you will know him when you see him because you will have seen him before. I know this sounds strange, but consider it a puzzle, if you like.

"When the time comes, you will know what I mean. But remember, tell no one of these, even if you are asked if you have such. It is very important. Do not fail me in this, my dear, or you will most certainly regret it. No, no questions. I am thirsty—too much talking. Now fetch me some tea, girl. I am waiting."

The early morning departure was difficult, and many tears were shed in the gray light. Geanninia thought the girl must be relieved at some level to have passed the farewells and, at last, be on the road.

As the diminutive figure of the House-keeper, her tall employer, and the golden dog shrank from sight, Marsia was finally able to turn around and tend more closely to her horse and the road, with no one remaining to be seen who could be waved to.

After a time, the Head-Mistress spoke. "You are quiet this morning, Marsia. Have you any questions for me I could address for you?"

Mistress Geanninia spent some time waiting for a reply.

"I have only one I am thinking of, Head-Mistress," the girl said in a soft voice. "The boy I … the image I saw last eve; the one I'm said to marry. Know you, perchance, his name?"

Appendices

Imperial Cinnian Family Tree 420

Molly-o'-the-Willows Family Tree 421

The Lay of Man 422

Character Log 426

Glossary: *Lingua Imperatoria* 446

Discussion Questions 454

Excerpt from Book Four:
Thaddeus and the Ancient One 457

Meet Louis Sauvain 461

How to Work with Louis Sauvain 462

Book One: *Thaddeus of Beewicke* 463

Book Two: *Thaddeus and the Master* 464

Next from Louis Sauvain 465

Imperial Cinnian
Family Tree

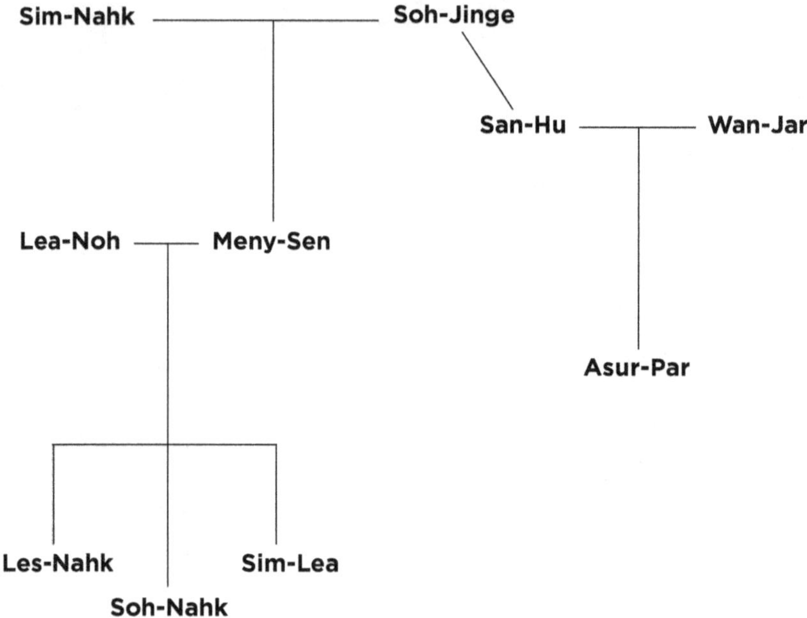

Molly-o'-the-Willow's Family Tree

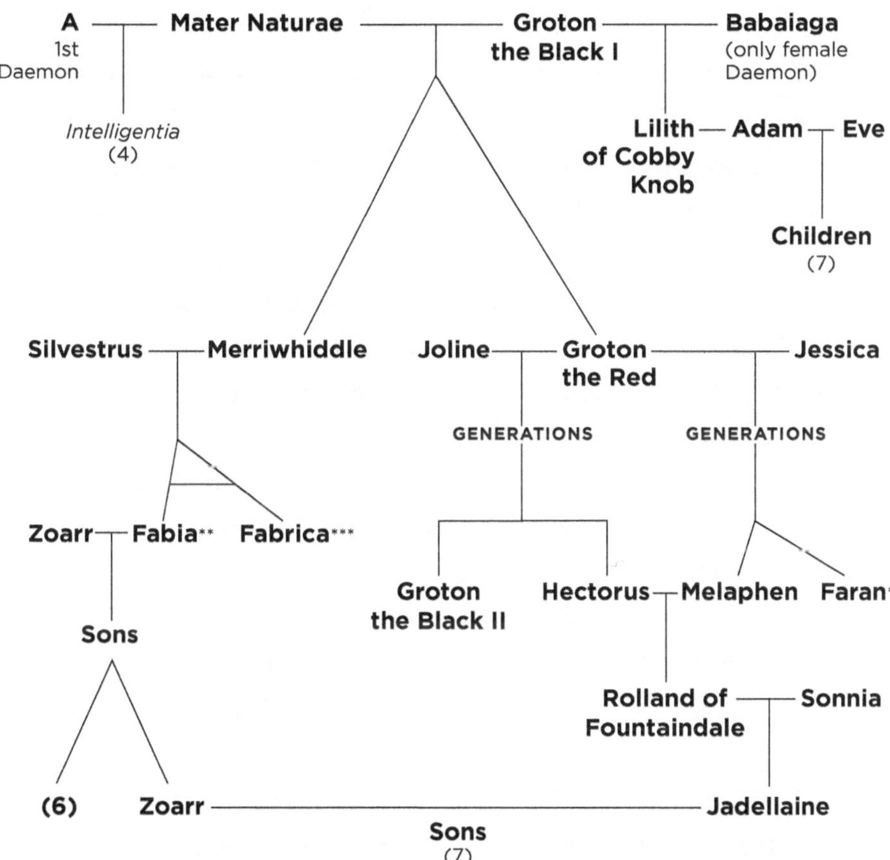

*fostered by Specus and Coqua, last of their race

** (aka) Molly-o'-the-Willows I, *Regina Mauretesiarum*—tutored by
Groton the Black II

*** died of abuse in childhood—avenged by Groton the Black II

The Lay of Man

Or, how it was that Man came to be on the Earth, taken from one of the oldest preserved texts of the Sacred Writings.

verything began with the Sun. It was the Sun who organized Everything and gave form and sustenance to Everything at the Beginning, even more so than now. After all was in place, the Sun shone down full upon the Land, and the Eldest arose in the South and walked the Earth.

They were the First Men of the Sun, and the Sun blessed them, and they multiplied. And they always remained in the South. But the Eldest were small, slight and shy. They had no Speech, knew not of Fire and were often taken by the wild beasts that lived there.

Time passed, and those Eldest who remained begat the Great-fathers of Man, who were larger, but ill-favored and also had none of Man's Speech. And the Land remained quiet.

These Great-fathers of Man saw that the Eldest were small and weak, and they slew them and ate them, and what Eldest had survived the wild beasts were consumed by the Great-fathers of Man until none were left living.

The Great-fathers of Man did try to live in harmony with the Life around them, but the land was harsh, and the Sun tested them and was set against them because they had eaten the Eldest, who were no more.

Time passed, and some of the Great-fathers of Man decided to journey North to see other lands. So it came to pass, and they spread over our lands and other lands to the East. The Great-fathers of Man came to know Fire, but only its beginnings, so they could not shape it to their purposes.

More Time passed, and those of the Great-fathers of Man who remained in the South begat the Fathers of Man. But the Fathers of Man were great and brutish and fought with the Great-fathers of Man, seeking dominion over them. And the Fathers of Man had the victory and ate all the Great-fathers of Man who lived in the South till none were left—just as the Great-fathers of Man had, themselves, eaten the Eldest before them.

Then the Fathers of Man took council, one with another, for they had Speech, and the Land never knew quiet again. And the Fathers of Man knew Fire, more so than the Great-fathers of Man, and they could shape it somewhat.

And the Fathers of Man decided to go North and pursue the Great-fathers of Man who had gone before them, so they could have the final victory over them and eat them as well. And so they set forth. At first, the Fathers of Man pursued the Great-fathers of Man to the North and slew all they could find and ate them. But the Fathers of Man grew to love the North for itself because it was dark and cold, for the Fathers of Man were strong and hairy.

And they stayed in the North and brought the mighty beasts that lived there under their dominion and ate them as well. So, it was that the Fathers of Man abode in the North and pursued no longer the Great-fathers of Man, who had gone elsewhere, so that some yet lived.

Time passed again, and the Fathers of Man who had remained in the South came to beget Man. And Man flourished and grew in strength and numbers, and the Sun shone down upon Man with benevolence. And he prospered. And Man had Speech, as well—not only the Speech of the Fathers of Man, but the Speech of Song and Wisdom, which the Fathers of Man had not.

And Man took council with one another and found that the Fathers of Man were brutish and repellent and jealous of Man and wished to keep Food from Man and Water from Man and thus keep Man in sub-servience as a willful child. And Man said, "No! This shall not be!"

And so Man rose up and slew the Fathers of Man in the South but did not eat them, for that was not Man's way.

And when all the Fathers of Man had been slain in the South, Man held further council and decided that some of the Men of the Sun—for that is what they now called themselves—would remain in the South and tend to the Land there and abide with one another while others of Man would journey North and pursue the remaining Fathers of Man, for they reckoned that was where the Fathers of Man had gone, for Man wished to have sole dominion in all the Land. And so they assayed to slay all the Fathers of Man in the North as well, so that not one survived. And this they did.

Those of the Men of the Sun who remained in the South became marked by the Sun as His own. And those of Man who traveled North became marked by the Moon as Her own. And over Time, no little enmity arose between the Men of the Sun and the Men of the Moon, though the cause of this is unknown. But that is another story.

Man journeyed North and discovered the hiding places of the Fathers of Man, for the Fathers of Man had seen the approach of Man and had fled from Man, remembering how they had treated Man. But the Sun aided Man because the Sun was displeased that the Fathers of Man had eaten the Great-fathers of Man. And the Sun brought light and warmth to the North that had them not before.

And Man made cruel War upon the Fathers of Man and slew them in their tens and their hundreds and their thousands until none of the Fathers of Man were left living. And Man left the Fathers of Man dead in their fields and in their forests and in their caves, and the Fathers of Man were seen no more.

Time passed. Some of Man went further North and abided there and became the Men of the Ice. And some of Man went further West until they came to the Sea where they sought to wrestle with Her and subdue Her. And some of Man went East and there they found the last of the Great-fathers of Man.

But the Great-fathers of Man did not know Man and were frightened of Man and so waged war upon Man. But Man was mighty and cunning and now knew Fire and Wheel and Spear in all their aspects and attributes, and Man slew the Great-fathers of Man unto the very last one but did not eat them, for that was not Man's way.

And thus, Man's victories were soon beyond counting. And, in time, he came to sing of them and to write of them.

Then the Sun gave Man dominion over all he surveyed, whether for good or for ill, and thus it has been unto this very day.

Character Log

A

A The first and greatest Daemon. Said to be creator, by will alone, of all. The Wise consider that it is the character of the Daemon, unavoidably suffusing its creation with its own essence, that accounts for the imperfections observed everywhere in the Universe and in Man himself.

Adjurford A Sorcerer at the *Collegium Sorcerorum*. Second-in-command to **Portoman** during the Sorcerous raid on the capital of the Cin in the time of the Eastern invasion, occasioned by the greed of the last Emperor of the Farther Westlands, **Tyrannus Superbus**. Their original mission was to destroy the Tower of the Cin. However, following **Portoman**'s descent into madness, **Adjurford** assumed leadership of the small band of Sorcerers and succeeded in making away with the Tower instead. He was able to return to the *Collegium Sorcerorum* with all his men, including the severely compromised **Portoman**. Speculation later arose that a young **Silvestrus** of Somerset was a member of that party.

Adrocles Superstitious house-servant to **Sophia** and **Astonius** of Brightfield Manor.

Aephesto Chief Eunuch to the Court of the Graecolian Pashata who befriended **Molly o' the Willows** during her time of servitude in that place.

Aetas Master of Natural Philosophy at the *Collegium Sorcerorum*, who often felt compelled to point out the regular and repetitive nature of patterns.

Afarius Slighter and sicklier brother of **Arnius**. Classmate of **Thaddeus** of Beewicke. Strong interest in the Aesthetic.

Akireu Eldest of four feral children of **Thaddeus** of Beewicke, whose mother, **Ethne** of the Flowers of Sorrow, was the Beewickean's first love. Brought by servants of the vintner, **Ormerod**, to Fountaindale, he was sold to **Chiron**, Centaur and Horse-Master of the *Collegium Sorcerorum*. It is suggested he was then taken by **Chiron** to Fornia where he was raised and trained by the Centaur, until word of the boy's prowess reached the ears of **Marcus Quintessentialus**, regional Pro-Consul, whose favorable influence assured **Akireu** a place at the Academy of War.

Al-Donn *Aelvae*. Lieutenant to **Non-Dar**, Lord of the Greensward *Aelvae*. Favors acorn soup.

Alistair Profane member of a pair of black marble Gargoyle statues charged with guarding the main entrance to the *Collegium Sorcerorum*. Claimed by some to be, on occasion, both sentient and mobile.

Anders of Brightfield Manor. Only child of **Astonius** and **Sophia**, successful distillers near Meadsville. Intelligent and clever, well-tutored by his teachers and apprenticed to **Silvestrus** of the *Collegium Sorcerorum*. First of the three Brothers to **Thaddeus** of Beewicke. Later affianced to **Nannsi** of Zorbas in Graecolia. He is Cardinal Point—*Occidus* (West)—of the *Circuitus Octipes Magnus,* the Great Compass.

Annania   Resident of Beewicke, assistant to local baker. Later to wed **Barcus** of Poosia, replacement apprentice for **Thaddeus** of Beewicke.

Annis   Male servant to **Ormerod**, vintner of Figberry.

Antigonis   Monitor lizard. Familiar of **Silvestrus** of Somerset, he abides at the *Collegium Sorcerorum* in his Master's study. He has a special dietary predilection for soft-feathered, nocturnal avian predators, to the distress of some of the other Masters at the College.

Apiarius Magister   Chief Beekeeper of the Hives in Beewicke, having inherited the position from his father.

Aquilla Magna   Ancient God of Eagles said to foster significant enmity toward Dragons.

Arbuta   Sister to tavernkeeper **Dawber** of Bannock. She lives alone in a small manor on the Frantillian coast.

Arch-Iten   *Aelvae* Bow Master at the *Collegium Sorerorum* and cousin to **Non-Dar**, local Lord of the Greensward *Aelvae,* who are, by tradition, allied to the College.

Argentus Silverfoot   One of silver-haired and pointy-eared half-*Aelvae* twin cousins. He is in his first year of study at the *Collegium Sorcerorum.* Along with his twin, **Platinus**, he befriended **Thaddeus** of Beewicke and his three human Brothers.

Argus   Loyal hound, eager companion and early protector of **Thaddeus** of Beewicke.

Argutia   Intellect. One of the four daughters—the *Intelligentiae*—of **Mater Naturae,** who together are tasked with preventing the Daemons at the Earth's core from breaking through to the surface via the Tower of the Cin to ravage the planet.

Arnius   Apprentice and *Tironis* classmate of **Thaddeus**. Largest and slowest in his class but loyal to a fault.

Arrius Sextus   Emperor of Westlands some 1500 years before present. Father, **Quintus,** had been Commander of the Fleet and was noted for galley crew training. Daughter, **Serenea**, briefly engaged to **Iusti Mores** until his fortnight spent in the Eastern Tower. Emperor, however, became intrigued by **Mores'** stories of the vast treasures of the Cin.

Astonius   Master distiller and astute businessman at Brightfield Manor, he is husband to **Sophia** and father of **Anders.**

Asullus   Sentient mule, born in Cobbly Knob in the year of the Great Comet and chattel of the witch woman, **Lilith**. Achieved capacity of speech and other gifts through his Mistress's magicks and has not been silent since. Suspected father to **Asummus.**

Atreus   Albino Griffon, traditionally employed by Seniors at the *Collegium Sorcerorum* as access coordinator and personal assistant to his masters. In recent past, he has worked for both **Wil Rathboneson**, and, following, **Thaddeus** of Beewicke.

Attacondros   King of Red Dragons. Passionate suitor for the favors of **Mari** the Green, Queen of Sea Dragons. Frustrated by the failure of his suit, he pronounces a terrible curse upon the Green Queen, summoning the Red Tide.

Avolare   Second of four feral children of **Thaddeus**, mothered by **Caerulea**, *Regina Papilionum,* Queen of Butterflies. Tall for a butterfly, she is blonde-haired and blue-eyed with a bluish tint to her skin. Abhors silences in conversations.

B

Balsaalmer   Master Artificer, *Collegium Sorcerorum.* Has good-natured rivalry with Master Smith, **Fabricus.**

Barcus of Poosia. Recruited by **Apiarius Magister** of Beewicke as replacement for the abruptly absent **Thaddeus**. Over time, he gains the respect and confidence of Thaddeus' parents, **Hycynthya** and **Cedric.**

Barnabas Cleric and Brother of the Order. One of only a small number of members of the Holy Orders allowed by the Council to study and teach at the *Collegium Sorcerorum.* He has a passion for the study of Law and serves as an Administrator of the College.

Beatus   Master Sorcerer and current *Princeps Academiae, Collegium Sorcerorum.* Benign shepherd to his flock. Many believe that upon his retirement he is likely to be succeeded in that position by **Silvestrus** of Somerset.

Bede   Venerable Master Sorcerer and early *Princeps Academiae, Collegium Sorcerorum,* to whom **Silvestrus** of Somerset was apprenticed.

Bellis   Golden hunting dog rescued by the four Apprentices from a beating. She decides to travel with the boys on their journey. She is also said to be associated with a tawny-braided woman, a young girl and the blonde alpha female of a wide-ranging combined wolf and dog pack. Legends describe a similar personage—an ancient minor Goddess known as **Luperca.**

Binarius (aka **Digitus**) Professor of Mathematics. Undeterred by loss of facility with decimal system, borrows idea from alternate source—**Thaddeus** of Beewicke —to devise system of numbers based on two digits only. Predicts affiliation of blind eagle **Osiric** with **Thaddeus.** Later in life referred to as The Mad Hermit.

Blumena   Kindly laundress and nursery matron at the Fountaindale Thieves' Guild. She took especial interest in the career of **Molly o' the Willows**.

C

Caecus   Near-sighted Master Sorcerer, who, for reasons which are unclear, demonstrates strong ties to the current *Supremi* class of *Indiginae* at the *Collegium Sorcerorum.*

Caerulea   *Regina Papilionium*, blue Queen of Butterflies. Life mate to My Lord **Spadix**, *Rex Blattarum*, King of Moths, who is widely known to be both unfaithful to, yet jealous of, his Queen. Mother of **Avolare** by **Thaddeus** of Beewicke.

Callidus of Agilitium. Albeit left-handed, he was the most accomplished Apprentice in sword work of the *Imperium* but perished during the Invasion of the Cin. Some believe his weapons—a sword and shield marked with a 'Λ'— were eventually destined for **Thaddeus** of Beewicke.

Carlus (aka **Charles***). Minor Brown Daemon of the Lower Vale, whose existence was spared long ago by **Silvestrus** of Somerset following the loss of a mortal wager. Per agreement, **Silvestrus** can summon **Charles** to perform tasks—typically involving combat—with the proviso that the spoils of such contests are afterward the Daemon's to do with as he pleased.

Carolle   Former Governess to **Anders** of Brightfield at Brightfield Manor, whose niece, **Nyree**, took a fancy to her young charge.

Carthago of Cannae. He is a roustabout seaman. He is also the cousin of a cousin of **Pontius**, Magistrate of Vexare. His loyalties are to family, crew and the Goddess of Profit. He is said to be good with a knife but confesses that his ultimate goal is to marry, settle down in the town of Zama, give up his seafaring ways and raise a large family in peace—as soon as he can find the means.

Cartographus Cleric and Brother of the Order. One of only a small number of members of Holy Orders allowed by the Council to study and teach at the *Collegium Sorcerorum,* he has a passion for geography, maps, travel and travelers' tales and serves in the library of the College.

Catria   Personal maid to **Sophia** of Brightfield Manor.

Cedric   Assistant to *Apiarius Magister*, Keeper of the Hives at Beewicke. Married to **Hycynthya**, the old miller's daughter, and father of **Thaddeus**.

Celsius   Skilled Master of the Healing Arts at the *Collegium Sorcerorum*. Enjoys drama and attention, typically arriving levitated on a cloud of green smoke. He is eternally anxious concerning compensation for his services.

Cerafonus   Male servant at Brightfield Manor, under the direction of **Sennacis**.

Charles (aka **Carlus***).* Minor Brown Daemon of the Lower Vale, whose existence was spared long ago by **Silvestrus** of Somerset following the loss of a mortal wager. Per agreement, **Silvestrus** can summon **Charles** to perform tasks— typically involving combat—with the proviso that the spoils of such contests are afterward the Daemon's to do with as he pleased.

Chiron   Centaur and Horse-Master at the *Collegium Sorcerorum*. He is given the task of training Apprentices in the use of non-edged weapons and mounted combat. Later, he leaves the College to seek the baby, **Akireu**.

Cock-Roach   Mid-level Goblin commander of raiding party sent to capture **Thaddeus** of Beewicke

Coqua   Last living female of the Fathers of Man, wife to **Specus**. She later becomes adoptive mother of **Faran** of Fountaindale at the encouragement of **Silvestrus** of Somerset but dies in an attack on her home by local townsfolk bigots.

Corrigan the Mad   He is the alcoholic step-son of **Mattom**, Arch Druid of River's Wood community. From childhood, he was a darkly moody youth who jealously harbored suspicions regarding his playmate **Luperca**, with whom he shared his step-brother, **Madigan**.

D

Dawber   Tavernkeeper of Bannock. He longs to retire to his sister's estate in the South, especially following recent events in his inn.

Digitus (aka **Binarius**) Professor of Mathematics. He is responsible for the conception and development of the decimal system though some say he could have spent more time on the development of his social skills as well. Later in life referred to as The Mad Hermit.

Dog-Face   Mid-level Goblin commander of raiding party sent to capture **Thaddeus** of Beewicke

E

Ephemerus First new Apprentice recruited for the *Collegium Sorcerorum*
following the disastrous results of the invasion of the Cin by Westlands Emperor,
Tyrannus Superbus, one thousand years in the past. He had a penchant for
uttering obscure prophecy after consuming strong drink.

Eques Knight-Master and leader of the Battle-Masters of the *Collegium
Sorcerorum*. He is the most knowledgeable and skilled of the Combat Masters
in the use of edged weapons and armor.

Equus God of four-footed mammals. Faithfully bears **Mater Naturae** to any
place and any plane of her desire.

Eryops Ancient and evil giant Amphibian living in swampy land near the
Southwest caves of the forest surrounding the *Collegium Sorcerorum* who, for
his own reasons, reports the comings and goings of various folk in the forest to
Master **Perditus** of the College.

Ethne of Tarandon, Lady of the Flowers of Sorrow. Mistress of vintner, **Ormerod**
of Figberry and, later, mother of **Akireu** by **Thaddeus** of Beewicke. Perished
from consumption, which she passed onto her employer prior to her death.

F

Fabia One of twin girls born to the union of **Silvestrus** of Somerset and
Merriwhiddle of Martanius, who was allegedly sacrificed by her mother to the evil
sentient tree, **Garrungroot**, in return for power, immortality, and invulnerability.

Fabrica One of twin girls born to the union of **Silvestrus** of Somerset and
Merriwhiddle of Martanius, who was allegedly sacrificed by her mother to the evil
sentient tree, **Garrungroot**, in return for power, immortality and invulnerability.

Fabricus Master Smith, *Collegium Sorcerorum*. Has good-natured rivalry with
Master Artificer, **Balsaamer**.

Falswar Comptroller of the Thieve's Guild, Fountaindale.

Faran of Fountaindale. Redheaded adopted son of **Specus**, last of the Fathers
of Man and Master Cook to the *Collegium Sorcerorum,* and his wife, **Coqua**.
Unrecognized relationship to **Melaphan** of Fountaindale. Former leader of
Faran's Falcons, Young Thieves' Guild and later becoming Guild Master of the
Thieves' Guild of Fountaindale.

Fastus the Fowler. Reputed father of **Somada** by his lover, **Lallie**, servant to
Ormerod the vintner of Figberry.

Fondula Mate of **Iam** of the First, Keeper of the *Orbis Magnvs*.

G

Geanninia of Glascoton. Imposing Sorceress, Head-Mistress and Professor at the *Ludia*. She has been romantically linked with **Silvestrus** of Somerset in excess of a lifetime.

Geoffrey of the Broom. Lord, skilled warrior and commanding officer of the Iron Company of the *Arx Montium,* Mountaingaard, Defenders of the *Collegium Sorcerorum.* He has a long-held desire to retire to the South, marry well, and initiate a dynasty.

Georgus   Along with **Loffi**, is stablehand to **Ormerod**, the vintner of Figberry. He is one of the few servants remaining at the estate following the illness and death of his employer.

Glabrus   Erstwhile classmate of **Silvestrus** of Somerset at the *Collegium Sorcerorum* in those days before the Great Westlands' Invasion of the Lands of the Cin.

Glaustus   Master Sorcerer and excitable colleague of Master **Bede** (the venerable) *Princeps Academiae, Collegium Sorcerorum.* Leader of the College's War-Party favoring the Westlands' Invasion of the Cin, as decreed by **Tyrannus Superbus**, *Imperator Ultimus,* for reasons—some thought—relating more to advancement of Sorcery, the College, and himself, personally.

Groton II   Arms Master to Thieves' Guild, Fountaindale. Came to Fountaindale after losing niece placed in his care to violent son of Chief of Graecolian Family. Sometimes linked to later mysterious disappearance of this same Graecolian son. In Fountaindale, developed strong ties with **Molly o' the Willows** and took singular interest in teaching her the arts martial of self-defense. Died in a bar-room brawl claimed to have been a random occurrence.

Grunius   Master sergeant and second-in-command of the Iron Company. Stationed at *Arx Montium,* Mountaingaard, he is charged with limiting access to, and defending those in residence at, the *Collegium Sorcerorum.* Said to have developed conflict with **Lord Geoffrey's** replacement, Captain **Titus Labienus.**

H

Hadrout   Irascible Centaur. Formerly partnered with **Silvestrus** of Somerset in the recruitment of likely lads for the *Collegium Sorcerorum,* he resigned from that post following a dispute concerning the Centaur's lack of willingness to bear either the recruits or the Master Sorcerer on his back.

Hap-Sung   Mother of Prince **Zoarr**, and wife of **Zauda**, House of Abdomoolano, King of Mauretesia. Former acrobat and contortionist, she was originally employed at the Temple of the Seven Pleasures in the capital city, Mellisol.

Hectorus Seaman and lover of **Melaphan** of Fountaindale, a prostitute working for the Thieves' Guild. He was the biological father of **Rolland** of Fountaindale. Dark-haired, with a sinewy frame, several golden teeth, and tattoos. Good with a knife and horses.

Hycynthya Mother of **Thaddeus** by **Cedric**. She is the daughter of Beewicke's old miller and only survivor of a curse placed on her family when she was a child.

I

Iacus Fallen former Apprentice to **Silvestrus** of the *Collegium Sorcerorum*. Later, he becomes a leader of the Black Sorcerers, and serves as advisor to the Thieves' Guild, and others, for exorbitant fees. His fall allegedly linked to irregular approach to **Geanninia,** Head-Mistress of the *Ludia*.

Iam Last of the First—the initial tribe of modern human sentients spreading up from the Land of the Sun to occupy the northern continent. The First were the builders of the *Orbis Magnvs (Lapidum Pendentium)*, a structure of Standing Stones located in the northwest corner of the forest surround, itself adjacent to the *Collegium Sorcerorum*—a construction marked with twelve symbols, whose precise purpose is undetermined, but may be related to time and space management. Though the current *Orbis Magnvs* is now a ruin, this was not always thus. In fact, legend speaks of a connection between it and the land's other Standing Stones. **Iam** tends over the structure since the mysterious disappearance—all in one night—of all his people, save his wife **Fondula,** who remained with him until her death some time past. He is tattooed and wears an orange blanket, special beads and two Great Golden Crested Eagle feathers. His greatest virtue is patience. He has had a passing acquaintance with **Specus** and **Coqua,** and later developed a benevolent interest in the career of **Thaddeus** of Beewicke.

Ingenia Wisdom. One of the four daughters—the *Intelligentiae*—of **Mater Naturae**, who together are tasked with preventing the Daemons at the Earth's core from breaking through to the surface to ravage their Mother's planet.

Iohnus Fellow classmate of **Thaddeus** at the *Collegium Sorcerorum*. Has Spiritual bent.

J

Jadell Young daughter of **Zauda**, King of Mauretesia and his wife, Queen **Hap-Sung**. She is very close with her older brother, **Zoarr,** and loves to tease him. She lives under a cloud, however, having been declared at the time of her birth to carry a Mark of Doom according to a short-lived Court Soothsayer.

Janeiva Faithful House Manager to Professor **Smythe**, Dorset Downs. Holds Manor together with assistance from golden dog, **Daisy**, and keeps her employer from wandering aimlessly about.

K

Kenneth of Walworth County. Childhood sweetheart of **Melior,** who left him at the alter following a last minute, gut-wrenching decision by the girl who, instead, went on to become the *Mater Amplior* of the *Sorores Silentii*—the Convent of the Silent Sisters, a nursing division of the Holy Orders near Moorstown.

Ko-Thas *Aelvae* Lieutenant to Lord **Non-Dar**, whose tribe abides in the forest surrounding the *Collegium Sorcerorum.* He is said to have an excellent collection of silver-veined maple tree leaves.

L

Labienus Titus. Lieutenant sent by his old Commander, General **Iulius**, to assume command of *Arx Montium,* Mountaingaard, relieving Lord **Geoffrey** of the Broom, Captain of the Iron Company. He quickly falls into conflict with Sergeant **Grunius**, the fort's second-in-command.

Lallie Daughter to **Morella** and, with her, house-servant to **Ormerod**, the vintner of Figberry. Recently delivered of **Somada**, her daughter by the estate's fowler, **Fastus**, but then abruptly abandoned by the same after he was confronted by her mother, **Morella**, regarding his intentions. She nursed **Ethne**'s son, **Akireu**, by **Thaddeus** of Beewicke, along with her own daughter.

Liaisonia Mistress. Directress, Division of Student Relationships, the *Ludia.*

Lilith Witch-woman of Cobbly Knob, and third cousin to **Silvestrus** of Somerset. She is an animal trainer, and owner of the mule, **Asullus**. At the request of her cousin, she imbued **Asullus** with the ability to speak, an act generative of a peculiar and unintended consequence. Rival with girlfriend **Eve** for the affections of her man.

Lillia of Falling Stone. Formerly a nanny for a Lord's large household some fifteen hundred years in the past, she demonstrated unique capacities in early adolescence, thus capturing the attention of a local priest, through whose support she was eventually able to achieve admission to the College of Sorcerers. Later, she became engaged to **Longius** of Adventitia but disappeared one night under mysterious circumstances.

Lilyput Ancient green Goblin, House-Mistress of the *Collegium Sorcerorum.* She is uncommonly skilled with Sorcerous enchantments and unaccountably knowledgeable concerning Sorcerous prophecy and politics. She is rumored to have the special ability to appear simultaneously in diverse settings and to have a long-standing, albeit obscure, relationship with the College's spectre, **Brother Longbone.**

Logus   Determined Master of Logic, Rhetoric and Analysis, *Collegium Sorcerorum,* who tends to the long view.

Longbone   Brother. Doomed, as a result of a curse, to roam the Spaces Behind at the *Collegium Sorcerorum,* living forever, never eating, never drinking, and never having direct contact with others. Thought to have some obscure relationship with **Lilyput** and, at her behest, rumored to perform late-night punitive visits to the chambers of young boys who have demonstrated behavioral infractions of the College's Articles of Conduct and Comportment.

Longius of Adventitia. Apprentice at the *Collegium Sorcerorum* over fifteen hundred years in the past. Clever artificer and one of only a handful at the College who was ever able to discover the secret of the Spaces Behind. Afianced to **Lillia** of Falling Stone. However, he is said to have disappeared one night under mysterious circumstances.

Luctarus of the Empty Hand. Short, slight and usually dressed only in a partially wound sheet, he is, nevertheless, one of five Battle-Masters at the *Collegium Sorcerorum.* His specialty is unarmed combat and he carries a Medallion of Power inscribed with the ancient Symbol of Duality.

Lucus   Fellow classmate of **Thaddeus** at the *Collegium Sorcerorum.* Strong interest in healing arts but also has Spiritual bent.

Luperca   Ancient minor Goddess, usually found in the company of wolves. She is said to be able to take the form of a tawny-braided woman but is also apparently associated with a small girl and a Great Pack Leader. The mother of the fourth of four feral children, **Sacerdotia**, fathered by **Thaddeus** of Beewicke, to whom she is known as **Bellis.**

Lupus   Young wolf who hunts **Osiric.** Forestalled in his course by **Thaddeus** of Beewicke, who the pack member acknowledges as Consort to **Luperca.**

M

Macro   Enforcer personally loyal to **Faran** of the Thieves' Guild of Fountaindale.

Madigan   Arch Druid and Sachem, son of **Mattom**, Arch-Druid before him, and step-brother to **Corrigan** the Mad. He rules from the Holy Seat in River's Wood. He is a childhood friend of the current avatar of **Luperca**, the ancient Goddess associated with wolves. He is the custodian of the predictive power of the Ancient Oak, the Great Wheel.

Marcus   Fellow classmate of **Thaddeus** at the *Collegium Sorcerorum.* Has Spiritual bent.

Mari the Green. *Regina Draconum Marinarum*, Queen of Sea Dragons. As a young adult, she developed an interesting relationship with a young man off the coast of a small fishing village in Frantillia. Unfortunately, he eventually disappeared. Later, she became mother, by **Thaddeus** of Beewicke, of **Ultoris**, the half-dragon, who was, from conception, sworn to vendetta against **Attacondros** the Red. She is, additionally, thought to have some close relationship with the Old Woman of the Sea, coincidentally named **Mari,** as well as with a young Sea Siren bearing the same name also.

Marius Corporal, Iron Company, Mountaingaard. Right-hand to Sergeant **Grunius**.

Marsia of Dorset Downs, Northfast. She is the fourth of four daughters of a local teacher. A tall girl, with hip-length honey-gold hair, she carries a pair of green stones, split from a single source and said to have special properties. She was recruited to the *Ludia* by Mistress **Geanninia** and traveled with her, joining with **Nannsi**, **Sonnia**, and **Molly o' the Willows**, in turn. She has special knowledge of a future with **Thaddeus** of Beewicke and has determined not to shirk from it.

Mater Naturae Mother Nature. Important figure of prehistoric times, enraged at the violation of her Earth-avatar by Daemons from **Bellona**. In response, she has charged her four daughters, the *Intellegentiae*, with the task of thwarting any attempt by those same Daemons to win their freedom from the Earth's core—into which they were cast and entrapped—by escaping to the planet's surface. Also referred to as the Lady.

Mattias Fellow classmate of **Thaddeus** at the *Collegium Sorcerorum*. Has Spiritual bent.

Mattom   Former Chief, or Arch Druid and Sachem, at River's Wood. Father to **Madigan**, current Arch Druid at River's Wood and step-father to **Corrigan** the Mad. He was able to persuade **Luperca**, an ancient lupine Goddess, to bring to fruition her part in the Ring's Plan, assuming her child form for various periods of time so she and **Madigan** could be raised as youthful friends. Before his death, **Mattom** was able to pass on this knowledge to his son, the subsequent Chief Druid, **Madigan**.

Melaphan Fiery, redheaded prostitute and mother, by **Hectorus** the sailor, of **Rolland** of Fountaindale. Following the loss of her seaman before the birth of their child, she strove to devote her remaining time and energy to raising the baby boy. She was later slain by a drunken customer during the boy's infancy, and the responsibility for his care passed to **Faran** of Fountaindale. Cautious rumors hinted at some manner of special relationship between **Melaphan** and **Faran**. Some few even considered her demeanor, at times, otherworldly.

Melior *Mater Amplior.* Abbess of the convent of the *Sorores Silentii.* Early on, she was betrothed to **Kenneth** of Walworth County, but following a soul-searching retreat, gave up the prospect of a husband and family to enter a religious nursing order. An excellent and highly skilled healer, she always found issues involving human relationships versus the higher good to be a struggle.

Merriwhiddle of Martanius. Failed student of Sorcery, and competitor with **Geanninia** of Glascoton for the attentions of **Silvestrus** of Somerset. Convinced by that Sorcerer to allow him to accompany her to her homeland after she had left the *Ludia* in her unfulfilled fourth year, she became pregnant with twin girls **Fabia** and **Fabrica**. **Silvestrus** then abandoned her. In a rage and seeking revenge, she formed a compact with the evil Tree Spirit, **Garrungroot**, who promised her power, knowledge, invulnerability, and immortality in return for a terrible price.

Modus Porter of the *Collegium Sorcerorum.* He frequently traveled outside the *Collegium* to obtain supplies and deliver messages. He was recruited, over time, to perform various tasks for gold by Master **Perditus**.

Molly o' the Willows Orphan sold to **Faran** of Fountaindale of the Thieves Guild. She had an especial talent with the young and tended the children of the Guild's night-ladies with great affection. She was mentored by **Blumena** of housekeeping and was instructed in defensive arts by **Groton** of the House Guard. She developed a sentimental attachment to the stands of willows lining the banks of the River Fountaindale. She often expressed hesitation concerning relationships with those of differing social class.

Morad Arch-Daemon and father of **Morag**. Slain by **Silvestrus** of Somerset. The son has vowed vengeance.

Morag Arch-Daemon, who long cultivated a connection with the Cinnian Tower, after being placed by his kind in the land of the peoples who would come to be known as the Cin. However, he abruptly lost power when a ragtag band of Western Sorcerers, in a surprise maneuver at the height of battle, purloined the Tower, transporting it to, and securing it on, the grounds of the *Collegium Sorcerorum.* Has developed plan to corrupt a Master of the College in order to win his and his People's freedom.

Morella Mother of **Lallie** and servant to **Ormerod,** the vintner of Figberry. She held a low opinion of **Ethne** of Tarandon, **Omerod**'s Mistress, yet took **Ethne**'s only child to Fountaindale, after his mother's death, and kept him safe to await the advent of the Man-horse.

Mores Iusti Living some fifteen hundred years in the past, he is the youngest *Princeps Academiae* of the *Collegium Sorcerorum*, achieving the post with surprising ease. Once ensconced, he discovers the Places Behind and begins to indulge voyeuristic impulses concerning **Lillia** of Falling Stone, among others. In his fourth year of administration, he mysteriously vanishes, coinciding with the disappearance of **Lillia** herself, and her fellow student and love interest, **Longius** of Adventitia. Despite significant efforts, these absences were never fully explained nor were their bodies ever recovered.

Morod Daemon son of **Morag**. Ambitious, some say, to a fault.

Morphia Purple-winged and often somnific representative of *Spritae* family of the *Faerrae*. Such *Fey* are often sought after to accomplish tasks and fetch items. Some are said to be exquisitely sensitive to the addictive powers of *Pixae* honey, especially the strain found in Beewicke.

Myrtelee of Tarandon. Mother to **Ethne** of Tarandon. Peasant-woman to whom, at the height of a harsh winter, four women appeared, initially identifying themselves as faggot peddlers. This pretext was rather quickly abandoned, however, and the four visited upon the unsuspecting woman an annunciation that her daughter, at a certain time, would be given the choice of everlasting fame or long life. She was instructed to ensure that her daughter learn this pronouncement by heart.

N

Nannsi of Zorbas, Graecolia. Her father is a successful merchant. She is the only short and dark member of her sib line, resembling none of her brothers and sisters. Attentive to details, she objects to much that is "frivolous" in life. She searches for a soul-mate and puzzles over how to convince that person of their inevitability while simultaneously seeking the means to meet the requirements for Sorceress practice.

Nellia Village girl who, after becoming pregnant unexpectedly, suddenly left the village.

Non-Dar Lord of the Greensward *Aelvae* dwelling in the forest surrounding the *Collegium Sorcerorum*. He is traditionally the ally of the Sorcerers and a blood enemy of all Goblin-kind. He is often experienced as a bit stuffy and full of himself but is considered steadfast and handy to have around in any altercation.

Nyree Niece to **Carolle**, former Governess to **Anders** of Brightfield Manor. She was frequently at Brightfield over the summer months where she struck up a relationship with the boy thought to be troubling.

Nytus Former Grand Master of the Thieves' Guild of Fountaindale. Found slumped in his chair one morning with a red, corded silken scarf of highest quality lying in his lap. By the following week's end, **Faran**, recently returned from the East, had assumed the very same chair.

O

Orbis Sister. Chief librarian at the Convent of the Silent Sisters, who, through her research, was able to delve the existence and purpose of the Rings of Resonance.

Ormerod Well-regarded vintner of Figberry, whose purberry wine vintages are famous in the region. Long-time acquaintance of **Silvestrus** of Somerset. Has taken to mistress, **Ethne** of Fountaindale—a former woman of the night. He eventually succumbs to pulmonary consumption acquired from this same mistress.

Orsa Sharpest-eyed lookout of the Iron Company stationed at *Arx Montium*.

Osiric Great Golden Crested Eagle. Formerly Lord of his Kind but blinded in a forest fire while trying to save his mate, **Qinda**, and their fledglings. He subsequently developed enhanced and compensating senses of smell and hearing, and later becomes fast companion to **Thaddeus** of Beewicke.

P

Perditus of Skara-Brae. The youngest Master to sit on the Governing Council of the *Collegium Sorcerorum*. Unpopular, anti-social, yet brilliant and ambitious, he is a dedicated student of Eastern Magicks, especially their rumored links to otherworldly powers. He has made a life study of the Tower, the only known artifact extant in the Westlands to date from before the time of the great Invasion of the East.

Pertangus of Mauretesia. Life Arms-Master to the House of Abdomoolano. He traditionally considers the end product to have precedence over the means by which it is accomplished.

Pisca Mermaid and seer to the Court of **Mari** the Green, *Regina Draconum Marinarum*. She brought the Sea Dragon Queen's attention to patterns in the Stars foretelling the advent of a young Human male by whom the Queen would bear a child of great importance who would grow to avenge the mother of a great wrong. She met her doom at the claws of **Attacondros** the Red, frustrated suitor of her Mistress. It is speculated that she was first ravished, then devoured by this personage.

Piscellus Old man of the sea and captain of his own fishing boat. He has a distant relation to **Pontius**, Magistrate of Vexare, who engages him to provide both shelter and transportation back to Vexare for the Magistrate and his young charge, **Thaddeus** of Beewicke, at the conclusion of the adventure of the green dragon's treasure.

Platinus Silverfoot   One of silver-haired and pointy-eared half-*Aelvae*, twin cousins, he and his close kin, **Argentus**, befriend **Thaddeus** of Beewicke and his three human brothers in their first year at the College before, by chance, running afoul of one of the Masters of the College.

Polyphemus   Cyclops. Having been bested by **Noman**, and through a number of peculiar circumstances, he ends up having his vision restored but his head subsequently nailed to the door leading to the Hallway of the *Indiginae,* or Seniors, at the *Collegium Sorerorum.* He is charged with seeing that those in their last year of study are not unduly disturbed.

Pontius   Magistrate of Vexare, Frantillia. In his youth, he was a skilled guide to boats and ships both entering and leaving the local harbor, earning rank of Pilot. He has written to the *Collegium Sorcerorum* for assistance in combatting a recent infestation of Red Tide, suspected of being of arcane origin. He is made aware of the Green Dragon's treasure by **Thaddeus** of Beewicke and must devise a course of action that brings the greatest benefit to the greatest number of his constituency.

Portoman   Master Sorcerer, *Collegium Sorcerorum.* One of a company of Sorcerers volunteering to serve the Empire during the invasion of the lands of the Cin. It was **Portoman** who intuited that the Cin's unanticipated success in first repelling, then slaughtering the Imperial legions was related to a magical concentration of Dark Vigor stemming from the Tower, lodged in the enemy's capital city. He and his companions, therefore, contrived to steal away the Tower —but at great cost to **Portoman**'s sanity. He was eventually brought safely back to the College along with the mysterious Tower. His broken mind, however, never healed, despite best efforts, and he did not long survive his return. He was apprenticed to Master **Glaustus.**

Primus   First of three tutors engaged by **Sophia** and **Astonius** of Brightfield Manor to educate their only child, **Anders**. He is bilious in nature.

Protervus   Imp. He has been impressed as guardian of the pantry at the *Collegium Sorcerorum* due to the natural predilection of young boys for caloric surfeit regardless of time of day or night.

Providentia   Foresight. One of the four daughters—the *Intelligentiae*—of **Mater Naturae,** who together are tasked with preventing the Daemons at the Earth's core from breaking through to the surface to ravage the planet.

Psittaca   Four hundred-year-old parrot pledged to House Abdomoolano of the Kingdom of Mauretesia. She is presently assigned to Prince **Zoarr**, sole surviving heir to the Leopard Throne, currently in study at the *Collegium Sorcerorum.* The parrot can authentically assume the color and shape of similarly-sized objects and is also an exceptional verbal mimic.

Publius   Only son of **Tyrannus Superbus,** accompanying his father on the Westlands' campaign to the lands of the Cin. Legend suggests he was taken alive —along with the Emperor—at the conclusion of the last battle and was yet living when led away.

Pugiles   Identical twin brothers, bald, mustachioed, and tattooed, great of height and broad of shoulder. They are of the Rom People and formally worked in Carnivale, before hiring out to **Faran** of the Thieves' Guild, Fountaindale, as Protectors.

Pumilus of Upcrag.   Dwarf, Master of Small Arms, and one of five Battle-Masters of the *Collegium Sorcerorum.* He is the only dwarf on record known to speak with a lisp.

Q

Qinda   Great Golden Crested Eagle and life-mate to **Osiric**, Lord of his kind. She perished in a forest fire protecting her fledglings, while her spouse vainly tried to beat back the engulfing flames.

Quintessentialus Marcus, Pro-Consul. He was an early sponsor of **Akireu**, local student of **Chiron** the Horse-man. His endorsement secured his young protege a place at the Academy of War in Fornia, thus initiating the boy's formal military career.

R

Rastius   Master Sorcerer and Sergeant-of-Arms at the *Collegium Sorcerorum.* He is of large stature, second in volume only to Master Cook **Specus.**

Rathboneson, Wil *Indiginae* in Senior year at the *Collegium Sorcerorum.* He formerly studied under Master Sorcerer **Perditus** of Skara-Brae but was dismissed at the end of only one year. It was speculated that the Master may have mistaken him for another. He is a lover of horses and Captain of the *Supremi Pila Ludere* team. His room is guarded by the albino Griffon, **Atreus.**

Raugauld   Cook to the Iron Company, *Arx Montium*, at Mountaingaard. Makes passable bear stew.

Renditius   Trusted scout for Iron Company, *Arx Montium*, the Mountaingaard.

Ritia   Barracks manager, Iron Company, *Arx Montium*, the Mountaingaard.

Rolland of Fountaindale. Only surviving child of **Hectorus**, seaman and **Melaphan**, redheaded prostitute. He is a street thief, Excelsior-class, junior Thieves Guild, **Faran**'s Falcons. He is rumored to have some special relationship with the very same **Faran**. Later, he is apprenticed to **Silvestrus** of the *Collegium Sorcerorum.* He is the second of the three Brothers to **Thaddeus** of Beewicke. He engages in a personal rivalry with **Zoarr** of Mauretesia. **Rolland** is Cardinal Point—*Orientem* (East)—of the Great Compass.

Rufo   *Nom de Voyage* of **Rolland** of Fountaindale.

S

Sabata   One of group of original settlers on Southern Frantillia coastline who found the village that came to be known as Vexare. She was pregnant at the time of the settling.

Sacerdotia   Female cleric and fourth of four feral children of **Thaddeus** of Beewicke, by **Luperca**, Great Golden Wolf Pack leader. She is an Arch-Druidic priestess in her own right and a demi-wolf.

Sanadar   Loyal House Captain to the Court of **Zauda**, King of Mauretesia. He is an exceptionally large fellow with massive earrings, ample wit and a deep and hearty laugh. He favors peach brandy.

Sapientia   Wit. One of the four daughters—the *Intelligentiae*—of **Mater Naturae**, who together are tasked with preventing the Daemons at the Earth's core from breaking through to the surface to ravage the planet.

Secundus   Second of three tutors engaged by **Sophia** and **Astonius** of Brightfield Manor for the instruction of their son, **Anders**. He is phlegmatic in character.

Sennacis   House manager to **Sophia** and **Astonius** of Brightfield Manor estate. He is choleric in nature.

Sennead   Great Golden Crested Eagle, son of **Osiric**. He assumed the Lordship of his Tribe after his father's loss of vision in a forest fire. Subsequently, he implemented a policy of benign neglect toward the efforts of his sisters, who sought to comfort their father following his injury.

Serenea   Daughter of **Sextus Arrius**, Westlands Emperor some 1500 years before present. Distraught upon receiving letter from her love, **Iusti Mores**, that he was breaking off their engagement, following his fortnight spent in the Tower of the Cin.

Servilla   Faithful servant to **Sonnia** of Frantillia, sent to the *Ludia* to be with her mistress. Put to death by Goblins after defending her charge.

Shire Reeve   Chief officer of law enforcement in Fountaindale and surrounding communities.

Silvestrus of Somerset. Instructor at *Collegium Sorcerorum*, Apprenticed to Master **Bede**, whom he considered venerable. Early in his youth, he is known to have studied serpent habitats along the coast of southern Frantillia. At the time of the Invasion of the Cin, circa 8500, he was elected to the Sorcerers War Council in spite of his young age and thus accompanied the Imperial Army of the Invasion to the East. Following this disaster, **Silvestrus** became a tireless proponent of the Doctrine of Sorcerous Pan-semination. Over time, he was recruited as a Disciple by the Mother, serving Her will through the Four *Intelligentiae*. He was the father of twin girls by failed Sorceress Apprenticiatrix, **Merriwhiddle** of Martanius. He is currently affianced to **Geanninia** of Glascoton, Head-Mistress of the *Ludia*.

Sin-Dol *Aelvae*. He is a member of the Greensward tribe led by **Non-Dar**, who dwell in the forest surrounding the *Collegium Sorcerorum*. He has studied the procurement of the rare and elusive substance, ambrosia.

Smythe Professor and Instructor, University at Topian. Father to four daughters, the youngest of whom, **Marsia**—future *Coeur d'Orange* of **Thaddeus** of Beewicke —most closely resembles his dear departed wife. He makes his home at Dorset Downs with the vital assistance of his faithful House Manager, **Janeiva**, and equally faithful golden dog, **Daisy**.

Somada Infant daughter of **Lallie** by the fowler, **Fastus**, born one month before **Akireu**, son of **Ethne** by Thaddeus. **Lallie**, already nursing **Somada**, went on to nurse **Akireu** as well.

Sonnia of Frantillia. She is the second child and only daughter of a successful merchant who has spoiled her outrageously. Sea life was her major interest until she was recruited to become a Sorceress at the *Ludia*. She is of average height and typically wears her waist-length brown hair in a braid, but her brilliant smile is judged her best feature. If she has any faults, it may be her ambition and attention to classist positions.

Sophia Mistress of Brightfield Manor, wife to **Astonius** and mother of **Anders**, her only child. She is known for her superb business acumen.

Spadix *Rex Blattarum*, King of Moths, life-mate of **Caerulea**, *Regina Papilionum*, Queen of Butterflies. A Great Brown Moth, he is always referred to as "My Lord **Spadix**." He is particularly jealous of his wife's interest in others and so, tends to resent **Avolare**—daughter of **Caerulea** by **Thaddeus** of Beewicke —whom he believes, but cannot prove, is not his child. His moth dust is said to have certain special properties.

Specus The last surviving member of the Fathers of Man. Husband to **Coqua**, the last surviving woman of the Fathers of Man. Unable to have children, he adopted eight-year-old **Faran** in an arrangement orchestrated by **Silvestrus** of Somerset for the Sorcerer's own purposes. He possesses uncommon culinary skills. Following his wife's death, **Silvestrus** convinced him to travel to the *Collegium Sorcerorum* and assume the duties of Master Cook for the school. The Master Cook's physical features are striking and unlike those of any other living human being

Split-Eye Mid-level Goblin commander of raiding party sent to capture **Thaddeus** of Beewicke.

T

Tertius   Third of three tutors engaged by **Sophia** and **Astonius** of Brightfield Manor to educate their only child, **Anders**. Later dismissed following a reputed difficulty with the cook. He is sanguine in nature.

Thaddeus of Beewicke. Only child of **Cedric** and **Hycynthya**. He is apprenticed to **Silvestrus** of the *Collegium Sorcerorum*, and is lover to **Ethne** of Tarandon; **Caerulea,** *Regina Papilionum*; **Mari,** *Regina Draconum Marinarum;* and **Luperca,** Great Pack Leader, with resultant issue of **Akireu**, **Avolare**, **Ultoris**, and **Sacerdotia**, respectively. He later proposes to **Marsia** of Dorset Downs, Sorceress. After losing Belief, he is identified as **Thaddeus** the Faithless. He is the Cardinal point—*Septentrio* (North)—of the Great Compass.

Thra-gora   Beatific member of a pair of black marble Gargoyle statues charged with guarding the main entrance to the *Collegium Sorcerorum*. She is claimed by some to be, on occasion, both sentient and mobile.

Tigellinus   Enforcer personally loyal to **Faran** of the Thieves' Guild of Fountaindale.

Toomus   Proprietor *Locusta Ruber*, Vexare.

Turd-Open   Mid-level Goblin commander of raiding party sent to capture **Thaddeus** of Beewicke

Tyrannus Superbus   *Imperator Ultimus,* the last Emperor of the Westlands, reigning from the imperial capital at Fornia, who led—one thousand years in the past—a million-man army consisting of ninety-nine Imperial legions at full strength in the Invasion of the Cin of the East. The campaign, however, proved a disaster, ending in the total annihilation of the invading force by the Cin's employment of their Ancient Ones—skilled users of Magicks—thought to have been aided and abetted by Daemon-kind. Two of the very few survivors of the entire campaign later vouchsafed on oath that at the conclusion of the final battle, they witnessed the Emperor and his son, **Publius**, who had accompanied him on the campaign, being led off by the enemy.

U

Ulina   Older female servant to **Pontius**, Magistrate of Vexare.

Ultoris   Third feral child of **Thaddeus**. He is the son of **Mari** the Green, *Regina Draconum Marinarum,* Queen of Sea Dragons. He inherited, as dragons do, all the knowledge of his Mother during the period of his incubation. By the time of his hatching, his mother had perished due to poisoning from the Red Tide, leaving her son with the Burning of Vengeance toward his mother's slayer, the mighty **Attacondros** the Red.

V

Vaticinati Cleric and Brother of the Order. One of only a small number of members of the Holy Orders allowed by the Council to study and teach at the *Collegium Sorcerorum*, where he serves as Chief Librarian and Steward of Rare Documents.

Vespertiliolis Nickname, **Little Bat**, applied to **Osiric** for the development of his compensatory ability of echolocation following his loss of vision in a forest fire.

Z

Zauda King of Mauretesia, of the House of Abdomoolano, Married to **Hap-Sung**, seventh and only surviving wife, formerly acrobat and contortionist at the Temple of the Seven Pleasures, dedicated to Goddess Dyanya. He is father to **Zoarr**, Prince and sole surviving heir-apparent, and **Jadell**, Princess of that House.

Zoarr of Mauretesia, seventh, and only surviving, son of **Zauda**, House of Abdomoolano, King of Mauretesia, and **Hap-Sung,** former acrobat and contortionist. He is Apprentice to **Silvestrus** of the *Collegium Sorcerorum*, recruited one year earlier than the typical age as a result of regional political considerations. He is the third of the three Brothers to **Thaddeus** of Beewicke. He is a skilled student of the martial arts as well as musician. He later seeks to court **Molly o' the Willows**. He is the Cardinal point—*Meridies* (South)—of the Great Compass.

A

Glossary
Lingua Imperatoria

A

Ab—from

Abitus—departure; of a departure

Academiae—of, or pertaining to an academy, place of higher learning

Acini—of a grape

Ad—coming to, arriving at

Administer—manager

Adrogantia—hubris; nerve; chutzpah

Advenae—newcomers; those just beginning study

Advenarum—of, or pertaining to, those just beginning

Adversa—bad; unfortunate; adverse

Aelvae—largest of the *Faerrae*; bold warriors, archers without peer, excellent in sports

Aequinoctium—equinox

Aestas—Summer, in Summer

Alvis—from the bowels

Amazones—women warriors

Amici—friends

Amicus—male friend

Amores—affairs of the heart

Amplior—superior; larger

Anima—breath

Anni—of the year

Anno—in the year of

Antiqua—old

Anus—old woman

Apiarius—beekeeper

Aprilis—fourth month of the year

Aquila—eagle

Aquilo—North wind

Arbiter—referee; judge

Arbor—tree

Arborea—pertaining to a tree

Arcanum—secret

Argutiae—wit

Arx—arc; range

Ascende—ascend; rise

Atrium—hall

Auferre—take away

Auster—South wind

Autem — moreover, also

Autumnale—autumnal; pertaining to the fall

Aux--or

Ave—hello; goodbye; hail

B

Bellona—Sister to Mars, the God of War—also, Mars-sized body striking Earth early in its history, leading to the formation of the moon (*Luna*)

Blattarum—of the moths

Brevis—short

Bruma—winter solstice

C

Caeca—blind

Caelum—heaven

Caeruleus—blue

Calcitra—kick

Caninum—pertaining to dogs

Canis—dog

Cantare—singing

Canum—of dogs

Caput—head

Cardines—Cardinal, or major points of the compass (N, E, S, and W)

Cardinis—Cardinal, or major point of the compass (N, E, S, or W)

Castra—encampment

Castratus—castrated one

Caupona—inn

Centaurus—horse-man, Centaur

Cerealis—eighth month of the year

Cibus—food

Cincinni—curls

Circuitus—circular instrument, as a compass

Circulus—of a circle; circular

Cobolorum—of Goblins

Cogitatio—one's cognition, thinking process

Collegii—of a college

Collegio—college

Collegium—institution of higher learning for boys

Colobi—Goblins

Cometae—comet; of the comet

Commuta—transform

Concidit—give up; surrender; deny; cease

Condicio—proposal

Conloqui—talking; speaking

Conloquium—negotiation

Contrahe—shrink in size

Conventus—convent

Convivium—feast

Coquere—cooking

Coronifer—slave holding wreath over the head of the Triumphant, while speaking a formulaic warning in his/her ear

Cortina—cauldron

Creationis—of creation

Cultri—knives; cutlery

Cum—with

Custos—gatekeeper; guard

D

Daemon—Daemon

Daemonis—of a Daemon

Decem—ten

Defundat—may it pour forth

Destrue—destroy

Dicit—speaks

Diem—day

Dies—day

Discere—learning to

Dissimulator—camouflage artist

Dolorosa—of sorrow

Dolorosus—pain

Domina—lady; house-mistress

Dominus—head man; boss

Domo—going away from, or leaving, home

Dormi—sleep

Draco—dragon

Dracones—dragons

Draconis—of the dragon, dragon's

Draconum—of, or pertaining to, dragons

Duodecem—dozen

Duri—hard

E

Electiones—choices

Epulae—foods

Equitum—pertaining to a horse

Erroris—of error

Et—and

Eurus—East wind

Ex—from

Explicationes—explanations

Exitus—consequence

Extende—expand in size!

F

Facere—making

Facite—make; restore

Factum—making; rendering

Faerrae—one of the major orders of the Fey, who are divided into *Pixae*, *Spritae*, and *Aelvae* by increasing size

Faerrarum—of the *Faerrae*

Fatuus—fool

Faunus—non-human sentient animal

Februarius—second month of the year

Ferias—holidays

Festivus—festival

Fiat—let it become; make it so; let there be

Fides—a belief; faith

Florum—of flowers

Forfices—scissors

Fortuna—luck; fortune

Fuga —flight

Fur—thief

Furiae—the Furies

Furis—of the thief

Furum—of thieves

G

Gens—nation; kind; grouping

Globi—balls

Globulus—globe; sphere

H

Heus—hark; listen

Hominum—of men

I

Ianuam—doorway

Ianuario—of January

Ianuarius—first month of the year

Ignave—coward

Ignesce—ignite

Ignis—fire

Illos—them

Imitatrix—mimic

Impeditus—thwarted; the thwarted one

Imperator—Emperor

Imperatoria—Imperial

Imperia—of, or pertaining to, Empire

Imperii—of the Empire

Imperium—Empire

Impetus—attack

In—in; at

Incendat—let it catch fire!

Incipe—start; begin

Incipere—starting

Indigena—one already present at his or her study; one of the second, third, or fourth years at a school

Indigenae—those already present at their study; those of the second, third and fourth years at a school

Inferni—inhabitants of the infernal regions

Inflationis—inflation

Inflatus—inflated

Ingenia—cleverness

Ingenium—spirit of

Inquisitio—quest

Insanus—insane, mad

Insignia—insignia

Intellegis—do you understand?

Intelligentiae—mindful ones

Inter-Imperium—period between Empires, interregnum

Inverte—turn inside out

Invicti—victorious

Invictus—invincible

Iovius—seventh month of the year

Iter—journey

Iudex—judge

Iudicare—to judge the status of

Iudicium—judgment

Iunii—of the sixth month

Iunius—sixth month of the year

Iusti—high, just

Iuvenem—youth

L

Laesae—treason

Laevus—left-handed

Lapidum—of the stones

Lapis—stone

Latrina—toilet

Lavatio—washing

Legatum—bequest; legacy

Legere—read

Leges—law

Legio—legion

Leopardinus—of the leopard

Lex—law

Liberate—be free of bonds/restraints

Liberi—children

Librum—book

Ligate—bind

Limine—threshold

Lingua—language

Litterae—letters

Litterati—literate ones

Locus—place, place of

Locusta—lobster

Luctator—fighter using no weapons other than hands and/or feet

Ludere—play

Ludi—game

Ludia—institution of higher learning for girls

Ludos—classes

Luna—the moon

Lunares—men of the moon

Lunaris—man of the moon

Luperca—she-wolf; archaic goddess

Luporum—of wolves

M

Magister—master, expert, chief person

Magistrum—master, expert

Magna—great

Magni—great

Magnus—great

Maio—of May

Maius—fifth month of the year

Majestasis—Majesty

Maledictio—curse

Manes—ghost; undead

Marinarum—of Sea Dragons

Maritima—of the sea, marine

Martius—third month of the year

Mater—mother

Mathematica—of, or pertaining to, mathetics

Mathematicarum—of mathematics, mathematical

Matris—of the mother

Maximi—greatest ones

Mea—my

Media—mid

Medice—physician

Medici—of the physician

Mel—honey

Mellum—honey

Membrum—member

Memento—remember

Mense—in the month

Mercatura—purchase, a purchase

Meridianus—meridian

Meridies—South

Mille—thousand

Millibus—distant by thousands of paces

Minimi—least ones

Minor—minor

Mitra—religious headwear

Montium—of mountains

Monumentum—monument

Mores—morals

Mori—to die; to be mortal

Mortis—death

Mortui—dead

Mundus—world

N

Nasus—nose

Naturae—of Nature

Neglegere—breaking

Neptunius—tenth month of the year

Nihil—nothing

Nivei—snow

Nova—new

Nox—night; night's eve

Numeri—of number, numbers

Nuptiae—of marriage

O

Occasus—downfall

Occidentum—the West, Westlands

Occidus—the West

Octipes—eight-footed, eight-pointed

Omnino—wholly, entirely

Oratio—speech

Orbis—ring

Ordines—Ordinal, or minor points of the compass (NE, NW, SE, and SW)

Ordinis—Ordinal, or minor point of the compass (NE, NW, SE, or SW)

Oriens—East

Orientalis—Eastern

Orientalium—of Easterners

Orientem—of or pertaining to the East

Orientum—the East, Eastlands

P

Papiliones—butterflies

Papilionum—of the butterflies

Papyrus—paper

Parare—to prepare; preparing

Parthorum—of the Parthians

Passeum—paces, of paces

Passus—of paces

Patefacta—yielded up; given up; surrendered

Pax—peace

Pendentium—of those hanging

Per—through

Perditi—lost; perished

Peregrinus—foreign; stranger

Philologe—Scholar

Physica—woman engaged in Science

Pila—ball

Pilae—balls

Piscatorum—of the fish

Pistoris—of a baker

Pixae—smallest of the *Faerrae*; frequent pollinators. Said to enjoy gyre and gimble

Plutonius—eleventh month of the year

Populusque—and the People

Potestatem—power

Praecipiti—headlong

Praeterirns—leaving, departing

Prave—depraved one

Prima—main, primary

Primus—primary

Princeps—leader; chief person in charge

Procax—bully

Prodi—to go; get going; proceed

Prolatus—offer

Providentia—foresight

Prudens—rational

Puella—girl

Puellae—girls; dolls

Pueri—boys

Pueros—children

Pugil—boxer

Pugna—fighting

Pugnare—fighting

Pulchella—pretty; beautiful

Pulicium—of fleas

Purgata—cleansing

Pustula—pimple

Q

Qua—which, that

Quaesitor—inquisitor

Quaestor—official

Quartus—fourth one

Quercus—oak

R

Recludite—open!

Regina—queen

Regulos—rules

Rerum—of matters

Respica—look behind

Restitutum—restoration; restored

Reunion—reunion

Reus—guilty

Reveletur—disclosed

Reverte—revert to previous state!

Rex—king

Ruber—red

Rufus—red

Rumpite—swell to bursting

S

Sana—healthy

Sanguis—blood

Sanum—health

Sapo—soap

Saturnalia—annual farewell old year, welcome new year festival

Saturnius—twelfth month of the year

Saxum—rock

Scientia—science; scientific method

Secundi—those in the second year of study

Semper—always

Senatus—the Senate

Senex—old

Septentrio—North

Septentrionum—of, or pertaining to, North

Sepulchri—tombstone

Sepultura—burial

Sidera—planets

Silentii—of silence

Sine—without

Sint—let there be

Sis—may you be

Sit—let it be

Solares—Men of the Sun

Solaris—Man of the Sun

Solitarius—hermit

Solstitum—Summer solstice

Somnia—dreams

Sorcerorum—of, or pertaining to, Sorcers; corrupted word originally meaning Sorcerers. More properly *Sorcererorum*

Sordida—outdoor; trail; rough; common

Sorores—sisters

Spadix—brown

Speculi—of the mirror

Speculum—mirror

Specus—cave

Sphaerae—balls, spheres

Spiritus—spirit

Spritae—mid-sized *Faerrae;* often sought to accomplish tasks and fetch items

Spuma—foam at the mouth, as with soap

Statim—immediately

Statuis—statues

Stercus—feces; slang expression

Stola—woman's gown

Sub—under, preceding

Subtercollem—under hill

Supremi—those in the fourth, final year of study; the most advanced of a group

Supremorum—of those in the last year of study

Supremus—one in the fourth, final year of study

Surpema—woman in the fourth, final year of study; the most avanced of a group

T

Tace—silence, be silent!

Tauri—of the bull

Te—you

Terra—land

Tertii—those in the third year of study

Tertius—third one

Tirones—recruits, those of the first year of study

Tironis—recruit, one of the first year of study

Tres—three

Turre—tower

Turris—tower

U

Ultimus—last

Uranius—ninth month of the year

V

Venereus—of Venus, love

Veni—one come!

Venite—more than one come!

Vermes—worms

Vernum—spring

Vesanus—madman

Vesica—bladder

Vespertiliolis—little bat

Vestimenta—clothes

Via—road

Vicerunt—they have won

Vinarii—of the vintner

Vincite—entangle!

Vires—power

Virgines—virgins

Viridis—green

Vites—vines

Volans—flying one

Z

Zephyrus—West wind

Discussion Questions for
Book Three: *Thaddeus and the Daemon*

Book Club Leaders … contact Louis to participate in a special meeting to discuss the book; the concepts; and the evolution of the series. In-person gatherings are possible if you are in the Midwest and Louis is available. Otherwise, Zoom is always an option.

1. The Sorceresses' proposal for a Springtime meeting with their Sorcerer partners seems to hide their covert purpose—to meet the "Loving Relationship" requirement to practice Sorcery. Is this justified?

2. Asullus argues that Thaddeus, only 15 and still at school, is in no way prepared to be a father to an infant child and should be satisfied that others will raise his son. Is this acceptable?

3. Upon reading Ethne's Farewell Letter, Thaddeus immediately sets out to travel to her without regard to planning or provisions but with the knowledge that she is likely dead by this time. This seems both dangerous and irrational. Is it?

4. On his trip south, Thaddeus has relations with both Mari, the Dragon-Queen and Luperca, the Wolf-Goddess. He eventually confesses all of his four prior trysts to Marsia. She is quick to attribute his behavior to a need to fulfill the Prophecy. Is this warranted?

5. By the middle of the book, it is clear that all eight Sorcery Apprentices have intimately partnered. Though all are at least fifteen years old or older, should any have delayed their joining?

6. Is the violence done to Sonnia at the hands of the Goblins out of character with the rest of the story?

7. When Thaddeus loses all Sorcerous Belief, he can no longer perceive magical creatures, and sees in others only what is real. How can he still speak with Sorcerers or be injured by what he cannot detect?

8. Following the defeat of the Daemon, Lilyput's life-ending trauma is readily reversed. How is this possible?

9. The "Universal Stone Spell" affects all with the land of the *Collegium Sorcerorum,* yet how do Brother Long Bone and the Gargoyles survive?

10. Was Thaddeus wise to trust Mayor Pontius, the Pilot of Vexare, with the knowledge of the Dragon's Treasure? Is it likely the politician will keep his word?

Contact Louis for on-line or in-person book clubs, author visits,
or with general questions at:
414-248-0427
AuthorLouisSauvain@gmail.com
Protinus Press
Mailbox 225
3900 W. Brown Deer Road – Suite A
Milwaukee, WI 53209

Excerpt from Book Four:

THADDEUS AND THE ANCIENT ONE ...

Prologue

My Dearest Serenea,

I pray to the Gods every night that you are safe, still in love with me only, and receiving my letters. I am safe, remain in love with you only and have been getting your letters most regularly. The post system here in the Land of the Cin is both faithful and punctual. It is worth a runner's head that it be so —I've seen. The delays and uncertainties seem to have more to do with those territories bordering the Empire, I think, though here I imply no criticism toward your father. Please know that I do hope the Emperor is well in health and continues to smile upon his only daughter—and a most beauteous one she is.

My studies are going well under the Ancient One, Pan Lo. He is strict with me, but I believe he means it for my betterment. He tells me I am the first of the West who has come to the Cin for instruction in the Magicks. He has only one other student, his son, Los Tao. He and I are fast becoming as brothers. The language was a barrier at first, but our master spoke a word and laid a gesture over me, and now I understand all that is said and written. It has been a wondrous gift.

Tell your father that the riches of the East are beyond counting and cause his own Court to appear, well, austere. Again, I intend no criticism. He should come here with the

Court sometime and view it for himself. The amassed wealth of the Cin staggers the imagination.

But I have written principally to tell you of the success of my studies. The Ancient One says he has not seen one so young progress so rapidly along the Ninefold Path. I have, of late, been pestering him to let me spend the fortnight in the Tower, and I believe he may soon let me assay the task.

You see, there is a tower here called the structure of Power. It is of a singularly unattractive construction—a sickly, bilious yellow with a red cap, some thirty-three paces in height. It exudes a disturbing aura—or power—as Pan Lo describes it, hence its name. Sometimes lightnings flash from the top level. I am told the Tower has been here always. Also, that the capital, Cinoton, was built around the Tower due to its presence.

The Ancient One says that if a student is considered both worthy and ready by the Council of Nine, he is allowed to reside in the Tower for a two-week period of fasting and meditation —taking his sleep each night near the Hearth of Entrance. It is said that after such a time, his perceptions and powers are not uncommonly heightened. Some, it is also said, leave the time changed and are never again quite as they were.

But whatever the risk, I intend to try my hand at the task. Perhaps I will accrue sufficient wisdom to one day achieve my life-long goal of becoming the Princeps Academiae of the Collegium Sorcerorum. What a thrill that would be!

None of these wild fancies will, of course, be possible without you, my true love, beside me. I am not yet certain how I will convince the Emperor of the Westlands to relent and let the Jewel of His House go into the care of a poor student-of-no-name, but I will find a way, never fear. As long as you are with me, I can achieve anything.

Well, I must close this missive now if I'm to make the late afternoon runner.

Remember, I will love you always. One day, sooner than we know, we will be together forever. Then I will no longer have to gaze at you furtively from my prickly post in the hedge-bush under your balcony, but we will actually be joined as one. I so look forward to that day.

I end this, then, with all my love for my truest life's treasure.

Your ever willing servant,

Iusti

House of Mores

Serenea,

I write to end our relationship. It is not my intention to bring you hurt, but my studies now consume all my time and energy, leaving no space for anything else.

I find I have developed a remarkable clarity in thought since my vigil in the Tower. I see, now, things I never thought to see. I see that man is weak and corrupt, and it is now a question to me as to whether or not the majority of them even deserve to exist. I have come to think a great winnowing might improve the race—rid ourselves of all the chaff and parasites, so to say.

My life's great work lies in front of me, but I find I can no longer pursue it here. Unfortunately, my former master's son, Los Tao, interrupted me at a critical time in my new studies, and a dispute arose between us. I was compelled to silence his protests, lest he spread lies to others concerning my discoveries. So now, perforce, I judge it timely that I leave this country and return to the West. Though I do not believe they will easily find his body, nevertheless, my studies are far too important to be placed in abeyance while meddlesome old men come pestering me with their ignorant questions. In any event, my old master has nothing further to teach me. My new insights place me as far above him now, as he was above me when I first came to him as a learner.

I plan to return to the Westlands rather sooner than most would expect. I believe I fancy taking the position of Princeps Academiae at the Collegium Sorcerorum. It would suit my purposes and help me to advance my work more easily.

Therefore, farewell Serenea. My regards to your father, the Emperor. Please explain to him how things have changed. I trust he will not consider it necessary to interfere with my plans as I assume the life of an academic. I am sure we would both regret it.

Do not think to contact me further. There would be no point.

Mores

Meet Louis Sauvain

Using my background in health care, I've has always been interested in how people employ fantasy to escape their current circumstances; and sometimes, their pain. Before turning to writing full time, I knew that being distracted—be it for a few moments or many hours—created a tolerance for what was momentary unbearable.

As my retirement loomed, I was finally able to let my fingers flow as each character entered the scene and their epic stories flowed. And as they flowed, the characters spoke up, guiding how they would respond when scenarios were created. The muse on my shoulder was my high school English teacher who pushed me with her ever present red pencil and supported my creativity and love of words.

Now, writing epic fantasy, my books have become the salve for pain, relief and escapism to abandon, for the moment, this world and embrace, for a time, another; sometimes for myself … and always for those who are just looking for a worthy read.

Born and bred in the Midwest, I call Wisconsin home. My reveal … most of my ideas come from the shower when I ask my characters, "Okay, where are you going to take me today?"

My challenge becomes how to bring YOU—my readers—along so that you, too, can enjoy my path to completing each story line within each book. To me, that's gold.

LouisSauvain.com

How to Work with Louis Sauvain

Author **Louis Sauvain** is not only a gifted storyteller, but also a witty and fun speaker. Bring him to your organization either in-person or Zoom.

For **Book Clubs,** use his Discussion Questions as a starting point found within the Book tab on his website: *https://www.louissauvain.com/* Or, query your members and let them do the asking, sending him the questions their inquiring minds want answers to.

For **Libraries,** with over 80% of the population believing that they have a book in them, Louis would be delighted to lead a discussion on any one of his books: its creation; its story line; and his unique writing process; the process of creating a multiple book series; and how to create a fantasy world—either general or epic.

For **Authors and Writers,** Louis would be available to lead a discussion on writing fantasy; how to make a "mark" in the world of book marketing strategy; and when to use a pen name.

To check his availability, contact him directly or via his website.

414-248-0427

AuthorLouisSauvain@gmail.com

PROTINUS

Protinus Press

Mailbox 225

3900 W. Brown Deer Road – Suite A

Milwaukee, WI 53209

Follow him on:

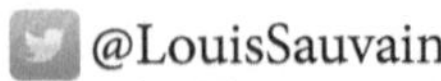 @LouisSauvain

 Instagram.com/LouisSauvain

Facebook.com/LouisSauvain

Thaddeus of Beewicke – Book One

Available at your favorite bookstore or amazon.com

Is life's pathway set for a person before they are born? Has a mission been predestined for the Chosen to undertake? Thaddeus is the first Apprentice of the Master Sorcerer, Silvestrus of Somerset, who was commissioned by a higher power to nurture him and seven others, guiding them onto the path of Sorcery when each entered their fourteenth year.

Thaddeus must fulfill a Prophecy that not only leads to his own self-discovery but holds the future fate of the world in his young hands.

Will he summon the will to break away from his familial expectations to seek this higher calling?

Will sorcery and, indeed, the world survive if he doesn't?

Will he understand and accept why he was chosen for the daunting tasks that await him?

THADDEUS AND THE MASTER – BOOK TWO

AVAILABLE AT YOUR FAVORITE BOOKSTORE OR AMAZON.COM

Coming to the College of Sorcery following a harrowing escape, Silvestrue of Somerset's first Apprentice, Thaddeus, must now bond with his Brothers to uncover an evil Master's treachery before the traitor and his Daemon Mentor can destroy the world they know.

Will he succeed in securing the Scholar, the Thief and the Prince to his cause despite their mutual distrust of each other?

Will the women of the Ludia choose to side with the young Sorcerers in their moment of dire peril?

Will the Golden Pack Leader reveal her true identity in time to thwart the approaching Goblin Horde?

Next from Louis Sauvain …

The Cinnian Tower Trilogy

Volume Four:
THADDEUS AND THE ANCIENT ONE

Volume Five:
THADDEUS AND THE EMPEROR

Volume Six:
THADDEUS THE FAITHLESS

available winter 2024